PENGUIN

Neil Hanson h..laimed
Mud, Blood an...nables:
The Autobiogra.................................erry Venables, the
current coach of ....football team, and *Team Tornado*
(Signet, 1995) with Gulf War pilots John Peters and John Nichol.

Neil Hanson lives in Ilkley, West Yorkshire, with his wife, Lynn,
and their son, Jack.

NEIL HANSON

The Vet

PENGUIN BOOKS
BBC BOOKS

PENGUIN BOOKS
BBC BOOKS

Published by the Penguin Group and BBC Worldwide Ltd
Penguin Books Ltd, 27 Wrights Lane, London W8 5 TZ, England
Penguin Books USA Inc., 375 Hudson Street, New York, New York 10014, USA
Penguin Books Australia Ltd, Ringwood, Victoria, Australia
Penguin Books Canada Ltd, 10 Alcorn Avenue, Toronto, Ontario, Canada M4V 3B2
Penguin Books (NZ) Ltd, 182–190 Wairau Road, Auckland 10, New Zealand

Penguin Books Ltd, Registered Offices: Harmondsworth, Middlesex, England

First published 1996

BBC ™ BBC used under licence

Set by Datix International Limited, Bungay, Suffolk
Printed in England by Clays Ltd, St Ives plc
Filmset in 10/12 pt Monophoto Sabon

Chapter 1

It was barely light as she drained the last of her coffee and stepped outside, closing the door of the cottage quietly behind her. She stood for a moment gazing out over the river, drinking in the beauty of a view which had yet to lapse into familiarity. There had been a frost in the night and every blade of grass was coated in white. Mist clung to the surface of the river, as wide and still as a lake.

Over the far shore, dawn was still reddening the sky, extinguishing the last of the stars and throwing the dark, tree-lined slopes into even deeper shadow. Apart from herself, the only visible living creature was a heron standing motionless in the shallows downstream, waiting for the receding tide to reveal its breakfast. There was no breath of wind, not a sound, not a movement.

She smiled to herself. If she needed any reminder that this was not London, the utter silence supplied it. Even in the dead of night in London there had been the noise of cars, lorries and police sirens, slamming doors and stumbling drunks, while the glow of the street lighting meant that no night was ever truly dark. Here a moonless, windless night was as black as coal and as quiet as a closed cathedral.

Rapt, she gazed at the river for a few more moments, then shivered and wrapped her coat tightly around her as she walked the few yards to the side of the narrow road winding through the village. There she stood waiting, her breath fogging in the cold morning air.

From a long way off, she heard the sound of Chris's Range Rover as he gunned it through the lanes, running late and speeding to make up time. He rounded the last corner and screeched to a halt in a flurry of gravel, headlights full on, cassette player blaring. The heron flapped disdainfully away downriver, as Chris leaned across to open the car door, his tousled black hair flopping across his forehead. 'Sorry I'm late, Jennifer, you must be freezing.'

'That's all right, Chris, I needed the time to adjust to my new surroundings.' He grinned, put the Range Rover into gear and drove off, his smile lighting up his face and making him appear far younger than a man approaching forty.

The car seemed to fill the twisting lane, yet Chris kept his foot down, speeding northwards along the river bank towards Whitton. From the corner of his eye he caught Jennifer wincing as he took another blind bend, their view completely obscured by the high earth banks and hedges towering even above the Range Rover's roof. 'Don't worry, Jennifer, these lanes are all one-way.'

She snorted, the laughter lines at the corner of her mouth deepening to two capital C's, then bit her lip nervously as another bend revealed a herd of Friesians ambling unconcernedly towards them, blocking the lane. 'Obviously no one told the cows.'

Chris had already spotted them and, braking to a crawl, began to inch past them, the cows rubbing against the sides of the car as they passed. As the tide of black and white rumps finally parted, they could see Whitton laid out below them. Jennifer leant forward in her seat, taking in the view. An old stone bridge crossed the river at the bottom of the town, from where the solid Georgian houses and Victorian villas rose in tiers up the steep hillsides. A dramatic railway viaduct cut the town in two, its arches crossing the valley in giant's strides. Cream- and lemon-coloured cottages clustered around the feet of its massive stone piers.

Jennifer's blonde hair was loosely tied back from her face and Chris watched her intently as she studied the view, his dark eyes scanning her profile. Finally he looked away, slipping the car into gear. 'I hate to interrupt the sight-seeing tour, but we're late as it is.'

'That's all right, I'm on holiday this morning, aren't I?' said Jennifer, stretching luxuriously as she sat back in her seat. 'You're the one who has to work.'

At the bottom of the hill a large, empty animal transporter rumbled into view, disturbing the morning quiet. They followed it down into the auction mart, already a hive of activity, a mêlée of men, animals and trucks. The maze of animal pens was crammed to bursting, mainly with sheep at this time of year, though there were still a few pens of calves.

The sellers, local farmers, kept a watchful eye on their stock and on each other. Chatting, smoking, all ages and all sizes, they leaned on the rails of the pens apparently at peace with the world, though their hawk-sharp eyes missed no sign of interest from any potential buyer. Were one to pause for even a second by their pens, they were on them in a flash, pointing out the finer points of their stock – noble breeding, perfect conformation, fine teeth and magnificent physiques – before returning to their mates, picking up the conversation as if they had never been away.

Chris parked the Range Rover among a battery of Land Rovers and four-wheel drives, most with small trailers empty of their loads. As he and Jennifer made their way across the yard towards the pens, the tailgates of the transporter slammed down and a mart hand released the catch on one of the gates to the sheep pens. Sheep spilled out into the narrow alley and a stream of them made their way up the ramp into the lower deck of the transporter, beginning a one-way journey that would end on a dinner table. The transporter was three tiers high and would not be leaving until all three decks were crammed full.

Jennifer took in the massed ranks of farmers, universally clad in drab shades of green and brown – the colours of the moors in winter. She gazed thoughtfully at her own, rather more colourful clothing for a moment, before asking, 'How many here are clients? Roughly.'

'Roughly?' said Chris. 'All of them. No, not quite, there's a few with Johnson over at Stowbridge. Some of the older ones here I remember from when I was a boy. Which they remind me of when it comes to paying their bills . . .'

'I wonder how they'll take to me; not just a woman vet, but a woman vet from London, it couldn't get much worse, could it?'

Chris laughed and glanced across at her, taking in her high cheekbones, the mischievous look in eyes that were a startling deep blue, and her slightly parted, soft red lips. A smile always seemed to be playing around the corners of her mouth, and even her slightly crooked nose – perhaps broken in a childhood accident – was oddly attractive. Her expression was open and direct. Only a melancholy, faraway look that sometimes slipped into her eyes hinted at past troubles. As she met his gaze, she gave him a quizzical look, head tilted slightly to one side. 'I don't think we'll be having any complaints from the farmers,' said Chris.

There was a silence, broken by Jennifer. 'Shouldn't you be getting to work?'

'Yes, yes,' said Chris, a little flustered. 'I'll clock in and if there are no immediate problems we can get a cup of coffee.' He took up station in the auction office, but had barely touched his coffee before he was called out.

'You the duty vet, Chris?' said one of two middle-aged farmers, their ruddy complexions a tribute in equal parts to a lifetime's work in the fresh air and to a lifetime's diet of bacon, butter, beer and whisky. 'I think one of my hoggs has broken its leg.'

In the narrow alley between two rows of pens, Chris sedated a ewe and put a resin cast on to its leg. Jennifer and the two farmers stood near by, watching closely. Chris packed his instruments away and straightened up. 'There you are, Brian, all done. She'll not be trying to jump out of pens again for a couple of weeks. Keep her indoors till you take the plaster off. That's twenty pounds, I'm afraid.'

There was a pregnant silence. The farmer looked first at Chris and then at the other farmer, from whom he had just bought the sheep. The other man looked impassively back at him, saying, 'I'm not paying, Brian, it's your animal now.'

'She was still yours when she jumped the pen.'

'No she was yours by then.'

'No, she's not mine until she's in the back of the truck.'

Chris glanced across towards Jennifer and winked. 'I'll put it on your bill then, Brian.' The two farmers continued to argue with each other, oblivious of anyone else, as Chris headed back towards the auction ring. Jennifer followed unhurriedly a few yards behind, taking in all the atmosphere of the sale.

As they entered the shabby brick building alongside the maze of animal pens, the voice of the auctioneer, magnified and distorted by the crackly sound system, rattled through the bids in a near-incomprehensible rush of words 'EEwanner wanner wanner – TEEwannner wanner wanner – YEEAWLdunn?' – Bang with the gavel – 'Lopsley, High Riddings. Lot 343. EEwanner wanner wanner . . .'

Jennifer followed Chris through the fringes of the crowd, drawing a few curious looks from the farmers draped comfortably over the rails at the edge of the circular, sawdust-strewn ring. The atmosphere was relaxed, routine. Some were selling, some just looking, keeping an eye on prices and filling in the time until the pubs near the mart opened for business, for auction day was as close as most of the farmers came to a day off. Once the serious business in the auction ring had been concluded, it was a chance to chat, catch up on the gossip and spend some of the 'luck money' from the sale ring.

As the auctioneer disposed of each lot from his perch on a dais above the ring, the handlers leapt into action, cajoling and prodding one lot of beasts out by one gate as the next half-dozen to be sold were ushered in by another. A young farmer, Neil Fairbrother, dark-haired and thin-faced with pale, washed-out blue eyes and a moody, slightly petulant expression, watched tense and anxious as his calves were herded into the ring. He either did not hear or ignored Chris's greeting as he and Jennifer passed by him on their way towards the car-park.

A couple of young buyers looked over Neil's calves. One turned to the other and muttered something, making a deprecating gesture as he indicated the animals. In a second Neil had confronted him, his face distorted with rage. 'What do you mean – they're not worth three hundred pounds?'

'They're underweight, they're no use to us,' said the buyer in a thick Black Country accent.

He started to move away but Neil grabbed his arm. 'Don't you dare tell me they're underweight, pal.'

'Let go of my arm.'

There was the briefest of pauses, then the buyer knocked away Neil's arm and punched him in the face, hard enough to draw a trickle of blood from Neil's nose. Before he could retaliate, a few of the nearby farmers had prised them apart, the moment over as quickly as it blew up. The buyers stalked off towards the far side of the ring, as the auctioneer's voice . . . '280. All done?' and the bang of his gavel announced that Neil's calves had been sold to another buyer. The look on Neil's face alone showed that the price was far less than he had hoped for. More upset than angry, he wiped some specks of blood from his face and pushed past Chris and Jennifer as they carried on towards the exit.

'What was all that about?' said Jennifer.

'Money, what else? They'll be lucky to make £5,000 this year, some of them. I'd not be in any of these fellers' shoes, that's for sure.'

As they left the mart, Chris glanced at his watch. 'Look, I've a couple of visits to make, do you want to come with me or be dropped off back at the practice?'

'I'll come with you, if that's all right. These grizzled old farmers round here have to meet the "new girl" some time, haven't they?'

Chris started the Range Rover and began to pull away, but he was forced to stamp on the brakes to avoid being hit as Neil stormed past in his battered pick-up, scattering gravel and crashing his gears as he swung out of the car-park and disappeared up the road.

'I used to think the drivers in London were bad,' said Jennifer. Chris smiled but said nothing as he let in the clutch and eased the Range Rover out into the morning traffic.

Neil drove fast up towards the hills to the north of Whitton, his trailer rattling and bouncing as he flung the pick-up through the bends and up the hills leading to his farm. He turned off down a lane at the moor edge towards a dilapidated farm, past a row of beech trees silhouetted against the sky, their shapes gnarled and twisted by the wind always keening over the moor.

The gate to the muddy farmyard was broken, hanging drunkenly by one hinge against the wall. A huddle of corrugated sheds stood on one side of the yard, facing a small, unlovely farmhouse, the paintwork peeling and the whitewash stained with damp. The sheds were even more dilapidated and surrounded by festering heaps of farmyard scrap. The farm had a few acres of pasture and meadow but most of its land was sour, waterlogged moorland, stretching up towards a ruined tin mine on the skyline.

Neil parked the pick-up and sluiced his face with water from the trough in the yard, trying to wash away his anger as well as the blood. He paused for a moment, composing his scowling features into a smile and then hurried towards the farmhouse, calling out, 'Debbie!' as he went in through the front door.

His wife came down the stairs, carrying some ironing. She was young and pretty, though her face was pale and her eyes dark-ringed with weariness. The faint rounding of her stomach suggested that she might be in the early stages of pregnancy. 'Debbie, we did all right,' said Neil, all smiles as he took off his coat. 'Three-fifty a head. Put it straight in the bank. That'll keep them quiet for a week or two.'

'Really? That's great,' said Debbie, though her voice and expression did not convey any enthusiasm. She followed him through to the kitchen, preoccupied and not responding to his chatter about the auction mart as he opened the fridge and helped himself to a bottle of beer.

Finally he fell silent and looked questioningly at her. 'Scott stopped by when he'd done,' said Debbie. 'He says six of the calves are scouring.'

Neil paused for a moment in the act of drinking. Then he shrugged and said, 'What would he know, eh?' but Debbie was not to be shaken off so easily.

'Neil. That's serious. They could die . . .'

He sighed and put down his bottle. 'I'll check them out, don't worry.'

'. . . And that feller from Hartley's phoned again. Says we still owe him for the last load of feed concentrate.'

'Never mind the feed concentrate,' he said, trying to keep the irritation out of his voice. 'Come here.' He picked her up, swinging her around and grinding his body into hers.

'Careful. I'm pregnant, you pillock.'

He moved towards the stairs, carrying her cradled in his arms. 'Time for your morning lie-down then, isn't it?'

She smiled at him then and wound her arms tightly around his neck as he carried her up the stairs and into their bedroom.

Chris and Jennifer had finished the morning calls and drove back to the practice, a low stone building with ivy smothering its gable end, standing on the outskirts of Whitton on the banks of the river. Steep, thickly wooded hillsides rose on either side of the river, opening out downstream into a vista stretching to the bridge that spanned the mouth of the estuary.

The practice building had once been a pumping station and it stood just below the weir which marked the end of the tidal river. At low tide, banks of glistening mud were exposed with the meandering courses of streams slithering like eels across them, but the tide was high as they drove down the hill and turned past the cedar standing sentinel on the corner. Two pure white swans drifted on the water lapping against the banks, their feathers ruffled by the first stirrings of a breeze.

Chris pulled up in the car-park, alongside the wooden loose-boxes in the yard. He grimaced as he saw his wife Patricia's car. 'Damn. Hope she hasn't been waiting too long.'

As they walked towards the entrance, the sound of their footsteps was lost in the murmur of the weir.

Inside the practice, Laura and Murray were cleaning up after an operation on a cat, which lay sleeping in its recovery cage. Murray was twenty-two, dark-haired and good-looking in a boyish way, his features still caught between youth and manhood. Fresh-faced and fresh out of veterinary college, his student humour entertained and irritated his colleagues in equal measure ... when they could discern the words masked by his Glaswegian accent.

Five years his senior, Laura was a local girl who had been with the practice since she qualified. She wore her dark hair swept back in a pony-tail and was plumply pretty, though there was a spark in her eyes which suggested a short temper.

'You remind me of a professor we had at college,' said Murray. 'Wielded a scalpel like a pickaxe. Looked a bit like you as well.'

'Gorgeous, was she then?'

'Who said it was a she?'

'Thanks.'

Laura went through into the reception area where Patricia and her girls, Charlotte and Abby, were waiting for Chris, while Maddy, grey-haired mother-hen to the practice, was as usual on the phone.

'Hello, love,' said Patricia, catching sight of Laura. 'Is Chris about?'

'I don't think so.'

'They probably got waylaid at market,' said Maddy, putting her hand over the phone for a moment.

Laura raised a quizzical eyebrow. 'And why does our new small animal specialist want to spend time at market?'

Murray wandered through, murmuring, 'It's funny how after

8

an operation, I always feel I could murder a steak and chips. Why d' you think that is?'

Laura and Maddy exchanged a look, but no one replied. 'How are the ticket sales going?' Laura asked Patricia.

She shrugged and crossed her fingers. 'You never know, we might even make a profit. Have you got yours yet, Murray?'

'Erm . . . I'll buy one on the door.'

'No you won't, you'll skive off. Twelve pounds, please.'

Murray looked round for help, but a row of stone faces greeted him. He sighed and fumbled for his wallet, playing up his Scots parsimony for all it was worth. 'Twelve pounds? And if I don't buy one, you get me the sack, right?'

'Includes a glass of wine.'

'Oh, a bargain, you should have said.'

Chris came hurrying in, scooping up the girls to give them a kiss. Jennifer, following behind, was waylaid by Patricia. 'Look, if there's anything you need for the cottage . . .'

'Like central heating?' said Jennifer. They both laughed.

Chris kissed Patricia, slipping his arm around her waist for a moment. They made a handsome couple, Jennifer thought. Chris ruggedly good-looking, Patricia, who was a couple of years older than him, very slim and elegant.

Chris took Abby by the hand. 'Right, all set?' But before he could reach the door, Maddy called him back.

'Oh, Chris. Neil Fairbrother just phoned. Says some of his calves are scouring. Can you call by this afternoon?'

'Phone him back and tell him I'll get up there by about . . .' he glanced at his watch '. . . five o'clock.'

'But you've got the PDs at McIntyre's at five.'

'Dammit.'

'Can't you go, Murray?' chipped in Laura.

'No, I've got a Ministry test on the Williams herd.'

There was a silence, broken by Chris. 'Jennifer, you can go. You can handle a case of scouring, can't you?'

Laura and Jennifer both looked at Chris in surprise.

'Erm . . . of course, I'd be happy to,' said Jennifer.

Laura compressed her lips in a characteristic expression of disapproval. 'Jennifer and I are supposed to be updating the drugs inventory this afternoon.'

'That can wait till tomorrow, can't it?' said Chris, ignoring the flash of anger in Laura's eyes as she turned away without speaking. 'Any problems, Jennifer, call me on the mobile. Right, come on, Abby.'

'Can't I come?' said Charlotte.

'Not this time, sweetheart, your turn will come soon,' said Patricia, ushering her out.

Jennifer asked Maddy for directions to Fairbrother's farm and then hurried out. Murray caught Laura's sour expression as she watched her go and tried, unsuccessfully, to soothe her. 'She has to make her first farm visit on her tod some time.'

Laura gave him a withering look and went back into the operating theatre.

Twenty minutes later, Jennifer pulled into the yard at Fairbrother's farm. She looked round for a moment, taking in the broken gate and general air of dereliction, before knocking on the front door of the farmhouse. After a moment the door opened and Neil appeared, with Debbie hovering in the background. Jennifer was a bit taken aback, recognizing him from the fracas in the auction mart.

'Mr Fairbrother?'

'Yeah?' said Neil, his face impassive.

'Oh, good morning,' said Jennifer brightly. 'I'm Mrs Holt. From the veterinary centre.'

'I know who you are. Where's Chris Lennox?'

This is not going to be easy, but don't lose your rag, Jennifer thought to herself. 'He's . . . erm . . . tied up. He's had to go to Plymouth.'

'What about Murray?'

'Busy. You got me, I'm afraid.'

'No offence, Mrs Holt, but I want Chris or Murray.'

'None taken, but I'm a fully qualified vet, Mr Fairbrother. You need have no worries.'

Neil just looked at her, saying nothing.

'It's me or no one, Mr Fairbrother.'

Debbie stepped to Neil's side and stared at Jennifer, whose welcoming smile was not returned.

After a long silence, Neil shrugged his shoulders and led the way across the yard to a small barn, dragging the sagging door open despite the squeal of protest from its hinges. Inside in the gloom were about twenty suckler calves and their mothers, wintering indoors in the cramped barn. The calves, three to four weeks old, had their own separate 'creep', running to their mothers when they wanted to suckle.

Jennifer began taking their temperatures as Neil and Debbie stood at one side, Neil's arms truculently folded. Jennifer finished and straightened up. 'They've got diarrhoea and a temperature all right. There are six scouring. These four aren't too bad, I'll show you how to tube them, but we'll have to take those two there back to the practice for treatment.'

'I don't know . . .' said Neil, concerned about the likely size of the bill.

'They'll be dead by tomorrow otherwise. I'll get you some bags from the car.'

Jennifer began to walk past them towards her car, then stopped and began to speak cautiously. 'Mr Fairbrother. I checked your records before I came up. The main reason why the calves are sick is because their mothers weren't vaccinated for Rotovirus last year.'

Debbie started at this and turned to stare at Neil.

'Yeah, well . . . that vaccine's bloody dear, isn't it?' spluttered Neil, trying to avoid Debbie's eye. 'And there's no guarantee it works either.'

Jennifer left an eloquent silence as she walked out of the barn. As Neil turned to Debbie, she marched out angrily before he could say anything.

Jennifer returned from her car with an electrolyte bag, which she quickly fixed up for one of the infected calves. She moved on to the second one and began trying to give it an antibiotic injection. As the calf jerked and struggled, Jennifer fought to hold it firmly against the side of the barn. She was about to put in the hypodermic when the calf twisted angrily away from her. Jennifer lost her balance and was hurled against the wall. She threw up her arm to protect herself and winced as it took the full impact.

She sat there for a moment composing herself, then looked across to Neil, who still stood there impassively, though a ghost of a smile played about his lips. Grimly determined, she got to her feet, grabbed hold of the calf again and this time managed to administer the jab successfully. She put the hypodermic back into her bag. 'Right, I'll need your help to get them into the trailer.' She caught Neil's scornful expression, but fought down her mounting anger and tried again, sweetly reasonable. 'If I were a man, I'd still need your help.'

As they loaded the calves into Neil's small trailer, Jennifer made a last effort to be friendly. 'I noticed you're fattening up a hundred or so lambs, Suffolk crosses? Do you want me to take a look at them, while I'm here?'

'Once they're weaned off their mothers, we call them hoggs not lambs,' said Neil, sarcastically. 'No thanks.'

Gritting her teeth, Jennifer nodded politely. 'I'll be back tomorrow to check up on the calves. With luck you shouldn't have to lose any. See you back at the practice. Bye.'

As Neil watched Jennifer drive out of the yard, Debbie came out of the farmhouse and confronted him, furious. 'You told me last summer you'd had those vaccinations done.'

'Yeah, well, I didn't, we didn't have the money.'

'So why didn't you tell me? Don't lie to me, Neil.'

Seeing his crestfallen face, she relented a little. 'We've got no money, how are we going to manage?'

'Easy, that's how. When the hoggs get sold off next month, you and me are going to be laughing. Go on, laugh.'

He tickled her and she laughed despite herself. He pulled her to him but both had faraway expressions as they gazed over each other's shoulders.

After circling the centre of Plymouth several times looking in vain for a parking place, Chris had given up and parked on a yellow line while he took Abby to find a dress for her first communion. The shop owner, a plump maternal woman in her early fifties, pulled out dress after dress, deepening Chris's confusion. He wished that Patricia was here to make the decision for him.

'When is your first communion, Abby?' asked the woman as she fitted her into yet another dress.

'Not for ages.'

'Next Sunday actually,' said Chris.

The woman stepped back to admire her handiwork and turned

to Chris for a comment. 'Erm ... delightful,' he said. 'Very pretty. What do you think, Abby?'

'I liked the first one.'

'What do you think?' Chris asked helplessly, turning to the shop owner.

'I think I agree with your daughter,' she said, giving him an understanding smile.

'Insurmountable odds, I give in.'

She laughed and turned back to Abby. 'Your mummy's going to love this dress.'

'No, she won't.'

Chris intercepted the shop owner's surprised look. 'It's all right. Abby's mother's a registered atheist, that's all.'

Chris paid the woman without blanching too much at the price, and was relieved to find that he did not also have to find the money for a parking ticket, since the car had miraculously escaped the attentions of the traffic wardens. They drove out of Plymouth past the banks of houses in pastel pinks, greens, yellows and whites, clambering up the hillsides like the tiers of a grandstand as if fighting for a glimpse of a precious sea view.

North of the last straggling suburbs they were out into rolling Devon countryside, the grass already impossibly green, even in the depths of winter. Abby chattered away incessantly while Chris smiled and nodded and gazed around him, enjoying the treat of a few hours away from ringing phones and demanding clients. Far ahead beyond Whitton, which lay hidden, nestled in a valley by the river, there were fleeting glimpses of the Dartmoor tors capping the brown, barren moors like seals basking on rocks. Nearer at hand the land was softer and gentler, curved and rounded like a pregnant woman, the soil as rich and red as blood and so fertile that even vertical slopes were thickly carpeted with vegetation.

He was whistling as he turned into the drive of his house, a cream-coloured Victorian semi-detached, standing high above the town with a view out over the rooftops to the tors. Patricia and Charlotte were in the garden, Patricia clearing weeds while Charlotte rummaged through the straw and hay in her rabbit's cage. When she saw Chris, she ran up the garden yelling, 'Hamlet's gone, Daddy, I can't find him.'

'He's only hiding under his bedding, trying to find some peace and quiet, I expect.'

Charlotte wheeled about and, seizing a stick, began trying to poke the bedding.

'Don't poke it like that, stupid,' said Abby.

'She's only trying to help, don't bully her,' said Patricia mildly. She raised a quizzical eyebrow at Chris.

'The dress is beautiful,' he said in answer to the unspoken question, 'but don't even ask the price.'

'She won't be too upset if I don't go to the communion?' asked Patricia quietly, looking across to Abby still arguing with Charlotte as they searched the rabbit cage.

'Not now, but maybe later in life.'

'What? Drugs, prostitution?'

'Probably.'

She smiled. 'In that case it's probably just as well that I've decided to go after all.'

He gave her a loving look. Patricia's principles were fiercely held, as her fellow councillors on Whitton Town Council had often discovered, and Chris knew what an effort it was for her to enter a church. He was about to kiss her, when he suddenly spotted the rabbit squatting in the drive by the car.

'Aha,' he said, pouncing on it and returning it to Charlotte. 'Here we are. Shall I put him in the oven for dinner?'

Charlotte's eyes filled with tears.

'Daddy was only joking, darling,' said Patricia hastily. 'I think.'

Chapter 2

Night had fallen by the time Jennifer got home. She let herself into the darkened cottage and picked her way past a pile of cardboard boxes in the hall. There were still crates and boxes stacked everywhere waiting to be unpacked, but the cottage already felt like home to her. She lit the fire and then ran a hot bath, sinking into it with a sigh of relief. She lay back and inspected the blue-black bruise on her arm, a souvenir of her battle with Neil Fairbrother's calf. She smiled to herself, not minding the scars of battle; she had enjoyed her day.

The sound of the front door roused her from her reverie. 'Steven, is that you? Put the kettle on, go on.'

A few minutes later she was sitting at the kitchen table in her dressing-gown, towelling her damp hair. Her son Steven, a sixteen-year-old trapped between the devil of adolescence and the deep blue sea of adulthood, already half a head taller than her, poured milk into two mugs of tea and handed her one. Jennifer glanced at him gratefully, noting for the thousandth time the eyes that Steven had inherited from her and the chin, nose and lips that could have been chiselled, unaltered, from his father.

She took a sip of her tea. 'So how was it?'

Steven shrugged as he leaned against the dresser, holding his mug of tea. 'OK. We got any grub in?'

'Sorry. I didn't have a moment. Why don't you order a Chinese and we'll go and collect it together?'

He ambled across to the window-sill and picked up the Chinese takeaway menu.

'You're not going to tell me about your karate class then?' said Jennifer.

He sighed heavily. 'It's not karate, it's escrima, it's completely different.'

She gave a mock bow in acknowledgement of her grievous error.

'It took an hour and a half to get back from Plymouth though,' added Steven.

'I know, love. We're going to have get used to not having everything on our doorstep.'

'We're going to have get used to a lot of things, Mum.'

'Yeah.' She caught the note of gloom in his voice and immediately tried to lighten the mood. 'You should see the shiner of a bruise I've got on my arm.'

'No thanks. "B" for two, I reckon,' said Steven, peering at the takeaway menu like a punter studying the raceform.

He was about to pick up the phone when it rang. 'Whitton 2684 . . . er . . . something 9,' said Steven, snatching it up. 'Yeah, hold on. Duty vet?' he inquired, looking at Jennifer.

She nodded and took the phone. 'Hello, Jennifer Holt speaking . . . Er, yes, but . . . Well, there's a surgery in the morning, I'm sure that . . . You see, the thing is our policy is not to make home visits at night unless it's a case of absolute necessity . . . Yes, yes. Where exactly are you, Mr Pritchard?'

She looked at Steven and then skywards. He grinned back at her.

She put the phone down and ran upstairs to dress, calling over her shoulder, 'I'm really sorry, Steven, I shouldn't be more than half an hour. I'll pick up the takeaway on the way back.' A few minutes later she was speeding through the darkened lanes, noting wryly that she was already mimicking Chris's cavalier driving technique.

The directions that she had been given led her to a bleak council estate on the edge of Whitton. It was not the kind of place she would have chosen to visit alone, least of all at night. Locking the car door, she looked nervously around. Suddenly the silence was pierced by a loud shout. She started as two skateboarders flew by and disappeared into the darkness. Her heart still thumping, she started to walk to a council house across the street.

Before she reached it, the front door opened and a man of about fifty, with the dishevelled, nervous look of a man long living alone, beckoned her in. His agitation was obvious as he led her through to the kitchen, where a small dog cowered at the bottom of a cupboard among a blanket and a couple of household slippers. It bared its teeth ferociously and barked angrily at them.

Jennifer got down on her hands and knees and peered into the cupboard, while the man stood behind her, anxiously peering over her shoulder.

'I can't go near Lucinda. She's been in there, barking her head off, for two days.'

'When was she last on heat, Mr Pritchard?'

'About six weeks ago, I think. She's not having a nervous breakdown, is she?'

'No. Do you know what the matter is with Lucinda? Hormone imbalance. She's convinced herself she was mated and those two carpet slippers are her new puppies. She'll protect those slippers like her life depended on it.'

While she was talking, Jennifer took out a hypodermic syringe and a muzzle.

'It won't hurt, will it?'

'That's why I use the muzzle.'

'I meant Lucinda.'

'I know,' smiled Jennifer. There was no answering smile, just a frantic look on Pritchard's face as Jennifer slipped the muzzle over the dog's head in one easy, practised motion and pulled her out, still barking and snarling, ready for the injection.

When she got back to the cottage, Steven was lounging on the sofa in the front room watching television.

'Hi. What's on?' said Jennifer, throwing her coat over the back of a chair and sinking down next to him.

'Did you get the takeaway?' countered Steven, ignoring her question as usual.

'Oh, blast it. I'm sorry, I completely forgot.'

She got up wearily and started to put her coat back on again. Steven strolled into the hall and watched her.

'I'm sorry, love, this is as unsettling a period for me as it is for you,' said Jennifer nervously, trying to gauge his mood. 'So for a while . . . well, we've got to help each other really, that's all.'

'Yeah,' replied Steven, deadpan.

He walked past her into the kitchen. She watched him ruefully for a second, then picked up the car keys and opened the front door.

'Mum.'

Jennifer turned round to see Steven smirking at her, holding up a tray full of Chinese takeaway dishes.

'You little bugger.'

'Don't expect your dinner on a tray every night, woman. I'm only sixteen, I've got anxieties of my own to work out.'

The next morning Jennifer was already in the stable block, checking on the two calves in the intensive care section, when Chris wandered in.

'Morning, Jennifer, how are they?'

Jennifer gave a 'so-so' gesture and carried on working.

'I've just had Debbie Fairbrother on the phone,' continued Chris.

'Yes, I'm going out there after morning surgery to change those drips.'

'That's why she called. They want me to do it.'

'Really?' said Jennifer, swivelling to look at him. 'Never mind, they'll get used to me after a couple of visits.'

'No, no, I'll go.'

Chris took a sudden interest in one of the calves as Jennifer stopped working and stared at him. 'She asked to see you rather than me and you agreed? Just like that?'

'This isn't London, Jen.'

'Don't patronize me, Chris. I have worked in a rural practice before. I know it was some years ago but . . .'

'I know that, but farm animals aren't pets, they're the farmer's livelihood. Continuity of care is something farmers hold very dear. I'm sorry if it upsets you but that's the way it is.'

'He who pays the piper, eh?'

Chris, in turn, now became irritated. 'Jennifer, you're a very experienced small animal vet. I didn't invite you to join the practice to do farm work.'

'I know, but that's not the point in this instance.'

'I think it is the point,' said Chris, with an air that indicated the subject was closed. 'Laura's leaving early for lunch today to go and look at a house, so ask Murray to help out in surgery if you need him.'

He walked out abruptly, leaving Jennifer staring angrily after him.

Chris's bad mood faded as he drove up into the hills to Fairbrother's farm. He liked Neil, regarding him as a friend as well as a client, and he admired his determination to make something of the farm, though he often wondered if Neil was really cut out for the job. He was too much of a dreamer to be a typical farmer and was already heavily in debt. Neil's father had gone under trying to make a go of the same farm and it had become almost an article of faith for Neil that he would make a success of it for the sake of his father's memory.

As Chris was driving up the last winding hill to the farm, Neil's sixteen-year-old part-time farm labourer, Scott, dropped off some winter feed to the ewes in the steep, hilly field behind the farm-house and then drove the battered old three-wheeler down into the yard. Neil was poring over some accounts on the kitchen table as Scott tapped on the back door. 'I've done, Mr Fairbrother.'

Neil ignored him, but as Scott shuffled from foot to foot, not quite sure what to say next, Debbie came through from the front room and spotted him.

'Oh, hello there, Scott. Neil paid you yet?'

Scott smiled with relief and shook his head shyly.

Debbie touched Neil's shoulder. 'Got any cash on you, love?'

'What do you think I am? Made of money?'

'We owe him for the week.'

'Yeah, well he can join the bloody queue, can't he?'

By now squirming with embarrassment, Scott called out, 'It's OK, Mrs Fairbrother, it'll hold till next time.'

'No it won't,' said Debbie. 'Give him some money, Neil.'

Neil addressed Scott directly for the first time. 'I'm sorry, mate, I don't happen to have any cash on me.' He turned to face Debbie. 'And if I don't pay for this feed concentrate today we'll get no more to fatten up those hoggs with. So leave us be.'

'I'll go now, don't worry,' said Scott, but Debbie and Neil were now locked into their own private argument and both ignored him.

'And whose fault is it they need fattening up indoors in the first place?' demanded Debbie. 'They should have been sold off months ago.'

'Don't you talk to me like that.'

'Give the lad the cash we owe him.'

'No, really,' pleaded Scott, 'I've got to get off to school now anyway.' He almost cried with relief when he heard Chris's Range Rover pulling into the yard.

Neil, suddenly all smiles, pushed past Scott to shake Chris's hand, greeting him with genuine pleasure. Scott climbed on to his trials bike and rode off down the track. Neil led Chris into the barn, talking animatedly about a parcel of nearby land that had just come up for rent. Chris replied in monosyllables, concentrating on his inspection of the infected calves, as Neil leant against one of the partitions and kept up his monologue.

'The word is he wants to sell off the farmhouse and rent out the land separately, right? I tell you something, Chris, another fifteen acres'd do me a treat, I've hardly room for my lambing ewes as it is.'

Chris paused in his work for a moment and looked hard at him. 'Neil. I don't want to put undue pressure on you but you do owe us nearly six hundred pounds. How can you think of renting more land when you're already in debt?'

Neil stopped, lost for words, and his jaw sagged even further when he saw Debbie standing in the entrance to the barn, holding a mug of coffee for Chris.

'I'll pay you off when the hoggs are sold, you know that, Chris,' muttered Neil, glancing nervously at Debbie and praying she had not overheard.

His prayers were not answered. Debbie walked over and handed Chris his coffee.

'Six hundred pounds, is that what we owe you?'

He nodded. She looked across at Neil, fighting to hold back her tears, then ran from the barn.

There was a long silence. Chris tidied up and got ready to go. 'The calves are going to be fine. You can pick the two up from the practice whenever you like. I'll see you later.' He paused for a moment, as if about to say more, then hurried away across the yard, leaving Neil staring after him. As Chris drove off, Neil listlessly picked up a spanner and began tinkering with a broken-down tractor at the bottom of the yard.

Debbie watched from the window for a long while, then came outside. Neil was invisible, working on the far side of the tractor. She called to him but there was no reply. Walking slowly around to the other side of the tractor, she saw Neil sitting on the ground, quite still, gazing sightlessly at a piece of metal in his hand. Bits of tractor engine lay on the ground all around him. He was crying silently.

'Neil . . .' said Debbie.

'I don't know where it goes.'

She went to him, sat on the ground and put her arms around him.

Neil was also on Jennifer's mind as she and Murray cleared up at the end of morning surgery, with Murray still trying to soothe her. 'They're a conservative bunch, farmers. None of them wanted to see me either when I first arrived here.'

'I still don't think Chris should have taken me off the case,' said Jennifer.

'Neil can be a difficult customer.'

'There's more to it than that. Chris doesn't want me to enjoy large animal work too much. Because I did rather sell myself to him as a high-powered small animal specialist, didn't I?'

Murray threw up his arms in mock horror. 'Don't tell me you've joined us under false pretences, Mrs Holt?'

He took her hand, play-acting the priest, but held on to it for a micro-second longer than the joke warranted. Jennifer looked at his hand and then at him, cocking an eyebrow until, embarrassed, he let her hand drop.

Point made, she resumed the conversation as if nothing had happened. 'Of course Laura would be happier if I were to do only large animal work.'

'No,' said Murray, 'that's not why Laura's edgy.'

'No? Why then?'

Murray hesitated for a second, unsure whether to continue, but Jennifer smiled encouragingly at him. 'Don't worry, I won't tittle-tattle.'

'Why do you think Chris took on someone as experienced as you rather than another vet of my age, say?'

'Like I said, to expand the small animal side of business.'

'It's more than that, Jenny. He wants you as a partner, obviously.'

It was not something that Jennifer had even considered, but as

she thought about it, she realized that Murray was right. 'I see . . .
and Laura of course is hoping to become a partner herself. Did
Chris say anything about this to you?'

'Of course not.'

'Listen, Murray, do me a wee favour, would you?'

He nodded encouragingly.

'Not "Jenny" please, I hate it. Jennifer or Jen.'

'Got it.'

'The trouble is : . . I really do prefer to work with large
animals.' She turned to a guinea-pig in a cage. 'No offence,
mate.'

While Murray and Jennifer were talking, Laura and her husband,
Alan, a solicitor in Whitton, had been looking round a house for
sale. It was a rambling old cottage with several outbuildings and a
perfect cottage garden. Alan tried to sound neutral as he said
goodbye to the owner but he could not hide the tremor of
excitement in his voice.

'Thank you so much. We'll phone the estate agent when we've
had a chance to think about it.'

The owner smiled and waved them off. Laura and Alan walked
away from the house but then stopped and looked back.

'It's absolutely beautiful,' said Laura.

'Isn't it?' He waited a moment, but then chivvied her eagerly,
his eyes shining in his round, cherubic face. 'Well . . . what do you
think?'

'Even if they drop the asking price, it's still outside our range.'

'I don't think so, really.'

Laura flashed him a look that Alan had grown to know well.

They walked in silence, a coolness developing rapidly between
them. Finally Alan could stand the silence no longer. 'What is it?'

'You know what it is. I don't want us to take out a whopping
mortgage. I'm going to need the loan facility from the bank to
invest in the practice.'

'He's not going to offer you a partnership, Laura,' Alan
interjected.

'We don't know that.'

He turned her around to face him and said gently, 'We do
know that. Since Jennifer arrived, he's let the whole matter drop,

hasn't he? He's got her lined up. Why else would he take on a vet of twelve years' experience?'

Laura looked at him for a moment in silence, then said, 'I think you should have more faith in me. I'm going to talk to Chris at the dinner tonight.'

'I don't think that's a good idea . . .' began Alan, but his voice trailed off into silence as she looked contemptuously at him and then strode off down the road, leaving him gazing forlornly after her.

Jennifer spent some time getting ready for the dinner. She put her hair up, looked at herself critically in the mirror, then shook her head and let her hair fall around her shoulders. She chose a discreetly sexy outfit, smoothed down her dress and stared at herself again in the mirror. She was pleased with what she saw, but frowned at a grey hair and yanked it out with a pair of tweezers.

She thought for a second and then walked through to Steven's room, where he was sitting hunched over his computer. Jennifer glanced around the obsessively tidy room, unlike her own, which had clothes and towels draped over every available surface. She went up to him and put her arms around him from behind.

'Mum!' said Steven crabbily.

'Affection never did anyone any harm, mate. How are you getting on with your megabytes and your input terminals this evening?'

Steven said nothing but leaned back in his chair and looked at her, resigned to the interruption.

'I think you should come with me tonight, Steven. I could do with the moral support.'

'But I haven't finished. Besides, I won't know anyone there, will I?'

'Whereas I'm about to meet all my closest friends, of course. Go on. I'll sneak you a lager.'

'Sorry.'

'Oh, all right. I don't blame you, I'm dreading it.'

She walked to the door, then stopped with an afterthought. 'Why don't you put some posters on the wall? This bedroom's tidier than mine, it's ridiculous. It's obvious where you get it from, of course. Your father used to follow me round with some Pledge and a duster.'

Steven did not share the joke and Jennifer was instantly contrite. 'Oh, I'm sorry. You do miss him, don't you?'

'I don't think about it.'

'Well, you should. You should talk about it too.'

As usual, Steven changed the subject. 'Are you not going to change for this dinner?'

'Huh, very funny. I'll see you later.'

She tousled his hair and went downstairs.

The dinner was being held in Whitton Town Hall, a granite, mock-Gothic Victorian pile, its chimneys rising like turrets above its crenellated walls. The only battles it had seen in its hundred-year history were political ones, however, and tonight it was hosting another joust, Patricia's fund-raising dinner in aid of a campaign against the building of a by-pass that would cut a swathe through the woods and green fields around Whitton.

As Jennifer walked into the bar, she saw Laura and Alan chatting to friends in a corner while Patricia and Chris, very much in host and hostess mode, were mingling with the guests. A local council-lor had cornered Chris but Patricia walked behind him and discreetly tugged his elbow. With a polite smile, Chris effortlessly disengaged and turned to Patricia, who muttered, 'He's Chair of the Education Committee. Don't let him start on public spending cuts, the man's a Neanderthal.'

As she began to move away, she paused, smiled fondly at him and whispered, 'I'm glad you're here, Chris. I value the moral support.'

'You know what they say. Behind every great woman . . .'

'. . . There's her therapist.'

Patricia moved on, and as Chris turned back to the group, the councillor looked him straight in the eye.

'Do you take your wife's position on the Education budget, Mr Lennox?'

'I might not if I knew what it was. But if I did know what it was, I wouldn't tell her I knew in case I disagreed with her. Even if I didn't. Disagree with her. Do you see?'

The councillor gave a weak, puzzled smile and Chris escaped

under the cover of the confusion. He had caught a glimpse of Jennifer looking lost in the crowd and worked his way over to her. He cast an admiring glance over her. 'I hardly recognized you.'

They moved to the bar and chatted over their drinks for a few minutes.

'How was your shopping expedition for the communion dress?' asked Jennifer.

'For something that's only worn once, it was extremely expensive.'

'I'm not a very religious person, I'm afraid.'

'Nor's Patricia. I'm not what you'd call a fanatic but I like to think there's something that separates us from the animal kingdom, apart from distemper and spongy brain disease.'

She smiled, but there was a brief, awkward silence. 'Look,' said Chris, 'I'd better circulate.'

'Er . . . Chris, in case I don't get a chance later, I wanted to say that . . .' began Jennifer.

'If it's about our difference of opinion this morning, forget it.'

'No, it's not that. I'm afraid I was rather "economical with the truth" at the interview. After so many years in the big city, I knew I'd never be offered a place in a rural practice if I said I wanted to work mainly with large animals, so I naturally said . . .'

'That you were happy to help build up my small animal business,' supplied Chris, completing the sentence for her.

'I mean, don't get me wrong, I am happy to do that, of course I am, but . . .' Jennifer's voice trailed off.

'But you want to do farm work and equine work as well?'

'Well, yes, but . . .'

'Then you can do it all, can't you? You'll just have to work bloody hard, that's all.'

Relieved and delighted, Jennifer threw him a dazzling smile.

Patricia joined them at the bar. 'Never again, I'm shattered.'

'Listen, Patricia, what exactly is this do about?' said Jennifer.

'Didn't anyone tell you?' said Patricia, her eyes sparkling with amusement. 'It's about the new by-pass they want to build.'

'Oh really? That's a good idea.'

Patricia smiled and shook her head.

'No, you're right, silly of me, a by-pass is a terrible idea,' laughed Jennifer.

Patricia checked her watch. 'Here goes.' She cleared her throat and banged on a table with a glass. 'Ladies and gentlemen! Will all those taking part in the fund-raising dinner please make their way into the dining-room. All those not taking part, don't think you'll get off scot-free, there'll be people coming round with buckets.'

As they sat down to eat, Neil was making his final rounds of the day at Fairbrother's farm. He checked the suckler calves and crossed the yard to the shed where the hoggs were kept. He swept his torch quickly around the shed and went out, closing the door. Everything seemed fine.

The noise of his footsteps faded away across the yard but inside the shed, above the rustle of the hoggs moving through the straw, there was the sound of water trickling steadily on to bare concrete. The rusted, ancient iron pipe bringing water to the trough lay broken on the ground and the trough was already dry, as the water ran uselessly away through the floor of the shed.

Chapter 3

Two days later, Chris and Murray were working in the operating theatre when Chris suddenly broke off from the operation. 'You don't think I made a mistake, do you?'

'With Jennifer? Why do you say that?'

'I don't know. A woman vet, a townie, a divorcee . . . I know Whitton's ready for a change, but we're not asking too much, are we?'

'Of Whitton or of Jennifer?'

'Both.'

'Probably,' grinned Murray. 'It'll be a laugh to see who cracks first, eh?'

Before Chris could reply, he heard a sudden commotion and went to investigate. As he went out into the corridor he could hear Neil arguing violently with Maddy.

'I'm telling you plain as day, you can't go in, Mr Fairbrother.'

'Why the bloody hell not?'

'What's the problem, Neil?' asked Chris, putting a restraining hand on his arm.

'I've come for the calves.'

'Well, you'll have to wait for a short while, I'm busy.'

'I haven't got all day, I've a farm to run.'

Chris took an even firmer grip on his arm and steered him outside on to the terrace by the river. 'Right, Neil, the first thing is that you are not to raise your voice to my staff – or to me – like that.'

'Yeah, well . . .' said Neil, as surly and truculent as a teenager.

'I mean it. Now the calves are fine, so what's the problem?'

Neil did not reply.

'Stubborn and argumentative, just like your dad,' said Chris. 'You can talk to me, Neil, now come on.'

'I ain't fed the hoggs for two days; there's no feed left.'

Chris stared at him aghast. 'Oh bloody hell, man, you must be crackers. They'll fetch nothing at the sales if you don't get them up to weight.'

'I know that,' said Neil angrily. 'What the hell do you think I am – an idiot?'

Chris gave him a world-weary look. 'I'll get some feed and come up tomorrow morning.'

'I can't afford to pay for any more.'

'I'll pay for the feed, you can owe me, don't worry. Now come on, let's get these calves loaded.'

When Neil got back to the farm, he found Steven helping Scott to load fodder for the sheep up on the pasture. Steven had made friends with Scott on his first day at his new school and he had come along with him, lured by the promise of a chance to mess about on the trials bike after Scott had finished his work.

Neil nodded curtly to Scott but scowled at Steven. 'He's just giving me a hand, Mr Fairbrother,' said Scott. 'It's OK, isn't it?'

Neil shrugged, scowled at Steven again, and then walked on across the yard without a word.

'Friendly, isn't he?' breathed Steven.

They foddered the sheep and then Scott took Steven rough-riding over the moor up to the old tin mine, plummeting down gullies and over ridges on the trials bike, as Steven hung on the back, whooping with excitement. As dusk was falling, they sat by the fence up on the hillside above the farm, sharing a can of lager.

'It's funny living in the country,' said Steven. 'Don't know if I like it yet. My mum says she's glad she's moved, but that's only because she's old. She'll be forty in a couple of years.'

'Yeah, mine too. Sad, isn't it?'

Steven gazed curiously at the sheds by the farmhouse. 'What's in those barns?'

'Hoggs – lambs. Come on, I'll show you, but keep quiet. If Mr Fairbrother catches us sneaking around he'll go berserk.'

They jumped on to the bike, freewheeling so as not to make a noise as they bumped down the rutted hillside.

The yard was in darkness but for the glow from the farmhouse kitchen. Scott led Steven to the barn, miming for him to keep quiet. He pulled the barn door closed behind them and switched on the light. They both froze in horror, staring at the scene confronting them. In the pool of light they could pick out one dead hogg after another, a carpet covering the shed floor. Among the dead hoggs, a few live ones stirred slowly.

'What's happened?' asked Steven, wide-eyed.

'I dunno. Let's get out of here,' said Scott, panic edging his voice as he switched off the light, shutting out the terrible sight. He grabbed Steven's arm and pulled him out of the door. They ran up the yard, pushing the bike.

'It must have been an accident, but don't tell anyone,' said Scott, peering anxiously over his shoulder. 'If Neil finds out we've been down here, he'll have us.'

'Who am I going to tell?' said Steven, shuddering at the thought of the dead hoggs.

'Come on,' said Scott. 'Let's go!'

He did not start the engine until they were out of the yard, but the farm dogs were already barking and the front door of the farmhouse swung open. Neil looked out but could see no sign of life. He called to the dogs to be quiet and was about to turn and go back inside when he heard Scott's bike, followed by the sound of the barn door, banging in the wind. He started to walk across the yard.

He came in through the kitchen door a few minutes later, walking like a zombie. He closed the door and leaned against it, his eyes staring sightlessly ahead. Debbie, watching television in the living-room, called to him, 'Neil? Was there anybody out there, then? Neil?'

He started and rubbed a hand over his face. 'Er . . . no. No, there wasn't.'

Scott had dropped Steven at the top of his lane and he hurried down between the high hedges, flinching as an owl winged silently across his path, a white ghost in the dark of the night. At the bottom of the lane, he stood for a moment, trying to compose his features as he looked out across the river, then quietly opened the cottage door and tiptoed in. He took off his jacket, hung it on the hook and started to creep upstairs, but froze as Jennifer came out of the kitchen, carrying a cup of tea.

She saw Steven and started. 'Oh, you gave me a fright. What are you sneaking upstairs for?'

Steven said nothing, but she saw the fear in his eyes. 'Steven, what's the matter?'

'Nothing. Tired, that's all.'

She wrinkled her nose at the smell of farmyard muck, still encrusting his shoes.

'Where have you been?'

'Nowhere.'

'I'm not prying,' she said, making her voice lighter and gentler, as she sensed his mounting anxiety. 'I'm just curious how your feet got covered in cowshit.'

Painfully slowly, Jennifer dragged the story from Steven as he sat on the stairs, still very distressed. She went over to him and held him to her. 'You did right to tell me, love. Now don't worry.'

He gave her a weak smile as she released him and picked up the phone. She dialled Chris's number and stood lost in thought as she let it ring and ring.

Chris's mobile phone lay on the dashboard of his car, parked outside Laura and Alan's pretty cottage in the shadow of the old stone viaduct. The phone rang insistently but went unheard by anyone above the hubbub of dinner party conversation.

Laura stood up to take some dishes back to the kitchen and Chris followed her through with another load. She took them from him and began to stack them by the sink, but as he turned to go back to the dining-room, she called after him, 'Chris, I've been meaning to ask . . .'

He stopped and turned to face her.

'You know how we were chatting before Christmas about the whole question of a partnership . . .'

He nodded, slightly discomfited.

'Well, I was wondering if you'd had any more thoughts on the matter.'

'To tell you the truth, Laura, I haven't. Perhaps I shouldn't have raised the matter before . . .'

'Before you'd had a chance to get to know Jennifer, you mean?' asked Laura testily.

'No, I was going to say before I'd found out if there was the demand to warrant a big injection of capital into the business.'

'There's no problem you know, on that front. The bank has promised me the loan any time I want it.'

'I know, I know.'

'Of course Jennifer has the capital already, doesn't she? From her share of her and her husband's business.'

'That's not relevant, Laura.'

'But are you going to offer her a partnership? I think I have a right to know, Chris.'

Before he could answer, Patricia put her head round the door. 'What are you two up to? Illicit snogging?'

Relieved, Chris put his arms around her, kissed her and marched her back into the dining-room. 'If there's sex to be done in't kitchen, it'll be thee and me, lassie,' he said, in a cod Yorkshire accent.

Laura did not share their amusement, staring angrily at Chris's retreating back. Out in the car, his mobile phone rang on unheeded.

Jennifer listened to the phone ring out a couple more times, then put it down and thought hard for a second. Abruptly she made up her mind and pulled on her coat. She kissed Steven's forehead as he still sat forlornly on the stairs, worrying his lip between his teeth. 'I won't be long,' said Jennifer, going out into the night. A moment later Steven heard the car drive off.

On the way up to Fairbrother's farm Jennifer rehearsed what she would say to Neil, but as she pulled into the yard, it was Debbie who parted the curtains and then opened the front door. 'What can we do for you at this time of night?' she asked coolly.

'Is your husband about, Mrs Fairbrother?'

Neil shouted through from the back room. 'Who is it, Debs?'

Jennifer raised her voice. 'It's Mrs Holt, I have to talk to you.'

By the time she had finished the sentence, Neil was at the front door. He threw it wide open and glared at her. 'What the hell do you want?'

'I think you know.'

'What's going on?' asked Debbie, looking from one angry face to the other.

Neil ignored her, still staring balefully at Jennifer. 'Get off my land. You're trespassing.'

'You have to show me the shed. It may not be too late.'

'Too late for what?' asked Debbie, panic beginning to edge her voice. 'What's happening, Neil?'

Again he ignored her. 'Get out!'

'Mr Fairbrother, I need to see.'

'You need to get back in that car and drive if you know what's good for you.'

Jennifer started across the yard towards the shed but Neil overhauled her and grabbed her roughly by the arm.

'I have to see them,' said Jennifer. 'Let go of my arm.'

Neil did not budge, tightening his grip, his fingers biting into her arm as he shouted, 'Get off my bloody land.'

Jennifer gave him a long look, then turned, pulling her arm away from him, and got back into her car. She drove off quickly, dirt spraying from the wheels as she sped up the lane, heading for the police station in the centre of Whitton.

Debbie stood silently on the farm doorstep, waiting for some word of explanation from Neil. He said nothing, gaze downcast but watching her warily through his eyelashes. Abruptly she strode away from the farmhouse towards the shed, ignoring his call, 'Debbie, don't.'

He started after her, but she reached the shed first. She opened the door and turned on the lights, reeling back as she saw the horror inside. Neil came quietly up, and stood a pace behind her in the doorway.

'They died of thirst,' he whispered listlessly. 'The pipe broke. I heard them bleating but I thought it was only because they were hungry.'

Debbie just stood there, mute and rigid with shock.

Chris was at the practice first thing the next morning, his mood as dark as the overcast sky. He and Jennifer carried on a furious argument on the terrace as Murray and Laura watched from a safe distance.

'It's my duty to report cruelty,' said Jennifer angrily, 'and Murray's and Laura's. Not just yours because you happen to be the boss.'

'These are my clients and you do not ever – do you understand – ever, barge on to their farms uninvited,' said Chris, banging his fist down on the wall in punctuation.

'Barge?'

'In the circumstances, I think Jen could be forgiven for acting hastily . . .' began Murray, trying to oil the troubled waters.

'I didn't act hastily,' said Jennifer rounding angrily on him.

'There were other ways of handling it,' said Laura smugly.

Jennifer flashed her a ferocious glare, but fought to calm the anger burning inside her. 'I had no choice,' she continued, more reasonably. 'The animals were suffering and he wouldn't let me see them.'

Laura's own anger was mounting, her bitterness spilling out at being passed over by Chris for a partnership. 'This isn't some ignorant inner-city yob maltreating his Rottweiler here. This is a working farmer who depends on his animals for his livelihood.'

'Laura . . .' pleaded Murray, but his voice was lost in the row.

'You think I don't know the difference?' said Jennifer bitterly.

'Do you know how much business we'd lose if clients began to see us as interfering busybodies out to cause trouble?' asked Chris.

'Clients!' exploded Jennifer. 'I may be new to rural practice and an ignorant townie but in my book animal welfare takes precedence over your balance sheet.'

Jennifer and Chris both stormed to their cars and roared off in a squeal of tyres and dust, leaving Murray and Laura standing there. Murray pulled a long face before going back indoors but Laura stayed outside, a smile playing around the corners of her mouth.

Jennifer and Chris ignored each other when they reached Fairbrother's farm, Jennifer tending to the surviving hoggs, giving them water and feeding them carefully with the concentrate that Chris had brought, while he stood off to one side, talking to Neil. As they talked, they watched a JCB excavating a large pit in the field in front of the farm. Next to the mound of earth was an equally big pile of bodies – the dead hoggs.

'What'll happen to me?' Neil asked quietly.

'The police will report it to the RSPCA, who'll decide whether to prosecute,' said Chris.

'Did she have to do that?'

'It is our legal duty to report cruelty, Neil, I'm afraid. You should've let Jennifer see the hoggs and told her what happened.'

'I never meant them to die. That pipe broke, that's all it was.'

33

'How come neither of you checked the animals?'

'I didn't want Debbie going in there, she's pregnant.'

'I see.'

'And I didn't want to see them, not if I couldn't feed them.'

There was a long silence, Neil gazing sightlessly ahead of him as the JCB repeatedly clawed at the dark red earth.

Jennifer walked over to them. 'I'm all done in there. There are half a dozen or so which are very weak, so I've put them apart. You'll need to keep a close eye on them.'

Neil nodded, avoiding her gaze. There was another uneasy silence as Jennifer looked at the pile of dead hoggs and then turned and went back to her car, acutely aware of Debbie watching her coldly from the front door of the farmhouse.

As Jennifer drove off, the JCB, having finished its excavations, began scooping up bucketfuls of dead hoggs, dumping the bodies into the pit as a man shovelled quicklime over and around them. They fell with soft thuds, their fleeces muffling the sound. Debbie turned away, biting her lip, and Neil walked round to the back of the farmhouse without a word, leaving Chris standing there as the JCB completed its grisly work, dumping soil back on top of the mountain of corpses.

When Chris got back to the practice, he found Jennifer sitting on a bench by the weir. She looked up as he walked over and sat down beside her. There was a momentary silence as both of them gazed out over the river.

'Eighty-three we buried,' said Chris.

Jennifer looked at him appraisingly. 'You know, I've never been able to harden myself to animal cruelty. I saw some things in London over the years you wouldn't credit. There's one thing you learn quickly. The English don't love their pets. They're sentimental about them, which is completely different.'

'Mindless cruelty's not confined to the big city.'

'I'm sure it's not.'

Chris took a deep breath. 'You did wrong, it's important that you understand that.'

'Important? You mean, for my future in Whitton?'

Chris did not reply.

'I didn't do wrong, Chris. Cruelty is indivisible. Of course

34

there are different explanations for cruelty – it can be wanton, it can be tragically accidental – but it's cruelty and it has to be stopped.'

'Occasionally I've had to threaten clients with reporting them to the RSPCA,' said Chris. 'It's very useful to have a third party so to speak, to help put a bit of pressure on. It usually does the trick too. But we are compromised in cruelty cases, Jennifer, that's the reality.'

'And what if it doesn't "do the trick"?'

'We cross that bridge when we get there.'

'For those eighty-three hoggs, it was already crossed, wasn't it?'

Chris looked thoughtfully at her for a moment and then got up and walked away as Jennifer put a hand to her eyes.

She was glad to get away at the end of the day, able to put the wrangles with Chris to one side as she submerged herself in mindless domesticity. She was cooking tea in the kitchen when she heard someone shouting outside. She turned off the radio. The shouting was clearer, a boy's voice, angrily calling, 'Steven! If you're in there, get out here.'

Jennifer looked out of the window and saw Scott. As she walked through to the hall, she saw Steven slip out of the house. Through the open front door, she could hear the argument outside.

'What's the matter?' asked Steven.

'You know bloody well what's the matter. You told her in there about those sheep.'

'I never did.'

'You're going to pay, I tell you. Neil's my mate and you grassed him up.'

'I never did.'

'I don't believe you, who else would have bloody well told her?'

'I didn't tell her!'

Jennifer stepped into the doorway. 'Yes, he did tell me. I forced him to. And we saved twenty of those lambs which would have been dead by teatime otherwise.'

Steven turned angrily to her, saying 'Mum . . .'

'Don't lie, stand up for yourself.'

He looked at her, with tears in his eyes, then muttered, 'You bastard,' and rushed past her into the house.

She recoiled, shocked, then glared at Scott, saying, 'Get off home, Scott.'

She closed the door and shouted up the stairs, worried. 'Steven?'

There was no reply. She went upstairs to his room and found him sitting on the bed, still tearful.

'You've messed up my life.'

'I've hardly done that, love,' said Jennifer, softly. 'You'll make it up with Scott, you'll see.'

'Moving here, I mean. What do you want to move so far from London for anyway? To get away from Dad, was it?'

Jennifer realized that this was more serious than she had thought. She sat on the bed a little way away from him and weighed her words carefully before she spoke. 'No, I didn't want to move all this way to get away from Dad. The offer from Chris was the only suitable one that came up. That's the honest truth.'

'It's still a long way to go back for the weekends though, isn't it?'

'Oh Steven, you can go back for a weekend to see Dad, of course you can. I wouldn't dream of stopping you.'

'Maybe I should go back for longer than a weekend.'

Surprised and hurt, Jennifer looked up at him. 'Is that what you'd like?'

He kept his eyes averted, talking almost to himself. 'He'd be pleased to have me live with him, wouldn't he?'

'Yeah, for about a fortnight.'

'He was right to walk out though, wasn't he? After what you did. He told me all about it, you know? You really hurt him.'

'I wounded his pride very badly, yes, but it doesn't compare to the pain he caused me over the years.'

She covered his hand with hers. 'I'll tell you all about it if you want but not right at this moment, eh? Its been a bad day for both of us. I'd better go and see how that meal's getting on.'

She went to the door but paused on the threshold. 'I shouldn't have interfered in your row with Scott, it was none of my business. I demand too much of you sometimes, I forget you're only sixteen.'

'You're so concerned about your new job you seem to forget most things,' he said stubbornly, turning his face away and rejecting the olive branch.

She gazed helplessly at the back of his head for a moment and then went out, closing the door quietly behind her as her eyes filled. She gritted her teeth and held the tears back determinedly as she went downstairs.

Chapter 4

As Maddy was sorting through some paperwork at the desk the next morning, Debbie came hurrying in from the bus-stop and stood by the counter, fidgeting nervously with the strap of her handbag.

Maddy smiled encouragingly. 'Can I help you?'

'I'm Mrs Fairbrother. I've come to see Mr Lennox.'

'I'm afraid he's out all morning, can anyone else help?' asked Maddy, but Debbie just shook her head, turned on her heel and rushed out again.

She was hurrying away from the building when Jennifer, loading equipment into the boot of her car, spotted her and called after her. Debbie looked back and hesitated for a moment, but then carried on.

'No, wait, please,' called Jennifer.

Debbie stopped, hesitantly, and stood there waiting.

'Is there anything I can do for you?' asked Jennifer as she came over to her.

'No, not really, it's . . .'

'Please. Let me help, if I can.'

Debbie looked doubtfully at her. 'Neil could go to prison for this, couldn't he?'

'That's extremely unlikely. Besides, there's no certainty the RSPCA will prosecute.'

'How would I cope if he went to prison? I'm going to have a baby.'

'Yes, Chris told me.'

'It was an accident, you know, those hoggs dying like that.' She looked guardedly at Jennifer. 'Everything's getting on top of him. One minute he's like a kid, full of dreams and whatnot and the next he's angry – he'd go mad if he knew I was here today.'

'Why did you come this morning?' asked Jennifer, her voice sympathetic.

'I was, er . . .' Debbie hesitated, then gave an imperceptible shrug of her shoulders and let the words tumble out. 'I was going to ask Chris to ask the RSPCA not to, you know, go on with this.'

'It's not Chris's decision really. It's theirs,' said Jennifer, not unkindly.

There was a silence.

'He can't cope,' said Debbie, resignation in her voice. 'Never has been able to. We'll never pay off our debts, not now. Just like his bloody father.'

'He wanted to succeed where Dad failed?'

'Stupid bugger, he was never cut out for it but I've never had the heart to tell him. Sorry to take up your time, Mrs Holt.'

Jennifer looked at her, unsure of what to say, but Debbie just turned and walked hopelessly away.

Jennifer went for a drink with Chris and Murray after work that night. She bought her round and returned to the table where the men were in a huddle. 'What are you two whispering about?' she said suspiciously.

'I bought a ticket, that's the main thing,' said Murray.

Chris snorted derisively, 'Out with some crumpet in Plymouth, I bet.'

Murray looked at Jennifer, embarrassed equally by the subject of the conversation and Chris's choice of words.

'Crumpet,' said Jennifer. 'Now there's a word I haven't heard in a good long while.'

'Don't start,' said Chris. 'You sound like Patricia.'

'By the way, Chris, I was expecting the RSPCA to have phoned by now. It's been two days now since I reported it.'

There was an uneasy silence. Jennifer looked up and caught Chris darting a look at Murray.

'What?' she asked.

Chris sighed. 'I called them this afternoon. I spoke to Dick Westerby – he's our man there – and I persuaded him not to proceed with the case. We both felt there were enough extenuating circumstances in this instance to warrant . . .'

He got no further with his explanation, because Jennifer abruptly got to her feet and walked out, leaving her drink untouched on the table. After exchanging another look with Murray, Chris got up and followed her hurriedly. Outside, Jennifer was already fumbling with her car keys.

'Wait!' called Chris, overhauling her. 'Jennifer, wait.'

She stopped and gazed levelly at him, though her jaw was clenched and her nails were digging into her palms.

'I persuaded the RSPCA to drop the case because that was the right thing to do,' said Chris. 'If you want to have a row about it, let's have a row about it and get it over with.'

'I don't want to have a row about it, which is why I left the bar.'

She turned and began to walk away from him again towards her car, but Chris persevered. 'I didn't phone them because Neil is a client, Jennifer. I did it because he's a friend. The hoggs are dead. It was a tragedy – an avoidable tragedy, yes – but there's no purpose served in grinding Neil into the dust.'

'I was going to persuade the RSPCA myself to drop the case,' she said angrily. 'I don't want to see that young couple torn apart, I'm not inhuman.'

'So what's the problem?' asked Chris bemused.

'I shouldn't have gone straight to the police. I should have talked it through with you first. I'm too anxious to make my mark.'

'If you agree with me, why are you upset?' asked Chris, both relieved and puzzled.

'Because . . . you did it behind my back.'

'I did it because this is my practice and I don't need anyone's permission to act on behalf of a client,' said Chris, exasperation again beginning to tinge his voice.

'I know you don't, Chris, but . . . I've been my own boss for nearly all of my professional life, I'm not used to having decisions taken over my head.'

'You're going to have to get used to it, aren't you?'

'Yes. But it'll take some adjusting . . . and I'm going to need your support.'

'I'll do my best,' he said, softening. 'I'll still bark orders at you every now and again but . . .'

'I'll try not to bark back.' She gave him a shy smile.

'You coming back in?'

She shook her head.

'OK. Goodnight.' Chris wandered back towards the pub as Jennifer unlocked her car but she lingered for a moment, looking thoughtfully after him as he disappeared inside.

When she got home, she found Steven standing on his bed fixing a poster to the wall. She stepped into the doorway. 'How can you sleep with that looking down at you?'

He turned round and grinned at her. 'It's better than this horrible wallpaper.'

'You've decided to stay then?'

'For the time being.'

She gave him a conspiratorial smile, then said, 'Sleep well,' and closed the door.

Chapter 5

Ten days later, Jennifer stood alongside Chris up at Fairbrother's farm. All Neil's stock and capital, the animals and the equipment, were on display for a couple of dozen farmers, browsing round, inspecting the wares. Neil stood off to one side, muttering to the auctioneer who would shortly start selling it all off.

'They call this the sad season,' said Chris, 'when the nights draw in.'

Jennifer looked around the desolate scene. 'It must be very lonely. I didn't expect it to end like this.'

He shrugged. 'It could've been worse.'

'Did Neil's father have to sell up too? Debbie mentioned him the other day.'

'It never got that far. He killed himself.'

Jennifer shivered, searched Chris's face for a second and then looked away. Chris kept his expression impassive and said nothing.

Debbie walked over to join them. She gave Chris a brief, bittersweet smile and then turned to Jennifer. 'Neil won't thank you for showing up today, but I will. Thanks for what you did.'

Jennifer flushed with embarrassment, realizing that Debbie thought she had called off the RSPCA. She gave Chris a sidelong glance but he had a faraway look and a half-smile on his lips as he gazed out over the fields. Jennifer turned back to Debbie, smiled and said, 'The least I could do.'

Debbie nodded and went back to stand alongside Neil, who looked past her towards Jennifer, expressionless and unsmiling. Chris intercepted the look and turned questioningly to Jennifer. She looked directly at Neil and made a small gesture of acknowledgement but he turned away without responding.

Chris said nothing as Jennifer let her gaze wander on across the crowd of farmers and the ramshackle buildings and up over the hills to the tors, standing out stark and black against the pale winter sky.

Chris and Jennifer did not wait for the sale. They made their way down the lane to Chris's car, past the clutter of parked Land Rovers and four-wheel drives.

'Fancy a day at the races today?' said Chris as he started the engine. 'I'm on-course vet at the meeting this afternoon. Patricia's coming as well. It might cheer us all up.'

'All right,' said Jennifer. 'Thanks, I'd like that.'

Whitton racecourse stood in the fields to the east of the town, a third division steeplechase course, its freshly painted white railings flanking a dilapidated concrete and steel grandstand – a refugee from the 1960s – sitting incongruously among the rolling green fields.

Chris stood talking into a two-way radio as the bookies shouted the odds and the tic-tac men waved their arms, semaphoring information to and fro across the Silver Ring. The crowd was a democratic mixture: old and young, men and women, a few high-rollers, swigging champagne and swallowing oysters from hampers in the boots of their Bentleys and Porsches, but far more farmers and factory workers, swallowing pints and pork pies before jostling the bookies' stands, eyeing the odds for the next race.

As the course announcer intoned the runners and riders over the public address system, in the sepulchral tones of a country parson announcing the next hymn, Jennifer made a bet with one of the bookies, backing Coolrain Star, a horse trained by a client of the practice.

She watched her ten-pound note disappear into the bookie's bulging leather satchel, took her ticket and pushed through the crowds to a tea stall, joining Patricia up in the grandstand just as the horses were being marshalled at the start. Patricia put down her binoculars and took a sip from the plastic cup of tea, grimacing at the taste.

'At least it's hot and wet.'

'What – the plastic or the tea?'

'What did you back?' asked Patricia.

'Hilary's horse – Coolrain Star.'

Patricia grimaced as she pointed towards the starting stalls. 'Do you get your money back if he doesn't start?'

Coolrain Star was the last horse to go in and was acting up and very restless, twice having to be turned away and led back. Finally the handlers succeeded in heaving and shoving him into the stalls, to the relief of his owner, Mark Shreeves, and his trainer, Hilary Coyle, watching from the rails.

Mark was in his late forties and slightly florid-faced, his once good looks now coarsened through drink. An outgoing, confident working-class man made good, he owned a small chain of local betting shops but his pride and joy were his racehorses, including Coolrain Star. Hilary, a single woman of thirty, ran a small stable of only a dozen horses — half of them Mark's — with the help of her father, Patrick, a retired steeplechase jockey. She needed a good result from Coolrain Star today and bit her lip in anxiety as the starter raised his flag.

'They're off!' boomed the PA, as the starter dropped his flag and the horses leaped from the stalls under the urging of their jockeys. Coolrain Star's jockey tucked him in behind the leaders, keeping clear of trouble and letting him run comfortably within himself. He cleared the jumps like a stag and looked full of running as they rounded the final turn.

His jockey pulled him to the outside and his long stride ate up the ground, overhauling the leaders one by one. Jennifer felt herself caught up in the mounting excitement as he swept to the front and won going away, the crowd roaring him home. Jennifer hugged Patricia in excitement, ridiculously pleased with her £50 win.

Jennifer's exhilaration was nothing to that of Hilary, who was practically turning cartwheels as Coolrain Star romped home, though her joy turned to anxiety when she saw him pull up quite sharply after crossing the finishing line. Chris had spotted the same worrying sign and was already in the winner's enclosure when Coolrain Star was led in, his flanks steaming.

Chris began examining the horse's legs as a crowd of well-wishers and back-slappers engulfed Mark and Hilary. As Mark accepted the congratulations, Hilary gave him a gentle reminder. 'You'd got no faith in the horse, I knew he'd come good.'

'About time too,' said the charmless Mark, 'after all the trouble he's been.'

Jennifer and Patricia appeared, Jennifer tucking her winnings into her purse. 'Well done, Hilary,' she said with feeling. 'What a fantastic win.'

'You must be the new vet,' interrupted Mark, before Hilary could reply. 'How do you do?'

'Jennifer Holt. I've been up to the stable once or twice.'

'So Hilary tells me.'

Jennifer's glance took in his chunky gold jewellery and diamond signet ring. 'He should earn you a lot of money.'

'I like the way this woman thinks,' said Mark to his circle of cronies.

Their laughter was interrupted by Chris, who was kneeling down, holding Coolrain Star's front leg. 'Mark, I think he's strained this tendon.'

'What? You sure?'

'I noticed he pulled up sharply at the end of the race. It's best you don't ride him out till he's settled down.'

'How long for, Chris? It's the middle of the season.'

'I don't know. We'll give him some bute and take another look tomorrow. In the meantime, keep that tendon cool.'

Mark's mood changed abruptly. He rounded on Hilary, complaining, 'He's been nothing but trouble. I should never have let you talk me into buying him.' Hilary said nothing, looking pointedly towards the sign reading 'Winner's Enclosure', but Mark just scowled and stomped off towards the bar.

Hilary sighed, thanked Chris and led Coolrain Star away.

'Come and have a celebration drink,' called Jennifer. 'I had a nice win thanks to you.'

But Hilary's clash with Mark had soured her appetite for celebrations and she just shook her head. 'Thanks anyway, but the sooner I get the horse back to the stables, the sooner he'll mend.'

Hilary's stables were ten miles east of Whitton on the windy, steep-sloping foothills below the moors. She lived with her father in a small stone house next to the stables, which were clean and well-maintained but very basic, with none of the expensive aids to training on which her wealthier peers could draw. All-weather gallops and swimming-pools for the horses were as much the stuff of dreams for Hilary as a mansion for herself.

She was completing the late-night check on her horses when her father limped into the stables. A widower in his mid-fifties, Patrick was a sad, lonely man, plagued by arthritis, the result of innumerable falls in his career as a jump jockey. His Irish accent remained as strong as the day he had left his home to make his fortune, but Hilary, born in England, had only the faintest Irish twang in her voice.

Hilary went to Coolrain Star's box and stroked his head. 'You overdid it a bit today, didn't you, boy?' She looked over her shoulder at Patrick. 'I wish you'd seen him, Dad, he was flying. You should have been there. My first result.'

Patrick just stared at the floor and said nothing.

Hilary studied him thoughtfully for a moment, then said accusingly, 'You didn't want to see Mark parade a winner, that's why you didn't go to the meeting.'

'No, no, I'm glad for the fellah. The result might earn him some respect in the racing world . . . at last.' He avoided Hilary's eye. 'Right, I'm off to my bed. Goodnight, girl.'

He smiled weakly at her and wandered back to the house as Hilary turned back to the horse, feeling the tendon anxiously.

Patricia, in her dressing-gown, was completing her own late-night checks, looking in on Abby and Charlotte, who were both fast asleep spreadeagled across their beds. She tucked them in and quietly closed the door. Chris was still at his desk downstairs, poring over figures and studying a spreadsheet on his computer. Patricia walked up behind him and kissed the top of his head.

He yawned and stretched, leaning back in his chair. 'I'm going to have to decide quicker than I was hoping to,' he said distractedly.

Patricia gazed blankly at him. 'Erm . . . no, I need a clue.'

'About offering a partnership to Jennifer. The cash flow's a real headache at the moment.'

'So offer her the partnership. She's got the money from the sale of her London business, hasn't she?'

'On its way apparently.'

'Listen, we're expanding and we need more capital,' said Patricia, adding, 'It's a nice problem to have,' as she saw his dubious look.

'Yes, I know,' said Chris, though his tone of voice suggested that he was anything but convinced. 'When it was just me doing the vetting and you doing everything else, I never worried about money. Now it's all I worry about.'

'OK then, let's sack everybody and go back to permanent night duty,' laughed Patricia.

'Laura won't like it,' said Chris gloomily, sinking deeper into his blue mood. 'She's expecting me to offer her the partnership.'

'Jennifer's better qualified.'

'But she's so headstrong.'

Patricia gave a slow smile. 'Aha. Attitude problem.'

'I wince sometimes when I hear how she talks to clients.'

'I wonder if this is only a problem because Jennifer happens to be a woman.'

He looked at her with a smile. 'Maybe that's all it is.'

'I think Jennifer would make a very good partner,' said Patricia with an air of finality. 'Don't be too long.' She kissed him and went upstairs to bed, leaving Chris lost in thought.

The object of his thoughts was out at Hilary's stables early the next morning, feeling the tendon on Coolrain Star as Hilary, Patrick and Mark looked on. Jennifer stood up and faced Mark. 'He's no better, Mr Shreeves, I'm sorry.'

'So what are you going to do about it?' asked Mark pugnaciously.

'I'll take a look with the ultrasound, that'll show us how much damage there is.'

'Bloody horse, he's had one medical problem after another,' said Mark, his irritation mounting. 'What about this meeting next week at Taunton?'

'Not a chance I'm afraid. That tendon could bow and he'd be out for good.'

'I want a second opinion . . . if you don't mind.'

Jennifer stiffened at the implied slight, but before she could respond, Hilary had stepped in. 'I mind, Mark. Jennifer is the professional, I think we should accept her judgement.'

There was a tense silence as Mark glared from one woman to the other.

Patrick nervously broke the silence. 'If he's going to be out for the rest of the season anyway, why don't we fire his tendons? At

47

least they'd give us no more trouble; it works more often than not . . .' Patrick lapsed into silence, cowed by a furious look from Hilary.

'Yeah, why not?' mused Mark, patting the horse's neck. 'Fire the front legs, tighten the tendons, we'd be getting no more complaints from you about the hard going then, boy, would we?'

'In which case, you will need to talk to another veterinary surgeon after all, Mr Shreeves,' said Jennifer. 'Applying red-hot irons to a horse's tendons to strengthen them is a barbaric practice and I won't do it. I'll happily scan the leg and begin a course of injections but I won't indulge in cruelty for the sake of increasing your prize money.'

Mark scowled and looked questioningly at Hilary. She returned his look, saying, 'I'm with Jennifer on this.'

Mark tried to make light of the situation, turning to Patrick and saying, 'I'm being taught horse sense by a townie vet and a woman to boot. There's a thing, Paddy, eh?'

Patrick chuckled weakly and Mark gave a short, humourless laugh, but his eyes were hard and unsmiling as he turned on his heel and walked away from the stable towards his car.

Jennifer looked thoughtfully at his retreating back, then picked up her things and headed for her car. 'I'll be back this afternoon with the ultrasound.'

'Yeah, thanks,' said Hilary. 'See you later,' but her eyes did not leave Patrick's face. 'You'd lick his boots if he asked you to,' she hissed as soon as Jennifer was out of earshot.

'We need his horses, Hilary . . .' began Patrick, but she cut him off.

'It's pathetic.'

'It wasn't me, girl, who fell for his fancy words now, was it?' asked Patrick mildly.

Hilary glared at him and then walked away.

Jennifer drove back down into Whitton, breaking into a smile as she saw the first snowdrops pushing through the grass around the cedar tree near the practice. It was the only sign of spring, for the day was grey, raw and cold and she shivered as she got out of the car and hurried into the building.

Alan was perched on a corner of the desk in reception, chatting aimlessly to Maddy and the nursing assistant, Clare, a tall, slim woman in her early twenties with a mischievous grin. She riffled through the pages of the appointments book, bored rigid with Alan's lumbering conversation, and was relieved when Chris wandered through and stopped for a polite word with him.

'How's this house move of yours going, Alan?'

'Did Laura not tell you? They've accepted our offer on that house we saw, the one out by Ivybridge.'

'Beats me why you're moving, it's delightful, your place,' said Chris, who, duty done, was already moving on, but Alan held him back, gabbling on about the house, despite Chris's patent lack of interest.

Laura appeared in the doorway from the surgery, leaving Clare to tidy up.

'The cottage is too small, that's the long and the short of it,' continued Alan, chuckling. 'Where are we going to put all those kids we're going to have?'

Laura looked up and hissed angrily, 'Alan!'

He gave Chris a weak smile and turned to face Laura. 'Oh, are you done? I'll go and wait in the car.'

'I'll just get cleaned up,' said Laura, every syllable dripping ice.

As Alan slunk out of the door she turned to speak to Chris, but he had seized the chance to make good his escape and was already in his office with the door firmly shut.

As soon as she reached their car, Laura began an argument that lasted throughout their weekly shopping run to the supermarket and continued in the car-park outside.

'You're making a fuss about nothing,' said Alan. 'What I say won't make any difference to Chris.'

'He's not going to offer me a partnership in the practice if he reckons I'm about to disappear for five years to have your children.'

'My children?' said Alan.

'He knows full well we can't afford a mortgage and the capital investment in the practice,' said Laura, ignoring the interruption.

'So why are we moving house?'

'Because you wanted to.'

'And you don't?'

Laura did not answer, shooting off at another tangent instead.

'It's like you're deliberately undermining me in front of him. Sometimes I really wonder if you wouldn't rather he made Jennifer a partner instead of me.'

She was speaking rhetorically but Alan's long, embarrassed silence showed her that it was actually true. She wheeled on him, ignoring a couple of shoppers who had paused to enjoy the free show. 'My God, you do. If Chris offers me the partnership, you're actually going to be disappointed, aren't you?'

Alan remained silent, shifting from foot to foot like a schoolboy caught stealing sweets.

Laura shook her head in disbelief. 'Well, that says it all really, doesn't it?'

'You're thirty-one, Laura. If we're going to have a family, when is it that you plan to start?'

'When I'm good and ready and not before,' said Laura, her eyes flashing as she got into the car, slamming the door behind her.

Visibly upset, Alan finally noticed the two shoppers, leaning on the handles of their shopping trolleys. They straightened up, embarrassed, as he glared at them.

'Wheels jammed on those trolleys, are they?'

Laura brooded throughout the afternoon, answering questions from her colleagues in a monosyllable and snapping angrily at one of Murray's customary feeble jokes. She waited until the others had gone home and, seeing a light under Chris's door, knocked softly. 'Chris?'

There was an answering mumble from inside and she went in to find him ploughing through the accounts.

'You wouldn't have time for a quick drink, would you?' asked Laura.

Chris sighed but then put down his pen and smiled at her. 'As long as you're paying.'

The pub was already crowded with drinkers, including Mark and a group of friends, obviously on their way back from a boozy day at the races. Chris steered Laura to a quieter table in a corner of the room. They sipped their drinks while Laura fidgeted nervously and then blurted out, 'Chris, you know what Alan was saying at lunchtime, about the house and kids . . .'

Chris interrupted her, laying a hand on her arm. 'Let me put your mind at rest, Laura. Unless I hear something from you direct, I don't pay it much heed.'

She smiled, relieved if not entirely convinced. 'Thanks. I have no intention of taking time off work to have children. Not for four or five years at least.'

'That's reassuring, I don't want to lose you,' said Chris, sinking back in his chair, thinking that the business of the meeting had been concluded, but Laura was not letting him off the hook that easily.

'But do you want me as a partner, Chris, that's the thing? I've been extremely loyal.'

'Beyond doubt.'

'And I've worked mightily hard in the last four years,' she continued, ignoring the interruption. 'Forgive me for being blunt . . . but maybe you owe it to me.'

Chris flushed a little but his voice was even as he said, 'Forcefully put.'

Laura waited impatiently but Chris only leaned back and took a mouthful of his drink.

'Am I too young or am I not a good enough vet?' asked Laura, relentless in her pursuit.

'Neither,' said Chris, now uncomfortable and irritated in equal measure.

'Then you've decided to offer the partnership to Jennifer, haven't you?'

'No, I haven't. But if I don't, I'll lose her, I know that.'

'But if you do . . . you'll lose me.'

Chris was taken aback by the ultimatum, though Laura's expression showed that it had come as something of a surprise to her too. She was searching for a way to continue when they were interrupted by Mark, weaving his way unsteadily to the table, his face even more flushed with drink than usual.

'Chris my old pal, that bloody woman of yours . . .' He broke off to patronize Laura, saying, 'Excuse me love,' and then turned his back on her again.

'Mark, this isn't quite the moment . . .' said Chris but Mark was unstoppable.

'Jennifer whatever-her-name-is laying down the law to me about how I'm to treat my own horses.'

Laura's sullen look began to fade; she at least was starting to enjoy Mark's discourse.

'She told me what happened and actually I fully support her decision,' said Chris.

'Downright rude she was,' continued Mark, unrelenting. 'I mean, how many years have we known each other, eh?'

Chris tried once more. 'Listen, Mark, let's chat about it in the morning.'

'No, you listen. I don't want that woman up at the stable again looking at any of my horses. Not if you value my custom. Sorry, but that's how it is.'

He wandered off back to his group of mates, leaving Chris staring unhappily at Laura. Had he not known better, he could have sworn that a look of triumph had flashed across her face.

Across the other side of town, Steven wandered out of the changing-room after a game of football. 'I'll see you outside, Scott,' he called over his shoulder. He had just come out of the door when he heard a burst of banging and crashing from the far end of the corridor. Two girls were standing around the drinks machine, while a third tried to liberate some cans of Coke. He recognized her as a girl from his class, Amanda Mulholland. She was sixteen and earthily pretty, with an in-your-face sense of humour and a sexual aura that had Steven and quite a few of his classmates gazing wistfully after her as she left the room, though most – including Steven – were too shy to approach her.

He paused in his tracks to watch her. Suddenly there was a shout. The girls ran giggling past Steven and ducked around the corner, but not before a furious woman teacher had appeared in the corridor. She stared after the girls and then strode up to Steven. 'Was that Amanda Mulholland?'

Steven shook his head. The teacher looked at him quizzically, her head tilted. 'Are you sure?'

'I know Amanda Mulholland,' said Steven. 'That wasn't her.'

The teacher continued to stare at him dubiously but had no option other than to believe him. She shook her head wearily and stalked back the way she had come. As she disappeared, Amanda stuck her head round the corner and looked back towards Steven. She gave him a smile that made him blush to the roots of his hair and chucked a can of Coke to him before disappearing again. Her laughter was still echoing down the corridor as Scott emerged from the changing-room.

'You're still here,' he said.

'Erm ... yeah. Fancy a drink?' asked Steven, holding up the can.

Steven was sitting at his desk the next morning, surrounded by the usual hubbub of the class before the teacher arrived, when Amanda strolled in with her friends. As she walked past Steven, she stopped and said loudly and deliberately, 'Thanks for last night, Steve. I won't forget it.'

She gave him a knowing smile and wandered on to her desk, leaving Steven blushing crimson as the other boys clustered around him. 'Have you really had sex with her?' asked one incredulously. Scott, who had spent the evening with Steven, playing football and then mucking about on the bike, was simply confused.

'What's she on about?'

Steven gave an embarrassed shrug, desperately trying to regain his composure.

Chapter 6

Chris and Jennifer stood in the X-ray room, studying Coolrain Star's ultrasound pictures. Jennifer frowned. 'A course of adequan should help, but he won't make that Taunton meeting.'

Chris nodded, preoccupied. 'You can tell Hilary. I'll let Mark know, I've got to phone him anyway.'

He put the pictures back in the folder but made no move to leave.

Jennifer looked up, slightly puzzled. 'You're very quiet this morning.'

'Mark was in the pub last night.' He took a deep breath. 'You weren't rude to him, I mean . . . all you told him was that you weren't prepared to fire Coolrain Star's tendons, right?'

'You have to ask?' said Jennifer quietly.

'No, of course, stupid of me. Sorry. He was drunk, he probably won't even remember saying it.'

There was a silence as Jennifer waited for him to continue. Finally she prompted him. 'Saying what?'

'He doesn't want you up at the stable. He doesn't want you to treat his horses.'

'And you told him . . . what?'

'I didn't tell him anything. Like I say, he'd been drinking.'

Jennifer's irritation was beginning to mount. 'And if he'd been sober, what would you have told him?'

Chris did not answer immediately, then blurted out, 'I don't know, Jen. He's an important client, he's friendly with other racehorse owners. Word gets around, you know?'

'What "word" is that then, Chris? That some stroppy new vet's rubbing your clients up the wrong way?'

'I have the highest regard for your clinical ability, Jennifer. You know that,' said Chris, skirting the issue.

'It's not enough.' She looked at him for a moment, then shook her head and said quietly, 'I'd better be getting to surgery.'

As she closed the door, Chris threw the folder down on the table, irritated both with the situation and with himself, for handling it so badly.

Still in a bad mood, Jennifer was loading some equipment into the boot of her car when Patricia pulled up and said, 'Hi.'

Jennifer gave her a perfunctory wave and turned back to the boot.

Patricia cocked an eyebrow. 'You OK?'

'Yup.'

'Jennifer, what's up?'

She paused and looked up. 'It's nothing. Really.'

Patricia smiled and said shrewdly, 'Chris giving you a hard time?'

Softening a little, Jennifer gave her a weak smile. 'How did you guess?'

'I've had a lot of practice.'

'I don't think he trusts me. To deal with the clients, I mean.'

'Are you talking about Mark Shreeves?' asked Patricia. 'Chris mentioned something last night.'

'Hardly anyone fires tendons these days. I was amazed Mark was even thinking seriously about it.'

'It's only that Mark's an important client. Or rather all the horse-owners are, it's where the money's to be made.'

'I know that, Patricia,' said Jennifer, patiently.

'Listen, it's not you. He's so bound up with the practice, he treads on people's feet and doesn't even know it half the time. He rates you highly, Jennifer.'

Jennifer gave her a dubious look. 'Funny way of showing it.'

'But it's true.'

'Then why won't he share anything?'

'Not exactly his strong point, I'm afraid.'

'He sees me as a threat. He's worried I'll undermine his authority.'

Patricia smiled, but said nothing.

'I'm right though, aren't I?'

'Take it as a compliment. I do,' laughed Patricia, winning a genuine smile for the first time from Jennifer.

Rain bucketed down that night, turning the streams into torrents, stained blood-red by the rich Devon soil washed out in the flood. Chris, duty vet for the night, peered myopically through the windscreen as he drove home from a call-out, speaking into a small dictaphone as he drove. 'Fourteenth. Stephensons. Examined ewe. Pregnancy toxima. Inject 20 mils dextrose IV 10% calcium sub cut. Visit fee. Twenty miles. Examination and drugs.'

He put the dictaphone down, glanced at his watch, then sighed as his mobile phone rang again. 'Sod's law,' he muttered. 'Lousy weather, twice as many call-outs.' He picked up the phone. 'Hello. Hi Andy, yes, yes, of course. I'll be up there shortly. Bye.'

He turned the car round in the mouth of a tiny, overgrown lane, by a white wooden signpost leaning drunkenly against the hedge. Its legend had long since been obliterated and it now stood, a white bony finger, pointing to nowhere. Chris smiled to himself. He had a not altogether serious theory that somewhere in the maze of high-banked, overgrown lanes around Whitton were tourists who had been driving round them in circles for years, lost to the world like Japanese soldiers hiding in the jungle since the end of the Second World War. Every time they reached a cross-roads, they would find that the legend on the signpost had been eroded away or broken off by local youths, who loved nothing more than confusing the tourists that they contemptuously referred to as 'grockles'.

Chris spent more time driving around the lanes than almost anyone in the county and even he still sometimes got lost, but he knew Andy Gallagher's farm well enough and threaded his way through the warren of lanes west of Whitton, pulling up in the yard of a whitewashed farm, nestling in a hollow, just across a meadow from the river. Normally it was sluggish and slow but tonight Chris could hear the river roaring past, swollen to an angry torrent. Drenched by the rain, he hurriedly took his gear out of the back of the Range Rover. Andy Gallagher shook his hand and led him to the cowshed.

A Friesian cow had just calved and its newly born calf already stood by its mother on weak, unsteady legs, but there was a pool of blood on the floor by the mother. Chris sighed again; this was going to be a long visit. 'How long ago did she calve?'

'Within the last hour.'

'Right. She's ruptured a uterine artery, so we don't have long. She'll need a blood transfusion.'

With Gallagher's help, Chris tethered a second cow near by and was taking blood from it with a cannula into a five-litre bag, when suddenly his mobile phone started to ring again.

He cursed and looked over his shoulder at Gallagher. 'You'd better answer that, Andy. In my coat pocket.'

Gallagher went to the coat and took out the mobile, but then looked helplessly at Chris, unsure of what to do next. 'Sorry, Chris, I'm not used to these.'

'Just press any button.'

He jabbed at a button with one of his thick fingers, reddened by a lifetime of outdoor work in all weathers, and spoke tentatively into the phone. 'Hello. No, it's Andy Gallagher here, Mrs Sinclair. Oh well, he's tied up at the moment.'

'Ask her what the problem is, would you?'

'Chris says what's the problem? Right. I see.' He put his hand over the phone and turned to Chris. 'She says Hilary Wright's phoned up with a suspected colic. The horse is sweating up badly.'

'Tell her she'll have to go out there herself. I don't know how long I'm going to be.'

While Chris began the blood transfusion and repaired the ruptured artery, Laura drove out towards Hilary's stables, peering anxiously through the windscreen, trying to follow the road through the teeming rain. She was also apprehensive about the visit, for she normally only looked after small animals and a colic was not something she had dealt with before.

As she pulled into the yard, Hilary hurried out to greet her, holding an umbrella. 'Thanks for coming.'

'That's all right, I only hope I can be of use.'

Hilary led her to Coolrain Star's box. 'He's been sweating and rolling for an hour or more and keeps looking at his flank where the pain is.'

Laura scanned the straw in the box. 'When did he last pass a motion?'

'No signs on the stable floor, as you can see. Twelve hours, I reckon.'

She looked worriedly at Laura who, visibly anxious, was trying to soothe the horse. She took a stethoscope out of her bag and tried to get nearer to him to take his pulse and feel his gut with her hand, but Coolrain Star thrashed about and started to kick.

'It's no good,' said Laura. 'I'm going to need some help.'

Roused from a doze on her sofa in front of the TV, Jennifer took Laura's call. She scribbled a quick note for Steven, who was out practising his martial arts in Plymouth, and then hurried out into the rain.

Twenty minutes later she joined Laura, Hilary and Patrick in Coolrain Star's box. She swiftly took charge, preparing an injection to sedate the horse, which was now even more agitated than before.

'The pulse rate's very high,' said Jennifer. 'How long has he been like this?'

'An hour. Two at most,' said Hilary.

'OK, my boy. We're going to get you settled down, before you do yourself an injury. Or any of us for that matter.'

With Laura and Hilary's help, Jennifer managed to get an injection into Coolrain Star and after waiting for him to quieten she did a series of tests, putting a stomach tube down his nose, tapping his abdomen and carrying out a rectal examination.

She worked with calm efficiency while Laura looked on, resentment mingling with admiration. 'Will he need an operation?' asked Laura.

'I'm not sure.'

'If you wait till you're sure, it'll be too late,' snapped Patrick.

'I'm aware of that, Patrick,' said Jennifer mildly. 'I want to take him back to the surgery and I'll decide there what to do next. OK, Hilary?'

'If you have to operate, what are his chances?'

'Fifty-fifty.'

'I'll fetch the box out.'

They got Coolrain Star loaded into the transporter and set off, Hilary driving while Jennifer and Laura stayed in the back to keep an eye on the horse. Jennifer called Clare on her mobile phone.

'Sorry to phone you this late, but we're going to need you in the surgery. Yes, a colic on Coolrain Star. Would you open the place up and get it ready? We'll be there in about twenty minutes. Thanks, bye.'

Jennifer and Laura sat in silence for a couple of minutes, bouncing around in the back of the transporter as Hilary drove as fast as the narrow lanes and filthy weather would allow.

Jennifer attempted some polite conversation. 'Had much interest in your house yet, Laura?'

'One or two people have viewed it but no offers.'

'Oh well.'

There was another silence, with Laura making no effort to keep the conversation going.

'It means a great deal to you, doesn't it – a partnership in the practice?' asked Jennifer, trying again.

Laura looked at her searchingly, seeking a hidden agenda behind the question, then said, 'This is my home town. You always want to be queen of the manor, it's only natural.'

'Yeah. I wouldn't want to stand in your way though.'

Laura looked at her quizzically for a moment. 'You didn't sell up and move two hundred miles to become an assistant vet though, did you, Jennifer?'

'I suppose not.'

There was another, longer silence, and a distinct frost in the atmosphere between them continuing all the way back to the practice.

The building was flooded with light, for Clare had already arrived and was preparing the operating theatre. Jennifer led Coolrain Star, still sedated, out of the transporter and through the pouring rain into the padded stable alongside the operating theatre. 'Everything ready, Clare?'

'Yes, I think so,' said Clare.

Jennifer carried out a further rectal test, frowning at the results. 'He's deteriorated. The gut's still obstructed. He could pull out of the colic on his own but if we leave him much longer and he doesn't, that'll be it.'

'Shouldn't we get Chris in?' said Laura. 'Just to be on the safe side.'

Jennifer paused for a second, then said, 'I don't think we need to. Hilary, do you trust my judgement on this?'

Hilary did not hesitate for a second. 'Yes.'

They manoeuvred Coolrain Star towards the operating table and strapped him against it while it stood vertical. Jennifer then administered the anaesthetic and they swung the hydraulic table into the horizontal. The horse lay still, unconscious. Jennifer began the operation, Clare assisting, while Laura watched the dials on the monitoring equipment. Hilary stood to one side, hands clenched and brow furrowed.

Concentrating fiercely, Jennifer felt calm and in control, working in silence except for terse commands and requests for information. The operation took over two hours. Finally Jennifer completed stitching the wound and stepped away from the operating table.

'Now what?' asked Hilary.

'Now we wait,' said Jennifer.

She pulled off her surgical cap and shook out her hair but left her gown on, leaning against the doorframe, tired but pleased with her work. Behind her, Laura and Clare sat quietly, while Hilary paced nervously to and fro.

An hour passed. 'How much longer, do you think?' asked Hilary.

'I don't know, love. Could be a while,' said Jennifer. 'Why don't you go home, get some sleep?'

'I couldn't sleep, I'm so nervous. What are his chances?'

Jennifer smiled and gave her a reassuring look. 'The same as when you last asked, five minutes ago.'

Hilary gave a rueful smile and leaned against the opposite wall for a moment. 'If he pulls through, he will race again, won't he?'

'No reason why he shouldn't, but not this season of course.'

Laura had walked through to check the dials and suddenly called excitedly, 'Pulse rate normal, he's awake.'

Hilary's face broke into a broad smile. She squeezed Jennifer's arm and then went to look at Coolrain Star.

The note that Jennifer had scribbled to Steven remained unread. He had been to his martial arts class in Plymouth and was concentrating hard amid the the rhythm and noise of the crashing escrima sticks. He did not notice as a face appeared at one of the windows. Amanda peered through the dirty window-pane, grinning at the spectacle inside.

When Steven came out of the hall about twenty minutes later, he saw Amanda on the other side of the road taking shelter from the teeming rain in a shop doorway. She waved to him and he crossed over and stood in the doorway next to her.

'What are you doing in Plymouth?' he asked.

'This and that,' said Amanda, airily. 'Do you want to go for a walk?'

'Why?'

'Something to do.'

He looked at her curiously. 'Were you just passing or what?'

She ignored the question, smiling at him and mimicking the action of the escrima. 'What's it for then, self-defence?'

'Martial arts. It's a whole philosophy.'

'Yeah? I'd rather carry a gun,' said Amanda, suddenly bored by the topic. 'It's cold, let's go somewhere.'

They wandered off towards the city centre, the rain bouncing from the pavements around them. By the time they found a burger bar, they were both drenched and sat at a table dripping water, their hair plastered to their heads. Amanda wolfed her burger as if she had not eaten in days. Steven broke off from his to inspect the state of his clothes underneath his jacket.

'The rain's got through. It's soaking.'

Amanda snorted. 'You looked a right pillock in those white pyjamas things.'

'Why were you watching?'

She smiled her slow, seductive smile but did not answer, taking an enormous mouthful from her burger instead.

Steven gazed at her, fascinated. 'Don't they feed you at home?'

'I'm the youngest of three sisters, right? If I didn't eat my food in about ten seconds flat one of them'd eat it for me.' Abruptly she changed the subject again. 'I know your mum.'

'You what?'

'Yeah. My dad looks after a dairy herd out by Corbridge.'

'You don't look like a farmer's daughter to me.'

'What do they look like then?'

Now it was Steven's turn for an abrupt change of subject. 'Did you come all the way to Plymouth to see me?'

Amanda smiled slyly but ignored the question. She gazed around the place, clocking the other customers, then looked straight at Steven. 'Do you fancy me then?'

He blushed but did not answer, despite Amanda's challenging, arousing stare. Instead he looked at the clock and said, 'It's stopped raining. What time's the last bus?'

'Twenty to eleven.'

They stayed in the burger bar, Amanda teasing and flirting with him as Steven told her about London and why they had moved to Devon. Finally he looked at the clock again, jumped to his feet and said, 'Come on or we'll miss the bus.' Amanda gave him an enigmatic smile and followed him out.

'What's funny?' asked Steven.

'Nothing,' said Amanda.

She rubbed the back of her hand gently against his and he shyly took her hand as they walked down the street.

When they got to the bus station, the stand for Whitton was deserted. The last bus had left half an hour earlier.

'I thought you said the last bus wasn't until twenty to eleven,' said Steven.

'I was wrong,' said Amanda innocently, a smile still playing around the corners of her mouth.

Steven tried to phone his mother from a call-box but the only reply came from the answerphone. 'We'll give it a few minutes,' he said, emerging from the box. 'She wasn't on call, so she can't be far away.'

They stood huddled together for ten minutes, Amanda stamping her feet against the cold, then Steven tried the call again. He came out of the phone-box shrugging his shoulders. 'She's still not in. I don't know where she is.'

'Well, we ain't got the money for a taxi.'

'We could hitch, I suppose.'

Amanda shook her head. 'I'm not allowed to hitchhike.'

'What are we going to do?'

Amanda shrugged.

'We could walk,' said Steven, but Amanda shook her head even more emphatically. 'Don't be stupid, it's twelve miles.'

They stood there in silence for a minute, Amanda cuddling into Steven as he gnawed his lip and tried to think what to do.

'Don't you like being with me then?' asked Amanda suddenly.

'Well, yeah . . . but it's a bus station in the middle of the night.'

'My auntie lives around here. We could stay with her.'

Steven flushed, looking slightly alarmed.

'Just till the first bus,' said Amanda, all wide-eyed innocence.

'We could watch TV, I suppose,' said Steven doubtfully.

'We could . . .'

They walked for about half a mile out of the city centre, into a large estate. Amanda paused at a street corner and said, 'Wait in that doorway there while I fix it up.' She kissed him, her lips warm and soft on his, and caught his bottom lip for a moment between her teeth, then smiled and sauntered nonchalantly across the road and up to the front door of a block of flats. After a few moments, a beam of light stabbed out as a middle-aged woman opened the door. 'Hi, Auntie Bridget, I've missed the last bus. Can I stay?'

'Course you can, dear,' said Bridget, giving her a welcoming kiss. 'Come on in.'

Amanda followed her into the flats and the door closed behind her, leaving Steven waiting apprehensively in the darkness.

Bridget chattered away inconsequentially as she bustled around, opening out a sofa-bed in her front room for Amanda. 'And how's Serena getting on at secretarial college?'

'All right, as far as I know. She doesn't talk about it much,' said Amanda, discreetly opening the curtains a fraction and peeking out. She closed them again and yawned noisily.

Bridget raised a quizzical eyebrow but said nothing except, 'Right. I'm off to my bed. If there's anything you want in the night, help yourself in the kitchen but don't clatter about. Now I'd better call your dad and tell him where you are.'

'I did already. From the bus station.'

'OK. Sleep well, pet, I'll wake you in the morning.'

'Goodnight, Auntie Bridget.'

Amanda smiled as the door closed. She waited until she heard Bridget go into her own room and shut the door, then went to the window and opened it, waving to Steven. He looked up, spotted her at the first-floor window and hurried across the road. Amanda leaned out of the window as he looked up at her, Romeo to her Juliet.

'How am I supposed to get up there?'

'Been in training, haven't you?'

Steven took an apprehensive look at the drainpipe next to the window, then began to climb.

Two minutes later, sweating with a combination of effort and nerves, he swung a leg over the window-sill. Amanda caught his arm and hauled him into the room, pulling him to her. Already flushed with exertion, he turned a deeper red as his eyes took in the double bed, already made up. 'Erm . . . do you fancy a coffee?'

'All right,' said Amanda, a little puzzled, heading for the kitchen.

An hour later they were still sitting fully clothed on the bed as Steven drank his fourth cup of coffee, concluding the story of his parents' split-up.

'. . . So I went off with my dad for the week on our own and he told me all about it.'

'Weren't you embarrassed?'

'No, not really. I was a bit confused but . . .'

'I would have been,' interrupted Amanda. 'My dad, talking about lovers and sex, I can't imagine it.'

They both laughed, then Steven fell silent as Amanda turned to face him. 'I'm quite tired, Steven.'

'Oh, are you?' said Steven nervously. 'I'm not. Not yet.'

'That's 'cos you've had four mugs of black coffee.'

He grinned. Amanda took his cup from him and put it on the floor, then leaned into him and kissed him. Steven responded and Amanda pulled him down on to the bed, lying beneath him, her tongue darting between his lips. She moaned softly as he kissed her neck and took his hand, guiding it to her breast, but as her own hand strayed towards his waistband, he broke off the kiss and pulled away from her.

Flushed and excited, Amanda looked at him incredulously. 'What's the matter?'

'Nothing.'

'You nervous?'

'Not really, no,' lied Steven.

Amanda propped herself up on one elbow. 'Well, are you gay?'

'No, I'm not gay. Well, at least not yet I'm not.'

They both smiled.

'It's just that . . . you know, with your Auntie Bridget in the next room . . . We can just talk, can't we?'

Amanda yawned. 'I suppose so.'

They fell asleep on top of the covers, both fully dressed and facing in opposite directions, and were still there the next morning, when the door opened and Auntie Bridget came in, carrying a small tray with two cups of tea on it.

Completely unfazed at the sight of Steven, she said brightly, 'Wake up, five past six.'

Amanda stirred and moaned. Steven sat bolt upright, shocked awake, staring straight at Bridget.

'I didn't know whether the young man took sugar or not.'

Steven blushed crimson but then forgot his embarrassment as he realized the time.

'It's daylight, come on,' he said, jumping up and shaking Amanda's arm. Bleary-eyed, Amanda followed, pausing to thank her aunt, who sent her on her way with a kiss and a knowing look. Steven hurried her down to the city centre to catch the first bus to Whitton.

Chapter 7

Coolrain Star stood unsteadily in the padded stable at the practice. Jennifer and the others watched him, all very tired, Clare trying unsuccessfully to stifle a yawn.

'You go home, love,' said Jennifer. 'There's nothing more to do here.'

Clare nodded gratefully and shuffled out, murmuring, 'Goodnight all. Good morning, rather.'

Hilary stroked the horse's face. 'How are you feeling, boy? Eh?'

'He's doing pretty good,' said Jennifer. 'Come on, let's leave him alone with his thoughts for a while.'

She took her by the arm and gently guided her away from the horse. Laura opened the stable door and the sunlight streamed in. They stepped out into the bright early morning.

Jennifer saw Hilary's transporter, standing on its own in the car park. 'I'd forgotten. Our cars are still up at your place.'

'I could drive you both up there now if you want,' said Hilary.

'I'm too tired,' said Laura. 'I'll stop by later. Is there anything more to do here, Jennifer?'

'No, I'll keep an eye on him. You go home.'

Laura started to walk away but stopped and turned back. 'Thanks for coming out last night.'

She and Jennifer exchanged tired smiles. It was the first sign of a slight thaw in Laura's previously unrelenting cold front and Jennifer was touched, for she knew what an effort even this small gesture must have been for her.

As Laura wandered off towards home, Jennifer made some coffee. She and Hilary sat wrapped against the cold, drinking it on the low wall overlooking the river. Still swollen with last night's rain, it swept past them, brown and swift, stained with peat and mud and carrying branches and even tree trunks on the flood. They sat silent for a minute just listening to the weir, normally a murmur, now a rolling thunder.

Hilary looked away from the river towards the stables. 'I'm not looking forward to telling Mark about the latest vet's bill.'

'How did you come to train his horses originally?' asked Jennifer.

Hilary pursed her lips and hesitated before replying. 'Through my dad. They go back thirty years those two. Believe it or not, Mark was once a jockey himself but he was never that good. Dad was better, he rode over two hundred winners. Mark used to hero-worship him; so Dad tells me anyway, but then Mark started to make the money and Dad's career took a dive. It's funny how their relationship has completely turned round.'

'Did you get started as a trainer when Mark asked you to look after his horses?'

Hilary nodded. 'Two years ago now. He saw it as a way of paying Dad back for all the good years.'

'So what is it with you two?'

Hilary looked sideways at her but then took a deep breath and carried on. 'I was very grateful for the opportunity to become a trainer and I . . . I showed it in the wrong way. We had a short scene together. It was a disaster of course, but he still resents the fact that I don't fancy him any more.'

Jennifer smiled sympathetically. 'When it comes to dealing with men, I think I'm the most ill-equipped woman in Christendom.' She squeezed Hilary's arm, then yawned and said, 'Look, I'm about ready to drop. You wouldn't give me a lift home in that, would you? I'll pop out later to pick the car up.'

'Sure.'

They ambled back to the transporter, arm in arm.

Jennifer dozed in the passenger seat as they drove through Whitton on their way to her cottage and it was Hilary who spotted Steven walking along the street.

'Isn't that Steven?'

Jennifer opened her eyes and stared at her pale-faced son. 'God, look at the state of him. It looks like he slept in those clothes. Drop me off here, will you, Hilary?'

As the transporter stopped, Jennifer jumped out and waved Hilary off. She turned to face Steven, who gave a start of surprise.

'Where on earth have you been?' asked Jennifer. 'Have you been out all night?'

'Well . . . sort of. No, not really.'

Jennifer saved the full-scale interrogation until they reached the cottage but began it as soon as she had closed the front door. 'Right, where were you?'

'I was with a friend,' said Steven sulkily.

Jennifer raised her eyes to the heavens. 'That's it, is it? "I was with a friend." Who? Scott? Do I know him? Were you with a friend . . . and a load of heroin addicts for example?'

'Don't be ridiculous,' said Steven.

'I worry about you.'

'You didn't know I was out. How could you be worried?'

'Don't be so pedantic!'

'If you must know, I stayed over at a friend's auntie's because we missed the last bus back to Whitton. There's a message – no, two messages – on the answerphone.'

'Fine. Phew. Like getting blood out of a stone.'

'Can I go and get changed now?'

Jennifer nodded and, off the hook, Steven ambled out of the kitchen. As he got to the bottom of the stairs, however, his mother's voice came floating after him.

'Steven. This friend . . . was it a boy or a girl?'

There was no reply. Jennifer smiled to herself, then gave another cavernous yawn and headed upstairs for a shower and a freshen-up.

Two hours later she was changed and back at the practice in answer to a call from Chris. The door to the equine unit stood open and she walked over, seeing Chris and Clare standing there with Coolrain Star. Even before she saw the horse, Jennifer could tell from Chris's concerned expression that the horse was in severe distress.

Chris looked up and saw her standing in the doorway. 'He has an ileus, I'm afraid. Severe.'

Jennifer looked at him sharply. 'You sure?'

He nodded. 'Tense bowel loops, pulse rate seventy-five. I tried a stomach tube and the gut's stopped functioning.'

She dug her nails into her palms. 'Dammit.'

'It happens, Jen. Not your fault. Even the best surgeon in the country . . .'

'Has he had painkillers?' asked Jennifer, clutching at straws.

'Yes. He's still in agony.' He straightened up and stepped away from the horse.

'We've no choice, I'm afraid.'

He walked past her out of the stable.

'I wish you'd phoned me earlier,' said Jennifer.

He stopped in his tracks, looked her full in the eye and said, 'Likewise.'

Stung, Jennifer turned to Coolrain Star and stroked him on the face, her cheeks burning.

Chris walked into his office, unlocked the safe and took out his revolver. He loaded it and walked out of the office and through reception as Murray, Laura, Clare and Maddy watched him go in silence. He shut the door and walked across to the equine unit. Jennifer stepped away from the horse as Chris stood framed in the entrance. He said nothing, but gave her a questioning look. She shook her head and walked out, standing alone in the car park, with her back to the buildings.

A few moments later, there was the single crack of a gunshot. It was audible inside the practice building and all four people froze momentarily before resuming their work. No one met another's eye. Jennifer stood stock still for a minute, then squared her shoulders and walked back into the practice. The others studiously busied themselves at their desks as she phoned for a taxi and then stood waiting in the entrance until it appeared.

Light rain was falling as the taxi pulled up at Hilary's stables. Lost in thought, Jennifer did not even notice. The driver turned to her, cleared his throat and then said tentatively, 'We've arrived, Miss.'

Jennifer came to with a start, looked around, then hurriedly got out of the taxi and paid it off.

Hilary came to the door all smiles, but one look at Jennifer's face told her what had happened. They sat at the kitchen table, Hilary pouring them both a large glass of wine. She drank hers in two gulps, refilled it and looked inquiringly at Jennifer, who shook her head, leaving hers untouched on the table.

Jennifer broke the silence. 'There was nothing more we could have done.'

'Sure. Here's to a once promising career as a trainer,' said Hilary, taking another large swig.

'You trained one winner, you can train another.'

'Yeah? When this gets out, my name's going to be mud. So when Mark takes the rest of his horses away, how am I going to get any more? Buy them myself?'

'Surely he wouldn't do that?'

'Just watch him.'

'It's not your fault. You have to fight for your name and your reputation, believe me I know.'

'What do you know?' asked Hilary, scornfully. 'Something goes wrong in your job, you shoot the horse and send the owner the bill.'

Jennifer winced but said nothing and Hilary, realizing she was being unfair, reached out a hand. 'Sorry.'

Jennifer sat at the table with her for an hour, Hilary growing more talkative and animated as the wine went steadily down.

'Let's get some fresh air,' suggested Jennifer, growing alarmed at the rate Hilary was drinking.

They walked in silence round to the stables but Hilary suddenly stopped. 'You know what Dad always said? There's no room for charity in this game. And he's right. I should never have accepted Mark's offer in the first place.'

'That's ridiculous . . .' began Jennifer.

'No, it's not. He only set me up in business so he could get me into bed . . . and Dad thought it was for old times' sake.' She was shouting by now, waving the empty wine bottle around to emphasize her words.

'Come on, love, calm down,' said Jennifer.

'Whatever made me think I could train a thoroughbred like Coolrain Star?' said Hilary, shifting moods with the effortless ease of the drunk. 'I probably overtrained him.'

'You didn't overtrain him.'

'Somebody has to be at fault and there's only me, isn't there?'

'Snap out of it, Hilary, stop feeling so damn sorry for yourself.'

Hilary rounded on her, furious. 'Why should I listen to you anyway? Why the hell did I take your word for it?'

'My word for what?'

'Chris should have been there last night.'

'It would have made no difference, Hilary,' said Jennifer patiently.

'How do I know? Maybe he might have done something else. Maybe Coolrain Star is only dead because of your incompetence.'

Jennifer stiffened as if she had been slapped. 'The colic was too far advanced,' she said flatly. 'I had to operate. I had no choice.'

'It's years since you worked with thoroughbreds, Jennifer. Maybe you've lost your touch?'

Too upset to speak, Jennifer gave her a long look, then wheeled around and walked briskly back towards her car. Involuntarily she slowed as she walked past Coolrain Star's empty box, wondering, despite herself, if Hilary was not right. Abruptly she quickened her pace again, got into her car and drove off. From an upstairs window, Patrick watched her go.

While Jennifer had been breaking the bad news to Hilary, Chris had taken on the equally daunting task of telling Mark. He phoned him at one of his betting shops and told him the news, arranging to meet for a drink that lunchtime to discuss it. As they walked down the street towards the pub, Mark was complaining, 'That's twelve thousand pounds up the Swanee, Chris. He's twelve grand's worth of bloody dogfood now.'

'He was destroyed on humane grounds – the insurance company won't quibble.'

Mark stopped and turned to face him. 'He wasn't covered.'

Chris was aghast. 'What?'

Mark shook his head, embarrassed. 'I forgot to renew the policy. I checked right after you phoned me and I couldn't believe it. I still can't.'

They walked on slowly.

'My best bloody horse. There was nothing else you could do, right? I mean, you had to operate, didn't you?'

'Yes. It wasn't me actually. Jennifer carried out the operation but she made the right . . .'

'But you supported her decision, yes?' interrupted Mark, his colour rising.

'I wasn't there.'

Mark again stopped in his tracks and grabbed Chris's arm, shouting, 'You weren't there? That woman cut open Coolrain Star and you weren't even bloody well there?'

'Calm down, Mark. Clinically she was absolutely right.'

Mark was far from calm, bellowing at the top of his voice. 'I told you. I told you to keep that townie vet away from my horses and now you've let her butcher my best thoroughbred!'

'She didn't butcher him . . .' began Chris, but Mark was beyond recall.

'OK. This is what I'm going to do. I'm going to get a second opinion. Another vet will do a post-mortem on Coolrain Star and if he tells me the operation was in any way botched, I'm going to take you and Whitton Veterinary Centre to the cleaners.'

'A P-M won't tell you anything I haven't told you already,' Chris countered, but Mark turned on his heel. 'I think I'll have this drink on my own, if you don't mind.'

He stalked off into the pub, leaving Chris standing on the pavement.

Mark's mood was not improved by a few whiskies. He went back to the betting shop in a foul temper, haranguing the manager over some triviality and reducing one of the counter girls to tears, and when the afternoon racing was over, he left the manager to cash up and drove up to the stables. He found Hilary and Patrick sorting through the tack in Coolrain Star's empty stable. Hilary had sobered up quickly and was pale, quiet, hung-over and full of remorse for abusing Jennifer.

'He was a good horse,' she told Mark. 'Temperamental, yes, but fast. It was bad luck. That's all it was.'

Mark shrugged dismissively. 'We'll see what the post-mortem shows up.'

'We did everything we could. Jennifer worked through the night, she was in no way to blame, and . . .'

He cut her off in mid-sentence. 'Save it, Hilary. I only stopped by to tell you I'll be taking my horses elsewhere. I would have phoned but I owe you and Paddy this much at least.'

Shock showed in Patrick's face but there was no surprise in Hilary's. 'Didn't waste much time, did you? Of course if you take them all away we'll go under,' she added, 'but you already knew that.'

'Please, Mark,' said Patrick. 'For old times' sake, give the lass another chance.'

Mark ignored him, facing Hilary. 'Racing's no world for you, girl. You'd be better off turning your hand to something else, believe me.'

As Mark walked back to his car, Hilary rounded on Patrick. 'Why can't you stand up to him, just once in your life?' She walked into the house, leaving Patrick standing there, dejected. She sat down in front of the TV but watched it sightlessly, taking nothing in.

A while later, Patrick came in, trying to mend fences. 'I'm going for a jar, do you fancy one?'

Without looking at him, she shook her head.

'When you were six years old,' said Patrick, speaking softly, almost as if talking to himself, 'you asked me to bring your mother back from the dead. When I said I couldn't, you didn't speak to me for two days. Disappointing a child always stays with you somehow.'

Still without looking at him, Hilary said coolly, 'You don't owe me anything, Dad.'

He looked at her profile for a moment and then left the room, closing the door quietly behind him.

Jennifer had stopped at home on the way back from the stables, too upset and exhausted to do anything more until she had grabbed a couple of hours' sleep. By the time she got back to the practice, Chris was already outside, loading up his car with drugs and equipment for the following day's rounds. He gave Jennifer a curt nod of acknowledgement but carried on working.

She walked over to him and asked, 'How did Mark take it?'

Chris shrugged. 'In the circumstances, you know . . .'

Jennifer looked at him warily, then said, 'I'm sorry I didn't phone you last night before I operated, Chris, but there wasn't much time.'

'That was the only reason, wasn't it?'

Jennifer did not answer.

'It's only that my second opinion would have strengthened our case.'

'What does that mean?'

Chris stopped arranging things in the boot and straightened up. 'Mark's threatened to take us to court.'

'What?'

'He's unlikely to win, but the effect on our business . . .'

Jennifer looked helplessly around, as if some explanation might be found among the trees on the river bank. 'But why? I don't understand.'

'Unfortunately you've given him an excuse for a charge of negligence.'

'Wait a sec,' said Jennifer, growing upset as she realized the drift of Chris's remarks. 'Are you saying that he wouldn't be threatening legal action if it was you who'd carried out the operation?'

'We'll never know, will we?'

'First Hilary, now you,' she said angrily. 'If you think I'm incompetent then say so.'

'I never said that.'

'You implied it, which is worse.'

'No, I didn't,' said Chris, nettled. 'Legally Mark has no case.'

'I'm not talking about the law, I'm talking about trust. Do you or don't you trust my judgement?'

'Not always, no,' said Chris, uncomfortable but determined not to evade the issue.

Jennifer's eyes filled with tears. She turned on her heel and walked off to her car rather than cry in front of him. Chris slammed the boot, a sick feeling in the pit of his stomach. He felt sorry for Jennifer but even sorrier for himself.

By the time she got home, Jennifer's mood had turned to anger. She walked into the front room, finding Steven and Scott watching MTV. They did not even look up but just carried on watching.

'Don't they teach you any manners at that school?' she asked, irritably.

They looked away from the screen momentarily, murmuring, 'Hi, Mum,' and 'Hello, Mrs Holt.'

'Time you were off home, Scott. Steven's got homework to do.' Without waiting for a reply, she strode to the television and switched it off.

Startled, Steven jumped up. 'What did you do that for?'

She ignored him, walking through to the kitchen and dumping her coat on the back of the chair. As she put the kettle on, she heard Steven saying goodbye to Scott. He walked into the kitchen and glared at her.

'You didn't have to be rude to him, you know? Just 'cos you're in a bad mood.'

Jennifer was in no mood for a discussion. 'Yeah, well, that's the advantage of being a grown-up, you can be rude to kids and claim you're doing it for their sake.'

'He's my friend, can't I even invite him home?'

'Don't get too used to the idea, that's all. It's not going to be home for long.'

'What?'

'Things aren't working out too well here, all right?'

'So you take it out on my friend.'

Jennifer made a great – and largely unsuccessful – effort to be reasonable. 'Typical of me, wanting to move out just when you're getting yourself together and everything.'

He grunted. 'You said it.'

'You'd be pleased if we moved back to London, wouldn't you? You're always moaning about how far away we are.'

'You always run away from problems, you do,' said Steven accusingly. 'Just like you and Dad.'

'Is that what you think? That I ran away from your father?'

'You made him very unhappy, Dad told me.'

'I was disappearing, Steven, in my own home. I felt like I was ceasing to exist.'

Steven said nothing in reply and she tried again, speaking less harshly. 'Please try to understand, sweetheart. I never stopped loving your father but we weren't right for each other.'

'Why don't you ever call him by his name?' cried Steven, rushing out and slamming the door behind him. Jennifer sank down in a seat at the table and put her head in her hands.

Laura filled Alan in on the day's events as they ate their dinner.

'You must be pretty pleased,' ventured Alan.

'I feel sorry for Jennifer, actually. It's not her fault all this, she did a bloody good job last night. I wish I could have done what she had to do.'

'Nevertheless this fiasco's bound to help your corner, isn't it?'

Laura shrugged. 'Maybe. Either way, I phoned the estate agent this afternoon.'

Alan paused with a forkful of food half-way to his mouth.

'I've withdrawn the offer on the house,' Laura continued, avoiding meeting his eyes, 'and I've taken this place off the market. A full partnership share in the practice'll come to near enough a hundred and twenty thousand pounds. I reckon the interest on that will cost me – us – quite enough to be going on with.'

Alan stared at her in shock. 'How could you do that without talking to me first?'·

'Because you'd never have agreed,' said Laura matter-of-factly, helping herself to more potatoes.

Alan was speechless with anger. He got up from the table and walked to the sink, dropping his plate noisily.

'Don't sulk,' said Laura laconically, 'it doesn't suit you.'

He whipped round, his moon face bewildered. 'I don't know what you want any more.'

'I want a partnership in the practice.'

'What about a partnership with me? Do you still want that?'

'Don't be ridiculous.'

'I mean it,' said Alan, emboldened for once by his anger. 'You don't want us to take important decisions together, you don't want us to have children.'

'I never said that.'

'So what is it exactly that you want out of our marriage?' he asked, the hurt showing plainly in his eyes.

Laura softened a fraction and went over to him. 'I'm sorry, I just couldn't face an argument about whether to move house or not, that's all it was. I don't want anything bad to happen to us.'

'Then trust me more, Laura, I'm not a fool.'

Almost uniquely among their circle of friends and acquaintances, Chris and Patricia were not feuding that night, though Chris was anything but relaxed as they lay in bed together. Patricia was reading but Chris just lay there, staring at the ceiling. After a few minutes, Patricia glanced across at him and said, 'I can hear your little brain whirring around from here.'

'A possible lawsuit, an untenable bank overdraft, a colleague I'm barely on speaking terms with . . . nothing wrong with the children I should know about?' said Chris melodramatically.

Patricia smiled and put down her book. 'So we were wrong about Jennifer, were we?'

'Maybe.'

'It won't stop me liking her though.'

'Me neither.'

'Maybe the problem is she's too good a vet,' said Patricia.

'How do you mean?'

'Too good to play second fiddle, that's all.'

'Yeah,' grunted Chris, rolling on to his side, facing away from her. Patricia put her book down and turned out the light, leaving Chris still staring into the darkness.

Chapter 8

Mark and Patrick arrived at the practice in Mark's car the next morning, followed by a beaten-up truck. Anderson, the knacker-man, jumped down from the truck as Chris came out of the equine unit to meet them all.

'Morning, Mark, Patrick, Mr Anderson,' said Chris warily, waiting to see which way Mark was going to jump today. 'The other vet'll do the post-mortem at your yard this afternoon, Mr Anderson. The horse is in there for you.'

'I'm sorry I went off the deep end at you yesterday, Chris,' said Mark.

'Forget it.'

'But I still have to have the horse looked at, I'm sure you appreciate . . .'

'Let me say one thing, though,' interrupted Chris. 'I've had a very good look at him myself and I know that Mrs Holt made the right clinical decision.'

'We'll soon see, won't we?'

Mark turned away and walked towards the stable with Anderson. Chris caught Patrick's eye and winked, winning a smile from him.

Through the window, Jennifer watched the men talking. Murray came up behind her and peered over her shoulder. 'The atmosphere here this morning. It's like there's been a death in the family,' said Murray, placing both feet firmly in his mouth.

Jennifer looked at him, raising an eyebrow.

'Er . . . sorry,' said Murray, realizing too late what he had said. 'The dust'll settle, Jen. You wait and see.'

'*Au contraire*, Murray, old love. It's being stirred up at this very minute.'

Jennifer turned to look outside again, her gaze locking with Patrick's as he saw her watching them. She turned away as she heard Anderson starting up the winch. The steel cable snaking from the truck tautened and strained, dragging the dead weight of Coolrain Star out of the stable.

Mark telephoned the other vet for his report late that afternoon. He listened in silence, worrying one of his knuckles between his teeth, as the vet embarked on a lengthy discourse, then interrupted impatiently. 'Right, I get the picture, thank you. No, no, don't bother with the written report. Just send your bill.' He hung up without waiting for a reply, rubbed his chin with his hand as he thought for a moment, then picked up his car keys from the desk and walked out of the office.

He drove east out of Whitton, the road climbing a ridge and dropping into a dark, thickly wooded valley, then climbing again, beginning the long haul up on to the moor. Mark branched off into a lane that burrowed and twisted beneath the canopy of the trees, an old 'hollow way', its surface sunk several feet below the level of the surrounding fields by centuries of erosion by wind, water and trampling feet. The steep banks were speckled with white snowdrops and yellow aconites, but Mark had no time for flowers; the only colours that interested him were on racing silks.

He swung into the yard of Hilary's stables, pasting an insincere smile to his features as he saw Hilary coming out of the stables. She greeted him warily and showed him into the kitchen, where he sat himself down at the table and looked pointedly at the kettle. She ignored the hint and remained standing, impassively waiting.

'I've been thinking, Hilary. What on earth is the point of going to all that fuss and bother of finding a new trainer to kill all my horses, when I've already got you to do it?' He chuckled at his own joke but Hilary did not join in, remaining stone-faced. He coughed nervously and began again, more seriously. 'The post-mortem confirmed that Mrs Holt wasn't responsible for Coolrain Star's sad demise.'

'I expected that.'

'I jumped the gun and I'm sorry.'

Hilary gave a faint smile but remained silent.

Mark drummed his fingers on the table-top and glanced around the kitchen. He was beginning to feel the uncomfortable silence and was glad when Patrick came in from the other room and stood alongside Hilary.

'Hello, Paddy. I thought you'd be down at the local by this time.'

Patrick also gave a faint smile but said nothing. Mark looked uneasily from one to the other of them.

Finally Hilary broke the silence. 'I've been thinking too, Mark. I'll keep your horses fit and well until you find another stable but I don't want to look after them.'

'Hilary . . .' said Mark, in a wheedling voice. 'Don't be like that.' He stood up, stepped towards her, and stroked her cheek. She recoiled as if she had been bitten by a snake.

'And I don't ever want to see you again,' she said, contempt in her eyes.

Mark flushed with anger. 'Come on, girl, what are you on about?' He turned to Patrick, sure of his support. 'Talk some sense into her, Paddy. You listen to your father now. Do you hear me?'

'I'm afraid she's right,' said Patrick.

Mark whirled around, surprise and fury battling for control of his features.

Patrick met his look without blinking. 'She'll be much better off without you. You're full of horseshit, you see. Always have been. You're as mediocre an owner as you were a jockey and that's the sad truth.'

Hilary smiled to herself as Mark, looking ready to explode, glared balefully at them both and then stormed out, slamming the door behind him with a crash. They heard him drive off in a screech of tyres. Hilary turned to face Patrick. They grinned at each other and she kissed him on the cheek.

Chris had been out with his family for the afternoon and the sun was already setting by the time he swung the Range Rover through the gate and pulled up in the drive.

'Come on, girls,' said Patricia, 'straight upstairs for your bath.' She opened the front door as Chris locked up the car and then started as she saw Jennifer sitting on the low wall. 'Oh. Hi, Jennifer. Do you want to come in for a drink?'

'No, better not, thanks. Chris, do you have a minute?'

'Er, sure, yeah,' said Chris nervously, glancing at Patricia.

She met his gaze, gave an imperceptible shrug of her shoulders and then said, 'In you go, girls. If you change your mind, Jennifer . . .'

They disappeared into the house, leaving Chris and Jennifer alone in the yard.

'Why don't we talk tomorrow? In the office,' said Chris coolly.

'This won't take long.'

'Did you come here to apologize?'

'Well . . .'

'There's no need really. Your clinical decision to operate was absolutely right.'

'But it might not have been. I didn't want your second opinion because I wanted to deal with Coolrain Star on my own, without you there.'

Chris tried to speak, but she silenced him with a gesture. 'In the past I'd never have been so arrogant as to do that, but after years of being an equal partner in business, I'm simply unable to work under somebody else. It's turning me into a bad vet.'

'Jennifer, you're not a bad vet, listen . . .'

Again she hushed him. 'There's more to being a good vet than wielding a scalpel. I committed a gross error of judgement. Who's to say it won't happen again?'

He shrugged his shoulders. 'Maybe.'

'It's also turning me into someone I don't particularly like. I'm much more accommodating than this normally, believe me.'

'I do believe you. Do you know what Patrick said this morning? "Can't be much fun having a vet about who's as good as you are and a whole lot prettier."'

Jennifer ignored the compliment. 'I feel very vulnerable here in Whitton, which is why I try too hard.'

'I'd hate to be in your position, anyone would,' said Chris, beginning to sense what was coming.

'It's not going to work, Chris. Me and the practice. You know that too, don't you?' He looked at her for a moment, then nodded.

They stood in silence for a few seconds.

'What will you do?' he asked.

'Go back to London. Set up a small animal practice on my own probably.'

'You'll hate it.'

She smiled ruefully and said, 'Yes, I will,' then walked back up the drive and out through the heavy wooden gates, without looking back. Chris stood for a long time, gazing after her, unaware of Patricia watching from the kitchen window.

Jennifer was still in her dressing-gown the next morning, pouring herself a cup of tea, when Steven appeared in the kitchen. She watched him carefully. 'Want some tea?'

He shook his head, not meeting her look. 'Late.' He grabbed an apple and headed hurriedly for the door.

'Aren't you even going to say goodbye?' said Jennifer, pursuing him down the hall. 'Steven?'

He ignored her, closing the front door behind him. Jennifer opened it again and stepped out into the porch, watching as he walked down the lane. Upset and preoccupied, she did not even register Chris's car pulling up until he wound down his window and said, 'Morning.'

She started. 'Oh, Chris. Sorry, I was . . .' She let the sentence trail off.

'Listen, I've been thinking,' said Chris. 'If you become my partner in the practice . . .' he paused for a second, then hurried on before she could reply, '. . . then you wouldn't be working under anyone else and you needn't turn into someone you don't particularly like. Simple.'

She looked at him thoughtfully, then gave a broad smile for the first time in days. 'Erm . . . do you want some breakfast?'

'No thanks, I've a visit to make.' He started to wind the window back up, then paused and said, 'You don't have to give me your answer immediately . . . teatime should do it.'

He grinned and drove off. Jennifer watched the car go down the lane and saw Chris slow as he passed Steven. He said something to him, then stopped and Steven hopped into the passenger seat. Jennifer smiled to herself as they drove off. She turned to go back inside, pausing at the sight of a heron, which normally priested the shore alone, standing surrounded by a congregation of oyster-catchers, all facing the river, expectantly waiting for the tide to turn.

*

Chris dropped Steven off at school and drove to the practice, humming to himself, but the sight of Laura's car in the car-park caused the tune to die on his lips and his smile to fade rapidly. He had an uneasy feeling that the ideal solution for himself and Jennifer would look very different from Laura's perspective.

He squared his shoulders and walked into reception, finding Laura chatting to Maddy. He smiled nervously, said, 'Laura, could I see you for a moment?' and led her into his office. He sat at his desk but Laura remained standing, hearing him out in silence as he laboured through his reasons for offering Jennifer a partnership. Her lips whitened as she compressed them in anger.

'Fine,' she said tartly. 'In that case, you have my notice. I'll be leaving as soon as you find a replacement.'

Chris looked at her helplessly. 'Won't you at least take a couple of weeks to think about it?'

'There's no point. Alan and I have already discussed what we would do in this situation.'

'I don't want to lose you, Laura.'

'You should have thought about that before you offered Jennifer a partnership,' she said furiously, her eyes flashing with anger.

'Do you think I didn't?' he retorted, then fought to get his own temper under control and went on soothingly, 'But you're only young, there's plenty of time. In three or four years the practice will be ready for another partner. In which case . . .'

'Who knows who else you might have brought in by then?' said Laura sarcastically.

'Laura, please . . .' began Chris, but there was a knock on the door and Murray opened it immediately, without waiting for an answer.

'Chris, I'm off to the McMahons, you wanted to have a chat first.'

'Yeah, but hang on a sec . . .' said Chris distractedly, pursuing Laura out of the door.

'No, you go ahead,' she said grimly. 'I've surgery to start up.'

Chris gazed wearily after her, then turned back to Murray, shaking his head.

As Jennifer came in a few minutes later, carrying a cat in a cat basket, she passed Chris in the corridor looking as if he was

83

running late for his own funeral. She carried on into the surgery and handed the cat over to Laura, who pursed her lips at the sight of her but only said, 'What's up with Asterix?'

'A wound inside his hind leg. Poor old Mrs Laker, she was in floods.'

Laura grunted and turned away, busying herself at the desk.

Jennifer studied her thoughtfully for a moment, then asked casually, 'What's up with Chris this morning?'

Laura stopped what she was doing and turned to face her. 'I've handed in my resignation.'

'You what?'

'I'm leaving.'

'Laura, that's crazy.'

She shook her head emphatically. 'My mind's made up.'

'You can't go just like that. I mean, this is terrible . . .'

'You feel guilty, you mean.'

'No . . . well, yes,' said Jennifer uncertainly. 'Yes, I do actually. If I thought you were going to leave the practice I would never have accepted Chris's offer.'

Laura snorted derisively. 'Yes, you would. I can do without the sympathy vote, thanks.'

She walked out of the room, leaving Jennifer standing there open-mouthed.

Chris had sent Murray off to the deer farm with a few words of encouragement. 'I've not met either of them but he seemed pleasant enough on the phone. They had trouble with their previous vet, apparently, so . . . be nice.'

'Oh, if I must,' said Murray, grinning. He drove out of Whitton towards Dartmoor, feeling the air turn colder and damper as he climbed steadily up through the hills, stopping occasionally to peer from his map to his scribbled sheet of directions.

Finally he turned off down a side road and muttered, 'Bingo,' as the hedgerows gave way to a new-looking chain-link fence, standing ten feet high and stretching away into the distance. A herd of rust-brown shapes could be seen patrolling the lower slopes of a thickly forested hillside.

Murray followed a sweeping drive up to the front of a fine manor house, where he was greeted by the owner, Peter

McMahon. He was expensively kitted out in a City financier's idea of what a gentleman farmer should wear – tweed jacket and plus-fours topped off with an oversize tweed cap. The cap was set at a jaunty angle, which further emphasized the habitual gloom of his expression, for despite his wealth he was a compulsive worrier. His wife Felicity, considerably younger, blonde, blue-eyed and extremely attractive, also came with them as they strolled up the field to inspect the herd.

Murray tried hard to concentrate on what Mr McMahon was saying but he was acutely conscious of Felicity staring at him, a smile playing around her lips. McMahon had only recently taken up deer-raising and though he was well versed in the theory – having read every available book and article on the subject – he had little practical experience.

At least we have that much in common, thought Murray, but he managed to turn his smile into an expression of sympathetic concern as McMahon led him towards a small group of grazing deer, confiding, 'I don't mind admitting it but I'm worried about these hinds, they're definitely underweight for their age.'

'Erm . . . they look pretty good to me, Mr McMahon.'

McMahon ignored the comment and continued in his lugubrious tones, 'It could be a mineral or vitamin deficiency, of course – in the feed or in the vegetation – and I'm extremely concerned that there might be yersinia in the herd.'

Murray did not have the faintest idea what he was talking about but played desperately for time. 'Yersinia? Er . . .'

'The pseudo-tubercular condition,' said McMahon, sighing heavily.

'I know,' lied Murray. 'Of course, yes . . . well, a simple test would put your mind at ease there. Why don't I come back tomorrow to collect some blood and dung samples?'

He smiled smugly at McMahon, whose face lit up with pleasure. 'You and I are going to get on famously. My previous veterinary surgeon – whom I had to let go unfortunately – was forever telling me the deer were absolutely fine when I knew perfectly well they weren't.'

A mobile phone began to ring. Both Murray and McMahon reached automatically for their pockets but it was McMahon's phone that was ringing. As he answered it, Murray retreated a few steps to give him some privacy. As he did so he heard Felicity's voice, speaking breathily in his ear.

'How long have you been in South Devon, Mr Wilson?'

Murray gave a little start of surprise, then turned to face her, saying nervously, 'About a year. Since I left veterinary college. In Glasgow.'

'And you don't find it too tame for you?' she asked, giving him a slow provocative smile. 'After Glasgow?'

He glanced nervously across at McMahon, who was still involved in his call, pacing to and fro as he barked instructions to his broker. 'Er . . . no, not really,' said Murray weakly. 'Not that I get out and about much, we're very busy . . .'

'Oh, I find that hard to believe,' said Felicity, stepping even closer to him. 'You strike me as a man who likes to party.'

Completely lost for words, Murray smiled helplessly back at her.

McMahon ended his call and strode over to Murray. 'Now, where were we?'

'Mr Wilson was telling me what a long way from home he feels,' said Felicity. 'It can feel very isolated here,' she said, holding Murray's eyes locked, like a stoat about to strike a rabbit, 'and it's frightening too sometimes; we can even hear the sirens from Princetown when a prisoner escapes.'

Glad of any excuse to break free of those hypnotic deep blue eyes, Murray turned to look up towards Dartmoor, dark and barren above them, a tide of moorland sweeping up to Hessary Tor, like the waves of a dark sea, breaking on a headland.

On a ridge below the tor lay an even more bleak and desolate place than the wind-swept moorland and granite tors. The grim, grey, granite walls of the prison towered over the village of Princetown, the houses huddled together in the lee of its walls like frightened children. A dusting of snow covered the ground and a cold wind whipped over the tops, driving grey cloud that clung to the prison walls like a shroud. The only sign of life on this cold, harsh morning was a grey-haired, careworn woman, standing by a battered, mud-covered estate car and looking expectantly towards the massive prison gates.

She waited, glancing repeatedly at her watch, the only sounds the wind and the metallic ticking of the car as the engine cooled. Finally she heard the rumble of heavy iron bolts and the clash of keys in steel locks. The gates swung ponderously open and a figure, dwarfed by the size of the gates, stepped outside, clutching a small suitcase in his hand. He glanced quickly around, a fair-haired, cocksure twenty-year-old, reassuring himself that the world was as it had been two years before, when he had last stood outside those prison walls, then walked briskly away from the building without looking back.

The woman straightened up and stood waiting for him, arms outstretched, ready to crush him to her in a hug, but he kept her at arm's length, kissing her lightly on the cheek, and giving her a big grin.

She looked at him critically. 'They've not been feeding you properly, Tom.'

'Keeping fit, Ma.'

He dropped his case on to the back seat of the car, turned back towards the prison and threw a defiant 'V' sign, then said, 'Let's get out of here, I've seen enough of this place for one life.'

As she drove off down the road, she leaned over and switched on the cassette player. Some rock music blared out and Tom smiled appreciatively at her.

'My favourite album.'

She watched him out of the corner of her eye as she drove. He was tense, sitting forward in his seat, staring straight ahead. His fists were clenched, beating out a tattoo on the dashboard in rhythm with the music, but as they left the moor behind and began to drop down through the foothills, he seemed to unwind, leaning back in his seat and looking around him, his mood lifting as the barren greys and browns of the moor gave way to the vibrant greens of pasture and meadow.

His animation increased as they neared their own farm and he took in every new fence post, every cow and calf, as they turned off the lane and drove into the farmyard. His mother walked into the house, leaving Tom standing in the yard, gazing around him, drinking in every detail and every lichen-covered stone. An old collie came bounding out of the barn, wagging its tail frantically, recognizing him instantly. Tom crouched down to pet the dog. 'Now Lucy, you remember me all right, don't you?'

His mother smiled at him from the farmhouse door. 'She's missed you, Tom.'

He nodded, then followed her into the house, the dog trotting at his heels. He walked upstairs and entered a small, sparsely furnished room. The collie followed him in and curled up patiently on the small rug, her eyes never leaving his face. Tom looked around for a moment and then, smiling to himself, he carefully opened and closed the door, an action he had not been allowed to perform for two years.

As he stood there, he heard the sound of a vehicle entering the yard. He went to the window and saw his father jump down off his battered old tractor, a thin, wiry, bearded man in his late fifties, with a truculent expression that suggested he spoke his mind and expected others to do the same.

He strode across the yard and into the house, going straight to the kitchen sink to clean up. 'That's almost the last of the barley feed, Stella,' he said, as he washed his hands.

She stopped cooking, and excitedly waited for him to ask about Tom. Instead he dried his hands, pulled a letter from an official-looking manila envelope lying on the table, and waved it at her.

'Did you see this?'

She shrugged her shoulders helplessly. 'What are we going to do? We'll have to pay.'

He shook his head, his face set into the stubborn, fixed expression she knew so well. 'I'm not throwing good money away. What do the Council ever do for us? Bureaucrats in breeches, that's all they are.' He dropped the letter in the bin. 'I'll teach them to threaten court action.'

Again she waited but he merely sat down at the table and started reading the paper. Finally she could bear the suspense no longer. 'Dick. Are you not even going to ask?'

'Ask what?'

'Your son's here, isn't he?'

'Oh. Right. How is he?'

'If you go up to his room, you'll see for yourself.'

'He'll be down soon enough, I expect.'

He went back to his paper as Stella noisily served up his lunch, banging his plate down on the table and muttering, 'Two years in prison. The least you can do is walk up a flight of stairs and say, "Hello".'

He picked up his knife and fork to start eating but then nodded wearily, stood up and went upstairs.

Tom was pinning a photograph cut from a magazine to the wall when Dick appeared in the open doorway. They looked at each other for a moment.

'Tom,' he said evenly.

'Dad,' said Tom, in the same neutral tone. There were no smiles and no physical contact between them, not even a handshake.

'I bet you're pleased to see the back of that place then?'

'Like a holiday camp. Only more fun.'

Dick frowned, unimpressed with Tom's bravado. 'Don't forget. You're only out on parole.' He looked at him for a while longer, then murmured, 'Well, erm ... welcome home,' and turned to go.

'Dad.'

'Yes?'

'I'll work. I mean, I'll pay my way.'

Dick nodded, gave a faint smile and then went back downstairs. After wolfing his lunch, he fished the official letter out of the bin, read it again, then dropped it back and headed purposefully out of the door. Stella heard him manoeuvring the tractor around the yard as he backed it up to the muckspreader. A few minutes later he drove out of the yard with a look of grim determination on his face.

Chapter 9

Patricia was seated at a table in a small committee room at the Town Hall with half a dozen councillors and council officials. As the sound of a tractor engine grew louder outside, they raised their voices to be heard.

'I see no reason why public parks shouldn't be subject to the same financial strictures as every other department,' said a councillor, his jowls quivering with righteous indignation.

'Perhaps we can get the kids to put 10p in a ticket machine when they want use a swing, Councillor Battersby,' suggested Patricia sarcastically.

'That's not helpful, Mrs Lennox.'

'I happen to think a public park which isn't free is no longer a public park. I'm old-fashioned that way, sorry.'

Another councillor butted in. 'Can we please get back to the matter at hand?' but at that moment all hell broke loose outside.

Dick had swung his tractor off the road into the car-park alongside the Town Hall. As an attendant came running over shouting, 'Oi, you can't park that there,' Dick revved up the engine and turned on the muckspreader. A thick spray of black, stinking, liquid slurry covered the parked cars, including a large black limo with the Mayor's crest on the front. Dick then began driving to and fro, spraying muck all over the front of the Town Hall. Officials dived to close the windows, but the stench was overpowering, even with them firmly shut.

Patricia and the others raced to the window and saw Dick grinning happily, spraying shit in all directions.

'That's my bloody BMW!' roared Battersby in anguish, and despite herself, Patricia burst out laughing.

She was still chuckling as Chris collected her from the Town Hall half an hour later.

'Is that all it was about?' asked Chris incredulously. 'His community charge bill?'

'Well, he does owe a few hundred quid.'

'He always was a stroppy old sod,' said Chris with feeling.

'What's a "sod"?' piped up Abby from the back seat.

'A clump of earth, darling,' said Patricia, shooting a warning look at Chris.

'He'll be let off with a caution anyway,' she said, as they came to a halt in their drive. 'I don't think the Leader of the Council fancies the publicity. I presume the liquid manure was pure, him being an organic farmer.' She chuckled at her own quip.

'He may be an organic farmer but he's only in it for the money, believe you me,' said Chris sourly.

'Now why can't he believe in the principle of organic farming and make money at the same time, what's wrong with that?'

'There's nothing wrong with it. Except I know Dick Sims.'

'I think you've got a grudge against him.'

'Why are you two arguing?' asked Abby.

Chris and Patricia exchanged guilty looks.

'Are we arguing?' said Chris. 'Yes, we are. Sorry.'

They went into the house, the girls disappearing upstairs as Chris and Patricia walked through to the kitchen.

'You may have a point anyway,' said Chris. 'I must be a bad judge of character.'

'Why, what do you mean?'

'Laura resigned this morning.'

'Oh, no.'

'She warned me that she would, but I never thought she'd actually do it.'

'She may be only acting on hurt pride,' said Patricia, putting a hand on his arm. 'You know what Laura's like, she can be very brittle.'

He nodded but looked unconvinced. 'I know, but perhaps I shouldn't have made Jennifer a partner so soon. She's only been with us five minutes . . .'

Patricia shook her head firmly and interrupted him. 'No, you're wrong.'

'We could delay the whole business.'

'No, Chris, you stick to your guns. The business needs a partner. Not next year – now. I'm sorry about Laura but there's too much of our lives invested in this to jeopardize everything for the sake of someone else's feelings.'

'You can be pretty ruthless when you want to be.'

Patricia, bridling at the implied criticism, gave him a very old-fashioned look.

Stella found Dick's exploits with the muckspreader much less amusing than Patricia had. 'What good would that have done for me then, if you'd been arrested?' she asked, as he sat at the table, chuckling to himself.

His smile only grew broader. 'Should have seen their faces. 'Specially that Deputy Mayor, he was puce he was.'

Stella could not help smiling herself at the thought, and turned away to hide it from him. She tried to be serious again. 'And what sort of example is that to set for Tom, eh? His first day out.'

Dick shrugged. 'The lad's old enough to know his own mind.'

'He's only twenty, Dick.'

As Tom came downstairs, Dick glanced up from his paper and offered a perfunctory nod of the head but Stella smiled warmly and said, 'I thought I'd give you a treat for your first meal, roast beef and all the trimmings.'

'I'm taking Lucy for a walk first. I'll stop by the Seven Stars for a pint.'

'It'll be ready by seven-thirty. You will be careful, won't you?' said Stella anxiously.

He smiled. 'Of the rabbits and night owls, is that?'

He whistled to the dog and walked down the lane to the village, strolling into the pub. The tiny stone-flagged bar was busy with people and he looked around, enjoying the laughter and buzz of conversation, then sat on a stool at the bar and ordered his first pint in two years. He sat quietly sipping his pint and savouring the atmosphere, Lucy sitting patiently at his feet.

As he looked around the room, Tom caught sight of three young men at the far side of the bar. He recognized them immediately. They were talking quite noisily, until one of them spotted Tom, then they nudged each other and fell silent, staring at him with no sign of friendliness on their faces. Tom held the look for a second and then looked away as the landlady leaned across the bar and said, 'Welcome back. Next one's on me, love.'

He smiled gratefully, but then glanced at the clock and said, 'Better not, my mum's cooking up something special.'

As the landlady moved away to the other end of the bar, Tom drained his pint, stood up, picked up Lucy's lead and walked out, watched by the three young men across the bar. He stepped out into the cool night air and paused, taking in the silence and the stars in the night sky, then started to walk slowly away from the pub. A voice from behind him pulled him up sharply.

'Well, well, if it isn't Whitton's hard man.'

Tom turned, looking back at the three men, then started walking away again up the road.

'Lost your bottle in there, did you then, Tom?' came the taunting voice.

'Piss off, dickhead,' said Tom contemptuously.

The leader pointed to Lucy. 'What have we got here then, lads?'

'Ugly, isn't it, Keith?' said one of them.

Keith stepped nearer to Lucy, who bared her teeth and barked at him.

'Don't you bark at me, you dirty little dog.'

'Don't push your luck,' said Tom, pulling the dog in close to his side and watching them warily.

Lucy barked louder and as Keith made a threatening move at the dog, she suddenly leapt forward and snapped at him, just catching his foot.

'Lucy!' said Tom, jerking her back on the leash, but with a shout of 'You little bastard!' Keith suddenly gave Lucy a savage boot.

The dog yelped in pain and Tom instantly forgot all his self-control and launched himself at Keith, screaming, 'You're dead!'

They traded punches and tumbled to the ground, grappling and cursing, but were quickly dragged apart by the other two, who pulled Keith towards their car.

Tom stood up, panting for breath and still furious, watched them get in the car and drive off, then turned to Lucy. The dog lay there whimpering in pain. He stroked her head and said, 'You're going to be all right, girl. We'll get you sorted,' and then ran back into the pub, asking the landlady, 'Have you got a number for a vet?'

'A vet? No, love, sorry.'

He turned to the bar and shouted, 'Anybody know a vet?'

Half an hour later, Jennifer drove into the car-park and saw Tom standing anxiously over the collie. Jennifer took her bag out of the car and walked quickly over to him. 'Tom Sims? I'm Mrs Holt from the veterinary centre. What's the dog's name?'

'Lucy.'

Jennifer crouched down. 'Easy now, Lucy. Let's have a look.' She handed Tom a torch. 'Hold that for me, would you?'

He shone the beam on Lucy, who yelped as Jennifer gently felt the back leg.

'She's broken her leg, I'm afraid,' said Jennifer. 'I'll give her a painkiller and we'll have to take her back to the practice and assess the damage.'

'She's going to be all right?'

'Let's hope. How did it happen?'

'Some drunk kicked her.'

Jennifer's glance took in the bruise on Tom's face and the dried blood around his nose but she said nothing.

Tom got into the back of the car and sat with Lucy's head cradled in his lap as Jennifer drove back to the practice, where she sedated the dog and X-rayed it. Tom waited impatiently as she pinned up the X-rays, studied them and then frowned.

'It's very bad news, Tom. She has a broken pelvis and a compound double fracture of the tibia. There, in her rear leg. The pelvic injury might heal in time but the fracture . . . that was one hefty kick. The kindest thing would be if I put her down.'

Tom shook his head vehemently.

'A simple overdose of anaesthetic,' said Jennifer. 'She won't feel a thing.'

'There's got to be something you can do for her. You can't just let her die.'

'Her injuries are very extensive.'

'But she's not some pig ready for the slaughterhouse, she's my dog. She's what I have.'

Jennifer smiled sympathetically but said, 'This is a rural practice, Tom. We're not geared up for complicated major surgery and there's no guarantee it would work anyway, she's very old.'

'Do it, please,' he implored.

She sighed. 'Even if we did operate, it wouldn't be cheap. We're probably looking at about four hundred pounds.'

Tom stared at her, aghast. 'Four hundred pounds?'

'Can't you afford that?'

Almost as if talking to himself, he said, 'You might as well have said four grand.'

'Isn't there anyone you could go to for help? Parents or anything?'

He shook his head. 'I don't want Lucy to die, Mrs Holt. Not yet a while. I'll get the money.'

Tom broached the subject with his father as they worked together, mucking out in the shed, early the next morning, but Dick rebuffed him calmly and matter-of-factly.

'She's too old, Tom, the vet said so herself, didn't she? Now let her go and be done with it.'

'So the answer's "No"?'

Dick stopped working and turned to face him. 'I'm sorry. Lucy was a good working dog but those days have long gone. This is a working farm, not a zoo.'

Stella had been eavesdropping on the conversation and, seeing the black look on Tom's face, she hastily joined in. 'Your father's right, Tom, I'm afraid. The operation might not even work either, you said.'

'I ain't seen nothing of her for two years.'

'Whose fault's that then?' asked Dick, irritated.

'You only ever think of yourself, don't you?' said Tom, turning angrily on his father.

Dick ignored the remark and carried on with his work, not wanting to be drawn into a big argument, but Tom was too upset to let it go.

'I'm right though, aren't I?' he said, appealing to his mother. 'If it doesn't suit him it doesn't get done.'

'Your father's thinking of us all here.'

Tom snorted. 'Money is all he thinks of.'

'The dog'd be all right anyways, if you hadn't gone out last night looking for trouble,' said Dick.

'I wasn't looking for trouble,' Tom answered, controlling his rising temper with an effort.

'Well now, that's the story of your life, isn't it?' sneered Dick.

Tom stared at him, hard-eyed, then hurled his shovel away, sending it clattering across the shed, and marched off out of the door and up the lane. Dick looked at Stella, shook his head wearily and then resumed work as she walked slowly back into the house and closed the door.

Tom's anger burned itself out as he walked down into Whitton, but he arrived at the practice not knowing what he was going to do or say. Jennifer greeted him brightly. 'The specialist says Lucy's fractures should be clean enough to knit together.'

Staring at the floor, Tom did not say anything.

Puzzled, Jennifer tried again. 'I'd better get started. Do you want to see her first?'

'The thing is . . .' began Tom in a dull monotone.

'What?'

He looked up helplessly. 'I ain't got the money.'

'You don't have to pay today.'

'I mean I don't have it. I can't pay for the operation.'

'Ah. That is a problem. Don't you have anyone who could help you out?'

Tom shook his head. 'There's something about me you should know, Mrs Holt. I left prison yesterday and they don't give you four hundred quid as a leaving present.'

Jennifer flashed a look at him from under her eyebrows. 'No. I don't suppose they do.'

She hesitated, unsure what to do. 'Perhaps in this case your mum and dad . . .'

'No. They won't. Do the operation, please.'

Jennifer hesitated. 'It's difficult, Tom. We're a business.'

'I don't want Lucy to die. You have to help her, there's no one else.'

Jennifer looked steadily at him for a few moments, then said, 'I'll have to talk to my partner.'

She found Chris collecting some drugs to load into his car and while Tom hovered in the background, she broached the subject. Chris heard her out in silence but then said, 'Why should we do the operation for nothing when Dick Sims can afford to pay for it?'

'Because Lucy belongs to Tom, and Tom can't afford to pay for it.'

'You're splitting hairs, Jen, the lad lives at home.'

Her voice softened. 'Come on, Chris. He comes out of prison, and his first day of freedom his poor collie is kicked half to death.'

Chris looked over his shoulder at Tom and then spoke more quietly. 'I don't see him as quite the deserving cause you do. Tom Sims was caught breaking into a warehouse, where he put some poor bugger of a night watchman into intensive care for a week.'

Jennifer was unfazed by the revelation. 'He's done his time, that's beside the point.'

'Yeah, it probably is,' Chris conceded, but then spoke with an air of finality. 'But if we give him an expensive operation for nothing, we can't give one to someone who really needs it.' He looked at his watch and said, 'I have to go.'

Jennifer watched him go, thought for a moment and then walked over to Tom. 'Right, I'd better get started.'

Tom's face broke into a broad grin as he took in what she had said. 'Shall I wait?'

'No,' said Jennifer. 'It's a long operation, you might as well go home. I'll phone you when it's over to let you know how we got on.'

Laura assisted Jennifer with the operation, which was long and difficult.

'I'm surprised Chris agreed for us to do this operation for free,' said Laura.

Jennifer glanced across the operating table at her, searching for a subtext. She shrugged. 'He didn't. I took a unilateral decision.'

'Oh well,' said Laura with leaden irony, 'as a partner you're allowed to, I suppose.'

Jennifer looked sharply at her. 'At least say that with a smile on your face,' but Laura just stared at her – unsmiling – and then looked back down at the dog.

Tom was feeding the calves in the cowshed when the call came through and Stella ran out to him.

'Mrs Holt just phoned, the operation went well and she thinks Lucy is going to be fine.'

He smiled and went back to work with renewed vigour. Stella walked outside, where Dick was hosing down the concrete apron in front of the cowshed. 'She sounds all right, this Mrs Holt,' said Stella brightly, as she picked up a yard brush and started sweeping the water away, 'operating on Lucy for nothing.'

'As long as she doesn't turn up next week demanding money.'

Stella stopped working, peeved at his attitude. 'Have some charity, Dick.'

Dick snorted. 'She works for Chris Lennox, remember, there's no love lost there.'

She put her hands on her hips and faced him, challengingly. 'That's nothing to do with this. You upset Tom and you had no right. He never started the trouble in the Seven Stars last night.'

'Oh, you were there, were you?' asked Dick sarcastically. 'He has to learn not to speak to his father that way.'

'He was concerned about Lucy, that's all. Go and talk to him. If only for my sake, please.'

Dick sighed and raised his eyes to heaven, but he turned the hose off and walked into the cowshed. Tom glanced warily at him, but carried on working.

'Those lads last night,' said Dick gruffly. 'Well known round here, they deserved a good hiding, I bet.'

Tom gave a faint smile but then pointed to the calves. 'They're poorly. They've got ringworm.'

Dick shook his head. 'The rings are almost dead, nothing to worry about.'

'What are you giving them for it?'

'Nothing.'

'Nothing?' said Tom incredulously.

Dick started to bluster defensively. 'They go for slaughter next week and then straight to the supermarket.'

'You've still got to give them something.'

'The medicine'd cost near enough two hundred pounds, it just ain't worth it.'

'What about the animals? Are they in pain?'

Dick was starting to lose his temper. 'They're not in pain, no.'

Tom looked at him in disbelief. 'You don't give a shit about Lucy, you don't give a shit about these calves.'

They stood shouting at each other across the shed.

'You go out of your way to make trouble, don't you?' demanded Dick.

'Nothing matters to you as long as you can make money,' said Tom, storming off for the second time that morning, but Stella intercepted him, saying quietly, 'Tom?'

'Those calves are sick and he don't give a damn.'

'Don't be ridiculous, of course he does.'

He snorted in derision and tried to push past her, but she held his arm to stop him. 'Don't make trouble for yourself, lad.'

'Why shouldn't I make trouble? It's all he thinks I do.'

'You've put your dad through a lot of pain. He's had to live with people talking behind his back about his only son being in prison. He's a proud man and it's not been easy.'

He shook his head angrily. 'Don't be so soft, he doesn't want me here.'

'Of course he does,' said Stella, but Tom just pulled his arm away and hurried off, still furious.

When Chris got back to the practice from his rounds and found out that Jennifer had carried out the operation after all, he was equally furious. Not wanting the others to overhear the argument, he led her out on to the terrace overlooking the river. The sound of the weir had no noticeably soothing effect upon him as he demanded angrily, 'Why spend valuable time and money on an old collie which won't last the night?'

'I don't know why you're so upset,' said Jennifer mildly.

'Because partners are supposed to decide things together.'

'Well, we left it in the air, so . . .'

'We did not leave it in the air,' Chris interrupted. 'I said "No".'

'Yes, well, I disagreed. You're going to have to get used to that.'

'What does that mean?' said Chris, raising his voice, then looking anxiously around to see if he had been overheard.

'It means we're equals in this, Chris, that's what you chose.'

They stared at each other without speaking as Chris's anger ebbed away. 'I did, didn't I?' he said finally.

Jennifer let out a long breath, then changed the subject slightly. 'Maddy tells me Dick Sims is an ex-client. Why "ex"?'

'We had a falling out. He bends the rules too much.'

'Do you want me to try to get some cash out of him for old Lucy?'

'No. Waste of time.'

Jennifer drove out to Dick's farm, with Lucy curled up in the back. Tom carried the dog into the house and bedded her down, then Jennifer gave her another injection as Tom stood anxiously by.

'She'll sleep a lot over the next couple of days, Tom,' said Jennifer, 'but if she seems feverish or if her nose gets warm, or if you're just worried about her at all, call the vet centre.' She stood up and started to pack her equipment away.

Tom hesitated for a moment, then blurted out, 'Mrs Holt, would you look at the calves while you're here? There's some ringworm.'

She looked at him doubtfully. 'I'm sure your father's dealing with it.'

He shook his head. 'He doesn't want to treat them, 'cos they're going for slaughter next week.'

'Well, it's not really done, Tom, I'm not his vet.'

Tom frowned and said nothing, but Jennifer softened, seeing his concern. 'All right, I'll have a word with him.'

'They're both out. Please.'

He led her out to the cowshed and stood behind her as she looked closely at one of the calves.

'Are you sure that he isn't giving them any sort of treatment?' asked Jennifer. 'Maybe he's giving them some homoeopathic medicine?'

Tom shook his head. 'He said it'd cost two hundred pounds to treat them and it ain't worth it.'

'There's nothing I can do now, I'll phone your dad this afternoon.'

'I'll save you the trouble,' said Dick, stepping into the shed.

Both of them started guiltily.

'You must be Mrs Holt,' said Dick.

'Mr Sims, I assure you . . .'

Dick ignored her, turning to Tom and demanding, 'What did you go behind my back for, Tom?'

'He didn't go behind your back,' said Jennifer, thinking on her feet. 'I brought Lucy home and I came in here out of curiosity. I'm not that familiar with organic farming methods, I didn't mean to pry.'

Tom gave her a grateful look as Dick stared suspiciously at her.

'Nevertheless, now I'm here,' said Jennifer, 'these calves should be treated.'

'The ringworm's on its way out, there's no need.'

'Tom tells me you have an exclusive contract with a supermarket. When are you hoping to deliver?'

'Wednesday week.'

Jennifer was taken aback. 'You can't deliver these calves next week, the ringworm's still contagious.'

'They're delivered without their hides, as carcasses,' said Dick, as if speaking to a child.

'If they come into contact with any other animals – in transit or in the abattoir – the ringworm will spread. You can't move them from here until the infection's completely disappeared,' said Jennifer firmly. 'You know the rules, Mr Sims.'

Dick stared at her insolently for a few moments, then said, 'Good day, Mrs Holt.'

Jennifer looked back at him, her eyes blazing, then turned on her heel and walked out.

When she got back to the practice she went straight in to see Chris. 'I don't know what we should do about it,' said Chris doubtfully, 'I don't even know which vet he's using these days.'

'Maybe I should go out there again,' said Jennifer, even more uncertainly. She shrugged helplessly and was about to go when Chris called her back.

'Jennifer. Erm . . . I was wondering how the arrangements are going with the sale of the London business?'

She laughed. 'You mean when do you get your money?'

He smiled back. 'It wouldn't half be handy.'

'I'm expecting some stuff from the accountants in London in the next couple of days. Why don't you pop round after work one evening and we can sort out some business?'

'It's a date.'

They walked through to reception together, where Murray was perched on the desk, speaking on the telephone. 'A fight? Oh dear, I am sorry.' He checked his watch. 'Er, yes, of course. Right.'

He hung up and turned to Chris. 'That was McMahon on the phone. A couple of his stags have been playing Terminator Two with each other. Sounds like one of them needs stitching and the other one might have to be dehorned.'

'Good luck,' said Chris.

'The thing is ... I've never actually taken an antler off a live stag before.'

'Neither have I,' said Chris, walking over to the shelves and rummaging about.

Murray looked hopefully at Jennifer, but she laughed and shook her head. 'Don't look at me. Everything I know about deer I got from watching *Bambi*.'

Chris turned round triumphantly, holding a book. He thrust it into Murray's hand, saying, 'It's all in there,' and was about to run for it, when Murray said, 'Chris, wait, there's something else.'

'What is it?'

Murray hesitated and glanced across at Jennifer. 'It's sort of ... private.'

Jennifer smiled. 'OK, I can take a hint. See you later.' She walked out, leaving the two of them alone.

'So, what is it, Murray?' asked Chris.

'It's ... I ... erm ...' He trailed off into silence. Chris looked pointedly at his watch.

Murray took a deep breath. 'The last time I went up there, I had a rather embarrassing moment with Felicity – Mrs McMahon.'

Chris raised an eyebrow at the use of the first name, but said nothing.

'I was getting some gear out of the back of my car and I saw her waving to me from one of the first-floor windows.'

'Doesn't sound too embarrassing to me,' said Chris, enjoying Murray's discomfiture.

'But just as Mr McMahon ...'

Chris interrupted. 'You're not on first name terms with him, then?'

Murray paused, flustered.

'Sorry, Murray, I was only winding you up,' said Chris. 'Go on.'

'... As Mr McMahon came out of the house, I saw Felicity still standing at the window looking down at me. Only she was half-naked. I almost dropped my syringes. McMahon told me I looked as though I'd just seen a ghost and turned round to see what I was looking at but she ducked out of sight just in time.'

'I see,' said Chris. 'Well, Murray, he could be a very good client for us. Just make sure the only things you touch have got antlers and you should be all right.'

He went back into his office, chuckling to himself. Murray made a face, then picked up his bag and his book and headed for the door, like a condemned man on his way to the gallows.

When Murray got up to the deer farm, there was no sign of either Mr or Mrs McMahon. He heaved a sigh of relief and walked up the field, carrying a dart gun and his medical bag. He found one of the huge wounded stags and stood looking at it thoughtfully. Its antler was broken and bleeding and it had a number of other cuts and abrasions. Murray put down the gun and his bag. He opened the book and began thumbing through its pages, frowning with concentration.

He did not notice Felicity approaching. 'Having trouble?' she asked, smiling sweetly.

Murray jumped and spun round. 'Oh . . . good afternoon, Mrs McMahon.'

'Please, Murray, don't be so formal, call me Felicity.'

He gulped, smiled weakly and looked hopefully around, in search of Mr McMahon, but there was no sign of him. 'Mr McMahon not about?'

'Safely out of harm's way, thank goodness. What happens now?'

'Erm . . . he's going to need stitching. But first he has to have an anaesthetic.'

Felicity took the book out of Murray's hands and started to thumb through it, standing dangerously close to him. 'You will tell me if I'm putting you off?' she said, flashing him a dazzling smile.

Murray gave her a wan smile in return. 'If I could have the book back, just for a minute.'

He leafed through the pages, acutely conscious of Felicity's steady gaze upon him, then put down the book and picked up the gun, firing a dart into the stag's rump. It bellowed and struggled for a minute, then lapsed into unconsciousness.

Murray went to work, growing in confidence as he dealt with

each of the stag's injuries in turn. Felicity stood near by, watching him. He looked round and again she smiled radiantly at him. Enjoying his work, his return smile was much less forced this time.

'Murray . . .' said Felicity.

'Uh huh?' said Murray, preoccupied with stitching a gash in the stag's chest.

'Do you find me attractive?'

Murray stopped in his tracks. His smile faded and he stammered incoherently. 'Yes . . . er . . . I mean . . . No . . . er.'

She stood right next to him, uncomfortably close, her breath warm and silky on his neck. 'I want you.'

'Mrs McMahon, really, I . . . I . . .'

'Don't be frightened, my husband needn't know.'

'I can't. I'm gay,' said Murray desperately.

Felicity recoiled in shock, but then she laughed and said, 'I don't believe you, I've seen the way you look at me.'

Murray was not sure how much longer professional etiquette could continue to win out over the stirring in his loins, but help was at hand.

McMahon's voice came booming across the field. 'Felicity, get in the house.'

They both started nervously, then Felicity gave Murray a slow, burning smile and adopted a meek expression as she turned to walk past her husband and back to the house.

Chris was standing waiting for him as Murray unloaded his car back at the practice. Murray smiled nervously. 'The dehorning went very well. I quite enjoyed the visit actually.'

'Apparently,' said Chris. 'Mr McMahon telephoned. He accused you of making love to his wife.'

'What?' laughed Murray. 'You're joking?'

'No, I'm not, I'm deadly serious,' said Chris. 'What happened?'

'Nothing happened. Of course nothing happened.'

Chris searched carefully for the right words. 'Murray, you have . . . you have a way about you. You like to flirt, don't you? I know you don't mean it seriously, but . . .'

'Chris, I did not flirt with Mrs McMahon. I'm sorry that you think I did.'

'I'm not saying you did but . . .'

'You want to know what happened?' asked Murray, aggrieved. 'I told you what happened last time I was there. This time, while I was working, she came straight up to me and asked me if . . . when I'd finished with the stag . . . if we could have sex together.'

Chris could not help but smile. 'She asked you that? Straight out? Was her husband there?'

'Of course he wasn't there. Yes, she did. I said "No", obviously. I told her . . .'

'What did you tell her?' asked Chris, now enjoying himself hugely.

'I told her I was gay.'

Chris burst out laughing. 'Well, now we know why McMahon gets through so many vets. His wife keeps chatting them up. I'll phone him back and suggest that from now on he finds a frumpy female vet to look after his deer.'

'Will that be all?' asked Murray grumpily.

'Yes. Well done with the treatment.'

Murray walked towards the practice, but paused with his hand on the door-handle, turned back and smiled. 'I was tempted though. She's gorgeous.'

Chapter 10

Stella, Dick and Tom were eating breakfast when they heard a car pull into the yard. Dick went to see who it was, and Stella and Tom heard, 'Ministry of Agriculture, Mr Sims. We've had a rather disturbing report,' before Dick slammed the door and went out into the yard. Bewildered, Stella looked at Tom, who shrugged his shoulders, though the nervous look on his face showed her that he knew why the man was there.

Twenty minutes later they heard the Ministry official's car drive out of the farmyard and Dick strode into the kitchen, again slamming the door behind him, his face distorted with rage. He glowered at Tom. 'A thousand pounds, that's what you cost me.'

'It's not my fault, I never knew she'd tell.'

'Should have thought of that first, you little hooligan, shouldn't you?'

Stella looked anxiously from one to the other of them. 'What did he say, Dick?'

'I can't deliver the calves. I've got to keep them here two weeks for a course of treatment.' He rounded on Tom again. 'The supermarket'll have to go elsewhere now. This could cost us the bloody contract.'

'How could you, Tom?' asked Stella, reproachfully.

'I never meant to grass on him,' he said helplessly.

'What did I do to get a son like you?' said Dick, his knuckles showing white on his huge fists.

Stella had a sinking feeling in the pit of her stomach. She tried to put a restraining hand on his arm, saying, 'Dick, don't. Calm down,' but he was past reasoning, stoking the fires of his own fury.

'You're nothing but trouble and always have been.'

Tom stood up abruptly. 'I don't have to listen to this crap.'

'You'll listen to what I decide you'll listen to,' said Dick, putting himself between Tom and the door.

'You threatening me?' said Tom.

'Leave it, the pair of you,' implored Stella, but both ignored her, eyes locked on each other, blood pounding, fists clenched.

'You raise your fist to me, lad, you'll see what comes.'

'Try it,' snarled Tom.

Stella pulled Tom away, crying, 'Stop it!'

He looked at her, then glanced back at his father and said, 'I'm not staying in this house.'

'You want to go – go,' said Dick, pointing to the door.

Tom pulled away from Stella and walked towards the door. 'You won't see me in this house again.'

'Good bloody riddance,' spat Dick.

Stella looked despairingly from one to the other. 'Shut up, Dick. Tom, where are you going?'

Tom stooped and picked Lucy out of her basket. 'Anywhere, as long as it's away from him.'

'You can't take Lucy, she's poorly, for God's sake,' said Stella, but as Tom hesitated, Dick yelled, 'Go. Get out! And take that mangy animal with you!'

Tom took a last look back and then hurried out, carrying the dog wrapped in a piece of blanket. Stella ran to the door, calling, 'Tom! Come back, please. Tom!' But he was gone. She looked across to Dick, who slumped heavily into a chair. He sat there in total silence for some minutes, then raised his head and said, 'Once word gets out, the supermarket'll pull out of the deal, you see if they don't.'

'It hasn't come to that yet.'

There was another long silence.

'Maybe we were too old for him,' said Stella in a faraway voice. 'The last time I felt like this, we had a visit from the police.'

She looked at Dick, who avoided her gaze.

Tom walked straight to the practice, carrying the dog in his arms. Maddy was alone in reception when he appeared.

'Where's Mrs Holt?' he said, a cold anger in his eyes.

'She's busy. Can I help you?'

'No. I want to see her now.'

'I'm sorry, you'll have to wait.'

Tom ignored her, putting the dog down on a chair and walking through towards the back.

'Wait!' shouted Maddy anxiously, but just then, Tom pushed open the door of Jennifer's office.

He stared sullenly at her, speaking in a low and threatening voice. 'What did you go and do that for, eh?'

Maddy looked nervously at Jennifer. 'Shall I call the police?'

'No, it's OK,' said Jennifer.

Maddy gave her a dubious look, but retreated to reception.

'Now, Tom,' said Jennifer, 'what's the problem?'

'You reported us, and now I've got nowhere to live.'

'What are you talking about?' she asked, baffled.

'You sent those Ministry people round.'

'No, I never did, Tom,' she said, frowning and thinking rapidly. 'Look, I'm very busy at the moment, wait in reception, I'll be out in five minutes.'

'Are you telling me what to do?'

He took a step nearer to her and Jennifer flinched involuntarily, seeing another side of him for the first time, but she kept her voice even as she said, 'Are you threatening me?'

He did not reply.

'Get out of here,' she said, anger overcoming her fear.

'My dad threw me out the house 'cos of you.'

'Out!'

He ignored her and stepped even closer, blocking the escape route to the door. 'I don't like people who do that.'

'I'm going to call the police,' said Jennifer, now really frightened but determined not to show it.

After a long moment, his stare boring into her, he muttered, 'Don't bother,' turned and walked out.

As he left, Chris, summoned by Maddy, came hurrying down the corridor. 'What's going on?' he asked, but Tom hurried out of the building.

Chris turned to Jennifer. 'Jen?'

She went to the window, visibly shaken, but did not reply.

'What happened?' said Chris. 'Tell me.'

'I've just had that – that lout threatening me. How could you do that?'

Chris stared blankly at her. 'What?'

'You reported Dick Sims to MAFF and you didn't even bloody well tell me.'

'Hang on, Jen . . .'

'I'm dealing with this family, Tom is my client.'

'Calm down,' said Chris, imperturbably. 'I reported Dick to stop him moving those calves.'

'Why did you just report him, why didn't you go and see him first?'

'Because there was absolutely no point. I know Dick Sims of old, I've had to report him before for this sort of thing.'

'That's no excuse. You could have told me.'

Now Chris was beginning to get annoyed. 'I made a unilateral decision. You're going to have to get used to that.' Jennifer bristled as she recognized her own words being quoted back at her, but she bit her tongue, controlling her anger before she spoke again. Chris walked out of the room, but she counted to ten and then followed him, finding him in the X-ray room.

As she appeared at the door, he glanced up and pointed to the X-rays hanging on the screen. 'Mrs Freeman's colt. Looks like a dislocated shoulder.'

Jennifer waited a moment or two, then spoke softly. 'We have a problem, Chris.'

He shrugged. 'Things'll settle.'

'I'm not sure in your heart of hearts that you want me here.'

He looked across at her guardedly, waiting for her to continue.

'As a partner, that is. I know how worried you are about the practice, about money and everything, but you never share your worries. You probably do with Patricia, but never with me. You see me as a threat, but I don't know why.'

'I didn't realize how hard it would be . . . you as a partner I mean. I resent this – all this . . .' He swept an arm around, taking in the building. 'I built it from scratch, I mean literally. I physically converted this building from an empty shell with my own hands. For the first year of business I worked from five-thirty in the morning to ten at night. Because we had nothing, Patricia and me. A bank loan, a three-month-old baby and a handful of clients who'd have left me at the drop of a hat if I hadn't been good enough. I know you and your husband ran a business too, but it isn't the same in the city. Reputation and word of mouth mean everything here.'

Jennifer smiled, and spoke gently, patiently. 'I understand all that but it's no excuse. I'm an ally here, not the enemy. I admire what you've done here and I want to be part of it.'

Chris paused and thought hard, then admitted, 'I have been giving you a hard time, I'm sorry. I've let the pressure get to me. I made the decision to expand the business and now I'm scared stiff that it'll collapse around my ears.'

She put her hand on his arm and looked into his eyes. 'I won't let it collapse, there's too much at stake – for me I mean. I've started a new life here and I'm going to make it work.'

'You will too, won't you?'

'If you let me.'

She looked down at her hand and, embarrassed, she withdrew it, then smiled at him and left the room. He watched her go and stood staring after her, the light from the screen casting dark shadows across his face.

When Jennifer got home that night, she poured herself a stiff drink then dialled a London number. Coming down the stairs on his way to the kitchen, Steven heard her voice coming indistinctly from the front room. He stopped and listened.

'I'm not being unreasonable . . . I want it settled, that's all . . . OK, yes . . . if you would, I'd be really grateful . . . fine, yes, of course I will. Bye.'

Steven hurried on into the kitchen. There was a long silence and then the door opened and Jennifer came in. When she saw him she put on a cheerful face and said, 'He sends you lots of love and he's looking forward to seeing you in a couple of weeks.'

He gave her a disbelieving look. 'I hate that tone you use when you talk to him. Like you're whingeing.'

Hurt, her cheerful mask slipped. 'Sometimes your father likes to make me grovel and that's when I whinge.'

Steven went to the fridge, helped himself to a Coke and sat down at the table. Determined to be positive, she tried again. 'But things are pretty good between your dad and me at the moment. We're sorting out all the business matters. And soon I'll be a fully fledged partner in the practice.'

Steven said nothing and did not look up.

'You're pleased about that, aren't you, Steven?'

'Yeah, sure,' said Steven, in a voice dripping boredom.

'At least it means we're staying in Whitton. You want that, don't you?'

'Uh huh.'

Jennifer sat down next to him. 'What is it? Tell me.'

'It's nothing really, it's just . . .' Steven broke off, embarrassed. 'Once you and him have sorted out all this money stuff . . . I mean, that only leaves me, doesn't it? As the sort of last link between you.'

Jennifer put her hand on his, but said nothing, her silence confirming Steven's statement. He pulled his hand away from hers and said abruptly, 'I've got to go, Amanda's asked me over to her place tonight – to meet the family.' He rolled his eyes, then walked out, leaving Jennifer still seated at the table, staring at the wall.

Steven walked up to the top of the lane and caught a bus south, asking the driver, 'Tell me when we get to Yelverbridge, please.' He peered at a set of directions written in Amanda's round, girlish scrawl as the single-decker bus rattled through deserted lanes and tiny villages, with Steven its only passenger for most of the journey. Finally the bus halted at a crossroads.

'Here y'are,' said the driver.

Steven got off and stood waiting for his eyes to get accustomed to the darkness as the bus disappeared down the lane, then set off up a side lane, the road seeming to glow faintly in the starlight. Every time it disappeared under a canopy of trees, however, Steven was groping his way forward, guided mainly by the sound of his shoes on the tarmac. Several times he blundered off into the mud at the side of the road.

Somehow he found the even narrower lane, rough and rutted with grass sprouting in the middle, that led down towards Amanda's farm, and as he got nearer he could smell a faint salt tang in the air and heard the low rumble of the surf breaking unseen on the shore beyond the cliffs. As he rounded a corner, he saw the warm glow of light from the farmhouse and smelt the sweet and sour stink of silage from the cowsheds near by. He knocked on the door and Amanda came running to open it. She looked Steven over in the light streaming from inside and laughed. 'They must have looked smart when you put them on.'

Ruefully Steven looked down, examining his shoes and trousers, now caked in mud.

He followed her into the house, and as Amanda opened the living-room door they were enveloped in noise and mayhem. The whole family was there, Amanda's father, Frankie, her mother, Noreen, and her two older sisters, Pamela and Serena, and all of them were talking – or shouting – at once.

'This is Steven,' said Amanda, but no one heard her. Noreen and Serena were trying to lay the table and arguing at the same time as Serena wiped a fork on her sleeve to polish it up.

'Don't do that, it's disgusting,' said Noreen.

'It's OK, I'm sitting here.'

Frankie, a Frank Sinatra fan and keen amateur musician still dreaming of his big break, even in his early fifties, was demanding, 'Who's been at my Tony Bennett album?'

'No one'd listen to that if you paid them,' said Pamela, laughing.

'Pamela gave it to Oxfam,' yelled Serena.

'I did not!' screamed Pamela, as Frankie rounded on her furiously. 'She was joking, Dad.'

'Don't tease your father, Serena,' said Noreen.

Steven looked on apprehensively from the doorway, standing close to Amanda for protection. They were still completely ignored.

'THIS IS STEVEN!' shouted Amanda at the top of her voice.

There was a stunned silence as the entire family froze and stared at him.

Nervously, Steven attempted a smile.

'Come and sit down, Steven,' said Noreen. 'Tea's just ready.' The normal volume of noise immediately resumed, with everyone talking, arguing and laughing at once as they dished up the meal, while Steven sat quietly in the middle of it all. 'Don't stand on ceremony, Steven,' said Noreen, as the family fell on the food like starving men, piling their plates high with scant regard for social niceties. Noreen, playing hostess, filled up Steven's cup as soon as he drank from it, while Frankie expounded his theories of popular music to him, delighted to have a captive audience.

'Now Bing Crosby, he was your original sophisticated crooner . . .'

'Original sophisticated crap more like,' yelled Serena. She and Pamela collapsed with laughter, but Frankie continued magisterially, ignoring the interruption.

'. . . Whereas Frank – Sinatra that is, of course – he was more of your pop star, your heart-throb, you know what I mean?'

'My mum says Frank Sinatra's just a senile old gangster who doesn't know when to retire,' said Steven, emboldened by the disrespectful banter from Frankie's daughters.

A hush fell on the room, as Frankie sat there open-mouthed, shell-shocked. Steven was aghast.

'He . . . he was only joking, Dad,' said Amanda hastily.

Steven took his cue. 'I was only joking, Mr Mulholland. I'm sorry.'

Frankie immediately recovered his equilibrium. 'You had me going there for a minute,' he said, slapping him on the back. 'Call me "Frankie", please. After Frank Sinatra, of course. My real name's Lionel.'

Steven smiled politely, acutely aware of Pamela and Serena giggling at his embarrassment.

After finishing the meal, Steven retreated gratefully to the porch with Amanda. 'How are you getting home?' she asked.

'I've got some money for a minicab.'

Amanda snorted with laughter. 'Minicab! This isn't London, Steven, you won't get a minicab to come out here. They'd never find the place for a start.'

'Oh.'

She leaned into his chest and they began to kiss passionately as she wound her arms tightly around his neck. After a few minutes, Amanda broke off and whispered breathlessly in his ear, 'Stay here the night. With me.'

'No I . . . I don't want to,' said Steven uneasily.

'You scared? Don't be scared.'

'It's not that . . .'

A look of realization dawned on Amanda's face. 'You've never done it, have you?'

He shook his head, embarrassed.

'I have but only once. This time it'll be much better,' she said firmly.

'I really don't want to. Not here.'

'But I thought – what is it?'

'I just don't, that's all,' said Steven, growing more uncomfortable by the minute.

'Shit. I thought you fancied me,' said Amanda, turning away.

'I do,' stammered Steven. 'It's just . . . I don't want to do it like this.'

'You might as well go home then,' she said, pushing him in the chest and turning to go back into the house.

'Wait,' called Steven. 'I really do fancy you and I want us to sleep together. I just don't want to do it with twenty-seven members of your family under the same roof.'

She half-turned back towards him, pouting as she spoke. 'Maybe I've changed my mind.'

'Please, Amanda, don't say that.'

'I'll think about it.'

She smiled her slow seductive smile and then closed the door.

As Steven threaded his way back through the warren of dark lanes, Tom was sitting in a shelter on the sea-front, his dog cradled in his lap. He shivered in the cool breeze from the sea and set off walking back up towards the town. He found a shop doorway, sheltered from the wind and hunched down. He felt the dog's nose. It was warm and she was panting heavily. The cast on her leg was also burning hot. He wrapped the dog tightly in his own coat and huddled down in the cold, trying to get to sleep.

He was waiting at the practice the next morning when Jennifer arrived. She gave him a hard look as he told her, 'Lucy's sick again, she's been panting like that all night and the cast feels hot.'

'Wait there,' she said shortly and carried the dog through to the back, leaving Tom sitting in reception, with Maddy keeping a wary eye on him.

Jennifer carefully felt Lucy's leg, then turned to Laura. 'It's osteomyelitis, I can feel the heat.'

'She'll need another operation then.'

Jennifer walked back to reception with Laura. Tom stood up, still avoiding her gaze.

'She's got bacterial infection via the implants,' said Jennifer flatly, 'it was always a possibility.'

Tom said nothing, waiting impassively.

'You've got a bloody nerve coming back here,' hissed Jennifer. 'I could have reported you for threatening me. I don't imagine your parole officer would have been over the moon.'

'I was upset about Lucy, you know . . .' said Tom uncomfortably, shifting from foot to foot.

'You assumed I'd reported your father. You couldn't give me the benefit of the doubt, could you? So why the hell should anyone give you the benefit of the doubt? Did your dad really throw you out of the house or did you simply fly off the handle at him like you did at me?'

'I'm sorry,' said Tom, dragging the words out of himself.

She stood there for a moment, staring at him with distaste, and when she spoke, her voice was hard-edged. 'Lucy will need another operation to remove the bone particles. I can do it for about a hundred and fifty pounds.'

'I haven't got any money.'

'That's your problem. I'll keep her in overnight, come back in the morning.'

'But I can't pay for it.'

'Then I'll have to put Lucy to sleep.'

Laura whipped round to look at her, shocked. 'He said sorry, Jen,' she said quietly, but Jennifer ignored her. Tom looked hopefully at Laura for a moment, then turned and went out through the door, leaving Laura and Maddy still staring at Jennifer in surprise.

While Jennifer remained intransigent towards Tom, Chris was showing signs of softening towards Tom's father. He had gone out to the farm on the Ministry's instructions and was administering oral antibiotics to the infected calves. Dick stood glumly a few feet away.

'You're enjoying this, aren't you?' he asked.

Chris shook his head. 'I never enjoy being asked by MAFF to arrive uninvited on a farmer's property.'

'This could do me a lot of damage.'

'You should have treated the ringworm then, shouldn't you?'

Dick hesitated, obviously having something else on his mind but finding it difficult to say. He took a deep breath. 'Look, Chris . . . er, Mr Lennox . . . we've had our differences I know, but . . .

there's no way you could have a word with MAFF, is there, and get them to keep quiet about all this?'

Chris thought for a moment, also struggling to say what was on his mind. 'Perhaps I was hasty. I should have spoken to you first. I'll see what I can do.'

'Thanks.'

'But get your act together, Mr Sims.'

Dick nodded gratefully as Chris resumed work.

Neither of them heard the phone ring in the farm. Stella answered it, glanced nervously towards the cowshed and then said, 'Yes, of course, Tom, where?'

She met him at the Seven Stars and sat having a drink while Tom wolfed down the pie and chips she had bought him, as if he hadn't eaten in days.

'What about Lucy's operation?' asked Tom, his mouth full of food.

'I could give you the money,' said Stella, 'but I'm not going to.'

'Will you ask Dad for me then?'

'No. You'll have to ask him yourself.'

He stopped eating for a moment and looked at her, horrified. 'I can't. Not after the things he said.'

'He was upset, and he was right to be, but he is concerned about you and he wants you home.'

'How can I go home?'

'You look him in the eye and tell him you're sorry, that's how.'

Tom shook his head. 'I can't do that.'

Stella looked at him, then got up and walked out, leaving him staring after her.

Stella said nothing about the meeting to Dick when she got home. She carried on with her work throughout the afternoon, occasionally glancing hopefully up the empty lane. Just as darkness was falling, she saw a figure walking down towards the farm. She went outside, standing in the pool of light spilling from the doorway, and watched Tom cross the yard to where Dick stood, hosing down his wellies. He stopped a little way away from Dick and waited.

Dick glanced up at him and then went back to cleaning his wellies. 'You've come home for your dinner, I expect. You had your mother worried sick.'

'I can see I'm not wanted,' said Tom impatiently, already turning to start walking back up the lane.

Stella ran into the yard, calling, 'Tom, wait!'

He stopped but jerked his head towards his father. 'He doesn't want me here.'

'Yes, he does.' She turned to look over her shoulder at Dick. 'The lad's got something to say.'

Dick stopped what he was doing and said gruffly, 'Spit it out then.'

Tom hesitated, but under his mother's promptings, he finally said, 'This is your farm . . . and I did wrong.'

'You did,' said Dick evenly.

'I'm sorry.'

'But it'll be your farm one day,' said his father, his face breaking into a broad grin, 'now you've come home.'

Tom still hesitated. 'Lucy needs another operation.'

'Your mum told me.' He looked across to Stella, then back to Tom. 'Tell you what I'll do, Tom. I'll lend you the money to pay for her and you can pay me back out of your wages.' He smiled and Tom returned the smile for the first time.

Dick walked over to him and put his arms round him awkwardly, a gesture that he had not used for a long time. Stella's eyes brimmed with tears, but she said nothing.

'I'd better phone the vet centre and let them know,' said Tom, but before going inside he took the evening paper out of his pocket and gave it to Stella. 'Seen this?'

As Stella started to read, Tom turned back to his father and said, 'But if this was my farm already, I'd have got the vet in for those calves.'

For once Dick smiled and did not fight for the last word. 'That's your lookout.'

Stella interrupted him, chuckling, 'Hey look at this.'

She held up the paper for Dick to see. Across the front page was a picture of him and the muckspreader, surrounded by people in the car-park.

'I like this bit,' she said. 'Opposition councillor Patricia Lennox said, "All things need fertilizer to grow. Since the present Council have wilted and run out of ideas, perhaps a shower of shit will do them some good."'

They all laughed as Tom went into the house to phone the practice.

Chapter 11

Under the reproachful stares of Laura and Maddy, Jennifer had already decided to carry out the operation anyway, but she did not tell Tom that when he called. She finished the evening surgery and then began the operation, with Laura assisting. By the time Lucy was safely restored to her cage to sleep off the anaesthetic, Jennifer was ready to drop from exhaustion. She thought of phoning Chris to put off their meeting until another night but then took her hand away from the phone. She had an hour to spare, time enough for a shower and some food to revive her.

As she came in through the front door, she heard MTV booming out from the front room. She shuddered but picked up her mail and wandered through to the kitchen, yelling, 'Evening!' above the din.

There was an answering shout from Steven.

She poured herself a glass of wine and sat at the table, opening a bulky envelope. As she read the letter, her expression changed and her anger began to rise. She slammed the letter hard down on the table, gnawing her knuckle as she tried to think what to do.

Just then the door opened and Steven came in. Jennifer put on an instant smile for him but he regarded her suspiciously, catching an ember of her previous expression.

'Is that the business stuff from Dad?'

'Yeah,' said Jennifer noncommittally.

'Everything all right?'

'Sure. How did you get on with Amanda?'

Steven's mood changed in an instant. 'Do you know what's worse than being sixteen? It's being sixteen and having a mother who wants an action replay on everything you do.'

He walked out again and Jennifer's false smile disappeared as quickly as it had come. She refilled her glass and reread the letter.

She was still sitting at the table gazing into space forty minutes later, when the doorbell rang. Chris was standing on the step, holding a bottle of wine. When he saw Jennifer still in her work clothes, he hesitated. 'I'm not early, am I?'

'No, no, come in,' said Jennifer listlessly.

She took his wine and led him through to the kitchen, pouring him a glass from her own, nearly empty bottle. 'Have you eaten?'

'Yeah, sure.'

'Good, 'cos I'm not up to cooking.'

He waited for a few moments, sipping his wine and studying her face, then said, 'What's the problem, Jen?'

She pointed to the bundle of papers on the table. 'I was under the impression – naïve little me – that our business, once sold, was going to be split fifty-fifty. But somehow I was misinformed. Somehow it's a sixty-five/thirty-five split, that's all to do with the . . .' she glanced down at the letter, '. . . proportional equity stake of the original capital investment.'

He saw her eyes fill with tears and said gently, 'You can fight it, Jen.'

'I don't want to fight it. I want that man out of my life.' She did not want to cry in front of him, so she stood up and went to the sink, rinsing out a cup for want of anything better to do. 'You know what's so disappointing?' she said. 'Even from a distance, he can still hurt me. How long does it take to forget someone?'

'You never really do,' said Chris. 'You wake up one morning and it doesn't hurt any more, that's all that happens.'

'I'll have to get a bank loan to make up the shortfall,' she said, her voice breaking. 'There'll be no difficulty, don't worry.'

She still did not look round, but Chris got up and went up over to her, hesitantly putting his arm around her shoulder. She smiled gratefully up at him but at that moment the door opened and Steven walked in. He stood there, taking in the scene.

Embarrassed, Chris dropped his arm from Jennifer's shoulders.

'What is it, Mum?' asked Steven.

'Nothing. Don't worry, I'm all right.'

'Is it about the letter?'

'No, no.'

'It seems your father's been a shade devious with the business arrangements,' said Chris.

Steven rounded on him, furious. 'And who the hell are you to talk about my dad like that?'

He stormed out, slamming the door behind him.

Chris looked wretchedly at Jennifer. 'I'm so sorry, I . . .'

'Well, that's a bucketful of brownie points you've just squandered,' smiled Jennifer, her eyes still red-rimmed. 'You'd better have another drink.'

He shook his head. 'I think I'd better go, before I do any more damage.'

As Jennifer showed Chris out, she could hear Steven's music thumping upstairs. She went up and knocked on his door. There was no reply but after waiting a minute, she opened the door and when he still did not acknowledge her, she went over, turned the music right down and sat down on his bed next to him.

He looked up at her. 'Has he gone?'

'Yes.'

'Is he your boyfriend now?'

'No, of course not. Chris is my partner. And a friend.'

He considered that, then asked, 'Why did you lie to me about the letter?'

'Because I don't like criticizing your father in front of you. I know how uncomfortable it makes you feel. He's your dad and I'll never ask you to take sides between us.'

Steven did not acknowledge the remark at all, merely picking up the remote control and turning up the volume again. Jennifer took the hint and left the room.

While Chris was at Jennifer's, Patricia had also been out visiting. She sat at Laura's kitchen table, trying to reassure her. 'I've been married to a vet for ten years, Laura, I understand Alan's feelings completely, but you have to decide – he has to decide – do you fight it or go with it.'

'I didn't resign because of pressure from Alan, Patricia. I resigned because . . .'

Patricia completed the sentence for her. 'Because you felt insulted. You deserved a partnership, so why the hell didn't Chris offer you one?'

Laura looked at her, surprised. 'So why didn't he?'

'Because Jennifer's a better candidate.' As Patricia saw the sour expression forming on Laura's face, she hurried on, 'But the practice needs you too, Laura. You're an excellent small animal vet and an integral part of the team.'

Laura nodded, but said in a small voice, 'But I've resigned.'

'Yes, well ... I've had a thought about that. Why don't you ask Chris if he'd make you an associate partner? You wouldn't have capital invested in the practice but it does mean a small share of the profits.'

Laura looked at her thoughtfully for a second, then a slow smile started to spread across her face.

Patricia looked at her watch. 'I'd better be getting back.' As she stood up, she winked at Laura and said, 'That idea never came from me, by the way. In fact I wasn't even here.'

They exchanged a conspiratorial smile.

By the time Patricia got home, Laura had already phoned and left a message on the answerphone for Chris. Smiling to herself, Patricia sat down on the sofa and picked up a book. When Chris got home, she buried her nose even deeper in her book as he played back the message. She looked up and caught his eye as the message ended: '. . . So have a think about the idea, Chris, and perhaps we can talk about it tomorrow. That's all, really. Bye now.'

He turned to Patricia. 'Well. Not such a bad compromise. What do you think?'

'Mmm,' said Patricia, as if considering it for the very first time. 'Worth thinking about seriously.'

'I wonder where she got the idea from,' said Chris, suspiciously. 'Jennifer, I suppose.'

Patricia yawned and stretched. 'Or maybe Alan,' she said innocently.

'I knew she'd see sense,' said Chris, smiling broadly. 'I'm going to have a huge drink.'

'And I'm going to join you.'

Dick and Tom were already waiting patiently in reception when Chris got to work in the morning. He stopped to exchange a few words with Dick, their conversation less forced and stilted than on their previous meeting. Tom remained silent, his eyes fixed on the corridor, waiting apprehensively for Jennifer to bring Lucy through. After a few minutes she came through from surgery carrying the collie wrapped in a blanket.

Tom stood up immediately and went over to her, staring at the dog. Her leg was still bandaged, but she seemed alert and well enough, her tail thumping against the blanket as she saw Tom.

'She'll need to take it easy for a while,' warned Jennifer. 'An indestructible old girl, though, isn't she?' She glanced across to Chris, who inclined his head in acknowledgement of the point.

Tom carried the dog out to his father's car, but Dick hung back to walk alongside Jennifer. 'Give me a ring if you're worried at all,' she said.

'Right,' said Dick. He looked furtively towards the car and saw Tom absorbed in getting Lucy settled. 'Oh, between you and me . . .' He pulled a roll of notes out of his pocket. 'There's five hundred and fifty pounds there. For both operations.'

'You don't have to,' said Jennifer, more than a little surprised. 'I did agree to do the first one for free.'

'Nothing's for free, Mrs Holt. Not in our business,' said Dick, smiling as he clambered into the driving seat.

She watched them drive off, then tapped the money thoughtfully in her palm as she wandered back inside the practice.

Jennifer was on her way through reception, heading for home that night, when the telephone rang. Maddy answered it, then covered the receiver with her hand. 'It's for you, Jennifer – your husband.'

Jennifer grimaced, but took the phone as Maddy studiously busied herself tidying up some papers on her desk. She could not help overhearing Jennifer's half of the conversation, however, and it was obvious that the call did not bring welcome news.

'Thought of some new way to cheat me? . . . Save your breath, I'm not interested . . . You're not serious . . . You can't do this to him, he's been looking forward to it for weeks . . . You bastard – and you don't even have the guts to tell him yourself, do you?' She slammed the phone down, gave Maddy an embarrassed look and hurried out.

She had steeled herself for a confrontation with Steven when she got home, but the cottage was in darkness, a light flashing on the answerphone the only trace of her son. 'I'm at Amanda's, back later, bye.'

Steven was curled up on Amanda's sofa, holding her at arm's length while he asked nervously, 'Are you sure they won't be back till late?'

Amanda rolled her eyes. 'For the third time, yes, I'm sure. Dad's down at the village hall with his band, rehearsing for Pamela's party, and Mum, Serena and Pamela are all out getting pissed. They won't be back till well after closing time, so relax.'

She leaned over and kissed him long and hard, her fingers nimbly unbuttoning his shirt. She ran her hands over his chest, moaning softly as Steven's breathing grew faster and heavier, then pulled away from him, placing her fingers lightly on his lips.

'What's up?' asked Steven.

Amanda smiled her long, slow smile. 'Nothing. Come upstairs.'

Later, in the darkness of her room, they lay tangled together, sweat drying on their skin. 'Your first time,' smiled Amanda, punctuating her words with kisses, 'You'll always remember me now.'

They made love again, more tenderly, less urgently, and then lay curled in each other's arms, not even speaking, just feeling the glow of each other's bodies.

Suddenly there was the sound of a key turning in the lock downstairs. They leapt out of bed in a panic, throwing their clothes on, and tiptoed to the top of the stairs, freezing as they saw Noreen, Pamela and Serena staring up at them. There was a long silence as the three of them took in Steven and Amanda's ruffled clothes and flushed faces, then they burst into shrieks of drunken laughter. Steven blushed crimson, but Amanda squeezed his hand and led him nonchalantly downstairs, ignoring the bar- racking from her mother and sisters, who were still hooting with laughter.

Steven and Amanda stood on the porch, not even noticing the freezing cold, reluctant to let the evening end. 'I've got to go,' said Steven three times, but each time he let himself be drawn back to her for another kiss. Finally she pushed him gently in the chest, gave him a smile that sent the blood pounding through his veins again and whispered, 'It was great, wasn't it? See you tomorrow.'

She watched as he walked up the lane, laughing quietly as he broke into a trot and jumped in the air as he ran. 'Looks quite pleased with himself, doesn't he?' chuckled Noreen, coming up quietly behind her. Amanda jumped, then nodded shyly.

'Er . . . Amanda, love,' said Noreen, 'are you and Steven . . . you know?'

'What? Using condoms, early withdrawal or the rhythm method?'

Noreen smiled benignly. 'Just don't tell your dad, he'll have a seizure.'

Amanda grinned back at her mother, hugged her and went inside.

Jennifer was still up, waiting for him, when Steven got back. He came jauntily into the kitchen. 'Hi, Mum.'

'Hi, you're late. I made some spaghetti carbonara. Your favourite. Well, one of them I can actually cook. I can warm it up if you like.'

'I'll eat it cold,' said Steven. 'I'm starving.'

He shovelled himself a plateful from the stove and sat at the table wolfing it down, while Jennifer watched him, a puzzled smile on her face. He finished it in two minutes flat, pushed the plate away and looked at his watch.

'Thanks, Mum. Er . . . I've got an essay to write for tomorrow, I'd better make a start.'

She nodded distractedly, and he shot her a curious glance, surprised that there was no outburst about neglecting his homework to spend the evening at Amanda's.

'Steven. Erm . . . your dad phoned me at the practice this afternoon. I'm afraid he can't do this weekend. He says he's very sorry but he's extremely busy at the moment.'

Steven glared at her. 'Yeah? Why didn't he phone me here?'

She shrugged.

'Are you sure you didn't phone him and suggest the idea?' said Steven, venting his disappointment and frustration on her.

'That's an awful thing to say. I'd never do that, you know I wouldn't.'

He ran out of the kitchen and disappeared upstairs.

'Steven!' called Jennifer, but there was no reply, only the sound of his bedroom door slamming shut.

As Frankie got up early the next morning, Noreen turned over, groaned and opened an eye like a poached egg. Frankie chuckled. 'Good night, was it?'

She groaned again.

'I'll get you a cup of tea and an aspirin when I've milked.' He went downstairs and out into the freezing dawn, and was at work in the milking parlour, moving from cow to cow with practised ease, when he heard the door open and saw his boss, Simon Dunning, standing in the doorway.

Only twenty-five, Simon was very young to be the manager of such a large estate, and though he was a graduate of Cirencester Agricultural College, his other qualification as nephew of the owner was the one that had got him the job. Frankie had been working as cowman for the estate, looking after the 250-strong dairy herd, long before Simon became estate manager, but though Simon's lack of experience often amused him, Frankie did not resent him.

Frankie greeted him in surprise. 'Morning, Mr Dunning. Early for you to be up and about.'

'I couldn't sleep, Frankie. I've a lot on my mind, so I thought I'd get an early start.'

Frankie nodded and carried on with his work. Simon watched him for a minute then said, 'The milk yield's still falling steadily.'

'I know,' said Frankie. 'There's a few cows with a touch of mastitis, but these antibiotics'll see to it, don't worry.' He gestured to the ointment he was rubbing into the teats of one of the cows.

'Do you want me to get Chris Lennox in?'

'No, don't bother, I've enough antibiotics to see me through.'

'Good,' said Simon. 'That's saved me a few quid at least.' His wan smile quickly faded and he went on hastily, nervously tapping his foot against a steel tank as he spoke. 'Frankie, listen, things are very tight financially at the moment. I'm having to rely on the income from the dairy herd . . .'

'Don't worry yourself, Mr Dunning,' said Frankie soothingly. 'The yield'll be back to normal in no time at all, I give you my word.'

'You're a good man, Frankie,' said Simon, turning to go.

'You and Mrs Dunning are coming to the party, aren't you?'

'Wouldn't miss it for the world. Right, I must go. I've got the bank manager coming to see me at nine and I have to get some figures ready for him.'

Simon walked out of the cowshed, disturbing a flock of rooks which flapped lazily away across the fields, cawing half-heartedly at him. He drove back up the lane and followed the main road for half a mile before branching off into the sweeping drive that led to the manor house, a very minor stately home, at the heart of the thousand-acre estate. The manor house was reserved for his uncle's use, though he rarely visited the estate and Simon lived with his wife, Stephanie, and their three-month-old baby girl in a flat in the converted stables which also housed the estate office.

Simon went straight there and pored over figures until the bank manager arrived. The manager made no concessions to the country in his style of dress, wearing a chalk-striped grey suit and black leather shoes and carrying a black briefcase. He stepped carefully around the puddles and mud in the yard and entered the office. He emerged half an hour later, accompanied by Simon who showed him to his car, all smiles. The smiles faded as soon as the man drove off, however, and he stomped up the stairs to his flat in a foul mood.

'God almighty, they charge exorbitant rates of interest and expect you to be grateful for them lending you the money,' yelled Simon, causing the baby, cradled in Stephanie's arms, to burst out crying.

Stephanie, her nerves already frayed from a difficult morning, rounded on him. 'Look what you've done, idiot.'

'I'm sorry, I'm sorry, I'm sorry,' he said, not sounding it.

'What's the problem?'

'Everything's the problem. The bottom's fallen out of the barley market, the store calves aren't ready for sale and now the bloody milk yield's falling. I'm not making this place pay, Steph, and that's my job.'

'Why don't you write to Uncle Larry?'

He glared at her and answered emphatically, 'No. What's he going to think if I go running cap in hand at the first sign of trouble?'

He turned moodily away from her, fiddling with some papers on the table, while Stephanie, upset, continued to try to soothe the baby.

*

Relations were much less strained at Frankie's house, where Pamela was standing wobbling precariously on a chair, being fitted for her wedding dress. Amanda, Serena and Noreen were helping out Auntie Bridget who, as dressmaker-in-chief, was pinning the dress. The TV was blaring in the background but could make no impression on the bedlam generated by the five women, who were shouting and laughing at the tops of their voices.

'Oh, that's beautiful, Pam, you look a million dollars,' said Noreen proudly. Serena gave Pamela a sly look. 'Pity Lee won't appreciate it.'

'Gerroff you,' said Pamela indignantly. 'He's got taste, has Lee.'

'Yeah, in lager maybe.'

'Now girls,' chided Noreen. 'Frankie, what do you think?'

Frankie was sitting in a corner, his face buried in the newspaper, though he was not reading it but gazing pensively into the middle distance. He shook himself and said, 'What? Oh ... it's beautiful.'

'At least people'll know you're up the spout, Pam,' said Amanda, laughing at her bulge straining against the material.

'Amanda, hush it,' said Noreen.

'Come here, you.' Pamela made an unsuccessful attempt to grab Amanda and nearly fell over in the process. 'Where's that beanpole of a youth you call your boyfriend?'

'Better than having a beergut,' laughed Amanda, sauntering out.

'Pamela, will you keep still and let Auntie Bridget measure you up?' demanded Noreen.

Pamela did so, muttering, 'I'll faint in the aisle if it's any bloody tighter.'

Serena smirked. 'How can you marry in white with your track record?'

'Look who's talking,' said Pamela.

While they were still arguing, Frankie got up, put his paper down and walked through to the kitchen where Amanda was laying the table.

'We're about to eat,' said Amanda, as Frankie headed for the back door.

'Not hungry.'

Amanda followed him outside. He walked into the milking

parlour, checked the level in the bulk tank and strode purposefully towards some churns.

'What are you being so grumpy for?' asked Amanda.

He jumped when he heard her voice, stepping guiltily away from the churns. 'Things on my mind, that's all.' He made a visible effort to lighten up. 'Doesn't your sister look a treat now?'

Amanda nodded. 'You'll be pleased to see the back of her, I bet.'

'Yeah. Who'll be next up, eh? You?'

She giggled. 'Get off with you.'

'Well, I can't see Serena getting wed in a hurry. Likes the good life too much that one.'

'Where did she get that from I wonder?' said Amanda cheekily.

'Your young man'll be coming to the party, I suppose?'

'Yeah. What d'you think of him?'

Frankie shrugged. 'Seems all right.'

'I know he doesn't say much . . .'

''Course he doesn't say much. Men don't get a word in edge-ways in our house.'

Frankie waited until Amanda had crossed the yard back to the house and then went back to the churns. He took the lid off one, carried it to the bulk tank and poured the milk into it, then returned for a second churn, looking furtively around as he did so.

Chapter 12

An unmarked police car arrived at the practice the next day, and Chief Inspector Cowan of the Devon Constabulary got out and smoothed down his uniform before leaning into the back of the car and pulling out a large cardboard box. He walked towards the practice entrance, puffing with the effort of carrying the box.

Murray was delivering the punchline of a joke to Chris and Maddy as Cowan came through the door. 'No, I'm here to check the plumbing!' There was a burst of laughter, but the sight of a senior policeman was enough to dispel it instantly. As Maddy hastily cleared away the remains of their lunchtime sandwiches, Chris put on a polite, welcoming smile. 'How may I help you, er . . . ?'

'Chief Inspector Cowan.'

'Chris Lennox, how d'you do?'

Cowan nodded and then wordlessly proffered the box to Chris. He peered inside.

'Ah. A Vietnamese pot-bellied pig, no less. Where was he found?'

'Oh, he's not lost,' said Cowan, 'he's mine. It's his eye.'

'What's his name?' asked Murray.

'Ho Chi Minh.'

Jennifer and Laura had wandered through from the surgery area, and as duty vets they took instant charge while Cowan hovered nervously to one side.

'Looks like an entropion,' said Laura. She turned to Cowan. 'That's an ingrowing eyelid. He'll need an operation, I'm afraid, but there's nothing to worry about.'

'Can I stay and watch? He's very important to me.'

Laura and Jennifer exchanged a quick look then shrugged their shoulders. 'Don't see why not,' said Laura.

As they disappeared into the back, Simon burst in through the front door with a face like thunder. 'Chris, I want a word.'

'OK, Simon,' said Chris mildly.

'Not here, outside.' Simon turned and walked out again without waiting for a reply. Chris glanced at Murray and Maddy and raised an eyebrow but followed Simon outside.

He found him pacing angrily up and down the car-park. 'The Milk Marque have been on to me. They've dumped 30,000 litres.' Simon spat the words out. 'They found antibiotics in it. Antibiotics prescribed by you, I might add.'

'Whoa, slow down,' said Chris. 'Now what's happened? What's Frankie done?'

'He's put contaminated milk in the bulk tank, that's what he's done, so they've binned the lot. With penalties, we're looking at over a thousand pounds.'

Chris stared at him in bafflement. 'I don't understand. Why are you telling me all this?'

'Because you're his bloody vet, why do you think?' shouted Simon.

'Now wait a minute, Simon. I may be Frankie's vet but I am not responsible for the way he runs his milk parlour. I don't even know what he was using antibiotics for. I haven't seen him in ages.'

'There's some mastitis in the herd.'

'So what did Frankie say?'

'I haven't spoken to him yet.'

Chris raised an eyebrow. 'Well, perhaps it would be a good idea to go see him and find out. I'll come with you.'

'This is all I needed, I tell you. On top of everything,' said Simon dramatically as he walked towards his car.

Noreen had taken the call from the Milk Marque at the farm and gone to find Frankie. He was spreading muck in the fields by the sea, a trail of seagulls following behind him, swooping on the muck like beggars at a banquet. He cut the engine and walked over to her, blanching as she told him about the call.

She stared at him in disbelief. 'What on earth made you do it?'

Frankie shrugged. 'It seemed right at the time.'

'That's no bloody reason,' said Noreen furiously.

'Simon Dunning's my boss and he was in a pickle.'

'You've got us into trouble as well now, Frankie,' said Noreen.

'He needed our help.'

'And what about us, eh? Your family.'

Frankie gazed around him helplessly. 'Have you forgotten what it was like when I was a tenant farmer? Lying awake all night thinking about bills, breaking out in a cold sweat if a cow coughed.'

'I remember,' said Noreen, 'but I remember too that there was no one around prepared to carry the can for us like you seem to be for him.'

Frankie did not reply. Still angry, she stared at him for a long moment and then turned to go, stopping as she looked back towards the farm and saw two vehicles turning down the lane. She pointed to them. 'Time to face the music, Frankie.'

Frankie drove his tractor back to the farm, to find Chris and Simon already standing by the bulk tank.

'Why didn't you get me in?' Chris asked quietly.

'I had some antibiotics left over from the last time, so . . .'

Chris shook his head wearily. 'You broke the law as well as the rules, Frankie. You're supposed to throw the milk away, not put it in with the healthy stuff.'

'I know, I was hoping they wouldn't detect it.'

Frankie fell silent, staring at the ground. Chris waited a few moments and then said, 'Are you going to tell me why?'

Frankie looked cautiously at Simon. 'The milk yield's down and Mr Dunning's under a lot of pressure at the moment.'

Simon started nervously and hissed, 'I didn't tell you to break the law.'

'No, I know but . . .'

'How could you do something so bloody stupid?' demanded Simon.

Chris shot a look at Simon, then turned to Frankie again. 'How much is the yield down? And for how long?'

'About three thousand litres a day for the last fortnight.'

'Is the silage up to scratch?'

Frankie nodded.

Chris looked puzzled. 'The mastitis shouldn't cause a drop of that amount. I think we should do some blood tests on the herd.'

Simon groaned. 'More expense. Is that really necessary?'

'The problem may be serious or it may be nothing at all, we don't know yet. Look, I know vet services are pricey but not to do tests – or even to cancel routine tests like you did with the IBR vaccination – is a false economy.'

Simon snorted his disagreement. 'If I agreed to every so-called routine vaccination and test you recommended, you'd be camped out on this estate permanently.'

Chris ignored him and spoke to Frankie. 'What about the milking machine, have you at least tested that?'

As Frankie shook his head, Chris raised his eyes to heaven. Frankie glanced uncertainly at Simon and then said, 'I'll run it this afternoon.'

'Right. I'd better be off,' said Chris. 'See you both at the party this evening.'

As Chris walked away, Simon rounded furiously on Frankie. 'You've cost me a thousand quid. I'm taking it out of your wages.' He stalked off to his car, leaving Frankie staring miserably after him.

He finished his work and did the evening milking before steeling himself to tell Noreen what Simon had said. He broached the subject as they changed for Pamela's party, standing in his under-wear squinting into the bedroom mirror as he adjusted his tie. His outfit had been the height of fashion in 1958 and might be again – if he lived long enough – but just now it gave him the look of an ageing escapee from *Happy Days*.

'I did wrong, so I'm not complaining,' said Frankie.

Noreen paused half-way into her tights and glared at him. 'You never complain, that's your trouble, but it's outrageous.'

'I lost him the money, didn't I?'

'Only because you were trying to help him. And to take it out of your wages. How are we going to manage, Frankie, tell me that?'

Frankie shrugged. 'We'll manage somehow. Let's not fret about a few hundred quid tonight of all nights.'

'But we can't afford it.'

'We'll marry Serena off to a millionaire.'

She ignored his feeble joke. 'You have to stop thinking of others.'

'That's what I am, Noreen, I'm not going to change now.'

A pain stabbed through his head and he winced and grabbed his forehead.

'What's the matter?' asked Noreen anxiously.

'Headache, that's all. It's OK.'

Serena opened the door and looked in. 'Ma, we ought to be going.' She looked across at Frankie, immaculately dressed from the waist up but still wandering round in his underpants. 'You not wearing trousers tonight then, Dad?' Frankie smiled at himself in the mirror and started to sing 'You make me feel so young'.

Jennifer was also pretty pleased with her reflection. She stood in front of a full-length mirror in her bedroom, smoothed down her dress, nodded with satisfaction and then called, 'Steven. Are you nearly ready?'

There was no reply. She walked down the landing but his bedroom was empty. She looked down the stairwell, calling, 'Steven?'

He was standing at the bottom of the stairs and replied without looking. 'I'm ready.'

Puzzled, Jennifer came downstairs. 'The jacket looks good on you.'

Again he did not reply. He walked to the front door, opened it and stood there waiting.

'Are you all right?' asked Jennifer, peering at him.

'We're going to be late.' He walked out into the night and Jennifer shrugged, turned off the light and followed him. There was a stiff frost and pale moonlight seeped through the mist hanging over the river. 'Too beautiful a night for another argument,' she muttered, following Steven to the car.

As she drove, she punched out the number of the practice on her mobile phone. 'Murray? Hi, it's Jen. Don't forget Chief Inspector Cowan is picking up Ho Chi Minh tonight. He said he might be a little late, but he'll definitely be there, so don't leave until he's been. OK, yes, and you.' She hung up chuckling to herself, but her smile faded as she saw Steven, still stony-faced, staring straight ahead into the darkness.

Murray went back to his paperwork for a few minutes then, bored, he dropped his pen and opened the back door, stepping on to the terrace for some fresh air. The shaft of light from the doorway illuminated a dog fox, foraging for frogs or mice on the far bank of the river. It froze for an instant, staring straight at

Murray, and then padded unhurriedly away, pausing to look back over its shoulder before disappearing behind a clump of alders. Murray peered into the dark shadows beyond the alders for several minutes but the fox was lost to sight. The only other movement in the still, frosty air was the water tumbling over the weir, glowing with a faint luminescence as it frothed white at the foot of the weir, then fading back to velvet black as it flowed away down towards the sea.

Murray heard a car pull up at the front of the practice and turned to go inside, leaving the back door ajar. Chief Inspector Cowan was already talking to a baffled-looking Clare. 'I've come for Ho Chi Minh.'

'I'm sorry?'

'He's had an operation.'

Clare gave him a blank smile and said, 'I'll fetch Mr Wilson.'

'He says he wants Ho Ho something,' whispered Clare as Murray appeared.

'He's a pot-bellied Vietnamese. The pig, that is, not the Chief Inspector,' said Murray, giving Cowan an ingratiating smile. 'I'll just go and collect him.'

Cowan looked at the posters on the walls and then at his watch, as the minutes ticked by with no sign of Murray returning, although there were the sounds of doors and cupboards being opened and closed.

Clare glanced up to see Cowan staring at her, drumming his fingers impatiently.

'What did you say his name was?' she asked nervously.

'Ho Chi Minh.'

There was another lengthy pause before Murray reappeared. 'Ah, Chief Inspector. I'm afraid you won't be able to take your pig home just yet.'

Cowan rose to his feet, baffled and anxious. 'But the lady vet said he'd be fine . . .'

'He is fine, he's fully recovered, it's just that he's . . . he's . . . he really ought to stay in overnight . . . for safety.'

Partly reassured, Cowan stepped towards the doorway leading through to the back.

'But I would like to see him if I can.'

'No,' said Murray, blocking his path. 'You can't.'

Clare gave him a look which suggested the men in white coats might be arriving at any minute. 'Let the officer see his pig, Murray.'

Murray shook his head, floundering on. 'I . . . I completely forgot, you see. Mrs Holt left instructions for Ho Chi Minh to be kept in total darkness for twenty-four hours. Because of the eye operation.'

Clare gave him another perplexed look.

'I'll come back tomorrow then,' said Cowan reluctantly, getting ready to leave.

'Tomorrow will be grand,' said Murray, almost sobbing with relief. He held the door open for Cowan, then shut and bolted it behind him.

'What the . . . ?' began Clare, but Murray shook his head and led her silently through to the recovery room. He pointed to the cage, standing empty, its door wide open. He then pointed dramatically to the back door, still ajar.

Clare groaned. 'Oh, no.'

'I'm afraid so,' said Murray. 'Ho Chi Minh's done a runner. You start looking outside, I'll phone for the cavalry.'

The doors of the village hall were open, spilling warm yellow light into the darkness as Jennifer and Steven walked up the path. Frankie's band, the Blue Notes – Frankie on vocals, Barry on double bass, Tom on piano, Ringo on drums and Snoo on rhythm guitar – were setting up on stage. Jennifer spotted Chris and Patricia at the bar and went over to join them, but Steven caught sight of Amanda and disappeared in the opposite direction.

As Jennifer reached the bar, Chris's mobile phone started to ring. He pulled it out of his pocket.

'Hello? What? Well, it can't have got very far, for God's sake, it's not a greyhound. No, I can't, you lost it, you find it. No, no. Well, just find it and put it back, OK?' He hung up and shoved his phone irritably back into his pocket.

'What's the matter?' asked Patricia and Jennifer in unison.

Chris shook his head. 'Don't ask.'

Noreen stopped to say 'Hello' at that point, which saved him from further explanations. They chatted for a minute, but when Simon and Stephanie came and stood next to them at the bar,

Noreen glared at them and walked away. Chris, Patricia and Jennifer exchanged puzzled looks and Stephanie did a double-take, then pulled Simon to one side asking, 'What's wrong with Noreen?'

Simon flushed. 'She's got a lot on her mind, that's all. Don't worry about it.'

She looked at him suspiciously and repeated the question. 'Simon, what's wrong with her?'

'I . . . I docked Frankie's wages.'

'What?' she shouted, then dropped her voice as the people at the bar turned to stare at them. 'How could you dock his wages? The day of his daughter's party. No wonder Noreen froze me out. We shouldn't even be here.'

'I had no choice, Steph. He's cost me a fortune.'

She ignored him. 'A loyal worker, a friend . . .'

'Oh come on,' interrupted Simon. 'A friend? He's just an employee.'

'No, he is a friend,' said Stephanie icily. 'As is Noreen. She really helped me with the baby, or have you forgotten that?'

'I'm trying to run a business,' blustered Simon.

She put her hand on her arm and looked him in the eyes. 'Simon, don't let this job turn you into something you're not.'

Shamefaced, he dropped his gaze and muttered, 'All right. I'll go and see him tomorrow. I'll make it up with him.'

'Good. Meanwhile, maybe we should go. I don't think the atmosphere is going to get any friendlier.'

They drank up and pushed their way through the crowded hall towards the exit, brushing past Steven and Amanda, who were huddled together on a bench at the side.

'If it's me, I want to know what I've done,' said Amanda, looking accusingly at Steven.

'If what's you?'

'This suicidal expression you've been wearing.'

'It's not you, all right?' he said moodily.

She slid closer to him on the bench and whispered softly in his ear, 'Come on, Steven. What is it?'

'I was going to spend half-term with my dad but he's changed his mind. There's been trouble between him and Mum over money and things.'

'Do you want to see him?'

'Of course I do.'

She thought for a few moments. 'Why did they split up?'

'She ran off with another bloke.'

'Really?' said Amanda excitedly, glancing across at Jennifer.

'Not for long though, she came back, but they still argued all the time.'

She shrugged. 'I'm lucky with mine, I suppose.'

'After they split up it was a bit weird at first but in the end I got to enjoy it; it was like having two homes.'

Amanda looked shrewdly at him. 'I tell you what, I wouldn't let my mum stand in the way of me and my dad.'

She fell silent as Steven took in what she had said. Then he turned to her, smiling for the first time that evening. 'Come on, let's nick a bottle of wine and go back to your place.'

Jennifer watched them sneaking out of the hall. 'I hear your Steven and Frankie's youngest are something of an item,' said Patricia, following her gaze.

Jennifer nodded. 'Suddenly I'm the mother of a man who's having sex. I feel fifty years old.'

Patricia laughed. 'Why don't you and Chris have a dance, and see if you can shed a few years? He's dying to dance but I'm full of flu and just not up to it.'

'Well . . .' said Jennifer, looking hesitantly at Chris.

'Go on,' said Patricia.

As they stood up, however, a massive, beaming farmer, weighing at least twenty-three stone, appeared at Jennifer's elbow. 'Mrs Holt, would you give me the pleasure of this dance?'

She exchanged a quick glance with Chris, who nodded and sat down.

'Yes, of course,' said Jennifer, taking the floor as the Blue Notes struck up. By the end of the song, the farmer was sweating profusely. Jennifer thanked him and beat a hasty retreat back to the table, leaving him mopping his brow with a red and white spotted handkerchief, the size of a small sheet.

'My turn now,' said Chris, steering Jennifer back on to the floor. The Blue Notes began to play 'My Funny Valentine', Frankie's voice caressing the lyric. Chris and Jennifer hesitated, slightly embarrassed at being on the floor for a slow, smoochy number, then danced close together, not speaking. Jennifer caught Patricia's eye and they exchanged a smile, but Jennifer still pulled slightly away from Chris, feeling a little awkward.

As the song ended, they hovered, waiting for the next number, but then saw Frankie mopping his brow and walking off stage.

'We'd better . . .' began Chris.

'Of course,' said Jennifer.

Out of sight of the guests, Frankie slumped down on a chair, sweating and grey-faced. Noreen came hurrying up, sat next to him and touched his brow.

'You're feverish, Frankie, I want you home immediately.'

'I can't, we've another set to do.'

'The boys won't mind,' she said firmly. 'I'll get someone to drop you off home.'

Amanda and Steven were so busy on the sofa that they did not hear the car dropping Frankie off and had a frantic scramble to do up their clothes when they heard his key in the lock. They were standing up, red-faced but not too dishevelled, when Frankie walked into the living-room.

'What's the matter, Dad?' asked Amanda. 'What are you doing home?'

Frankie ignored her and looked at Steven. 'You'd better get off home now, lad.'

'What?' said Amanda. 'Why should he go home?'

'Don't argue, do as you're told.'

'It's OK, I'll go,' said Steven nervously, but Amanda grabbed his hand and stood her ground. 'No, stay. What's up with you, Dad?'

'I don't want you using this house as a hotel.'

'Oh come on . . .' began Amanda, but Frankie cut her off. 'Leave it,' he said, in a threatening voice that she had never heard him use before. She stared at him, upset and shocked, as Steven muttered, 'It's all right, I'll go.'

As Amanda said goodbye to Steven, Frankie sat down heavily in a chair, wiping his brow, which was clammy with cold sweat. She came back into the room and glared at Frankie accusingly. 'What the hell's eating you, Dad?'

'Go to your room and leave me alone.'

'I'm not a child,' said Amanda defiantly. 'Don't you order me about. If I want to bring someone back, that's my lookout.'

'Get out of here, girl, will you,' cursed Frankie, his voice hoarse.

Her eyes filling with tears, Amanda ran out of the room, slamming the door behind her. Still sweating heavily, Frankie lay back and closed his eyes for a moment, then prised himself out of his chair and stumbled upstairs to bed.

Amanda was having breakfast, leafing through a magazine, when Frankie came downstairs the next morning and sat down across the table from her. He was very pale and still had a film of sweat on his forehead. Amanda ignored him, carrying on reading.

He looked carefully at her and then poured himself some tea. 'You want a refill?'

'No thanks,' said Amanda neutrally, without looking up.

'What's that you're reading?'

'Magazine.' She buried her nose deeper in it.

Frankie took a deep breath and tried again. 'Did you see Ringo's ten-minute drum solo last night?'

She shook her head, still not looking up.

'You must have left by then. He got so carried away he let go of a drumstick; it hit Mrs McIver smack in the gob.'

Amanda tried very hard not to smile but failed. She looked up at last and grinned at him, recognizing, if not entirely accepting, his way of saying sorry for the previous night. He grinned back at her.

Noreen, nursing a hangover, came in from the other room. She checked, surprised to see Frankie sitting there, and said, 'Will you go back to bed please, you've a temperature of over a hundred.'

'I've cows to milk, Noreen.'

'Well, will you at least let me call the doctor?'

He shook his head. 'It's only flu, it'll pass.'

Frankie got up and wandered listlessly out of the house as Noreen sat down at the table, shaking her throbbing head.

Over at Jennifer and Steven's house Jennifer was running late, hurrying to collect her things as she munched on an apple. Steven sat at the table, saying nothing and ignoring her.

'Make sure you close the back door before you leave, OK?' said Jennifer. 'Bye now.'

There was no reply.

She stopped with her hand on the door-handle and turned back. 'Ten-year-olds sulk, Steven. Not sixteen-year-olds who think they're adults.'

He looked up, but still said nothing.

'You've obviously decided it's all my fault that your father doesn't want to see you,' continued Jennifer. 'Fine. If there's anything else wrong with the world you happen to hold me responsible for, you will let me know, won't you?'

She walked out, her sarcasm a waste of breath. Steven waited until he heard her drive off, then went to the cupboard under the stairs and pulled out a small suitcase. He stepped into the porch, locked the door and hurried away up the lane.

When Jennifer arrived at work, she found the place in bedlam as Chris, Maddy, Clare and Murray turned the practice upside down for the fourth or fifth time, in the increasingly desperate hope that the pig might magically have turned up since the last time they looked.

Finally Chris called a halt. 'Let's face it, it isn't here. Assuming it can walk at about five miles an hour it could be anywhere this side of Exeter by now.'

'Or squashed flat on the A38,' said Murray helpfully.

'Thanks for those words of hope, Murray,' said Chris testily. 'For that you can do a house-to-house search in the local vicinity.'

'But that'll take all day.'

Chris smiled evilly. 'Yes it will, won't it?'

'Why don't we call the police?' said Maddy.

There was dead silence as the others all looked at her.

'Er . . . no, that wasn't such a good idea, was it?' she said, flushing.

The phone rang and Maddy gratefully answered it. 'Chris, it's Frankie Mulholland. He wonders if you could get out to him some time today?'

Chris looked across at Jennifer. 'It'll be about the mastitis. Could you do it? I'm really tied up.'

'Looking for a pot-bellied pig, no doubt,' laughed Jennifer, heading for the door.

She drove out towards Frankie's farm, determinedly putting her problems with Steven out of her mind as she enjoyed the morning sunshine. Daffodils studded the hillsides, and though the hedgerows were still bare as whips, the air above them seemed to shimmer in a haze as if at any moment the buds would burst into leaf. She drove slowly, looking around her, revelling in the countryside.

Jennifer's cheerful mood did not survive long at Frankie's farm, however. She paused in her examination of one cow and turned to him. 'There are some signs of an infection in the womb. When did she abort exactly?'

'Eight days ago.'

Her jaw dropped. 'Why didn't you report it to us? It's a legal requirement, Mr Mulholland.'

'I didn't want Mr Dunning to know he's been losing calves,' said Frankie uncomfortably. 'He's enough problems as it is.'

Jennifer stopped work and stood up. 'Calves? How many abortions have there been?'

Frankie hesitated, like a barman caught with his hand in the till. 'Er . . . five.'

'And you've had a fall in milk yield too?'

He nodded.

Jennifer tried to keep her expression neutral, but her mind was racing. 'Look,' she said carefully, 'there might be a connection. I'll have a chat with Mr Lennox and get back to you later. I'll take a blood sample with me and in the meantime I'll give her some antibiotics.'

'Right,' said Frankie, starting to turn away.

'And . . . how are you in yourself, Mr Mulholland?' asked Jennifer. 'Are you well?' She tried not to betray her anxiety as she waited for the answer.

Frankie looked at her suspiciously. 'I'm absolutely fine, and call me Frankie, please. Seeing as we're almost related now.'

She smiled. 'Frankie then. You sing beautifully by the way.'

Jennifer kept up the small talk for a couple of minutes then said, 'I really must be going now, Mr Mul . . . Frankie. I've got to do these tests. I'll give you a call later on.'

In contrast to her journey up to the farm, her drive back to the practice was anything but unhurried. She was bottling some blood to send to the Ministry's labs for testing when Murray came in, exhausted.

'Don't ever go knocking on doors asking if people have seen a black pot-bellied pig,' he sighed dramatically, draping himself across the desk. 'They talk back to you like you're a victim of care in the community.'

Jennifer was concentrating hard on labelling the blood samples and did not reply.

'I speak . . . but she doesn't hear,' said Murray.

Jennifer grunted. 'Frankie Mulholland's herd's having an abortion storm. With a drop in milk yield too, it could be lepto, couldn't it?'

'Could be a lot of other things as well,' said Murray. 'Besides, the herd's tested every year, how could they have caught it?'

'Loads of ways.'

Murray paused and asked casually, 'How's Frankie feeling?'

Jennifer stopped work and glanced at him quizzically.

'Leptospirosis is infectious, yes?' said Murray.

She nodded. 'He says he's fine.'

'Well, that's all right then . . . though farmers do, don't they, even when they're not.' He dragged his body reluctantly off the desk. 'I'd better give Chris a pig update.'

'He's not back from visits yet.'

'Right.' He gave another theatrical sigh. 'I shall return to the porcine quest, this time with Clare for moral support.'

He went out, dragging his feet.

Jennifer heard Chris arrive back about half an hour later and went out to meet him in the car-park as he was starting to unload his gear.

'Any sign of Ho Chi Minh?' he asked hopefully.

'Nope. Murray's gone off again, this time with Clare. Listen, Chris, I'm a bit worried about Frankie's herd. There have been five recent abortions. Did you know?'

Chris looked up, worried. 'No, I didn't know that.'

'Neither does Simon Dunning and nor do MAFF for that matter.'

He frowned and shook his head. 'Stupid bugger.'

'I think it's lepto. I've sent a sample off. At least Frankie's well though, so . . .'

'But he isn't,' interrupted Chris, now quite alarmed. 'He went home early last night with a fever. I presumed it was this flu that Patricia had. I'm going to get out to the farm and do a full herd profile,' he said abruptly, slamming the boot of his car.

'Do you want me to come with you?'

'No, don't worry,' said Chris, getting into the Range Rover and driving off hurriedly.

Chapter 13

Amanda had been hanging around at the end of school, waiting for Steven. When she saw Scott walking down the corridor with a group of his friends, she hurried after him. 'Scott. Didn't Steven come in today?'

'No, he's probably got a hangover from your sister's party,' laughed Scott.

'Won't be the only one.' She tried to sound casual. 'He didn't tell you he was going anywhere, did he?'

'You sound like his mum, Amanda. He's bunked off school for a day, that's all.'

She shrugged, embarrassed. 'Yeah, probably. See you.' She smiled and wandered off.

'Has he shagged her yet?' whispered one of Scott's friends.

'Course he has,' said Scott loftily. 'That's why she's all worried about him. Girls do that, you see. They play hard to get but when you've got them, they turn into your mother,' he added, turning into Woody Allen.

Amanda got off the school bus at the top of her lane and wandered moodily down to the house. She opened the door and called, 'Mum, Dad,' but there was no reply and she wandered into the kitchen and put the kettle on. She took a mug of tea for Frankie out to the byre. Peering into the gloom, she called, 'Dad? Where are you? Dad?'

She looked around and suddenly caught sight of her father's body, lying face down in the straw in the corner of the byre. The mug fell from her fingers, shattering on the concrete floor as she screamed, an agonized, ululating wail of grief. She ran to him, pulling at his arm and shaking him. There was no response, but when she turned him over, though he lay as still as a corpse, there was a faint, ragged pulse and she could hear the hoarse whisper of his breathing. She dropped his hand as if it had burned her and ran frantically from the byre towards the house.

As Chris sped through the lanes towards Frankie's farm, he had to brake violently to avoid an ambulance coming the other way at top speed, blue light flashing. He drove on towards the farm, filled with a grim foreboding. As he pulled into the yard, Amanda came running from the house. 'They've taken Dad to hospital.'

'Which one?'

'Derriford. What's the matter with him, Mr Lennox?'

The tears welled up in her eyes and Chris held her to comfort her. 'Is your mum with him?' he asked.

She nodded. 'They phoned her at the drop-in centre. She's going straight there.'

'I'm going to go to the hospital. Do you want to come with me?'

She shook her head. 'I've got to wait for Pam and Serena.'

Chris gently took his arm from round her. 'Don't worry, your dad'll be OK.' He drove off back up the lane, but as he looked in the mirror, he could see her forlorn figure, a little girl once more, standing alone in the middle of the yard, gazing after him.

Jennifer had just got in from work, dumping her coat over the banisters, when she saw a note by the phone. She picked it up and read it, then groaned aloud. She was about to call Steven's father when the phone rang.

'Jen, it's Chris. Bad news I'm afraid. Frankie's collapsed and been taken to Derriford. I'm on my way there now. Would you get out to his farm and do the herd profile?'

'Of course.'

'Send the blood samples straight off to MAFF for lepto tests. Oh, and you'd better call in on Simon Dunning, let him know what's happened.'

'What do you know about lepto in humans?'

'About as much as you.'

Chris had phoned ahead to the hospital and a senior houseman met him at the desk. They walked quickly down a long corridor. 'He's in a coma and his kidneys are failing,' said the houseman. 'We're running tests but it's almost certainly leptospiral meningitis. Does he wear protective clothing when he's milking?'

'None of them do.'

He shook his head wearily. 'What do they expect? They're

constantly exposed to the urine spray. Were you treating the cows for lepto?'

There was a brief hesitation before Chris replied. 'We didn't know they were infected.'

The houseman said nothing in reply but he gave Chris a questioning look as they hurried into the intensive care unit. Frankie lay deathly white and unconscious on the bed, surrounded by a battery of machines. The flickering dials and green traces were the only signs of life. Noreen sat by his bed, staring intently at his face. She did not look round as Chris pulled up another chair and sat beside her.

Unaware of the drama taking place at the hospital, Murray and Clare plodded on around the streets of Whitton, looking for Ho Chi Minh. As yet another door was slammed in their faces, Murray saw a police car coming round the corner. A young WPC in the car was holding a Vietnamese pot-bellied pig on her lap.

Murray and Clare exchanged glances. 'Come on,' said Murray. They sprinted down into the town centre and arrived at the police station in time to see the WPC and Ho Chi Minh disappearing through a side door.

Murray ran to the door and rapped frantically on it but the WPC was already out of earshot. Murray cursed, kicked the door and turned round to see a policeman giving him a hostile stare. Murray smiled sheepishly and then walked briskly past him and in through the the front door of the police station. Two minutes later he was walking hurriedly down a corridor with the WPC from the police car.

'And you won't tell your governor where you found the pig, will you?' said Murray anxiously.

They turned a corner and ran slap into Chief Inspector Cowan.

'Ah!' said Murray, his eyes rolling wildly.

'Oh, Mr . . . er . . .'

'Wilson,' said Murray dutifully.

'Quite. I'm afraid I can't come and collect Ho Chi Minh until tomorrow now, will that be all right?'

Murray's eyes stopped revolving and a look of beatific tranquillity spread across his face. 'Perfect,' he murmured, 'perfect.'

'Can I help you at all?' asked Cowan.

Murray's look changed again instantly to one of mounting panic. 'What? No, er . . . I'm . . .'

The WPC rescued him from his predicament. 'Mr Wilson thinks he might have witnessed a robbery, sir. I'm taking a statement.'

Murray threw her a look of immense gratitude, noting for the first time what a very attractive WPC she was.

Half an hour later Murray returned with his car and parked it at the back of the police station. He and the WPC surreptitiously loaded Ho Chi Minh and Murray closed the boot, heaving a sigh of relief. 'I can't thank you enough, you've really saved my life there.'

'That's all right,' said the WPC, smiling. 'If I ever develop rabies, I'll expect free treatment.'

Murray was about to get into the car but hesitated, turning back to the WPC.

'Look . . . erm . . . I was wondering if . . . er . . . you were doing anything on Saturday? Maybe I could buy you a drink, you know, by way of a thank you?'

The WPC gave him a quizzical look, thought for a second, then flashed him a smile.

'Why not?'

'Where shall I pick you up?'

'Why don't we meet in the Drake about eight? I'm working Saturday afternoon, so I can go straight there.'

'In your uniform?'

She shook her head, giving him a teasing smile. 'No. I do take it off occasionally.'

'It's a date,' said Murray, getting back in the car and driving off feeling ridiculously pleased with himself. On his way back to the practice, he phoned Chris on his mobile, saying excitedly, 'We've found the pig,' as soon as he answered.

'Murray, this isn't the moment,' said Chris. 'I'll talk to you later.'

'Why, what's wrong?' asked Murray.

'I'll talk to you later,' Chris repeated and then cut him off.

He stood in the hospital corridor talking quietly to Jennifer as they sipped plastic cups of tea from a machine. Noreen, Amanda,

Serena and Pamela sat in an impersonal waiting area just up the corridor, all staring into space, lost in their own private thoughts.

'Simon Dunning's not really to blame though, is he?' murmured Jennifer.

'But are we?' said Chris. 'That's the question.'

Jennifer darted a look at Frankie's family. 'Come on, Chris. If Frankie didn't tell us about the abortions, how were we supposed to know? You wouldn't even have known about the drop in milk yield if Dunning hadn't come stomping round to the practice.'

Chris shrugged, unconvinced.

They walked back down the corridor to join Noreen and the girls. Jennifer sat next to Amanda, taking her hand. 'Steven would be here but he's done a bunk.'

Amanda looked up inquiringly.

'He's gone to see his dad.'

Amanda started to cry quietly.

'The thing is,' she sniffed, 'Dad was rude to Steven the last time he saw him and Dad isn't like that.'

Jennifer held her close as she cried. Over Amanda's shoulder, she saw the senior houseman coming along the corridor. He walked up to Noreen, touched her shoulder gently and shook his head slowly as she looked up. 'Mrs Mulholland . . . I'm so sorry.'

An hour later Chris put Noreen and the girls into a taxi to go home. He and Jennifer stood watching as the rear lights disappeared into the darkness. He sighed heavily. 'I don't know about you, but I need a drink.'

They walked over the road to a pub and found a quiet corner. Chris swallowed half his drink in one gulp, then gazed moodily at the table top. 'Why didn't I take blood samples at my first visit? Why didn't I ask Frankie if he'd had any abortions?'

'Chris, stop torturing yourself,' said Jennifer, laying a hand on his arm. 'We can only act on what clients choose to tell us. We're not social workers.'

Chris looked down at her hand as she took it away, unselfconsciously, to take another sip of her drink. Chris drained his, then made an effort to lighten the atmosphere saying briskly, 'Time for home I think.'

They left the pub and got into his car. He was about to start the engine when he saw that Jennifer still had something preying on her mind. 'What is it?'

She shivered. 'The look on Amanda's face when the doctor told them that Frankie was dead.'

He nodded. There was a long silence. Finally he asked, 'Did you get hold of Steven?'

She shook her head. 'He's never gone off without telling me first – across town, let alone two hundred miles.'

'He's sixteen . . .' began Chris.

'No. He's punishing me for leaving his dad and for moving down here.'

'How would you take it if he told you he wanted to live with his father?'

'Unbelievably badly, but I couldn't stop him.'

'He's not likely to, though, is he?'

She shrugged helplessly. 'Steven's also the man in my life really. Once he leaves home . . . in my whole adult life I've never lived alone and the thought terrifies me.'

He smiled sympathetically. 'You'll find someone, Jen. Even in dear old Whitton.'

She shook her head. 'To find someone you have to look.'

'And you're not looking?'

She looked at Chris and he met her gaze but then glanced hurriedly away, muttering, 'We'd better be getting back.'

He started up the car, but as Jennifer gazed unseeingly out of the side window, Chris looked back at her for a long moment before driving off.

After he had dropped off Jennifer, Chris drove slowly home and slipped quietly into the house. He paused to look up the stairs at the glow from the bedroom and then walked into the lounge and poured himself a drink. He sat down in the near-darkness, lost in thought.

The door opened quietly and Patricia appeared in her dressing-gown. 'I phoned the hospital,' she said. 'They told me you'd left hours ago.'

'I was . . . I was held up,' he said evasively.

'You might have called, I was worried.'

Chris shrugged.

'You weren't on duty this evening,' said Patricia. 'How was I to know nothing had happened to you?'

He roused himself from his reverie. 'I'm sorry.'

'You should call, Chris,' said Patricia insistently. 'I'm not nagging, but . . .'

'I know. I stopped and had something to eat . . . on my own.'

'Oh, right,' she said uncertainly. 'Well?'

'Well what?'

'How's Frankie, of course? They wouldn't tell me over the phone.'

He looked up at her. 'He's dead.'

Chris was out at Frankie's farm early the next morning, working his way slowly through the herd, carrying out the immunization with a Ministry official. There was a cold wind blowing and rain slanted across the yard, drenching the men despite their waterproofs.

Noreen stood watching from her bedroom window, beside a bed that had not been slept in. She turned away and moved slowly as if in a fog, out of the room and down the stairs. Amanda, Pamela and Serena all lay asleep in each other's arms on the sofa in the front room, the dying embers of the log fire still glowing faintly. Noreen moved silently into the kitchen and mechanically started to fill the kettle.

A car pulled up in the yard. Simon and Stephanie got out and walked across to Chris. 'What a business,' said Simon, glancing nervously towards the farmhouse as he turned up the collar of his Barbour jacket.

'One of those things,' said Chris.

'I spoke to MAFF already and they say it isn't my fault,' said Simon.

Chris paused in his work and gave him a look dripping with contempt. 'That's OK then.'

'Frankie lied to us, you see, about the abortions, about the protective clothing. He told me he was using it and . . .'

'Mr Dunning,' said Chris slowly, 'I really don't care exactly whose fault it is at the moment, and if I were you, I'd worry more about Frankie's family.' He turned his back and moved on to the next cow.

Simon flushed, catching Stephanie's withering look. 'I'm only trying to do my best,' he muttered defensively.

'Best for who?' she snorted. 'For Noreen? For me? Oh, forget it, it's not worth it.' She headed back to the car, leaving him standing there alone.

When Chris had finished his work, he hesitated outside the farmhouse, then turned away and walked to his car, not knowing what he could say or do to help Noreen but feeling a vague sense of guilt that he had not spoken to her.

The lanes were empty of traffic, wet and glistening with grey water dripping incessantly from the trees, as he drove slowly back towards Whitton, the dull thud of his windscreen wipers sounding like a funeral drum.

Steven had returned in time for Frankie's funeral, but he and Jennifer kept up a war of words as they got ready.

'I'm not asking you tell to tales on him, Steven,' said Jennifer. 'I'm only concerned that he looked after you properly, that's all.'

Steven gave her a cynical look. 'And if he didn't, you'd be as chuffed as hell.'

'No, I wouldn't. It's not a competition for your loyalty.'

'Isn't it?'

'Well, it isn't from my side. I promise.'

Steven continued to look disbelievingly at her. The doorbell rang but Jennifer made no move to answer it. 'You had a terrible time, didn't you?'

Steven did not answer but his expression showed that she had scored a direct hit. Finally he said, 'Shouldn't we answer the door?' and turned away.

Chris stood on the doorstep while Patricia waited in the Range Rover. As Jennifer greeted him, Chris seemed about to say something, then changed his mind and hurried back to the car.

They drove across town to the crematorium, a dull post-war building next to an industrial estate on the edge of town. The Blue Notes quietly played a slow Sinatra number as the mourners filed in, filling the room. Frankie's coffin stood in front of the altar, a single wreath of white lilies lying on its lid. Steven caught Amanda's eye as she sat in the front row but she turned away without any sign of recognition.

After the service, the mourners all filed outside and exchanged funeral clichés as they waited for their turn to utter a few words of condolence to Noreen and her family. Jennifer looked around the crowd, then turned to Chris, whispering, 'You'd have thought Simon Dunning would have had the decency to show up.'

Chris nodded. 'Guilty conscience, no doubt.'

Steven saw the family getting ready to leave and ran over to speak to Amanda. She waited, her mouth set in a hard line.

'I'm really sorry,' said Steven awkwardly.

'Yeah. So are we.'

'The thing is . . .' began Steven, but Amanda cut him off.

'It doesn't matter.'

'I wish I'd been here,' he said miserably.

'Yeah.' She walked away, leaving Steven upset and confused.

He did not speak except for monosyllables all the way home, and disappeared upstairs while Jennifer was saying goodbye to Chris and Patricia. She left him alone and busied herself cleaning the house and then making dinner. He had still not come downstairs and eventually she went up, finding him in his room, staring at his computer.

'Your dinner's ready,' said Jennifer.

He looked round briefly. 'Not hungry really.'

She sat on the bed, but after another quick glance Steven went back to the computer.

'I have a confession to make,' said Jennifer. 'You were right. I was quite pleased you had a bad time with your dad. We do compete for your loyalty. No matter how hard you try not to, you can't help it. I'm sorry.'

She waited for a few seconds, then got up and moved to the door. 'Don't be long, it'll get cold.'

'There was a woman in the house,' said Steven, not looking at her. 'That's why he didn't want me for the weekend – because I'd be in the way with the new girlfriend about.'

Jennifer tried not to let her surprise show. She watched him closely, realized he was on the verge of tears and went to him, crushing him in her arms. 'It doesn't mean he doesn't love you. He's trying to get his life together, that's all.'

'It's not that,' said Steven, through his tears.

'What then? Tell me.'

'If he wants a new girlfriend, it means he doesn't want you back.'

'No, sweetheart, he doesn't want me back, and I don't want to go back.'

'Not ever?'

'Not ever.'

She held him closer, rocking him in her arms.

Noreen had let it be known that she and the girls would be in the Drake Inn on the Saturday night. It was both a wake for Frankie and a farewell to their neighbours, for on behalf of the estate, as estate managers must do, Simon had moved with brutal speed, serving an eviction notice to have Frankie's tied cottage empty for the new cowman who was already looking after the herd. When Jennifer and Steven arrived, the bar was already busy, though there was no sign of Noreen and the girls.

Murray and Alice, the WPC whose name he had now discovered, were seated at a corner table. 'My boss sends his regards by the way,' said Alice, a malicious gleam in her eye.

Murray looked at her suspiciously. 'Oh. He made me feel a bit of a prat actually. When he came to pick the pig up, he said, "I only wondered why you brought him all the way back here when you could just as easily have left him at the police station for me."'

Alice spluttered into her drink.

'The people who found him happened to be friends of his,' continued Murray. 'Small world, isn't it?'

'He's all right anyway, the old sod.'

Murray gave her a look of mock seriousness. 'That's no way to talk about your commanding officer.'

'Oh, I can,' smiled Alice, 'he's also my dad.'

It was Murray's turn to choke on his drink.

'It is a small world, isn't it?' said Alice, laughing.

As Noreen, Amanda, Serena, Patricia and her fiancé Lee all came into the bar, the conversation died. Everyone turned to give them a smile of encouragement, knowing what a show of family strength this was. Then, embarrassed by the silence, everyone started talking at once. Noreen sat at a table, a faint smile on her face as she acknowledged the greetings of her friends and neighbours.

Jennifer and Steven walked over to them. Amanda looked up and said, ''Evening, Mrs Holt,' then took Steven by the arm and led him off to the side of the room.

Jennifer smiled at Noreen. 'It's good to see you all here.'

'Thank you, Mrs Holt,' said Noreen, still with the faint smile in place, though her eyes were red-rimmed.

'Chris tells me you'll be leaving the farm.'

'None of us would want to live there without Frankie. Pamela's with Lee now anyway and Serena'll soon be off too. So Amanda and me'll stay with my sister for a while, till we find somewhere permanent.'

'In Whitton?'

'No, no. In Leeds.'

It was a shock to Jennifer and, looking across to Steven, she could tell from his face that Amanda had just broken the same news to him.

'Leeds?' said Steven.

'Yeah,' said Amanda flatly. 'What's it like?'

'It's miles away, that's what it's like,' said Steven gloomily. 'What about you and me then?'

Amanda shrugged. 'We could meet up in the holidays.'

'Yeah,' said Steven but the look on both their faces showed how unlikely that would be.

Steven turned and pushed his way out of the bar and, forlorn, Amanda came back to the table. 'I've got to be with my mum, Mrs Holt,' she said.

Jennifer gave her an understanding smile and squeezed her arm. 'Of course you have. He'll understand that in time, but you're his first love, Amanda, right now he's so wrapped up in his own sense of loss that he cannot even see yours. He's only sixteen.'

'So am I, Mrs Holt,' said Amanda, sitting down next to her mother and putting an arm around her.

As Jennifer drove home, Steven sat in silence in the passenger seat, brooding.

'I know you won't want to hear this now, Steven, but the clichés really are true . . .' She got no further.

'You're right,' said Steven testily. 'I don't want to hear it.'

Jennifer was about to reply, when she gasped and braked hard as she came round a bend to find the road blocked by makeshift barriers with a man waving a torch to and fro.

She wound down the window as he walked alongside the car.

'What is it?' she asked. 'An accident?'

The man laughed. 'Only if you'd crashed into the barriers. It's more of a local tradition as you might say – a harness race.' He eyed Jennifer's mobile phone on the dashboard. 'I wouldn't bother phoning the police, it'll all be over and we'll all be on our way home – including you – long before they get here anyway.'

'I wasn't thinking of it,' said Jennifer. 'I've never seen a harness race before. Are you coming, Steven?' He shook his head sulkily and sank lower into his seat, while Jennifer got out of the car and walked to the barrier.

Beyond it was a mile-long, straight stretch of road, lit by torches, lamps and the headlights of cars parked all along the verge. Two white posts stuck in the grass at the side of the road marked the finishing line. Two horses harnessed to metal traps were just visible in the lights at the far end of the course.

As Jennifer looked around, she could see a handful of other women but the crowd milling about was predominantly male. A group clustered around an unofficial bookie, with thick wads of notes changing hands. A man in his late twenties, big and easy-going, placed a hundred-pound bet.

'No need to ask which one you're backing, Jim,' said the bookie.

The man grinned. 'It breaks my heart to take your money, Dave, but Ninja's a flying machine. You'd have to shoot her to stop her winning.'

The bookie gave an enigmatic smile, as several other punters crowded in, eager to get their money on.

'Which horse is which?' Jennifer asked the man beside her.

'Ninja is the one on the left with the white blaze – that's Jim Cronin's nag,' he said, pointing to the big man who had just placed the bet. 'The other is Starfire. I don't know much about him, his owner comes from over Honiton way.'

There was the sound of a car horn from the far end of the course, answered by a blast from a car near the finishing line.

Then there was a shout as the two horses set off, their drivers sitting low in the sulkies, flicking out their long, thin whips to crack them around the horses' flanks. The crowd scattered to the sides of the road, leaving an avenue barely wide enough for the two sulkies, racing wheel to wheel.

Jennifer was caught up in the excitement as the trotting horses high-stepped down the course, their hooves clattering on the tarmac and the wheels of the sulkies whirring. She could hear Jim Cronin's voice booming above the shouts of the crowd, but Starfire pulled steadily away and finished a good couple of lengths clear of Ninja. The sulkies flashed across the line and clattered to a halt, only yards from the barrier.

As a few punters collected their winnings, others were already demolishing the barriers and the first cars were pulling away. Jennifer turned and walked back to her car. Behind her, Jim exchanged a wry look with the bookie Dave, as he walked over to Ninja. Dave clapped him on the shoulder as he passed. 'Good race that, Jim.'

'Glad someone thought so,' said Jim, trying to muster a smile. 'That's just cleaned me out.'

Dave flashed a thick roll of notes. 'Starfire couldn't lose.' He winked and tapped the side of his nose. 'Cortico, James.'

'You what?'

'Steroids.'

Dave grinned and moved off through the crowd as Jim stroked Ninja's flank, looking thoughtfully at Starfire's triumphant owner.

Chapter 14

Murray came sprinting into the practice late the following afternoon, carrying a dog wrapped in a blanket. Clare and Chris were standing in reception as he burst through the door.

'Has Laura gone?' said Murray.

'Yeah. What happened?' asked Clare, hurrying forward to open the door of the surgery for him.

'He got caught in some barbed wire,' said Murray, laying the dog carefully on the operating table. He looked up at Clare and asked, 'Er . . . were you off?'

Clare nodded. 'But I don't mind staying.'

He gave her a grateful look.

As Murray examined the dog's wounds, Chris stuck his head round the door. 'Do we know who the dog belongs to?'

Murray pointed to the dog's neck. 'There's a tag.'

'Then ring to check the owners can pay for treatment, yeah?'

'Right you are,' said Murray, as Chris disappeared, heading for home.

Clare slipped the tag off the dog's collar and scanned the number, then picked up the phone as Murray changed into a gown for the operation. 'This telephone has been temporarily taken out of service,' she said, mimicking the android tones of the recorded voice as she replaced the handset. She peered at the tag again. 'Cronin. It could be Jim Cronin, I suppose, he lives in Beresford.'

'Do you know him?'

'Sort of. He works as a beater sometimes at Dad's shoots.'

'There speaks the Lady Chatterley of Whitton,' said Murray.

'In your dreams, Murray,' laughed Clare.

He looked away and busied himself with the dog, but she was almost sure that he was blushing.

There was a brief silence, then Murray said, 'Oh, sod it, it's only going to be thirty-five quid at the most, they're bound to be able to pay,' and picked up a syringe.

'I love it when you're masterful,' said Clare huskily, then ruined it by bursting out laughing.

Murray had recovered his poise and grinned flirtatiously as he wielded the syringe and then stitched the dog's wounds.

'By the way,' said Clare casually, 'Dad wants to know if you're still on for Saturday.'

'I think I'm supposed to be on call.'

'Wimp,' she snorted dismissively. 'I've seen worse things in shorts than your legs.'

'Oh, all right,' he said wearily. 'I'll ask Jennifer if she'll swap.'

'Shorts?'

'No, duties.'

'I think she's still here,' said Clare helpfully. 'I'll ask her if she's got a moment.' She sauntered out, pausing in the doorway to look back over her shoulder, catching Murray staring after her. Her smile deepened as he again flushed and dropped his eyes.

'Damn, damn, damn,' Murray muttered to himself, as she disappeared down the corridor.

A few moments later he heard two pairs of heels clacking on the linoleum. Jennifer put her head round the door as Clare hovered in the background, smiling mischievously. Murray stepped towards Jennifer and gave a courtly flourish with his hand. 'Jennifer, may I say how ravishing you're looking today?'

Jennifer fixed him with a beady eye. 'And may I say the answer is "no", Murray?'

He simulated wounded pride. 'Have I asked you for anything?'

'Not yet.'

He sighed. 'OK. Could you take first call for me this weekend?' he asked, his voice oozing treacle. 'Swap it for any inconvenient date you like.'

'What's the occasion?'

'Erm . . . Clare's dad has asked me to make up the numbers for a rugby match.'

Amused, Jennifer raised an eyebrow at Clare. 'I didn't think you played rugby, Murray.'

'I don't. Please?'

'OK.' She scanned her diary. 'Now, how about that tricky dehorning at the Burmans?'

He groaned. 'You drive a hard bargain.'

'Only when I can smell fresh meat.'

She winked at Clare and walked back down the corridor.

Murray left Clare to tidy up after the operation and carried the still drowsy dog out to his car. He drove up a narrow, twisting valley out of Whitton and emerged on to Roborough Down, a wide expanse of scrubland crossed by stone-lined leats, built by Drake to bring water across the moors to Plymouth and still in use four centuries later.

The yellow gorse studding the scrubland flamed to orange and red as it caught the rays of the setting sun. Murray turned off the road into the village of Beresford and pulled up outside a small terraced council house. Carrying the sedated dog, he walked up the path and rang the doorbell.

A girl of six opened the door, then stood there hesitantly, staring shyly at him.

'Oh, hello,' said Murray. 'Is your mummy or daddy in?'

The girl regarded him gravely for a moment, then called, 'Mum, it's Ben.'

'No, I'm called Murray.'

'I meant the dog, silly.'

The girl's mother, Dawn Cronin, a pale, downtrodden-looking woman in her mid-twenties, appeared at the door. She looked suspiciously at Murray.

'Mrs Cronin?'

She nodded.

'Erm . . . I'm Murray Wilson from the Whitton Veterinary Centre. I'm afraid your dog – Ben is it? – got into a bit of a fight with some barbed wire. I did try to ring but the phone seemed to be out of order.'

She shrugged. 'We've been cut off. Come in.'

She showed him into the living-room. It was cheaply furnished and chaotically but comfortably strewn with kid's toys and drying clothes. Jim Cronin lay sprawled on the sofa, reading the *Mirror* sports pages with half an eye on the TV and on his year-old baby, who was spreadeagled across his chest, fast asleep. The little girl returned to the television and stared intently at it, but a young boy who had been sitting at the table stood up anxiously as soon as he saw the dog in Murray's arms. 'Is he all right?'

'He'll be fine,' said Murray. 'He's just a bit dopey at the minute, we had to stitch a couple of cuts.'

'I bet you didn't even know he'd got out, did you, Matthew?' said his mother accusingly.

'Has he got a basket?' asked Murray, beginning to feel the weight of the dog in his arms. She jerked her head towards the back door. 'In the yard.'

'Can't we keep him inside tonight, Mum?' appealed Matthew.

She shook her head firmly. 'No, you know Ryan's chest is bad.' She looked across at Murray, explaining, 'The baby's allergic to the hair.'

Jim, who had been watching the conversation like a spectator at Wimbledon, swinging his head to and fro, roused himself and said, 'Matthew, do you want to show Doctor . . .'

Murray smiled. 'Call me Murray, please.' Matthew led him out to the yard, which backed on to open countryside, a spacious contrast to the cramped interior of the house. The dog-run was enclosed in chicken wire with a home-made kennel, knocked together from pieces of scrap wood, at one end. There was also a ramshackle shed-cum-stable and a bit of the open scrubland had been haphazardly – and probably illegally – fenced off as a paddock for the trotting horse.

'Who does the horse belong to, Matthew?' asked Murray, as he fixed a protective collar around the dog's neck.

'Me.'

'It's not your dad's?'

'Jim's not my dad,' said Matthew, matter-of-factly. 'He's Tara and Ryan's dad. Ninja's mine. Ben's mine and all.'

'Lots of pets you've got,' said Murray.

Matthew looked at him scornfully. 'Ninja's not a pet. She races.' He nodded at an upended sulkie propped against the shed.

Murray finished fixing the collar and stood back. 'There, that'll stop Ben scratching his stitches open.'

Matthew smiled for the first time. 'Space dog.'

Murray smiled back as Jim joined them outside saying, 'Thanks for bringing him round.'

'No problem, I live just down the road.'

Jim hesitated for a second. 'I was wondering, while you're here, if you'd have a look at Ninja,' he said, nodding at the horse.

'Why, what's the problem?'

'She's been off her feed lately.'

Matthew looked at him, puzzled. 'She ate what I gave her this morning.'

Jim ignored him.

As Murray gave the horse a cursory examination, Jim casually said, 'One of my mates, the vet gave his horse corti something.'

'Cortico?' asked Murray.

'That's it, worked wonders,' said Jim.

'Well, I'd only give cortico for an allergy and from what I can see, that's not her problem. You'll have to call me out during the day to do a proper examination.'

'And you'd charge me for that,' said Jim slyly.

'I'm afraid so.'

'So how much do I owe you for tonight?'

Embarrassed as always by the subject of money, Murray ummed and aahed, glanced at their shabby clothes and finally said, 'Oh, um, twenty-five pounds.' Jim took some notes from his back pocket but had to scrape the final pound together from his loose change. Even more embarrassed, Murray walked with them round the side of the house to his car. 'Matthew knows what to do to keep Ben's wounds clean, don't you?' he asked.

Matthew nodded.

'Good, bring him in at the end of the week for his top-up antibiotics.'

He drove back across the Down in the gathering darkness and pulled up outside his flat. When he walked inside, he shivered in the cold, checked the thermostat on the wall and turned up the heating. The flat was sparsely furnished and surprisingly tidy for a bachelor flat, apart from the remains of Murray's breakfast – a box of cereal, a half-empty milk bottle and a bowl and spoon – still lying on the coffee table.

Still with his coat on, he started to tidy them away into the kitchen, then changed his mind, wearily shaking his head and pouring himself a bowl of cereal. He sat down on the sofa, turning on the TV with the remote control, and listlessly zapped from channel to channel as he ate his spartan meal.

Breakfast TV was blaring out at the Cronins' the next morning.

Dawn gave Ryan some baby cough mixture, while Tara sat mesmerized watching the cartoons. Dawn called out to Matthew, who was out in the back yard. 'You're going to be late for school. How many more times?'

Matthew grunted and carried on stroking Ben, who was still wearing his space-dog collar.

Jim, bleary-eyed with sleep, was feeding Ninja, who was eating hungrily from a bucket.

'Ben needs to go for his injection,' said Matthew. 'Murray said.'

Dawn came into the yard with Tara. 'Nice try, Matthew. Come on, your sister's ready.'

Matthew reluctantly took Tara's hand and dragged her towards the gate.

Jim looked across at him and said, 'I'll take Ben in, Matt.'

'I'm still coming to the race tonight, aren't I?' asked Matthew.

'We'll see,' said Dawn, with a warning look at Jim.

'Oh, Mum, you promised.'

'I said I'd see.'

He stood by the gate, his face clouding. 'You said I could.'

Dawn lost patience and shouted, 'School. Now.'

He went out through the gate, kicking at the ground, still with Tara in tow.

Jim watched him go, then said, 'Give him a break, eh, Dawn? He's been looking forward to it.'

'I suppose so.' She paused. 'You'll take Ryan with you when you go to the vet's, won't you?'

He smiled. 'Nah, I thought I'd leave him here with a box of matches to play with. Come here.'

She went to him and they kissed, but she quickly broke away, exclaiming, 'Oh bugger, I forgot to get bleach. I'll have to get it on the way in.'

'They should get their own bloody bleach, what they pay you to clean their poxy office.'

'I get it back out of petty cash. What are you going to pay the vet with, anyway?'

'I paid when he came round the other night,' he said awkwardly.

'How much?'

'Twenty-five quid.'

She blenched. 'Jim!'

He shrugged and tried to laugh it off. 'It's all right. Ninja's going to come in tonight, I can feel it in my water.'

She snorted. 'That's what you said about Ryan – "Another girl, I can feel it in my water." We're late with the gas, they'll be cutting that off next.'

He kissed her again. 'Don't worry so much.'

'Someone's got to.'

Jim dropped Dawn off for work in his beaten-up old van, then drove on to the practice. He cradled Ryan in the crook of his arm as he led Ben into the surgery on a leash. He walked up to the counter. 'Morning, is Murray in?'

Maddy looked up. 'I'm sorry, no, he's not at the moment. Can anyone else help?'

'I'm Jim Cronin, I was told to bring the dog in for a jab.'

'Oh, right, if you take a seat, Mrs Sinclair will do that for you.'

Jim waited a few minutes before Laura appeared and led him through to the surgery. While she gave the dog an injection, Jim glanced around the room, his gaze lingering on the drugs cabinet.

'He should be fine now, Mr Cronin. The wounds are healing well and the antibiotics will make sure there's no infection, won't they, boy?' said Laura, ruffling the dog's fur.

'He'll know not to be so daft next time. By the way, is the young bloke in?' inquired Jim, elaborately casual. 'The one who looked after him first?'

'Murray, you mean?'

'Yeah, that's him.'

'No, he's out on a call, I'm afraid.'

There was a knock and Maddy stuck her head round the door. 'Sorry to interrupt.'

With an apologetic smile, Laura walked over to the door.

'I've got Mrs Benson on the phone,' murmured Maddy, to groans from Laura. 'She's worried that two of the kittens seem to have stopped suckling altogether.'

'Tell her it's really important she gives the mother a bit of peace. She may not be feeding them because she doesn't like being watched.' She sighed. 'I've already told her all this.'

Maddy nodded and disappeared.

'Sorry,' said Laura, turning back to Jim, 'you wanted to see Murray about something?'

'Er, yeah, when he was out at our house the other night, he had a look at my horse and said he'd give it something because it was allergic. Cortico, I think he said it was. He told me to collect it when I brought Ben in.'

There was another knock on the door and Maddy reappeared. 'Mrs Benson is insisting on a visit.'

Laura raised her eyes to heaven. 'Oh, put her through, I'll talk to her.'

Jim smiled sympathetically at her as Maddy went back to reception. Laura unlocked the cabinet and pulled out a box of cortico. Her extension started to ring and she handed it quickly to Jim, saying, 'Here you go. Just let Maddy know on the way out and she'll send you the bill.'

As Jim left, Laura picked up the phone with a long-suffering look. 'Hello . . . yes, Mrs Benson . . .'

Jim was grooming Ninja in the shed when Matthew got home from school. He called, 'School all right, Matt?' Matthew nodded and walked moodily into the shed.

'Get me some water for her, will you?' said Jim. 'Oh, and your mum says it's all right for you to come to the race.'

Matthew's demeanour changed in an instant. He picked up the empty bucket and ran out of the shed, thrilled. Jim watched him go, then whipped out the packet of cortico and fed Ninja a handful of the pills.

After dark they loaded Ninja into the trailer and drove out to the same section of road, which was already marked out with cars lining the verges. Jim parked the van and helped Matthew and Ninja's rider get the horse backed into the sulkie, but then saw Dave a short way off. Muttering, 'Stay here a minute, Matt,' he walked over to him.

The two men talked for a few seconds, then walked over to Jim's van. Curious, Matthew edged towards them. Dave wandered around it, poking at the rust patches, then said, 'Call it four hundred.'

Jim shook his head. 'Four hundred and fifty.'

'Four hundred and twenty,' said Dave, pretending to turn away.

'All right,' said Jim reluctantly, then took some cash from his pocket. 'With that then.'

Dave counted the money and made a note in his book. 'A round four hundred and fifty on Ninja to win.' He glanced up and caught Matthew watching him intently. 'This your lad, Jim?'

Embarrassed that Matthew had witnessed the transaction, Jim said, 'Yeah, well, Dawn's, you know. Ninja's owner, aren't you, Matthew?'

Dave smiled, then leaned conspiratorially in towards Jim. 'You hear about Brighton Rock the other night?'

'No.'

'They'd bunged him something to bring him down.'

'What?' said Jim.

Dave shrugged. 'Paracetamol, codeine, whatever. Anyway they'd given him a bit too much. Everyone's ready, they're off – and Brighton Rock doesn't even start.'

'On paracetamol?' asked Jim incredulously.

'Straight up. We all had to go home.'

Jim smiled disbelievingly, but Matthew stood there with eyes like saucers, avidly taking it all in.

Jim put his hand on Matthew's shoulder and guided him to the roadside. 'Come on Matt. Not much point coming if you can't see anything, is there?'

They stood impatiently waiting for the start, Jim gnawing at a knuckle with nerves. Finally the car horns sounded and moments later there was a shout from the start as the two horses raced away, the wheels of the sulkies whirring behind them. As Matthew and Jim shouted themselves hoarse, Ninja steadily pulled away from the other horse.

Matthew and Jim were both wild with excitement, shouting and hugging each other as Ninja sped past towards the finish line, but the driver of the other sulkie strayed too close to the edge of the road and as a wheel caught in the grass verge, the sulkie tipped over. The driver was catapulted out of his seat into the soft mud of the ditch at the side of the road, but the horse crashed heavily on to the tarmac. The driver crawled out of the ditch and got shakily to his feet but the horse was writhing in agony on the road. Matthew watched its struggles in horror, tears stinging his eyes, until Jim led him away, his own excitement unabated by the accident. 'Come on, Matt, let's congratulate Ninja.'

Matthew looked back towards the fallen horse as a crowd of men gathered around it, hiding it from his view. A few men slapped Jim on the back and shook his hand as he strode purposefully over to Dave, who put a brave face on his losses. 'Looks like you won't be walking home after all,' he said, as he counted out a stack of notes into Jim's hand. He jerked his head towards the scene back along the road. 'The other one's dog meat I reckon.'

Jim dropped Matthew off at home and bedded down Ninja in the shed, before heading for the pub, but while he was out celebrating the victory, Matthew lay awake in his bed, staring at the ceiling as images of the crippled horse flashed before his eyes.

Jim was still snoring when Dawn got up the next morning. Carrying Ryan on one arm, she made his breakfast, using her one free hand with practised skill. Tara, as usual, sat transfixed by the cartoons on the television. As she walked over to the table, Dawn saw a note from Jim, reading: 'Told you!' It was pinned to a pile of £10 notes. She smiled, looking out of the kitchen window towards Matthew, still in his pyjamas, who was scooping some feed out of a bucket and trying to give it to Ninja. The horse was uninterested, however, and Matthew came into the house looking puzzled. 'Ninja's not eating.'

Dawn smiled, the sight of £120 in cash doing wonders for her mood. 'She's probably tired; you'd be tired if you'd run a race pulling that thing,' she said, nodding towards the sulkie. She pointed at the money on the table. 'She did all right though, eh?'

Matthew nodded, but his face showed no animation.

'You were late enough back,' she said brightly. 'I didn't even hear you come in.' There was no response and she tried again. 'Was it like you thought it would be, seeing her race?'

'It was all right,' said Matthew, very subdued.

Dawn stared at him, baffled. 'What's up?'

'Nothing.'

She felt his forehead with her hand. 'You're not hot.'

He pushed her hand away. 'Mum, you know when Jim gave Ninja to me, he said that she belonged to me and everything, didn't he?'

'You know he did,' she said. 'What's brought this on?'

'Nothing,' said Matthew, walking out of the kitchen and going upstairs, leaving her gazing after him, even more puzzled.

Patricia was also up early that morning, already dressed and brushing her hair at the dressing-table mirror, when Chris woke. He watched her for a couple of seconds before she realized he was awake.

'What happened to our lie-in?' demanded Chris sleepily.

'You stay in bed, love, I've got too much to do,' said Patricia, coming over to the bed and planting a long, loving kiss on his lips. 'Happy birthday.'

They kissed again, Chris enveloping Patricia in the duvet, but they were interrupted by a chorus from outside the bedroom door.

'Happy birthday, Daddy!'

Chris sighed with resignation and Patricia smiled and disentangled herself as Abby and Charlotte came running into the room, clutching cards and parcels. Patricia picked up her hairbrush again. 'Breakfast in bed as a birthday treat?'

He looked at the clock. 'No, I've got to go out to Brabourne's to sign off some heifers he's exporting.'

A couple of hours later, Chris pulled up at Brabourne's farm, a hi-tech cattle establishment, equipped with brand new machinery and laid out to the latest specifications. It was gleamingly clean and as functional and profitable – and as soulless – as a new factory on an industrial estate. Alec Brabourne met Chris in the yard, a bombastic individual, florid-faced and expensively dressed, successful and accustomed to getting his own way.

Chris began inspecting the pedigree heifers as Brabourne watched impatiently, clutching some official forms. He offered Chris a pen to sign them, but something about the heifers was giving him pause and he ignored the proffered pen. He completed his inspection, thought for a moment and then shook his head.

'They can't go Alec, I'm sorry. The foul in the foot isn't completely clear.'

'But they're due out for export today.'

'It'll be ten days tops.'

Brabourne stared at him angrily, his already high colour darkening another couple of tones. 'That might be too late. For all I know, the Czechs might call the whole thing off, then I'm out of pocket four grand a heifer. It's been a hell of a deal to set up.'

Chris tried to pacify him. 'They're not going to get embryo transfer stock from just anywhere, they'll wait.'

'We'll have to see, won't we?' He paused and gave Chris a calculating stare. 'Johnsons at Corbridge might not take such a hard line on this.'

Chris kept his own anger firmly in check. 'I'd be sorry to lose your custom, Alec, but I'm not risking my LVI certification.'

Brabourne swore and stalked off, slamming a gate furiously behind him.

As Chris headed for home, Murray was approaching the rugby club with all the enthusiasm of a Christian about to face the lions. He muttered a nervous greeting to Alan, who was a regular player for the team, then changed in silence, putting on his borrowed rugby strip – several sizes too large for him. As he emerged from the changing-room, his pre-match nerves were not soothed by the realization that he was by some distance the least imposing physical specimen on either side.

Clare was standing outside, surrounded by a knot of players, and with a pang of jealousy, Murray saw that she was flirting with them every bit as enthusiastically as she did with him. Spotting Murray, she broke away to greet him with a wolf whistle. 'Not bad for a stick insect.'

There was a burst of laughter from the other players, but she walked over to him and said, much softer, 'Dad's really grateful, Murray.'

He smiled and glanced over towards the knot of spectators, but was distracted by the sight of an enormous player from the opposing team psyching himself up for the game by head-butting the door to the changing-rooms. He looked at Murray and gave him an evil grin. Murray shuddered and hastily averted his eyes as Alan walked past and slapped him on the back. 'It's egg-shaped and you pass it backwards, Murray.' He paused, took in Murray's pale face and expression of pure terror, and said, 'Don't worry, we'll hide you on the wing.' Murray smiled weakly and followed him on to the field.

The match had been in progress for ten minutes and Murray

was beginning to relax, not having been within ten yards of the ball – or an opponent – so far. Just then, however, the opposition stand-off hoisted a steepling kick, a towering 'up and under'. To Murray's horror, he saw that it was heading his way. 'Yours, Murray,' called Alan encouragingly, and Murray ran uncertainly towards it. As the ball plummeted into – and through – his arms, he was hit simultaneously by several players, including the gorilla he had seen before the match, who smacked him in the throat with his forearm, then followed through with his head. Murray saw the same ugly, scarred forehead that had been nutting the changing-room come thudding into his face.

Murray and the ball hit the ground at the same time, travelling in opposite directions, and there was a groan of disgust from his team-mates at his incompetence. He lay with his face squashed in the mud, blood seeping from a gash over his eye, and saw the ball trickle out of play and stop at Laura and Clare's feet as they watched from the touchline. If Murray hoped for a little of the milk of human kindness from them, he was sadly mistaken.

Laura looked at him contemptuously and then turned to Clare. 'Your dad should have asked me to fill in. I could play better than that.'

Murray sighed and dragged himself back to his feet, nursing his wounded head.

The rest of the game was one long uninterrupted nightmare. Wherever he tried to hide, the ball sought him out, and wherever the ball was, some big, ugly and violent opponents were never far behind. Sore, bruised and knackered, he staggered off the field at the final whistle and into the warm embrace of a hot bath.

Slightly recovered by the time he had dressed, he surveyed himself anxiously in the changing-room mirror. The cut over his eye was still weeping blood, the edges of the wound gaping open. The thought of spending his Saturday evening sitting waiting for hours in the outpatients' department of the hospital had no appeal whatsoever. He went in search of Clare, finding her surrounded by a circle of players. 'Clare, can you do me a favour?' asked Murray, drawing her to one side. 'Can you stitch this cut over my eye?'

Clare laughed. 'I'm a nursing assistant in a vet's practice, not a doctor, Murray. The only things I help stitch have fur and four legs.'

'Come on,' pleaded Murray. 'I don't want to trail all the way to Plymouth and waste two or three hours for the sake of a couple of stitches.'

'All right then,' Clare relented, 'but don't blame me if you're scarred for life.'

Murray fetched his veterinary bag from the car and Clare sat him down in the deserted changing-room, asking, 'Do you need a double brandy as an anaesthetic?'

'Er ... no,' said Murray doubtfully, gritting his teeth. 'It probably won't hurt much.'

Clare swabbed the wound and pinched the edges together, concentrating hard, the tip of her tongue just showing between her lips. Murray gazed at her face, framed by a tangle of long dark hair and tantalizingly close to his. He had flirted with Clare constantly since joining the practice but had never tried to take things any further than that. Now as he sat there looking into her dark brown eyes, he discovered that he had an overwhelming urge to kiss her.

He was considering the implications of this exciting new discovery when Clare put in the first stitch. He winced, but stifled the indrawn breath and tried to smile.

'One more should do it,' said Clare, 'it's only a tiny cut.'

She put in the second stitch, as Murray continued to stare mesmerized at her face.

Switching her gaze from his eyebrow, Clare intercepted Murray's look. She gave a slow smile, tilting her head to one side, and as she spoke, Murray could feel her breath, warm and gentle on his cheek. 'Why, Murray,' she chuckled. 'For a moment there, I could have sworn you wanted to kiss me.'

'For a moment I could have sworn it too,' said Murray, reddening.

She leaned in towards him a fraction more, her lips parting slightly, then pulled tantalizingly out of reach, her smile deepening. 'I couldn't allow it though, I'd be struck off the register if I started a relationship with a patient.' She strolled out of the room. 'I'll be up in the bar, when you've finished admiring my handiwork.'

Murray gazed longingly after her, then got to his feet with

difficulty and studied himself in the mirror. He glanced at the two neat little stitches above his eyebrow but then stared thoughtfully into his own eyes for a long moment, before following Clare upstairs.

The bar was heaving with rugby players and spectators. Starving hungry, Murray found a table and fed ravenously on a pie and chips.

'Don't they feed you at home?' said Clare, wandering over to his table.

Murray shook his head. 'I can't remember the last time I had a decent meal.' He crammed in another mouthful.

'Lost without a little woman to tend the hearth, are we?' sneered Clare.

'Excuse me, Ms Sexist,' said Murray, pushing his empty plate away, 'I happen to be rather a fine cook. I just never get the time to do it – well, it's the shopping more than the cooking really.'

Clare gave him a sceptical look. 'Can't see you in a pinny somehow.'

'If you're free tonight, I'll prove it and cook for you.'

She glanced towards a player standing near by. 'Can't do tonight, sorry.'

'Tomorrow then?'

'You're on.'

Murray's face broke into a broad smile; the day had – almost – been worth the pain on the rugby field. Clare went back to join her date for the night, and after a jealous glare in his direction Murray drained his drink and nodded his goodbyes to the players, ignoring the smirk from the opposition gorilla.

Murray walked stiffly out and drove home, limping slowly towards his front door as he gave himself up to his bruises. He was going through his pockets, looking for his key, and did not see Matthew waiting in the shadows by the door until he was almost on top of him.

Murray started, saying, 'My God, Matthew, what is it?'

'You've got to come, Ninja's sick. She's not eating. She hasn't touched her feed-bucket.'

'Your horse? Well, I'm not on call, you see, Matthew. You're supposed to ring the practice and one of the other vets will come out. It's my night off.'

Matthew looked at him steadily but said nothing.

'How long have you been waiting here anyway?'

'Not that long,' said Matthew disconsolately. He turned and began to trudge away.

Murray watched him go, compassion and fatigue battling for the upper hand. Finally he called, 'Hang on, Matthew, since it's you.'

Matthew turned, beaming, and ran back.

Murray had to move some stuff from the passenger seat of his car to make room for Matthew, who sat with the veterinary bag on his lap. He looked over at Murray, noting the cut over his eye. 'Did somebody hit you?'

It took Murray a second to remember the cut. He felt it gingerly with his fingers. 'No, er, well, yes, but we were playing rugby so it doesn't count.'

They pulled up outside Matthew's house and he led him round to the stable. Jim came hurrying out of the back door. 'Sorry to drag you out here but she's racing Monday. We can't afford to let her go sick.'

'No worries,' said Murray. 'How's the dog?'

'Oh, he's fine,' said Jim. 'The lady vet didn't mention I'd brought him in, then?'

He waited anxiously for the reply, but Murray was already preoccupied with the horse and noticed nothing. 'No, she didn't,' he said. 'Now, Ninja does seem a bit under the weather, doesn't she?'

'Worms, isn't it?' said Jim.

'Off her food, slightly anaemic, coat's dull – looks like worms, yes. I'd like to do a blood test to be sure, though.'

'How much is that?' asked Jim, long-faced.

'Forty quid, then you're looking at another forty for treatment on top of that.'

'Forget it,' said Jim. 'We just don't have that sort of money.' He sighed to himself. 'And there was me thinking the other night was the start of a winning streak.'

Murray thought hard, aware of Matthew watching him intently, full of confidence in him. 'There is something,' he finally said, reluctantly. 'It's a drug called Ziromec. I could give Ninja an injection, and if she is suffering from worms, it'll clear them up by tomorrow.'

'How much will it cost?'

'Ten pounds.'

Jim smiled with relief. 'And if you give her the injection she'll be fit for Monday?'

Murray nodded. 'Go for it then,' said Jim exultantly.

'You should know that it's not licensed here, Mr Cronin, but a lot of vets use it.'

'It's worth a try, though, if she's going to be fit to run. Eh, Matt?' Jim smiled at Matthew, who did not respond.

'She's not on any other medication, is she?' asked Murray, as he prepared the injection.

'Er . . . no, no,' said Jim shiftily. 'I'll er . . . I'll get you the ten quid.'

As Murray gave Ninja the injection, Matthew wrestled with his thoughts and suddenly blurted out, 'I don't want Ninja to race.'

'Mmm?' grunted Murray, concentrating on his job, but then, realizing what Matthew had said, he looked up in surprise. 'Why not?'

'They said it was going to be sent for dog food,' said Matthew, close to tears.

'What was?'

'This other horse at the race we went to. It got hurt really bad.'

'Have you told Jim?'

'Told me what?' said Jim, coming back with the money.

Murray looked expectantly at Matthew but he stayed silent and finally Murray filled the gap. 'Matthew's worried that Ninja might be injured if she races. Apparently you saw a horse get hurt?'

'Yeah, there was a bit of an accident. There's nothing to worry about, Matt, we've got a good driver and Ninja's not getting in anyone's way at the moment.'

Matthew appealed to Murray. 'Can't you tell him?'

'I'm sure Jim wouldn't race Ninja if it wasn't safe,' said Murray gently.

Matthew looked from one to the other, then shouted defiantly at Jim, 'You can't have her.'

'If she's fit, Matt, she's racing,' said Jim easily.

'But she's mine. If I say she can't race you can't make her.'

Jim grinned and winked at Murray, but not being taken

seriously drove Matthew wild. He pushed Jim in the chest, shouting, 'You're a lying bastard! You said you'd give her to me. You didn't mean it. It was just a lie, you liar!' as he ran sobbing out of the shed.

Murray looked concerned, but Jim did not turn a hair. 'Don't worry, he goes off like that sometimes. It never lasts long.'

Unconvinced, Murray cleared up his equipment and set off wearily for home, thanking his stars that Jennifer, not he, was on first call that night.

Even as he was thinking that, Jennifer was taking a call. 'I see, OK. I'll be there as soon as I can.' She hung up, smiled apologetically at Steven and headed for the door. 'Sorry love, I've got to go.'

'You'll be back in time to give me a lift to Scott's, won't you?'

'Hopefully. I am on call, love, I can't be sure.'

Steven glowered at her. 'We're supposed to be going to a party. I did tell you.'

'I remember now, I'm sorry.' She pulled a crumpled £20 note out of her purse. 'Here. Call a taxi if I'm not back in time.'

Jennifer sped along the lanes in her car, racing for a stud farm where a newborn foal was ailing fast. After only a few weeks, Jennifer was already driving as fast and furiously as Chris – normal vet driving as he described it. She was trying to dial a number on her mobile at the same time but was driving through a blind spot on the network and could not get it to work. Distracted, she took a corner late and the car slid across the road, crashing into a gatepost.

The engine stalled. Swearing, she got out of the car. She stared at the smashed headlamp, crumpled bonnet and the gatepost leaning drunkenly to one side. She got back in the car and tried to start it without success. She looked at the useless mobile phone, sighed, got out of the car again, and began walking up the drive towards the glow of light from the farmhouse. She knocked on the door, and as it swung open said, 'Sorry to bother you, I'm afraid I've bashed my car into your gate. Do you mind if I use the phone?'

Chapter 15

Chris was sitting down to a birthday supper with Patricia, Charlotte and Abby when the phone rang. He had been opening his present from Patricia, a pair of expensive walking boots. She watched his face anxiously. 'Are those the ones you wanted, because the shop said you could take them back . . .'

Chris shut her up with a kiss. 'They're exactly the ones I wanted. Thanks, love.'

He had already put them on, despite her half-hearted protests, and clomped over to the phone wearing them. 'No, you were right to call, Jennifer,' he said. 'Don't worry, it can't be helped. Where are you?' He frowned. 'Yes, I do know it, I'll be round as soon as I can.'

Patricia pulled a face as he put the phone down. 'On your birthday as well.'

'I know.'

Chris was already sitting in the Range Rover when he noticed he was still wearing his new hiking boots. He started to get out again, then muttered, 'Oh, what the hell,' and drove off. He arrived at the farm fifteen minutes later, approaching the door in some trepidation. His knock was answered by Jennifer, with Alec Brabourne close behind.

'Chris, this is Mr Brabourne,' said Jennifer.

'Alec, please,' said Brabourne. 'Hello, Chris.'

'You two know each other?' said Jennifer, surprised.

'Oh, yes,' said Chris.

He sat in the house for an uncomfortable ten minutes while Jennifer finished her drink, chatting animatedly to Brabourne, who then came outside to wave them off.

'He was loving that,' said Chris sourly as he drove away. 'I bet he'll make us pay through the nose for his bloody gate.'

'Oh, come on, Chris, he's a lovely bloke.'

Chris snorted. 'Lovely if you're blonde, maybe.'

They drove on to the stud farm, where the owner, Lesley, a middle-aged woman, well-dressed in a tweedy, huntin', shootin' and fishin' kind of way, was waiting apprehensively. They hurriedly examined the foal, which lay flat in a stall, too weak even to raise its head.

'We'd better start cross-matching from the other horses,' said Chris, but Jennifer shook her head firmly. 'It's too late for that.'

Chris gave Lesley a slightly embarrassed smile, not overjoyed at having a difference of professional opinion in front of a client. 'It's the only chance he's got, Jen.'

Again she shook her head. 'No, we could wash away the plasma proteins in the mother's blood and replace the faulty fractions.'

Chris caught Lesley's bemused look and smiled. 'Sorry, Lesley. Basically the foal is like a baby with blue blood syndrome. Normally we'd find a match from another horse and give it a total blood transfusion, but we don't have time. The best shot is to take blood from the mother and wash the antibodies from it.'

'How do you do that?'

Chris gave Jennifer a look as if to say, 'Yes, how do you do that?' but Jennifer had no doubts. 'There has got to be a path lab at one of the hospitals that'll do it for us.'

'At this time of night?' said Chris.

She shrugged, said, 'It's worth a try,' and started to fix up the equipment to take blood from the foal's mother. Chris still hesitated, but Jennifer had no doubts. She turned to Lesley. 'We'll need about six litres from May Queen.'

Chris finally nodded to himself as much as to Jennifer and said, 'Right, I'll start phoning round the hospitals.'

Close to midnight, Jennifer and Chris were wandering down a deserted hospital corridor in search of a coffee machine. They had handed the mare's blood in to the path lab for treatment and they could do nothing more until that had been completed. They were both giggly from tiredness and the adrenalin of working at top speed, racing around trying to save the foal.

'That poor man,' laughed Jennifer. 'Did you see his face when you said it was horse's blood?'

'He must have thought NHS cuts were taking on a new dimension.'

'Next of kin – May Queen!'

They calmed down as they walked along the drab, echoing corridor and there was a momentary silence between them.

Chris glanced at her. 'You could go home . . .'

'So could you,' said Jennifer. 'I'm the one on call, after all.'

'And miss all the fun? Anyway, you need the car.'

'That's true, I'd forgotten.'

She glanced down and noticed his footwear for the first time, then looked at him quizzically. 'Were you about to go out on a hike when I rang?'

Chris looked down at his feet. 'Oh, lord, I should ring Patricia.' He hesitated for a moment, explaining, 'These were my birthday present.'

'Oh Chris,' said Jennifer, mortified at breaking up his birthday party. 'I forgot. I'm sorry, dragging you away when you were celebrating.'

'Don't worry about it.'

'Happy birthday, anyway.'

'Thanks.' There was an awkward silence, broken by Chris. 'Right. I'll find a phone.'

They waited for over an hour, and when Chris went to the lab to find out how much longer it would be, he arrived back fuming at being patronized by the doctor.

'How much longer?' asked Jennifer.

'They can't say,' said Chris irritably. 'The thing about doctors is they always have to prove they know more than you. Every doctor I've ever come across has been the same.'

Jennifer sat there in thoughtful silence for a few moments, but shook herself out of it as she became aware of Chris watching her. 'Sorry, Chris, I was just thinking you were right . . . I um . . . I was involved with a doctor, when my marriage broke down.' She spoke haltingly, as if half talking to herself.

Chris nodded but stayed silent, encouraging her to continue.

'I quite liked him being . . . arrogant, I suppose. It saved me having to think, him deciding things.' She paused and flushed, flicking a quick look at Chris. 'That sounds awful, doesn't it? Sorry, I don't know how we got on to this . . .'

'It's fine,' said Chris gently.

She gave him a grateful look. 'Steven blames me for things going wrong with his father, the affair I mean.'

'Have you talked about it?'

'I've tried, but I end up making it sound like some . . . painful duty.' She paused, then hurried on. 'You know: "Things were so bad at home that I was driven into the arms of another man" . . . as if there was no pleasure, or excitement – and there was. I mean, it was great, in some ways. Not just the sex – the secrecy . . . everything. Of course, on one level, it was to do with my marriage failing but on another it wasn't and I can't explain that to Steven.'

'You can't expect him to understand at his age.'

'I don't know. I think he's put his finger on it in a way; I was selfish.'

'Is that always such a bad thing? You sound like you're being a bit hard on yourself.'

She shrugged, but then tried to lighten the mood. 'So. How many Hail Marys?'

They exchanged smiles but another pregnant silence grew between them, with Jennifer very aware of Chris's eyes searching her face. Abruptly he got up and walked back down the corridor. 'I'm going to try the lab again.'

It was another forty minutes before the lab finished cleansing the blood. Jennifer phoned ahead to warn Lesley that they were on their way while Chris collected the blood and signed the paperwork, then they hurried out into the night. Chris drove fast even by his normally reckless standards, but in the early hours of the morning there was no traffic and they arrived swiftly – and safely – at the stud farm, where Lesley stood waiting in the doorway of the stable. Chris and Jennifer leapt out and ran towards her.

When they had finished transfusing the blood, Jennifer stayed with the foal as Chris picked up the empty blood bags and started to take them outside.

'Vital signs look good,' said Jennifer.

'Yeah, but you'd better keep an eye on him,' said Chris. 'There's still the possibility of circulatory collapse. After a fall in blood pressure like that, it's the classic shock event.' When he walked back into the stable a minute later, however, he saw Jennifer and Lesley with smiles as wide as the stable door, watching the foal cross unsteadily to his mother and start to suckle.

As they drove home, they were both still elated by the foal's recovery, laughing and talking animatedly. 'Incredible, wasn't it?' said Jennifer, her eyes shining.

Chris nodded emphatically. 'I mean, I knew the theory but I've never seen it done.'

Jennifer smiled. 'To tell you the truth I hadn't either. I thought I'd better not mention it before.'

'I'm glad you didn't,' chuckled Chris. 'You'd better take the car, as you're still on call – I hope Murray is going to make this up to you.'

He pulled up outside his house, but there was a pause, neither of them really wanting the evening to end. Finally he said, 'Well, I'd better say goodnight then.'

'Goodnight . . . and thanks again, Chris.'

'No problem. 'Night.'

Chris tiptoed upstairs and padded quietly around the dark bedroom, trying to get undressed without waking Patricia. As he got into bed, however, Patricia jumped, exclaiming, 'Oh! Cold feet.'

'Sorry.'

'That's the worst bit,' she murmured sleepily. 'Was it a nightmare?'

'No,' said Chris, still running on adrenalin, 'it was this haemolytic foal out at the stud, we had to give it a transfusion. It worked like a dream though, Pat, you know, one minute, it's at death's door, then . . . I tell you, just now and then you see an animal recover like that and you feel like . . .'

'God?' she interjected, amused by Chris's enthusiasm.

He stopped, feeling a little foolish, and muttered, 'Sorry.'

'No, it's nice. It's not often I hear you so excited about work.'

She put a warm arm around him and drifted slowly back to sleep, but Chris still lay wide awake, staring at the ceiling.

Matthew Cronin was also wide awake as the church clock struck three. He got out of bed and pulled on his clothes, peering anxiously at Tara, but she slept on. He opened his door soundlessly, listened to the deep, even breathing coming from Jim and

Dawn's room and then sneaked downstairs. Standing on a chair, he reached up to a high shelf in the kitchen cupboard and took down the bottle of Ryan's cough medicine and a container of aspirin.

He let himself out of the house and padded across the yard to the shed, where he switched on the lamp Jim used at the flapping races and emptied the cough medicine and the aspirins into Ninja's feed-bucket. He offered it to the horse several times but she would not take it. In the end, he put the bucket down on the floor, switched off the lamp and went back to bed, hoping she would eat it during the night. An hour or so later he was woken by the sound of Ninja whinnying in distress. Matthew rolled over and put his head under the pillow, but he could still hear her whinnying pitifully.

Jim was up early the next morning, greeting Ben, now fully recovered, who jumped around him playfully as Jim put some food in his dish. He went outside and opened up the stable. Ninja stood weak, droopy and sweating, her coat steaming in the cold morning air, and when she moved, she hobbled painfully across the shed, lame in one leg. There was blood on the floor and wall. Jim rushed into the house, gabbling at Dawn, 'Will next door let us use their phone?'

'I suppose so,' she said. 'What's up?' But Jim was already sprinting from the house.

Bleary-eyed, Jennifer dragged herself from her bed to answer the call and drove carefully out to the Cronins' house, her normal high-speed driving abandoned in terror at the thought of wrecking Chris's car as well as her own. When she got there, she surveyed the wreckage of the horse's shed. Ninja had kicked her straw all over the place and her feed-bucket lay tipped and trampled on the floor.

Jennifer examined the horse carefully. 'It looks like she's severed the tendon as well.'

'How's she done that?' asked Jim.

'She could have had a convulsion. Look at her eyes. Nystagmus, flickering, that's a sign ... You say Murray had a look at her yesterday?'

'Yeah, he gave her a shot.'

'What of, do you know?' said Jennifer, careful to sound neutral.

He thought for a moment. 'Ziro something? They've all got funny names, haven't they?'

A slight tightening of Jennifer's lips was the only outward sign of surprise that she gave, and brooding over the state of his horse, Jim did not notice.

'All right,' said Jennifer. 'We'll have to get the horse down to the practice for X-ray.' They loaded Ninja carefully into Jim's trailer, while Matthew hovered uneasily in the background.

As soon as Jim had left the practice, Jennifer phoned Murray and called him in. She was viewing the X-rays of Ninja's leg when he arrived. She came straight to the point. 'Did you give the horse Ziromec intravenously?'

He nodded sheepishly.

Her tone softened a little, sympathetic but still insistent. 'I just don't understand why.'

'You know it can work wonders.'

'Yes, but it's risky. It can cause a reaction.'

'I'm hardly the only vet who's used it,' said Murray defensively.

Jennifer frowned. 'There's a practice rule against it, you know that. Besides, you weren't even sure if it was worms.'

'They couldn't afford a blood test. I had to do something.' He was almost pleading with her.

'No, you didn't. You felt pressured into having an answer, but it's better to admit you're not sure than end up with a mess like this.'

'Here endeth the second lesson,' said Murray, but then hastily apologized, realizing his flippant tone was wildly inappropriate. 'Sorry, Jen. I know it's serious.' He paused, then said hurriedly, 'I'd be really grateful if you didn't mention this to Chris.'

She shook her head as he looked beseechingly at her. 'I'm sorry, Murray, I'm afraid you're going to have to face the music on this one, and you'd better let the family know how much it'll cost to operate.'

Murray left the practice like a condemned man walking to face a firing squad and drove out to the Cronins'. Dawn and Jim sat at the kitchen table as Murray paced nervously around, explaining Ninja's injuries and the treatment she would need.

'How much?' asked Dawn.

Murray hesitated. 'Er ... seven hundred. Seven hundred pounds.'

Dawn was incredulous. 'Seven hundred pounds?'

He nodded miserably. 'It's a tricky operation, I'm afraid.'

'There's just no way we've got that sort of money,' said Jim.

'I'll talk to Chris, the practice may be able to come to some arrangement.'

'But even with the operation, she's not going to be fit for racing, is she?'

'No, she isn't. I'm sorry.'

Jim's face had crumpled like an empty crisp packet. 'We can't afford to keep her if she doesn't race,' he said dully.

'Of course. Well, I'll leave you to think about it,' said Murray, moving towards the door.

Dawn looked pointedly at Jim. He hesitated, then said reluctantly, 'There's no need. You may as well put her down.'

Feeling terrible, Murray murmured something and left. As Dawn closed the door, she saw Matthew, who had been listening to their conversation from the stairs.

'Can't Murray do something?' he asked plaintively.

She shook her head. 'We can't afford to keep her, love. It's kinder just to put her to sleep.'

She tried to put her arms round Matthew to comfort him but he shook her off. 'I'll work, I'll get a job, I'll get the money.'

'No, it's too much.'

'But it's my fault,' he sobbed.

'Don't be soft,' said Jim.

'You don't know, I poisoned her. Last night, I gave her Ryan's cough medicine and some aspirins, like the man at the flapping said, just so she'd be too slow to race. I didn't mean her to get hurt. I just wanted to stop her racing.'

Jim's face darkened with fury. 'You stupid little bastard.'

Matthew cowered, fully expecting Jim to hit him but Jim punched the wall in his anger instead. As he did so, Matthew ran past them out of the house.

'Matthew!' shouted Dawn, then turned to Jim, her voice dripping with sarcasm. 'That was clever.'

Jim nursed his hand, his fury already abated and feeling contrite about scaring Matthew. He rushed outside, calling to him, but the boy had already hopped over the fence that separated Ninja's paddock from the open heathland and was off, running as fast as he could, tears staining his cheeks. He disappeared among the gorse as Jim, out of breath, gave up the chase.

Matthew wandered over the Down for hours, then, tired and hungry, he walked down into Whitton, keeping well away from his home and the main roads. He had just enough money for a couple of chocolate bars, but having wolfed them down he was still ravenous. He wandered the streets for a while, then, nervous of being spotted, he went back up to the Down.

Nightfall found him on the edge of Whitton. His thin pullover gave little protection from the cold and he was shivering as he entered the yard of a small warehouse. He walked slowly round the building, pausing at a chained and padlocked double door. The chain was loose enough to leave a slight gap when he tried the door, just big enough for him to squeeze through. Inside, the warehouse was silent and dark. His stomach rumbling, Matthew huddled into a space between some packing cases, and rested his weary head on his arms.

He woke with a start, hearing footsteps outside. Terrified, he got up and scrabbled his way further into the warehouse but knocked over a packing case in the dark. It fell to the ground with a thud, the sound reverberating around the building. He froze as a torch swept round the room, catching him huddled in the beam like a frightened rabbit before an onrushing car.

A beam of light stabbed out into the darkness outside Murray's house as he answered the door to Clare. She looked stunning in a dark green satin dress, and her long, lustrous dark hair, which she normally kept up at work, swung around her bare shoulders. Murray's normally easy charm seemed a little forced as he greeted her, however, and she asked nervously, 'Am I too early?'

'No,' he said hastily. 'Come in, come in. Abandon hope all ye who enter here.'

He showed her through to the kitchen, where dinner was still under construction, and Clare opened the bottle of wine she had brought, pouring it into the mismatched, service station glasses that Murray produced with an apologetic smile.

She looked around the flat, teasing him gently. 'I'm a bit disappointed. No mirrored ceiling? No waterbed?'

'No, but I've got the torture equipment in the wardrobe.'

Murray eventually pronounced himself satisfied with dinner and they sat down to eat. As he did not possess a dining table, they sat on the floor, eating from the coffee table. Murray began to unwind a little as Clare enthused about the food and flirted with him deliciously. He poured some more wine.

'I should warn you that if you're trying to get me drunk, Murray . . .' said Clare, 'it's working.'

She flashed an inviting smile at him as she collected the plates together and stood up. Murray got to his feet as well, stood looking at her for a moment and then suddenly kissed her. She responded as enthusiastically as the stack of plates she was carrying would allow, giggling, 'Can I put the plates down first, please?' He released her for a second, but as they resumed kissing, the doorbell rang.

Cursing, Murray broke off the clinch and went to the door. Jim Cronin was standing on the step.

'Mr Cronin,' said Murray grumpily.

'Matthew's not with you, is he?' asked Jim, nodding to Clare over Murray's shoulder.

'No.'

'I thought he might have turned up here, if he's scared to come home.'

'Why, what's happened?' said Murray.

'We had a bit of a barny about his horse. The stupid little bugger tried to nobble it last night.'

'What did he give the horse, do you know?' asked Murray anxiously.

'Codeine linctus and paracetamol – what we had in the house.'

There was a pause. Murray said nothing.

'Anyway, let us know if you see him, eh?' said Jim, turning to go.

'Of course. I hope he turns up soon.'

'Probably will,' said Jim doubtfully, 'now he's given us all a good scare. Sorry to bother you.'

Murray shut the door, very preoccupied. 'I hope Matthew's OK,' said Clare, 'but I don't get why he wanted to nobble his own horse.'

'He'd got it in his head that the horse was going to be injured if she raced. I suppose he was just trying to stop her.'

'Why did Jim think Matthew would be with you anyway?'

'Oh, he's taken a bit of a shine to me,' said Murray uncomfortably.

'No accounting for taste,' laughed Clare, turning to face him, expecting to pick up from where they had left off before Jim arrived, but Murray did not respond.

She waited a moment, then resumed the conversation. 'His dad used to knock him about, you know – well, both Matthew and Dawn actually. It got so bad when he was a toddler they had to take him into care.'

'It wasn't Matthew's fault about the horse; it was mine,' said Murray miserably, averting his gaze. 'I gave it Ziromec last night.'

Clare stared at him aghast. 'And the Cronins don't even know? Murray, how could you?'

'Well, of course I intend to say something . . . there just hasn't been time,' said Murray lamely. There was a long silence. Murray stared at his hands, ashamed of himself. 'Er . . . Clare,' he began, but she cut him off coldly.

'I'd better be going. Thanks for dinner.' She got her coat and went hurriedly, leaving Murray staring miserably at the debris from the dinner and cursing himself for his own stupidity.

When Jim got back to his house, Dawn looked up hopefully, but seeing his grim expression, she quickly looked away again, tears once more starting in her eyes.

'You want me to go and ring the police?' asked Jim.

She nodded. 'You'll have to.' She sniffed back the tears. 'I could see there was something up with him all day yesterday but he wouldn't tell me what. He'll talk to you before he'll talk to me. I know I'm a cow to him sometimes but I don't mean to be.'

'He knows that,' said Jim tenderly.

'Does he? It's just the way I catch him watching me sometimes, like he hates me. He looks so much like his father, you know? I know it's not his fault.' Her shoulders shook with sobs, and Jim went to her and held her to him.

When her sobbing quietened, he kissed her forehead and said, 'I'll just slip next door and phone the police, I won't be a minute.' He was back in not much more, saying excitedly, 'They've found him, he's down at the police station, they just picked him up.'

Dawn scrambled for her coat and they hurried out of the door.

Ten minutes later they were standing at the counter of the police station.

'A security guard found him in a warehouse,' said the desk sergeant. 'Matthew tells us you'd had a bit of a family row.'

They nodded sheepishly.

'Well, we may want to bring him back in and give him a formal caution,' said the sergeant, 'but I very much doubt if we'll be pressing charges . . . though whether you tell Matthew that at this stage is up to you.'

Another officer brought Matthew through to the desk, looking pale and very frightened, and Dawn wrapped her arms around him and led him outside.

'I wasn't going to take nothing, honest,' said Matthew, tearfully. 'I just got in 'cos I was cold and there wasn't anywhere to rest.'

Dawn shushed him gently. 'I know. Don't get yourself in a state. I believe you.' She hugged him tightly to her as they walked towards the van.

After a sleepless night, Murray was up early the next morning. He dressed carefully and drove over to the Cronins' house without even stopping to eat breakfast, fearing that he would lose his nerve if he delayed. Jim, as genial as ever, led him through to the living-room. Murray glanced nervously from Jim to Dawn, then launched abruptly into his speech. 'Mr Cronin, Mrs Cronin, you should know that Ninja's injury . . .' He paused, gulped and carried on. 'It is possible that the injection I gave her could have caused her to go into convulsions. I'm . . . well, obviously I'm very sorry about the whole thing.'

Jim and Dawn took this information slowly on board. 'So it was your fault?' said Jim.

Murray squirmed. 'Possibly. Now, I have an idea that'll be less distressing for Matthew than having to put Ninja down. If the practice pays for the operation to repair her tendon, there's a shelter in Bridgecombe that may take her when they've got a place free. So if you could see your way to keeping her until then . . .'

'Now hold on a minute,' said Jim, his geniality rapidly evaporating. 'I've lost my horse and the money I could make out of her and now you're asking me a favour?'

'Well, for Matthew's sake if nothing else,' said Murray helplessly, aware that things were sliding out of his control.

Dawn spoke for the first time. 'I reckon we're owed some compensation, if it's your fault. What does your boss say?'

Murray blanched. The last thing he wanted to happen was to have Jim and Dawn confronting Chris. 'You'd . . . um . . . you'd have to speak to him about it.'

'Don't worry,' said Dawn. 'We will.'

Murray was appalled at the turn of events. 'I really can't say how sorry I am about this,' he spluttered, looking hopefully from face to face, but neither Dawn nor Jim were giving an inch.

'That's not going to help us, is it?' said Dawn.

Murray drove into the practice with a sick feeling inside him and went straight in to see Chris, who greeted him with a smile that soon became a frown and then an expression of barely controlled fury. 'You know my thoughts about using Ziromec that way and you flagrantly ignored practice policy, for no good reason that I can see. And then to admit you were responsible to the Cronins . . .' He pushed his hands through his hair in despair and disbelief. 'I just don't believe you could be so naïve. Never, ever, admit liability – it's practically the first rule of vetting. What the hell was going through your tiny mind, Murray?'

Murray started to offer a defence, but seeing Chris's face, he thought better of it and muttered, 'I don't know . . . I suppose I wanted to help them out.'

'Can they actually pay for the operation?' asked Chris wearily.

'No. I wondered . . . since the practice bears some responsibility for the horse's injury, whether you'd consider us shouldering the cost,' ventured Murray hesitantly.

'The practice?' shouted Chris. 'The practice bears no responsibility for you deciding to play miracle worker and screwing up.'

'OK, take it out of my wages,' said Murray hurriedly.

'Over seven hundred quid?'

'If you're willing to get it in instalments, take it out of my wages. Seriously.'

'And after the operation?' asked Chris, calming down slightly.

'I was going to ring the shelter out at Bridgecombe.'

'And what are you going to do if they don't have a place straight away? Keep the horse in your flat?'

'I'll sort something out.'

'You'd better do, Murray. It can't stay here – this isn't the bloody donkey sanctuary.' Chris took a deep breath, then spoke less angrily. 'Right. You'd better tell Jennifer that she's due to operate, hadn't you?'

Murray nodded, mumbled something incoherent and stumbled out.

Jim and Dawn had left Matthew to sleep on, and it was late morning when he came downstairs. Matthew looked at Jim nervously, flinching slightly as he looked up and saw him. 'Where's Mum?' he asked.

'She's gone to work,' said Jim gently. 'She said to let you sleep. Not every day she lets you skive off school, is it?' The attempt at friendliness was forced, but still welcome, and Matthew relaxed imperceptibly.

'Look, Matt,' Jim went on, 'I'm sorry I lost it about Ninja. It wasn't your fault. I knew that really, I was just, you know, a bit worried about her.'

Matthew gave him a disbelieving look.

'It was that injection Murray gave her,' Jim went on hurriedly. 'He came round to tell us first thing. I'm going round to see her at the vet's and sort things out. Do you want to come?'

Matthew hesitated. 'Are you still going to turn her into dog meat?' he demanded.

'No.' There was a brief silence. 'Better get dressed, eh?'

Matthew turned and ran upstairs.

Clare was cleaning up after the operation and keeping an eye on the recovering Ninja when Murray wandered in. They greeted each other awkwardly with forced smiles, the previous night's events still fresh in both their minds.

'She's looking good,' said Clare with unnatural heartiness. 'Jennifer was pleased with the way it went.'

'Good.' There was an awkward pause as Murray wrestled with himself, wanting to say more but afraid of exacerbating an already delicate situation. In the end he opted for silence and with an apologetic smile, turned to go.

'Murray.' He stopped expectantly. 'Maddy wanted a word with you.' She softened her tone a little, as she saw another doom-laden look cross his face. 'Don't look so worried, I don't think it was serious.'

'She's about the only person left in Devon that I've not managed to piss off.'

'Yet . . .' said Clare, giving him a genuinely warm smile.

When Murray stuck his nose into reception, Maddy collared him instantly. 'It's just for my accounts,' she said, as she tapped through a display on her computer, 'if you're paying for this operation on the Cronin's horse?'

He nodded glumly.

'I wasn't sure what I should wipe from my records,' she continued breezily. 'There are charges outstanding for a top-up antibiotic injection and a cortico prescription from Laura, should they go on too?'

'Yeah, just charge the lot to me,' said Murray wearily. As he turned to go, however, a sudden thought held him back. 'Cortico? Are you sure?' He went back to look at Maddy's screen.

'Mmm, yes, there you are,' said Maddy. 'It was for the horse's allergy or something.'

'The horse isn't allergic,' said Murray, hurrying through to Laura's office.

When Jim arrived with Matthew a few minutes later, Murray was in an altogether more cheerful mood.

Matthew acknowledged him coldly and warily, as Jim said, 'He wanted to see Ninja if that's all right.'

'Of course,' said Murray. 'She's just perking up.'

He led them to the stable where Ninja was recovering and Matthew stroked her muzzle and fed her some horse pellets, which she took hungrily.

'You'll be able to visit her at Bridgecombe whenever you want,' said Murray. 'I know it's not the same as having her at home, but . . .'

Matthew said nothing.

'Did Jim tell you it wasn't your fault she hurt herself?' said Murray.

'Yeah,' muttered Matthew in a low voice, turning his face away.

'I told him what happened,' said Jim.

There was a long silence, then Murray began to speak again, ostensibly addressing Matthew, though his words were equally for Jim's benefit. 'We'll never know exactly what happened. A lot of things could have caused Ninja's accident. Not what you gave her, but she could have reacted badly because of something else in her system. That's why I asked Jim whether Ninja was on any other medication before I injected her.'

He broke off and looked directly and unblinkingly into Jim's eyes.

'Erm . . . she wasn't,' said Jim, weakly and unconvincingly.

Murray went on relentlessly. 'No, that's what you said. If she had been, though, say someone had slipped her a steroid, like . . . I don't know . . . cortico for example . . .' he glanced sharply at Jim again, '. . . it could have made a big difference. I'm sure people can get hold of them easily enough.'

Jim's demeanour had changed in the space of a few seconds from cocksure, arrogant indifference to an expression of embarrassment and fright. He looked pleadingly at Murray, glancing towards Matthew.

Murray let him stew for a few more seconds, then said lightly, 'Still, the important thing now is what's best for the horse and for Matthew, isn't it?'

Jim nodded, shamefaced, but said nothing.

He let Matthew pet the horse for a few more minutes, then said, 'We'd better be getting back, Matt.'

Matthew looked at Murray. 'Can I come and see her tomorrow?'

'Of course.'

'Then you'll have her at home for a few weeks, before she goes off to this shelter,' said Jim.

Murray inclined his head towards him, in acknowledgement of his implicit offer.

'And before you ask,' added Jim, 'we can't keep her after that.'

'I know. But I'll be able to see her.'

He turned to go, but Jim called him back. 'What do you say to Murray, then?'

Matthew stared at him blankly. 'What?'

'Thank you,' prompted Jim.

'But it was his fault,' said Matthew, completely bewildered by Jim's volte-face.

'It was the medicine's fault, not his,' said Jim. 'Sometimes there are just accidents.' He paused, waiting, then prompted him again. 'Well?'

'Thank you,' said Matthew, grudgingly and reluctantly, still not meeting Murray's eyes. He walked outside, but Murray and Jim exchanged a long, meaningful look before Jim turned to follow him.

When Murray walked back into the practice Chris was leaning against the desk, waiting for him. He raised a quizzical eyebrow. 'All sorted then?'

'Yeah,' said Murray happily. 'Jim Cronin has agreed to take the horse back until there's a place at the shelter. I don't think they'll be taking it any further.'

'So Laura was saying,' said Chris. 'Good. Fancy a drink?'

Murray did a double-take, slightly surprised at Chris's friendliness. He took him up on the offer readily, however. 'I could certainly do with one.' He hesitated for a moment, then asked, 'If the family had decided to sue or demand compensation, or whatever, what would you have done?'

'Backed you, of course,' said Chris matter-of-factly.

'Really?'

'Naturally. We all make mistakes.'

'Nobody's perfect after all, eh?' said Murray, his old cockiness beginning to reassert itself.

'That's right, Murray,' said Chris drily, 'but just keep trying.'

Chapter 16

Murray was not the only one to have made a mistake, for Laura's failure to tell Alan about the offer of an associate partnership had gone down like a lead balloon with him. When she finally broke the news, they began an argument over breakfast that continued all the way through the early morning traffic into work. By the time Alan pulled into the practice car-park to drop her off, the atmosphere between them was poisonous. Laura leaned across to kiss him on the cheek, as she always did, but he did not respond.

She looked at him quizzically. 'You're not helping to defend anybody in court today, are you? If you are, I don't fancy their chances much.'

Her effort at humour fell on completely barren ground. 'Are you getting out?' asked Alan, staring straight ahead through the windscreen.

'How long's this going to last?' asked Laura.

There was no reply. She sighed, exasperated. 'It's like living with a six-year-old.'

Once more he failed to rise to the bait, pompously stating, 'I've work to do, Laura.'

'Look,' she said. 'Are you pissed off because I talked to Chris about the associate partnership idea before I talked to you? Or are you actually pissed off because you don't want me working here at all?'

Alan looked pointedly at his watch. 'We've discussed this over and over.'

She stared at him in exasperation. 'I'm not going to be your little woman at home, Alan. As Patricia says, if you're married to a vet, you fight it or go with it.'

'Did you talk to Patricia about us?' he demanded.

She shrugged. 'What does it matter?'

'It matters.'

'Alan, listen . . .' Laura began, but he just leaned across, opened the door and gave her a hostile stare. She opened her mouth to say something else, but then shook her head resignedly and got out of the car. He drove off without a backward look.

When he reached his office, the receptionist greeted him with, 'Good morning. Mr Harris wants to see you at once.'

Alan groaned, 'That's all I need,' but he walked straight down the corridor to the senior partner's office. Harris looked up at Alan's knock, flashed his mirthless smile and said, 'Sit down.'

'If this is about the Dixon conveyancing,' said Alan guiltily, 'I think I know how we can solve it.'

Harris waved that problem away with a flick of his hand. 'Never mind that, Alan. The marine technology firm we look after, Butler and Linney's, have a subsidiary in Birmingham, Alabama, involved in a takeover. They want someone from here to go over there with their business people and accountants, at least until the takeover goes through.'

Alan looked blank. 'I haven't had much to do with Butler and Linney's. Why haven't you asked Deirdre?'

'Because she has to look after this end of things,' said Harris testily. 'I want you to go. You're the right person for the job.'

'Thank you. I'm flattered.'

'So you should be. This is a big opportunity for you, Alan. And for us too, I might add.'

Alan nodded. 'Er . . . how long would it be for?'

'Five months, six at most.'

'And if I agree, when would you like me to go?'

Harris raised an eyebrow at Alan's use of 'if' but said nothing except, 'We'd want you to leave on Monday.'

'I'll talk it over with Laura and let you know.'

Harris dismissed him with a small gesture of impatience and Alan walked back down the corridor, thinking furiously.

He brooded on it all morning, staring sightlessly at the documents in front of him, then paced around Whitton throughout his lunch hour. Finally he stopped dead in the street, turned round and hurried back to work. Harris's secretary looked up surprised as Alan reappeared. 'He's still at lunch, Alan.'

'Never mind, I'll wait.'

When Harris came in a few minutes later and saw Alan waiting for him, his face cracked into a dry smile, like a fissure in a dried-up river bed. 'Ah, Alan, you've made the decision? Good, good, come in.'

He sat down behind his desk and said encouragingly, 'Well?'

'Mr Harris, this may be extreme folly, but I really don't want to go to Alabama for six months.'

Harris's smile disappeared as abruptly as switching off a light. 'These are very important clients, Alan. What shall I tell them – that one of our juniors can't be bothered to help steer them through a critical business move?'

'It's not that I can't be bothered . . .' began Alan.

'You're passing up a tremendous opportunity. What if another similar opening occurs in a few months' time? I'd be disinclined to approach you again.'

'I appreciate the offer, believe me, but . . .'

'But what?' said Harris irritably.

'I love my wife . . . and I don't want to be away from her for so long.'

'Why, did Laura threaten to leave you or some such?'

'No. I haven't even told her about it.'

Harris stared at Alan for a second, his eyes cold and hooded, then switched his attention to the paperwork on his desk muttering, 'I'm sure you've work to do,' without looking up again.

Alan took the hint and left.

Laura arrived home that night expecting a continuation of the morning's row. Instead she found the table already laid, candles burning and soft music playing. Alan kissed her, put a glass in her hand and said, 'Dinner's almost ready, why not have a quiet few minutes with the paper?'

Laura gladly accepted the peace offering. Neither of them referred to the row and Alan did not mention his conversations with Harris. They sat facing each other across the table, smiling often as they ate.

'Why don't we do this more often?' said Laura, pushing her plate away and leaning back in her chair.

'Then it wouldn't be special.'

'This is special, isn't it?' said Laura, taking his hand.

'Very.'

'How "very"?' she asked, smiling as she bent to kiss the inside of his wrist. 'Show me.'

'Later,' said Alan, putting down his knife and fork.

'Now,' said Laura, running her fingers lightly down his arm.

'I haven't finished.'

'I don't care.'

Laura held out her hand, giving him a slow, sultry smile. He pushed his chair back and she led him over to the rug in front of the open fire. They stood for a moment, kissing.

'What's for dessert?' said Laura.

'Crème brulée. It'll get cold.'

'It's already cold,' said Laura, starting to unbutton his shirt. She smiled, sliding down on to the rug with him.

Alan was already up and dressed when Laura woke the next morning. She could hear him whistling as he moved around the kitchen and she smiled fondly to herself as she rolled out of bed and padded through to the bathroom. She was standing at the basin in her dressing-gown, brushing her teeth, when Alan came in, clutching a letter in his hand. She smiled through the toothpaste at his reflection in the mirror, but Alan's returning stare was anything but friendly.

She hastily spat out the toothpaste and turned to face him. 'What on earth's wrong? You look as if you've just been invited to your own funeral.'

He threw the letter down beside her. It was addressed to her, giving final details of a two-day small animals course she was due to attend that weekend. She had been postponing telling him that bit of news, waiting for the arguments about her associate partnership to die down. Now she had left it too late.

She gave him an uneasy smile. 'It's only two days.'

'Only?' snorted Alan. 'It's the whole weekend.'

'I know, but that's not such a problem, is it? There's always next weekend.'

He turned to go, speechless with fury.

Laura was baffled at his reaction. 'You're not even going to talk about it?'

'I'm late.'

She glanced at her watch. 'No, you're not.' She paused, choosing her words carefully. 'We need to talk, Alan. I want to sort this out.'

Alan turned back to face her. 'You're right, I'm not late at all. I just don't want to talk about it. You've made up your mind as usual. If you want to go on the course, go on the course.'

'For heaven's sake Alan, it's only two days, not a lifetime.'

'Go for a fortnight for all I care.'

Laura stopped dead in her tracks, stunned. Alan picked up the letter and brandished it at her, like a prosecutor producing Exhibit A, his voice laden with bitterness and sarcasm. 'I mean, when were you going to mention this, Laura, Saturday morning? A quick call from the station, or a carrier pigeon when you got there?'

She tried to keep her cool, knowing that she was in the wrong but genuinely baffled by his reaction to such a trivial matter. 'I'm sorry. I should have told you sooner, but the way things have been between us recently, it just never seemed to be the right moment.'

Alan ignored the tentatively proffered olive branch. 'Anyway,' he lied, 'I've already made arrangements for this weekend.'

'Oh, so it's all right for you to do it without telling me?' demanded Laura.

There was an angry silence, the previous night's loving intimacy already a distant memory.

'The course is booked,' said Laura flatly.

'So cancel it.'

She shook her head. 'It's important.'

'So's this weekend,' said Alan, as petulant as a little boy, his round face white with anger.

Laura paused again before replying, struggling desperately to make some sense of Alan's over-reaction. She shrugged helplessly. 'I'm sorry, I just don't see what the problem is, Alan. Whatever it is you want to do this weekend, surely we can do it next weekend instead?'

'I'm busy next weekend,' he spat. 'I've booked myself on a two-day small animals course.' He hurled the letter down in disgust and stormed out, slamming the door behind him.

Laura stared at the door, infuriated and utterly baffled.

She was still preoccupied with Alan's behaviour when she got to work, and was almost run over as she stepped in front of a car pulling into the car-park at the practice. The driver smiled understandingly and waved her on but was rewarded only by a ferocious glare from Laura, who stalked off into the practice with a face like thunder, barely acknowledging Jennifer's greeting as she came out to meet the man, a Ministry of Agriculture, Fisheries and Food official.

He got out of his car and strode purposefully towards the building, a handsome, confident man in his mid-thirties.

'Jennifer Holt,' said Jennifer, smiling and extending her hand.

'Michael, Michael Fleet. I'm not late?'

She shook her head. 'No, I'm early.' She glanced at her watch, adding, 'So are you, as a matter of fact.'

He smiled and heaved an exaggerated sigh of relief for Jennifer's benefit. 'You wouldn't believe this. I got lost.'

'I'd have waited,' said Jennifer, already liking his direct and confident manner.

'I hate being late. Gives the wrong impression.' He smiled ruefully. 'Though I already seem to have done that with your colleague.'

Jennifer laughed. 'Don't worry, it's nothing personal, she almost bit my head off on her way in.'

Michael laughed as well, looking at her with frank appreciation. Then he said briskly, 'Right, down to work. Did Chris tell you what we're doing?'

'Just that you're assessing my application for Local Veterinary Inspector status. You want to see me do a decent TB test?'

'It's a couple of farm visits. Nothing to worry about.'

'Time for coffee?'

He checked his watch ostentatiously and shook his head. 'Not really.' Then he cracked a smile. 'One sugar in mine.'

They were finishing their coffee when Chris came hurrying through, carrying bits of equipment to his car. He paused to shake Michael's hand.

'We're going up to High Lane, Chris, to take some TB samples,' said Jennifer.

Chris stared at her blankly.

'My LVI certificate?' prompted Jennifer. 'My assessment?'

'Oh, yeah. Sorry,' said Chris absently. 'Look, excuse me, I'll have to dash, I'm late already.'

As he turned to go, a stray thought struck him. He called to

Maddy, who covered the mouthpiece of the phone and raised her eyebrows inquiringly.

'Moors End Farm?' said Chris.

She nodded. 'Don't worry. I've asked Murray to do it.'

Chris hurried for the door, calling to Jennifer and Michael, 'I'll see you both later . . . and don't worry, Jennifer, he's all right.'

'She's already passed her first test,' said Michael, holding up his coffee mug. 'Best one I've had all morning.'

As Jennifer and Michael followed Chris out, Murray appeared from the back, holding a package. 'Has Chris gone?' he asked Maddy.

'Only just. You might catch him if you run,' said Maddy, but then shrugged her shoulders and smiled as they both heard Chris's Range Rover driving off. 'On second thoughts, I don't think you can run fast enough.'

'Are you sure these antibiotics are right?' asked Murray, gesturing to the package. 'You could treat a dozen pigs with pneumonia with this lot.'

Maddy raised an eyebrow. 'The repeat prescription for Moors End Farm?'

'Yeah.'

'Must be right, it's a repeat prescription.'

'All this?' repeated Murray, showing her the boxful.

Maddy glanced casually at the drugs. 'He knows what he's doing, Murray, that's what Chris always gives him.'

Murray hesitated, then shrugged his shoulders. 'OK, you're the boss – or at least, he is.' He smiled and wandered out to the carpark, still clutching the box.

Jennifer and Michael were just setting off on the short drive to a dairy farm on the outskirts of Whitton. The farmer moved a cow down into a makeshift crush, then stood watching as impassively as the beast itself, while Jennifer prepared the TB testing kit.

Michael stood off to one side, occasionally making a note in his notebook. 'When were they last tested?' he asked.

'April,' said Jennifer, still busy with the kit. 'Chris did the heifers in May. There were two reactors, your lot cleared them.'

She straightened up and advanced on the cow, carrying clippers for shaving the fur from two sites on its neck. At the first touch of the clippers, however, the cow reacted as if it had been jabbed with an electric cattle prod, shying away from her.

'Come on. Come on,' muttered Jennifer, acutely aware of the scrutiny from Michael and the farmer. 'Come on, you silly cow.'

'Do you want a hand?' asked Michael.

She shook her head. 'No thanks, I'm fine.'

After a little coaxing and a bit of sheer brute force, Jennifer managed to hold the cow still for long enough to clip the fur. She measured the thickness of the flesh with a pair of callipers and then fired the 'gun', injecting a controlled dose of TB into each of the sites. She worked swiftly, without fuss, and then stepped back, patting the cow hard. 'Well, I don't know about you, love, but I never felt a thing.' The cow ignored the joke, but Michael smiled appreciatively.

Jennifer packed up quickly, and she and Michael chatted animatedly as they drove up towards Dartmoor, turning off into a village just below the edge of the moor, where the mournful baying of hounds announced the presence of the hunt kennels long before they came into view.

'What attracted you to large animal work?' asked Michael.

Jennifer glanced at him suspiciously, searching for signs of male chauvinism in the question. Satisfied, she shrugged and replied, 'I like a challenge. I got sick of messing with dogs, cats and hamsters . . . One or two other reasons.' Abruptly she changed the subject. 'You're sure you don't mind a quick detour to the hunt kennels? It's Laura's client but I said I'd take it for her. We like to keep them sweet, they take all the carcasses around here.'

'It's fine,' said Michael, gazing appreciatively at Jennifer's profile as she drove down the lane. He was in no hurry at all to bring her assessment to an end. 'By the way, what were they?' he asked.

She looked sharply at him then shook her head, smiling gravely. 'The other reasons? I wouldn't want to bore you with the details.'

She pulled up by the kennels, ending Michael's line of questioning for the moment at least. As they got out of the car the kennel manager, Sarah Hallam, came across the yard to meet them. Grey-haired and patrician, used to getting her own way without question, she surveyed Jennifer with barely concealed displeasure.

'I don't think we've met?' she said coolly.

'Jennifer Holt,' said Jennifer, extending her hand. 'How do you do.'

Sarah pointedly ignored the proffered hand, saying even more icily, 'Where is Laura?'

'She, er . . . she got held up this morning, Mrs Hallam.'

Sarah clicked her tongue in disapproval.

'She sends her apologies,' continued Jennifer, gritting her teeth but determined to stay polite. 'I can understand if you'd rather wait, but Laura said you thought it might be urgent.'

Sarah hesitated, still not entirely happy with Jennifer. As she pondered, a knackerman's lorry laden with pig and cattle carcasses started backing into the yard, its path blocked by Jennifer's car.

Sarah abruptly made up her mind. She gestured towards an archway. 'The kennel's through there. You'll have to move the car first.' She turned on her heel and stalked off towards the kennels without looking back.

Jennifer exchanged a meaningful look with Michael as she went to move the car.

The hounds redoubled their barking as Jennifer and Michael followed Sarah into the kennels. Jennifer examined a sick foxhound pup, listening to its breathing through a stethoscope and taking the animal's temperature. Sarah stood with arms folded, watching critically as Jennifer worked.

'How long has he been like this?' asked Jennifer.

Sarah unfolded her arms and spoke quickly and anxiously, like a mother describing her child's symptoms to his doctor. 'He was off his feed last night. He looked like he had a temperature so we put him in here. He'd not touched his feed this morning . . .' Her face softened as she looked indulgently at the pup, then resumed its stony mask.

Jennifer examined the thermometer. 'A bit on the high side. Not well, are you, mate?'

Sarah winced at the familiarity, even though it was with the pup.

'He is a bit off colour,' continued Jennifer imperturbably. 'I'll give him some antibiotics for now. Can I check on him tomorrow?'

'We've had jaundice,' said Sarah anxiously.

Jennifer shook her head and said firmly, 'It's an infection, Mrs Hallam. See how we go on with antibiotics. He should be right as rain by morning.'

As Jennifer drove back down from the kennels, she had to swerve to avoid Murray, running late and driving like a bat out of hell up towards Moors End Camp, a deserted barracks from the Second World War, silhouetted dramatically on the Dartmoor skyline. A JCB stood sentinel at the entrance to the camp, beside a signboard proudly advertising 'an exclusive development of executive-style homes'.

Slightly lower down the hill, in the yard of a rather less exclusive development – Moors End Farm – there was a cacophony of squeals as a hundred pigs were being loaded into the back of an articulated transporter. The farm's owner, Colin English, a bluff, no-nonsense character in his mid-thirties, herded pigs towards the vehicle, helped by his eleven-year-old son, Danny, while his wife, Elaine, watched from the sidelines.

Resourceful, ambitious and energetic, Colin took pride in the speed with which the pigs were loaded, but a single sow was disinclined to join its peers in the transporter. Colin was on it immediately, shouting, 'Hup, ya bloody thing! Don't give me a hard time.'

Elaine gave him some good-humoured barracking from the sidelines, calling with mock impatience, 'Come on, we haven't got all day!'

The sow reluctantly started to amble up the ramp and the transporter driver got out of his cab with the paperwork. Colin surveyed the scene in triumph, wiping the sweat from his brow. He turned to Elaine, executing a sweeping bow as he said, 'For my next miracle.'

As he was doing so, the sow had a last-minute change of mind and made a dash for freedom. Colin tried to block it but the sow produced a sidestep of which Jeremy Guscott would have been proud and left him sprawling in the mud as it sprinted back to the far end of the yard, squealing in triumph. Colin looked up ruefully, to see Elaine and the driver in fits of laughter.

'That's very impressive,' said Elaine, 'very impressive indeed.'

Colin got heavily to his feet and set off in pursuit of the recalcitrant sow.

Even while the transporter was still rumbling up the farm lane, Colin was already moving the next lot of fatteners into the recently vacated shed, packing them tightly into the stalls under the scrutiny of an audience of a hundred or so other pigs, all setting up a high-pitched, insistent clamour for food.

Elaine had changed into her best clothes to go shopping and stopped off in the shed on her way to the car.

Colin looked up. 'Are we all set for Sunday?'

She shook her head. 'He says he can't do it on Sunday. He's organized a bike ride with Mark and Andrew. You know what he's like with his friends,' she went on hurriedly, as she saw Colin's displeasure. 'I've told him you want to go out.'

Colin thought for a moment. 'Saturday?'

'Colin,' she said, exasperated.

He looked at her blankly.

'I'm seeing the land agent on Saturday.'

'What, all day?' he asked, confused.

Elaine looked up towards the camp on the skyline. 'Do you want to buy that land or not? They're not going to wait, Colin. I was going to make him an offer on Saturday. I thought we'd agreed all this. We need more land, just so's we can take care of this lot.' She gestured to the pigs.

'Can't you see him next week? I need a day out.'

She sighed indulgently. 'You've got no business sense.'

'I've got a beautiful wife, though.'

Elaine smiled despite herself.

'Look, I'll talk to him,' said Colin.

'Oh, no, you don't. I'll talk to him. You talk to Danny.' She checked her shopping list. 'Do you want anything?'

'How about a goodbye kiss?' Colin moved towards Elaine.

She took in his filthy overalls, stained with mud and pig muck, and began to retreat, giggling nervously. But the more she backed away, the more he wound her up by advancing. Elaine ended up cornered against the wall, pleading, 'Colin . . . Colin, I've just got changed,' panic and laughter battling for control of her voice.

Colin leaned against the wall, his arms either side of Elaine, preventing her escape. He kissed her lovingly, careful not to dirty her dress.

Elaine sighed, her voice laden with irony. 'And they say romance is dead. Now . . . do we need anything?'

'Yeah,' said Colin, deadpan. 'We've run out of bacon.'

Elaine looked around for something to throw, but was interrupted by Murray's appearance in the entrance of the shed. As Elaine made her escape, Colin strode forward to greet Murray. 'Mr Wilson, is it? You found us all right?'

Murray nodded and held up the box of antibiotics. 'I've brought these, but as I'm here, perhaps I can have a look at the infected animals?'

Colin led him to a stall at one side of the shed, a little away from the other pens. As he looked on anxiously, Murray examined five infected pigs, then peeled off his rubber gloves. 'They've had a lot of pneumonia?' he asked.

'Just this year . . . I don't know what to do. We can't seem to shake it off.'

Murray looked round the shed, glancing up to the roofing and taking in the pigs packed tightly together in their pens. 'The ventilation is poor, but part of your problem, at least, is that they're too close together.'

He paused, but Colin said nothing.

'How long have you been using antibiotics?'

Colin thought for a moment. 'This year.'

Murray raised an eyebrow. 'And Chris hasn't said anything?'

'They need spacing out, I know that. There are too many in here, but we're hoping to get some more land soon.'

'But if you farm this intensively, when one of them gets it, it spreads. You know you're losing money?'

'Tell me about it,' said Colin ironically. 'Look, I can manage with antibiotics. You know how it is – if I don't shift 'em fast . . .'

Murray nodded sympathetically, reluctant to give him too hard a time. 'But MAFF are starting to notice this sort of thing. They're saying overcrowding is a welfare issue.' He shrugged, unwilling to say more to a man who, after all, was one of Chris's clients, not his own. 'I can treat them, Colin, but you need to space them out more. It's up to you, mate.'

Murray thought for a moment, then spoke again, half to himself. 'I can't believe Chris hasn't said anything ... When was the last time you saw him?'

'Here? I can't remember ... some time last year,' said Colin, oblivious to Murray's incredulous stare.

Chapter 17

Jennifer and Michael had completed the morning rounds and were relaxing over a pub lunch. 'How am I doing?' asked Jennifer with a conspiratorial smile.

'We can call it quits now as far as I'm concerned,' said Michael.

'What, when I'm having all this fun?'

He smiled at her ironic tone. 'I thought you said you liked it?'

'I said it was a change from what I'm used to.'

'Ah yes, it's all coming back to me – you moved away, needed a challenge and didn't want to bore me with the details.'

She laughed. 'There's nothing to tell.'

'It's all right,' said Michael, easily. 'Just tell me to get lost.'

'I don't mind you asking. I had other reasons, they're just . . .' she smiled helplessly '. . . boring.'

'You're married?'

Jennifer glanced sharply at him, slightly discomfited by his directness. 'Separated.'

'Isn't it a pain in the arse?'

She laughed. 'You too?'

'Eighteen months and counting. It just feels like a lifetime.'

He gazed unseeingly out of the window for a moment, then, remembering himself, gave her a slightly embarrassed smile and asked, 'Kids?'

'One,' said Jennifer. 'Well, I'm not sure he's still a kid. In fact I'm not sure what he is. Other than the fact that whatever it is, it's suddenly taller than I am. How about you?'

'I'm taller than you too.' He put up a hand to defend himself as Jennifer threatened to throw her sandwich at him. 'All right, don't shoot. I knew you meant kids but no, I haven't got any. We weren't together long enough.'

A slightly uneasy silence fell between them; it was intimate ground for such new acquaintances. Michael looked up. 'You don't mind me asking?'

'I don't mind,' said Jennifer. 'It's nothing to be ashamed of. I just don't know why I'm telling you all this.'

'Jennifer, can I ... I er ... Can I be very honest?' asked Michael, blushing slightly.

Jennifer waited expectantly as Michael struggled to unburden himself of what had been on his mind since he first set eyes on her.

'Er ...' he began, but just then Jennifer's mobile phone started ringing. He swore under his breath in exasperation, causing Jennifer's smile to deepen as she picked up the phone.

The smile quickly faded. 'Hello? ... Yes, Maddy ... OK. No, don't worry, I'll go straight back there. Yes. Bye.' She hung up, and drained her drink, giving Michael an apologetic look.

'Urgent?' he asked.

'I'm afraid so.'

He nodded, resignedly. 'It's all right. I'll get myself a cab.'

'What did you want to ask me?'

'It doesn't matter, another time.'

Jennifer checked for a moment, as if about to say something herself, then changed her mind and hurried off, calling, 'Thanks, see you soon, I hope,' to Michael as she left. She drove straight back to the hunt kennels, setting off another hound chorus that brought Sarah hurrying out to investigate.

When she saw Jennifer, she scowled and stood blocking her way, even more hostile than she had been earlier. 'I'm sorry, but after what has happened, I don't want you anywhere near my animals. I asked to see Chris. Why should I see you? You said it was going to be all right.'

'I may have missed something, Mrs Hallam,' said Jennifer. 'If I could see the pup I'll see what I can do.'

She attempted to step past her but Sarah put a restraining hand on her arm, saying flatly, 'There's nothing you can do.'

Jennifer stopped, baffled.

'Didn't she tell you?' said Sarah. 'It's too late to treat it. I just want to know why it died.'

Jennifer took off her coat and headed purposefully for the kennels. It would need an autopsy to determine the cause of the pup's death, but she was determined not to overlook any potential signs of infection among the other dogs. She had been working hard for three-quarters of an hour when she heard a car pulling into the yard. She looked up and was less than pleased to see Chris heading her way. She gritted her teeth but went back to work on a foxhound bitch, listening to its chest through a stethoscope.

As Chris squatted down beside her, she took the stethoscope from her ears and gave him a cool and questioning look.

'Maddy told me,' he said, in answer to the unspoken question. 'I must have just missed you.' He paused, waiting for a thaw in the atmosphere, but went unrewarded. He tried again. 'Mike seems impressed . . .'

There was still no reaction from Jennifer, who carried on working, beginning to take a blood sample from the bitch.

'. . . So I wouldn't worry about Mrs Hallam.'

She looked up and said tersely, 'I wasn't.'

Chris nodded towards the bitch, his tone still warm and friendly. 'What is it?'

'I don't know. It should just be a routine infection. She's got two more with swollen throats, running a temperature. I don't know why the pup died.'

'Do you mind if I give you a hand?'

She looked up again, surprised and pleased that he had asked the question. 'I could do with it,' she admitted, smiling for the first time.

'I'll have a word with her as well,' said Chris, jerking his head towards Sarah, who was standing watching them from the gateway.

'What are you going to say?'

'I'll tell her it's a routine infection and we'll keep an eye on it,' he said airily, getting up and strolling back towards Sarah.

When Jennifer had finished checking the other dogs, she put the still, lifeless corpse of the pup into a black plastic bag and carried it to the boot of her car. She and Chris drove back to the practice in convoy and arrived back in reception giggling about Sarah.

'I thought you handled her really well,' said Chris, tongue firmly in cheek.

'You're wrong,' laughed Jennifer. 'I handled her brilliantly!'

Laura overheard them. 'Sarah?' she queried.

'You know you said there was a bitch with problems?' said Jennifer. 'I thought you were talking about the dog.'

Even Laura laughed. 'She's all right once you get to know her.'

'She's a good client too,' said Chris, 'despite her little character flaws.' He turned to Laura. 'A pup's died and she's got a couple more with signs of an infection. They'll probably be fine in a day or two but you know what she's like.' He looked hopefully at her. 'She likes you, Laura.'

'Yeah, I know,' said Laura heavily, knowing what Chris was angling at. 'I'll give her a ring in the morning.'

Maddy took a telephone call, then held her hand over the mouthpiece as she spoke to Laura. 'It's Alan. Do you want to take it in your room?'

Laura hesitated, embarrassed, then said, 'Er . . . no. Can you tell him I'm not here, Maddy?'

Jennifer and Chris exchanged a surprised look as Maddy, unflappable as ever, just uncovered the handset and said, 'Hello, Alan? If I had a brain I'd be dangerous. I've just remembered, she went out on a call a while ago. No, sorry, I don't. OK, 'bye.'

After she hung up, there was a silence, Laura staring at the wall and none of the others knowing quite what to say. Finally Chris cleared his throat. 'Jennifer's got the pup in the car, Laura. I wouldn't mind knowing what killed it. How are you fixed for an autopsy tomorrow?'

'Best invitation I've had all week,' said Laura dully.

Chris smiled abstractedly and wandered off towards his office. Jennifer studied Laura's profile for a few moments, then looked at her watch and said, 'I was going to ask if you fancied going out, Laura, for a drink or something.'

Laura looked round, surprised, and said hesitantly, 'No . . . thanks. Really.'

'You're sure?'

Laura hesitated, then said, 'No, I'm not sure, what's the "or something"?'

'How about dinner at my place?'

'You're on.'

They stopped at an off-licence and stocked up with wine, then drove on to the cottage, where Laura began uncorking the first bottle with a purposeful air while Jennifer started on dinner.

Steven stuck his head into the kitchen long enough to say, 'Hi Laura, don't cook for me Mum, I'm going out. Bye,' and was gone, the door slamming behind him.

Laura smiled. 'The man in your life.'

Jennifer nodded, but added, 'I think I nearly got asked out today.'

'Oh yeah?' said Laura, eager for the gossip.

'The man from the Ministry.'

'Really. I didn't get a proper look at him.'

'I did. It's a shame he didn't quite get round to it. I think he was just about to suggest something completely improper when Sarah bloody Hallam rang.'

They chatted on about trivia as they cooked and ate dinner, Laura needing to unburden herself but finding it difficult to open up to Jennifer. The wine was helping and by the time they were well down the second bottle both of them were slightly drunk.

'So,' said Jennifer finally, settling herself back in her chair. 'Problems with Alan?'

Laura nodded. 'I don't know what's wrong with him.' She paused, took another gulp of wine and looked at Jennifer from under her lashes before going on. 'It's been a nightmare these past few days.'

'Don't you feel you can talk to him?'

'Just at the moment, Jennifer, I . . .'

She broke off, then said hurriedly, 'You don't want to hear my problems. I should go.'

Jennifer shook her head, reached for the wine and filled Laura's glass. 'You don't have to go. Give him a ring. Tell him you're staying if you like, he's not going to mind.'

'At the moment I don't think he'd even notice,' said Laura, sinking back gratefully into the sofa.

She took another drink and murmured, 'I mean . . . I don't know where I am with him. A couple of weeks ago he was fine, now the slightest little thing he's on the ceiling. It was like talking to a stranger this morning.'

'What was it about?'

'The small animal course,' she said disbelievingly. 'It's ridiculous. How can you fall out over a sodding hamster?' She laughed despite herself. 'I thought we'd got past all this but he doesn't want me working. He wants me at home, preferably pregnant.' She smiled ruefully at Jennifer. 'And the way things are going, that would be a miracle.'

There was a pause, then they both started laughing together as Jennifer pulled the cork on another bottle of wine.

Chris was also drinking steadily as he and Colin, sat at a corner table in the Drake Manor, watching a darts match.

'You've got a good 'un there, you know,' said Colin, as Chris put another round of drinks down on the table. 'Your lad.'

'I don't think Murray sees himself as anyone's lad,' laughed Chris.

'I rather got that impression,' said Colin. 'You know he gave me a bollocking?'

Chris raised an eyebrow. 'No, what for?'

'Over-farming. He says that's why I'm getting so much disease. He's not wrong either.'

'You know what to do about it?'

'Win the lottery and get out of farming,' grinned Colin. 'Of course I know what to do – don't do it – but things are never that simple, are they? If you want to make decent money these days you have to keep shifting livestock.'

A loud cheer from the crowd around the dartboard ended the conversation.

'Great, that's us through to the final,' said Colin, draining his pint. 'That should be worth a few pints on the house – sup up, we might even get a lock-in.' He winked at Chris and headed for the bar.

By the time they left the Drake it was well after midnight and both men were drunk. Chris set off to walk home, steering an unsteady course down the street while Colin fell into the back of his waiting taxi. He was snoring by the time the taxi reached the farm and the driver had to shake him awake and then stand waiting while Colin fumbled blearily in his pockets, trying to sort out his change. He was too drunk for mental arithmetic and after dropping a handful of coins into the mud, he finally gave up and handed the driver a tenner, saying, 'Keep it.'

As the taxi pulled away, Colin lurched across the yard, singing to himself as he headed for the pig sheds to make his late-night check. Drunk as he was, the farming routine was too deeply ingrained to be overlooked. He leaned heavily against the wall of the shed, fumbling for his front-door key. Suddenly he stopped dead, instantly sober, staring wide-eyed at one of the pens. On the floor a few yards in front of him, two of the pigs lay dead.

Laura and Jennifer were both pale and slightly hungover when they got to work the next morning, but one glance at Chris told them that they were far from the worst sufferers. He stood nursing the hangover from hell, gripping the edge of the counter in reception like a seasick passenger clutching on to a ship's rail. Maddy gave him an old-fashioned look and turned to deal with a client, while Clare, more sympathetic, went to make some strong black coffee.

The phone on Maddy's desk began to ring, and seeing her tied up with the client, Laura leaned over to answer it. 'Vet centre . . . yes, she is. Is that Michael?'

Jennifer looked up to see Laura smiling knowingly at her.

'I don't know what he wants,' said Jennifer implausibly, taking the phone rather self-consciously as her colleagues suddenly remembered important business elsewhere.

Chris staggered through to his office and sat at his desk with his head in his hands, raising one hand in minimal acknowledgement as Clare brought him some coffee. 'Do you want some aspirin?' she asked solicitously.

He shook his head. 'Just the horse pistol.'

Murray put his head round the door as Clare left, saying loudly, 'Good night last night?' with just the hint of a malicious grin.

Chris held up his hand and shook his head, appealing for Murray to speak more quietly. He pulled himself together with an effort, took a sip of his coffee, shuddered and pushed it away. 'Right, Murray, you wanted to see me about Colin?'

Murray nodded, unsure of how to begin. 'Have you seen his drugs account?'

'What about it?'

'The quantity of drugs he's getting through?'

Chris gave him a quizzical look.

'This is a very sick farm, Chris.' Murray paused, reluctant to step on Chris's toes. 'He's not my client of course . . .'

Chris waved that away. 'It's all right, Murray, say what you have to say.'

'I dropped the stuff off yesterday as you asked, but he's using the antibiotics to combat the effects of poor management. By rights we should report him.'

'Do you think he'll do something about it?'

Murray took a deep breath. 'Look, that's not really the point. He said you'd not been down there for about seven months.' He dropped his gaze. 'Tell me to mind my own business, but I don't agree with him using a high volume of drugs on repeat prescription. Not with animals kept like that.' He paused and looked up again, challenging Chris with his eyes. 'Like I said, though, he's not my client . . .' He turned to go.

'Murray, wait,' called Chris. 'Thanks.'

Murray turned back to face him again. 'You're his friend, Chris. Why don't you pay him a friendly visit?'

Chris nodded and pushed back his chair. 'The air up there on the tops just might save my life.'

'It might,' laughed Murray, 'as long as you stay upwind of the pig sheds.'

Chris drove at half his usual breakneck speed up out of Whitton towards the moors, where the dull, barren brown of winter was already becoming tinged with green. The day was cool but fine and he drove with his window open, gulping down lungfuls of air, his head clearing slowly, painfully, with the fresh air. When he reached Moors End, he paused for a moment to watch the JCB, silhouetted against the sky, digging up clawfuls of earth like a heron stabbing its beak into the estuary mud.

Elaine and Colin were at work in the yard, with Colin nursing a hangover every bit as awful as Chris's. He looked up as Chris approached. 'Have you come to finish me off?' he asked.

Chris nodded. 'A bullet for each of us.'

'Now there's an opportunity,' said Elaine cheerily. 'Chris, when's Patricia coming to see me?'

'I know, I know, it's been ages . . .' he began.

'Well, don't make excuses,' said Elaine briskly, 'you know

where we live.' She smiled and went up to the house to make some coffee.

Chris watched her go, then turned to Colin. 'Doesn't change, does she?'

'Neither do you.'

Chris looked up, puzzled.

'Come on, Chris,' said Colin. 'This isn't just a social call, is it?'

Chris shook his head, slightly shamefaced.

'Come and have a look,' said Colin. 'You'll see I've already started to follow Murray's advice.' He led him into one of the sheds, where the pigs had been spread out a little, with some of them moved into the yard. 'I've started moving them, I just need a bit more time.' He eyed Chris nervously.

'They still need more room, though,' said Chris. 'You need more space, Colin. That's your answer – more sheds . . . But a lot of this is my fault, I should have been here more often.'

They walked back into the yard, and Chris broke off as he saw the carcasses of the dead pigs lying in a trailer.

'Yesterday,' said Colin, in answer to the unspoken question.

'Why didn't you report them?'

'I didn't find them till last night.'

Chris nodded, but then another thought struck him. 'You have told us about your other deaths, haven't you?'

'Yeah,' said Colin, a little too quickly. 'Well, most of 'em.'

He caught Chris's despairing look. 'I know, it's a health risk. I am trying, Chris. I'm going to build more sheds, as soon as that lot have finished, there's loads of land up there.' He gestured up towards Moors End Camp, where the JCB now sat silent on the skyline.

Colin turned to look at the carcasses and blurted out anxiously, 'It'll be fine though, won't it? If I do that?'

'Of course it will,' said Chris with a wry smile as he saw Colin's expression of disbelief. 'Trust me.'

'What, after last night?'

While Chris was up at Moors End, Laura and Jennifer were carrying out the autopsy on the foxhound pup. 'Very enlarged spleen,' said Laura, absorbed in her work. She paused, baffled for a moment. 'Have you seen this?'

Jennifer moved across to the operating table, looked down and shook her head slowly. 'Are we sure this is just an infection?'

Laura continued removing the dog's spleen, her conversation coming in isolated fragments. 'I want to take some more blood samples . . . Get smears to the VI Centre . . . See if they've got any better idea. There's a massive white blood cell count.' She was both puzzled and intrigued by the case, the dog's cadaver a particularly complex puzzle to be analysed and decoded.

'No idea what killed it yet?' asked Jennifer.

'To be honest, I haven't a clue, but it's something much more specific and deadly in its action than a routine infection.'

She stepped away from the table and pulled off her operating mask and gloves. 'I want Chris to look at the samples.'

He was not in his office and she went through to reception to see if he was back from his calls, but instead of Chris, she found Alan, who had just walked in from the car-park and was standing hesitantly, just inside the door. He hurried over to her, but she gave no sign of welcome, standing impassively waiting for him to speak.

He looked nervously around the busy reception area and asked, 'Can we talk? Somewhere else?'

'I'm busy,' said Laura flatly.

'No change there then,' said Alan, instantly regretting his bitter tone as Laura glared at him and then stepped through the door leading to the car-park. Alan followed her as she strode over to his car and opened the driver's door. She stood there pointedly waiting for him to go but Alan faced her and demanded, 'Where were you last night?'

Laura shook her head. 'We can't do this here.'

'Oh, well, that's all right then,' said Alan sarcastically.

'It was late . . .' she began wearily.

'You're telling me. Where were you?'

'Look, I'm sorry. I was going to phone, we were going to have one last drink. I don't know what happened . . .' She broke off. 'I can't believe you've come here.'

Alan flinched and looked away, hurt.

Laura drew breath and spoke in measured tones. 'Look, I should have told you where I was. I'm sorry.' She looked straight into his eyes. 'We can't go on like this.'

Alan returned the look wearily, suddenly spent. 'Do you know where I should have been next week? Birmingham. I know that doesn't sound much but that's Birmingham, Alabama, not the other one.'

He had her full attention. She waited for the explanation.

'American clients. They asked for me in person apparently, but I told them I didn't want it.'

Laura, stunned, said nothing.

'You can imagine how that went down ... how it looks,' continued Alan. 'The next thing I know is they're saying I won't get a partnership because I've got a conflict of interests. I'm compromised.'

'A conflict of interests?' queried Laura.

'I won't do anything that'll take me away from you.'

'Me? Why didn't you tell me, Alan?' asked Laura, dismayed.

He shrugged. 'I'm telling you now.'

There was a long silence. 'Look, there's no point in arguing,' said Alan, hopelessly. 'You're right, I shouldn't have bothered coming here, it was a stupid thing to do. Anyway, you've got things to do.' He gestured towards the practice and made to get into the car.

'Alan. What time will you be home tonight?' asked Laura, more gently.

'I'm not going into work. I've phoned in sick, taken the day off to sort a few things out. I mean, no one's going to miss me,' he added pathetically.

'If I get back as soon as I can?' asked Laura.

He nodded. 'I can't change my mind though.'

'I don't mean that. I mean . . . us.'

'Yeah, OK.'

Laura half smiled. 'It's a date then.'

She went back inside and carried on working on the autopsy and packing and checking samples for the VI Centre, throughout the afternoon and into the evening.

'Would you like me to stay on to help?' asked Jennifer anxiously, but Laura waved her away.

'No, you go and have a great time with the Man from the Ministry.'

Jennifer smiled and then hurried out, leaving Laura staring down a microscope.

She worked on methodically, staining a series of slides to test for increasingly obscure and unusual conditions and breaking off only to phone Alan and warn him that she would be late. She felt a momentary pang of guilt at his mournful tone down the phone but forgot it quickly as she again buried herself in her work.

Around nine o'clock, Chris tapped on the door and came in with a cup of coffee for them. Laura took hers gratefully, stretching and yawning and then rubbing her eyes.

'How's it going?' asked Chris gently.

She shrugged. 'Very enlarged spleen, inflammation of the liver. Lymph nodes were up. I've taken some swabs for culture and sent samples off to the VI.'

'But you still don't know what killed it?'

She smiled wearily. 'No, it must have been suicide.'

'Drink your coffee and go home.'

'Is that your prescription? Anyway, I've only got a couple more to do.'

Chris thought for a moment. 'Jaundice?'

She laughed. 'Are we talking about this or my marriage?'

'Anything you want to tell me about?'

'No, not really. Thanks. We've got some problems but we'll sort them out.'

He nodded and turned to go as Laura leaned over the microscope again. As she examined the slide, she stiffened and called urgently to Chris, her voice filling with fear. 'Chris . . . I think it's anthrax.'

Chris stopped in his tracks and turned back aghast. 'Are you sure?'

She nodded but gestured to the microscope. 'See for yourself.'

He peered down it, while Laura looked on in silence, then he abruptly stood up and strode over to the antibiotics cabinet and began frantically riffling through it, looking for penicillin.

He tried to brief Laura on the steps that they now had to take but he had difficulty marshalling his thoughts, for he was more than a little panicked, deeply aware of the dangers of anthrax infection. 'We need to tell the VI at Weybridge.'

'Look, er . . . if you're going down to the hunt kennels . . .' began Laura, but he interrupted.

'And can you get on to the HSE? They'll have to shut it down. MAFF will want to isolate the source.'

'So where's it come from?' asked Laura.

That brought him up short. He thought for a moment. 'It's a sporing bacillus. It lives in the soil, then when you break the ground . . .' He shuddered. 'The last case I heard of was in the corner of a field. Cattle. They found out later it had been used as a knacker's yard in the 1870s. Once it's in the soil, it stays there for at least a hundred years.'

'Do you think it's from carcasses the kennels have used for feed?'

Chris shrugged. 'It's so rare these days.' He began thinking aloud. 'Two dozen farms, a couple of smallholdings. They're all sending carcasses to the hunt kennel.'

'Are we in danger, Chris?' asked Laura, her eyes never moving from his face.

'Anthrax isn't that easy to catch.'

'That's not what I'm asking.'

He shook his head. 'I don't know.' He pulled a packet out of the cabinet and said abruptly, 'Two of these, now.'

'Penicillin?'

He shrugged. 'It works on pigs.'

They both smiled fleetingly at the gallows humour.

'You need an injection from your GP as well,' said Chris.

'There's also Jennifer. She helped with the autopsy,' explained Laura. Chris scooped up his jacket, shoving the penicillin into his pocket. 'Can you ring the others? Tell them what's happened? I'll take some penicillin to Jennifer.'

He turned to go, but she called out, 'Chris, wait a second.'

He paused, half-way out of the door.

'I need to go home for a few minutes, before I go to the kennels.'

He hesitated, then said, 'Of course, but as soon as you get hold of Murray, tell him to get started straight away and be there as quick as you can.'

Chris rushed out and drove off at top speed.

Chapter 18

Jennifer and Michael had only just got back from their night out. Michael pulled up outside the cottage, switched off the engine and looked appreciatively around, taking in the view of the river, shimmering in the moonlight.

'It might not be much . . .' said Jennifer.

'But it's a mortgage,' supplied Michael.

'It's not even that.' She glanced across at him, smiled and said, 'It's been a really great night.'

'Yes, it has, such a great night that it seems a pity to end it so soon . . . I suppose a coffee's out the question?'

They looked at each other for a long moment and then Jennifer said, 'Come on in.'

As she showed Michael in and closed the door, Steven came bounding down the stairs in his underpants. Jennifer looked up surprised, having expected him still to be out, but Steven was even more surprised to see Michael standing there. There was a pause as all three of them gaped at each other and then Jennifer, recovering her poise first, said, 'Er . . . Michael, this is Steven.' Michael, though every bit as fazed as Steven, masked it well, extending his hand confidently for a routine, masculine handshake as though greeting a strange man in his underpants was all in a day's work for him. 'Michael Fleet. Ministry of Agriculture.'

Chris pulled up outside the cottage a few minutes later. He moved hurriedly from the car and knocked on the door. As he waited for an answer, he glanced around him and recognized Michael's car, but before he could react, Jennifer had opened the door.

'I'm, er . . . sorry to disturb your evening,' said Chris, hesitating on the doorstep.

'You're not disturbing anything,' said Jennifer. 'Come in, I'll get you some coffee.'

Chris stepped into the hallway, murmuring a greeting to Michael but too taken up with the breaking crisis to be diverted for more than a second.

'Jennifer.' She stopped and looked round, startled by the gravity in his voice. 'The pup from the hunt kennel. It was anthrax.'

Her eyes widened in fear and she put a hand to her forehead, her mind racing.

'Yeah, I know,' he said quietly. 'Look, I'm sure everything's going to be fine, Jen. Honestly.' He unpacked the drugs. 'It's penicillin. I want you to take some, just as a precaution, and you need to see your GP first thing, all right?'

She nodded, numb with shock, as Michael cut in, 'Does the hunt kennel know?'

'I'm on my way there now,' said Chris, more sharply than necessary. 'I'm going to get the place sealed off, just as a precaution.'

He hesitated, confused by his reaction to Michael being in Jennifer's house but unable to dwell on it with so much else on his mind. He said hurriedly, 'Look, I've got to go. I'm sure it's nothing to worry about, Jennifer. I'll see you first thing in the morning, all right?'

As he turned to go, Jennifer followed him out. 'If you want any help . . .'

He said, 'No,' abruptly, then added, 'Thanks,' in a less harsh voice.

As he walked towards his car, Jennifer called after him. 'Chris. Are you all right?'

'Me?'

'Yeah.'

Chris stood, gazing stupidly at her. In all the panic he had not given a thought to himself and it took him a second to realize what Jennifer was talking about. Finally it clicked. He smiled and said, 'Yes. I'm fine,' waved and got into the Range Rover, driving off in a flurry of gravel.

The kennels were ablaze with light and Murray was already at work when Chris turned down the lane. Sarah hurried towards Chris as he began unloading kit and antibiotics from the boot. 'Tell me this isn't happening, Chris.'

Chris gave her an understanding smile. 'We'll do what we can, Mrs Hallam.'

'But anthrax? I mean, that's biological warfare.'

'It's a naturally occurring infection, which was then developed as a weapon. I'd like to give the horses an injection of antibiotics.'

She looked at him sharply. 'Can't you test them for it?'

Chris shook his head. 'We can test your carcasses. There isn't a test for anthrax in live animals. The disease has to show itself and that's only happened in the dogs. If we're lucky it'll end there.'

'And if we're not?'

Chris and Murray exchanged glances. Neither had an answer.

'The only anthrax vaccine is for military use,' said Murray carefully. 'The best we can do is treat them with penicillin.'

Sarah walked away from them, distraught, as Murray gestured around the yard saying, 'This is going to take all night.'

'Then the sooner we start . . .' said Chris grimly. 'We've got to isolate the source, Murray, and I want to inject all the horses. No sign of Laura yet?'

Murray shook his head.

'Can you get on to her then and give her a gentle hurry-up to come and give you a hand?'

Murray reached for his mobile phone as Chris headed for the stables.

Laura was still wearing her coat, standing in her kitchen. She was simultaneously sawing at a loaf with the breadknife to make a quick sandwich and trying to talk sympathetically to Alan about his job in the five minutes before she had to leave again.

'Are you sure you're all right?' said Alan.

'I'm fine. Honestly. Look, I'm sorry about this, we needed to talk.'

'It'll wait.'

She tried desperately to get her mind in the right frame. 'It's just a temporary setback, isn't it? They're not going to fire you?'

'They wouldn't do a thing like that . . . but I might have to resign.'

She stared at him, puzzled. 'They can't make you do that.'

He shrugged. 'The word's gone round. They don't think I'm committed. I won't get the partnership, everyone wants it. And of course everyone says they're squarely behind you, because that way the knife goes straight between the shoulder blades. I can stay for as long as I like but as far as the work goes it's downhill from here.'

'Is this what's been wrong?' asked Laura.

'You've noticed,' he said bitterly.

Laura looked up, still holding the breadknife. 'You know that whatever happens, Alan, I'll be right behind you.'

Touched, Alan looked longingly at Laura. He glanced down at the knife and smiled. 'Will you put that bloody knife down first?'

Laura grinned and dropped the knife, but as they kissed each other tenderly, the phone started ringing. Laura did not answer it immediately, giving Alan another kiss and a lingering look. Finally she picked up the phone. 'Yeah, I'll be right there, Murray.' She hung up, blew Alan a kiss and hurried out.

A bitterly cold wind was blowing off the moor at six the next morning, as Jennifer and Chris parked their cars in the yard of the kennels and walked across to join Murray and Laura, their faces grim and purposeful. Even the dogs seemed to share the sense of foreboding, for there was none of the hound chorus that usually greeted them, only silence. Jennifer had snatched a few hours' sleep, Chris a couple, but both Murray and Laura had worked through the night. They looked up wearily as Chris and Jennifer approached.

'We're about half-way through,' said Laura.

Chris looked at the mound of carcasses Murray had been testing and asked, 'Nothing so far?'

Murray shook his head and turned towards the next one.

'Careful,' said Chris.

Murray gave him a look and then took a sample from a dead pig, making a nick in the ear to take blood without exposing spores to the air.

Chris and Jennifer saw Sarah coming towards them and went to meet her.

'Nothing overnight?' asked Chris.

Sarah shook her head. 'They all seem fine . . . so far at least.'

She looked as if she had not slept either, and had lost all her customary haughtiness. Her face was pale and lined, and she darted looks nervously between Chris and Jennifer, seeking whatever reassurance she could find.

A Land Rover drove into the yard. Sarah looked questioningly at them, and Chris, recognizing the driver, said, 'Health and Safety.'

Just then Murray hurried across to where they were standing. 'Where are the pigs from, Mrs Hallam?'

'The pigs? Moors End.'

Murray closed his eyes for a second, then said flatly to Chris, 'There's anthrax in the first one.'

Stunned, Chris stood stock still for a second, then shook himself and began to bark out orders. 'There were two, Murray, test the other one as well. Jennifer, you'd better get back to the practice for morning surgery. Murray and Laura, you finish up here. I'll call MAFF and then go and see Colin at Moors End. I think it's my responsibility, don't you?'

Murray shifted uncomfortably but said nothing, and after a moment, Chris gave a wintry smile and then walked away, lost in thought.

By nine o'clock Murray had finished examining the carcasses. He had stripped off his mask and gown, and was carefully disposing of his gloves. Laura helped him pack away as Sarah joined them.

'We're finished,' said Laura.

'And other than the two pigs, there's no sign of any more infection,' added Murray.

'We're clear?' asked Sarah, confused.

Laura shook her head. 'Not exactly. Anthrax . . . it's like that. It comes and goes. Sometimes we don't know why.' She paused and gave her a sympathetic look. 'I'm afraid MAFF will still seal the kennels.'

Sarah stood lost in thought for a moment, confused and upset. 'I just don't understand. I never feed pigs to the dogs.'

'You've been using sheep and cattle for feed?' asked Laura.

'Cattle.'

'The anthrax spores come from the pigs,' said Murray. 'If there are breaks in the skin, they get into other carcasses. They could be inside anything that's been on the yard.'

Up at Moors End, Colin had waved Elaine and Danny off on a

shopping trip and was walking, whistling, across the yard, feeling that everything was right with the world, when he began to notice that it seemed strangely quiet. His step faltered and he looked around, trying to pinpoint the source of his mounting unease. Then he moved towards the sheds, breaking into a run. He flung the door open and reeled back as if he had been slapped in the face, seeing several pigs lying dead on the ground.

He turned and sprinted to the house, dialling the practice number frantically. 'Maddy . . . Colin English . . . Is Chris there? . . . Have you any idea when he'll be back?' He glanced out of the kitchen window and saw Chris's Range Rover pulling up in the yard. 'Never mind.' Colin dropped the phone without another word and ran out of the house to meet him.

'Chris, there's more dead, lots of them . . .' began Colin, but his words died in his throat as he saw the look on Chris's weary, haggard face.

Chris also registered the near-panic in Colin's eyes but could do nothing to soften the blow. 'I'm sorry, Colin, there's no easy way to say this. It's anthrax.'

Colin staggered and almost fell. 'Anthrax?'

'We've tested the carcasses from yesterday. There's an outbreak at the hunt kennels. We had no way of knowing until we'd done the tests.'

'Yeah, but . . .' began Colin, desperate for any straw to clutch. 'You're sure they're from here?'

Chris nodded. 'MAFF are going to seal the farm.'

Colin slumped against the doorframe. 'Well that's it, then, we're finished.'

Chris shook his head and said gently, 'It doesn't mean you're finished. They're not going to destroy healthy livestock. We can probably treat your infected animals. Even if it's in the soil, once MAFF isolate the source, they can deal with it.'

'How did it get there?' asked Colin, his face crumpled and hopeless.

'I've no idea.'

'What's going to happen?'

'They won't let you move any more animals for the time being.'

Colin stared dully at Chris, realization slowly sinking in. 'But if

I can't move livestock, Chris, I can't sell pigs. And if I can't sell pigs, then I'm finished.'

'Look, let's just take this one step at a time,' said Chris. 'There are some things we need to do straight away. Where are Elaine and Danny?'

Colin stopped open-mouthed, starting to panic. 'Elaine and Danny, they were on the yard all yesterday!'

'Where are they, Colin?' asked Chris, gently but firmly.

'They've gone shopping, I don't know where.'

'Then we'll try and find them at all the places they might be. Don't worry, there's no need to panic.'

Colin looked sceptically at him. There seemed every reason to panic, as Chris's demeanour confirmed. As they walked hurriedly into the house, Colin glanced up the lane to see the first MAFF vehicle turning in. MAFF officials, suited like spacemen, jumped out and began erecting barriers across the lane.

Colin phoned all the local shops and left messages for Elaine in each one, but there was no returning call and Elaine and Danny drove home to Moors End an hour later, blissfully unaware that anything was wrong. When they turned into the lane, however, Elaine had to brake sharply to avoid a moon-suited MAFF official, who stepped out in front of her.

She gasped, 'What the . . .' but suddenly everything was happening too fast for her, as more men in protective clothing surrounded the car and a police inspector ran towards them.

Elaine sat frozen, unable to take everything in, and Danny began to gibber with fright as the inspector shouted to her through the closed window.

'Can you move the car? Can you move the car back, please?'

'Stay here, Danny,' said Elaine abruptly, stepping out of the car. 'What's going on?' she demanded.

'Move the car back,' said the inspector.

'No, I won't. I bloody live here.'

'The farm is being sealed and cleaned.' He shot her a look. 'It's anthrax.'

Elaine pushed past him and ran down the lane.

Colin was wandering round the yard, bewildered and helpless, while MAFF personnel examined the pigs and Chris talked urgently to Michael. Colin heard the shouting up the lane and turned to see Elaine running towards him. He grabbed her to him as if his life depended on it. 'I tried to phone. Are you all right?'

Elaine did not reply, not knowing quite what to say, as she looked around her at the ruin of their farm. Colin tried to reassure her. 'There's no need to worry, love. Chris'll sort it out.'

She looked sharply at him. 'Is it true, Colin? Is it anthrax?'

He nodded.

'Then how can he sort it out?'

Chris moved across to join them, already defensive as he spoke to Elaine. 'I just thought there was a high level of infection, Elaine. I . . . we thought it was pneumonia.'

'Pneumonia! You're supposed to be our vet,' shouted Elaine, angrily shrugging off Colin's restraining hand. 'You were here a couple of days ago and everything seemed fine then, did it?'

'I didn't know it was anthrax.'

Elaine gave Colin a disbelieving look.

'It's not Chris's fault,' said Colin hastily. 'It's very rare and hard to diagnose.'

She ignored him, taking another long slow look around the wreckage of the farm.

'Is it as bad as it looks?' she finally asked.

Colin nodded. 'They're going to stop us moving livestock.'

Elaine blinked as she realized the implications. She looked at Chris. 'Will we have to leave?'

'No. It looks bad, but once they've isolated the source, things'll calm down. Look, why don't you stay with us, just for tonight?' As he saw the challenging look in Elaine's eye, he went on hurriedly, 'I know there's nothing to celebrate but I think it would be easier . . . with Danny . . .' He did not have to complete the sentence.

'Yeah, thanks, Chris,' said Colin hastily.

Chris intercepted a sharp look from Elaine to Colin and said, 'There's no point in staying with this going on, Elaine. There's nothing you can do.'

She gave a grudging nod.

'Collect some stuff for the night,' said Chris, 'and then we'll need to get you and Danny to the doctor. Just for a check-up, purely routine,' he added nervously as he saw Elaine's murderous look.

At sunset, Colin locked the house for the night, carrying an overnight bag and a carrier bag. He was alone on the yard, save for the MAFF guard who would stay there, keeping out intruders until the farm was declared safe again. Colin drove dejectedly down into Whitton and pulled up outside Chris and Patricia's house. Through the lighted window he could see Danny sitting on the floor doing a jigsaw with Abby and Charlotte. Elaine stood in the doorway, half watching the television news but really watching Danny.

Colin walked round to the door and rang the bell. Patricia opened it, expecting to see Chris, and did a double-take when she saw Colin standing on the doorstep, dishevelled and utterly exhausted. He tried to smile but could not manage it.

He looked past Patricia to where Elaine was standing at the end of the hallway and hurried to her, searching her face for the answer to his question.

'Danny?'

'He's all right,' said Elaine.

Colin hugged her, overjoyed. 'Thank God for that. Are you?'

'Yeah. She said if we started feeling ill we should ring the surgery and she'll come and see us.' She looked him over critically. 'How about you?'

He shrugged. 'I'm fine.'

He looked round at Patricia, who took the hint and disappeared into the living-room, leaving them alone. 'They've sealed the farm,' he said miserably. 'I'm sorry.'

'No point in being sorry,' said Elaine. 'If they've sealed the farm . . .'

'But we're due compensation.'

'And how long is that going to take?'

He shrugged. 'We'll be fine in a couple of days.'

She shook her head firmly. 'We'll be under in a couple of days. We're going to have to do something, Colin, but we're not going to be doing it here, not any more. If we can't move the livestock, we've got no cashflow. We can't expand anyway, because we can't use Moors End. They're not going to be selling that land now, and I don't think we'd want to buy it, do you?'

He shuddered but struggled to sound convincing as he argued. 'But even if the farm's finished, that doesn't mean we are. We can start again.'

Elaine gazed levelly at him. 'And how many times are we supposed to start again?'

He had no answer. He looked at Elaine, then dropped his gaze and put his head in his hands as his bravado evaporated.

Elaine took a deep breath, bracing herself for an argument. 'I've spoken to Derek.'

'Wales?' said Colin dismayed.

'I know, but it's not going to be for ever, is it? He's got work, just for now. He's looking for a pigman.'

'We can't just leave . . .' began Colin, but Elaine, losing patience, interrupted angrily.

'We're finished here, Colin. Can't you see that?'

She regretted her flash of temper instantly and went to him, holding him tight in her arms. Colin looked up to see Danny watching them from the doorway and made a show of being gruff. 'And how long have you been ear-wigging?'

'Are we going to Wales?' asked Danny.

'Me and your mum have got to talk about it, Danny.' He paused and glanced at Elaine. 'But I'm going to speak to your Uncle Derek.'

Danny's face lit up. 'Excellent!'

Colin gave a resigned smile. 'Well, that's that decided.'

He and Elaine looked at each other in silence for a few moments.

'We'll be all right, Colin,' said Elaine gently. 'It's a setback but it doesn't mean we're beaten.'

'Beaten? Us? That'll be the day.'

She hugged him again, but her smile faded as soon as her face was hidden from him. She stared unseeingly over his shoulder, thoughtful and sad.

Chris had been driving aimlessly for a couple of hours, going over and over the events of the last few days and their possible consequences. The more he thought about it, the more depressed he became. He imagined that he had been turning at random as he drove along, but he came out of his reverie with a start when he saw the JCB at Moors End outlined on the skyline against the setting sun.

He cursed and turned the Range Rover round, driving back down into Whitton. When he reached the practice it was still ablaze with light as Michael and the MAFF staff combed through the practice records. When Chris came through the door, Michael was standing with his back to him, holding out a computer printout to Jennifer and asking, 'Is this his drugs account?'

She glanced at it and said, 'Yeah ...' but broke off when she saw Chris.

Michael followed her gaze and smiled apologetically. Everything stopped as they all turned to look at Chris, then Michael broke the silence.

'Maddy said to use your office.'

Chris nodded, expressionless, and Michael disappeared inside, closing the door.

Chris stood there looking lost and broken, and Jennifer felt a wave of tenderness for him. 'Are you all right?' she asked.

'Yeah. Fine,' he said grimly, staring at the closed door of his office.

She gestured towards it. 'They're only checking Colin's records, trying to find out when the outbreak started.'

He nodded distractedly, scarcely seeming to hear her.

'This isn't your fault, Chris. You know that, don't you?'

'That's not the point,' he said wearily. 'I've been prescribing antibiotics.'

'But you weren't to know it was anthrax.'

'Jennifer, I haven't been there in over seven months. I've been repeat prescribing for the whole of that time.'

Jennifer was incredulous. She looked to Murray for confirmation. He nodded but tried to temper it, saying, 'Colin's been a client for years.'

'But you didn't see the animals?' asked Jennifer.

Chris shook his head. 'I left it up to Colin. You know how it is.' He shrugged, shamefacedly. 'Show me a vet who doesn't repeat prescribe.'

Jennifer let the silence speak for her.

'Look', said Chris, 'this doesn't involve you two. Why don't you go home?'

Jennifer shook her head. 'No, I'm staying.'

'I'd rather stay as well,' said Murray. 'I know I'm only the deckchair attendant but I'd rather go down with the ship.'

Chris smiled gratefully at them.

Jennifer and Chris began sorting through the file of past farm visit lab reports, hoping to find anything which might stand as evidence that he had visited Moors End in person at some time in the past year, but before they had got far, Michael appeared in the doorway. His face was impassive, giving no clues, as he said, 'Right, Chris, we're ready for you now.'

Chris straightened his shoulders as he followed him through, ready for the worst.

A MAFF staff member stood by his desk. Michael walked over to it and picked up a battered-looking book. He began leafing through it, glancing occasionally at Chris. 'We've isolated the source. It was recorded in this farm diary from June 1944.' He began reading, saying, 'You're not going to believe this: "Worse today than yesterday. Six suspected cases, three more dead in the night and all animals that had been strong and healthy. Wilson calling again this afternoon, but still at a loss."'

He closed the diary and put it back on the desk. 'Wilson was his vet. He thought it was pneumonia.' He shot Chris a quick glance. 'Then the army evacuated an entire camp overnight and two days later there was an outbreak of anthrax.'

'Not much changes, does it?' said Chris. 'What's going to happen to Colin?'

'As far as the farm's concerned? He'll be prevented from moving the livestock until the farm's free from anthrax. At least we know where it came from now . . . but it's early days.'

Chris looked down at the printout lying on the desk and Michael intercepted his glance. 'You can't be blamed for failing to spot anthrax, Chris. However . . .' He gestured to the printout.

Chris nodded. 'I've been repeat prescribing instead of knowing what was going on at his farm. I'm his vet and I lost track of the quantity of drugs he was using. I accept full responsibility.' He waited nervously for Michael's next move.

'We all make mistakes, Chris.'

Chris stiffened and looked at him sharply, but Michael was not being ironic or patronizing.

'I mean, for what it's worth, I think it was a mistake,' Michael went on, 'and as soon as you realized something was wrong, you tried to sort it out.'

Chris stared at him blankly, failing to take the hint first time.

'After Murray told you he was concerned,' prompted Michael, 'would it be fair to say you were just too busy to check . . . on this one, isolated occasion? If anyone asks?'

'Er, yes. It could be,' said Chris, his mind emerging slowly from its fog.

'Why don't we just say that, then?' said Michael, glancing at his colleague, who nodded, impassive.

Michael picked up his papers and prepared to leave, giving Chris a brief smile. 'I know it's a stupid thing to say, but don't worry.'

Chris managed a smile in return.

Jennifer left Chris alone in his office for an hour while she busied herself with her own work, but then, concerned, she tapped on his door and went in. Chris was knocking back a glass of whisky from a half-empty bottle sitting on his desk. He gave her a guilty smile as she asked, 'Are you all right?'

'Me? Tired. Worried. But not quite drunk. You should be at home.'

'You're the one who should be at home. Come on, I'll give you a lift.'

He stood up unsteadily and followed her out.

She tried to bolster his confidence as she drove him home, but Chris had only half his mind on the conversation, and not just because of his worries about Moors End. He was also very aware of – and aroused by – Jennifer sitting close to him, and was trying not to let it show.

'Anthrax is the last thing on anyone's mind, Chris,' said Jennifer. 'Nobody looks for it. You made a mistake, that's all.'

'You're sounding like Michael.'

Jennifer glanced inquiringly at him, wanting to know what Michael had said.

'I neglected Moors End but it was an isolated incident.' He looked across at Jennifer and half-raised his hand, wanting to touch her, but then let it fall back into his lap. 'Nice bloke, isn't he?' he said, trying to hide the jealous note in his voice.

Jennifer gave him a sideways look but carried on trying to lift him. 'Do you want to hear something funny? When you came round, he'd just walked in on Steven in his underpants . . . That's Steven in his underpants, not Michael. He said he wouldn't have minded only he thought Steven was my boyfriend.'

Chris gave a forced laugh as Jennifer turned into his road. 'Will you see him again?' he asked carefully.

'I'm not sure he'll see me,' smiled Jennifer. 'What do you think?'

'I think it's not up to me,' said Chris, in a voice that suggested he wished it was.

'You know what I think?' said Jennifer. 'It's more trouble than it's worth. I've just got out of one relationship. The last thing I want is another.'

Chris said nothing, becoming increasingly uncomfortable.

'Chris?' prompted Jennifer, as she pulled up outside his house.

'I don't know what you're asking me for.' He gazed longingly at her for a moment, then opened the car door. 'I'll see you tomorrow. Thanks for the lift.'

'Chris?' He checked and turned back towards her. 'You're not going to sit up all night thinking about this? I do worry about you sometimes.'

Chris smiled then leaned over to kiss Jennifer lightly. He pulled back for a second, looked into her eyes and then kissed her again, insistently. Jennifer began to respond, but then pushed him away, protesting.

There was an embarrassed silence. 'I'm sorry . . .' muttered Chris.

'What was that?' asked Jennifer, confused.

He shook his head. 'I'm sorry. I'd better go.'

'Chris?' He turned reluctantly to look at her. 'What was that?'

He gazed at her, not knowing what to say, then abruptly got out of the car, needing to get away from her as quickly as possible. He paused on the doorstep, about to turn and say something else, but Patricia opened the door, killing all prospect of further conversation. Jennifer drove off without looking up at Patricia, as Chris turned and walked past her into the house.

Patricia stared after him, puzzled, then closed the door, as Chris stood in the hall, desperately fighting for his equilibrium.

'Murray called,' said Patricia. 'What happened?'

'Yeah, sorry,' said Chris distractedly. 'I er . . . It'll be fine.

MAFF wanted to go through some records. There's nothing I can do, so there's no point in worrying.'

'Murray doesn't think it's that simple.'

'Murray?' said Chris uncomprehendingly, still reeling from the incident with Jennifer.

Patricia realized that he had not been listening. 'He's just come off the phone. Look, I know everyone repeat prescribes, Chris, but that's not how MAFF are going to see it.'

Chris suddenly could not take any more. 'Patricia,' he said irritably. 'Look, I'm sorry, I can't talk about this. Not right now.'

She looked up sharply at him but then said gently, 'Sorry. I wasn't thinking.'

Chris went upstairs, closed and locked the bathroom door behind him and leaned his forehead against the cool tiles, trying to stop his mind racing.

Chris went in to the practice early the next morning and paced around anxiously, waiting for Jennifer. By the time everyone else had arrived, she had not appeared. 'No sign of Jennifer, yet?' he asked Maddy for the third time. She glanced at her watch and gave him a puzzled smile. 'Give her a chance, it's only ten past nine.'

As she was speaking, Jennifer came in and walked up to the desk, brisk and business-like as usual. 'Morning, Maddy, can you get on to Taylor's and tell them I'll be twenty minutes?'

'Mathers phoned,' called Clare.

Jennifer nodded. 'I'll ring them from the car.'

She turned to go into her office, saying cautiously, 'Morning, Chris,' as she passed him.

'Hi.'

There was a brief embarrassed silence then she moved on. Chris stared stupidly after her until reality intruded, in the shape of Maddy with a stack of queried invoices.

'I'll look at those in a minute, Maddy,' he said, setting off after Jennifer.

She was gathering equipment together as he came into her office. He stood just inside the door. 'About last night, Jen. Do you think you could . . . forget it?'

She thought for a moment, then said, 'It's forgotten.' She snapped her bag shut and walked past him, down the corridor.

As she was crossing the car-park, Michael's car pulled into the yard. She stopped, surprised, and walked over to him. 'Hello, Michael, I thought you'd be tied up with Moors End.'

'I'm on my way there now, but I er . . . I thought you should know. I did some asking round yesterday. Chris might get a written warning, but no further action.'

'Thanks.'

'I never said that,' he went on, nervously. 'If you could keep it between you and Chris.'

'Of course.'

There was a silence. 'Look,' said Michael. 'I was going to say, we should go out again. I mean . . .'

Jennifer had already thought hard about it and made her decision. 'I'm sorry, Michael. I can't see it working. I don't want to waste your time and I don't want to lie. I'm not ready for this.'

'I know it's the wrong time to ask.'

'No, you're right.' She paused and gave a sad smile. 'It's . . . the wrong time to ask.'

Michael sighed and nodded, then drove slowly away.

Chris stood at his window, watching them talking from behind the blinds and imagining the worst. After Michael had driven off, Chris gazed unseen at Jennifer for a minute, then closed the blinds as if trying to shut her out of his mind for good.

Michael drove slowly up to Moors End. The farm was quiet but Murray was there, taking the temperatures of the pigs which had survived the outbreak. As Michael came over to him, Murray nodded towards one of the sheds. 'There's still some pneumonia. No more sign of anthrax . . . at least not yet.'

Michael gestured to another shed. 'With a bit of luck it'll be the same in there.'

Murray gave him a surprised look.

'It'll be days before we're certain,' said Michael. 'Anthrax comes and goes.'

They heard a diesel engine starting up and looked round to see the JCB up at Moors Ends Camp wheel around and start to move off the site.

'We've told them to stop digging,' said Michael. 'As long as the soil is not disturbed, there's a chance that the farm will stay clear. There's not much more we can do except wait.'

Murray glanced around the yard. 'He's finished, isn't he?'

Michael nodded, but said, 'He might get some compensation.'

Murray snorted. 'Pigs might fly.'

Chapter 19

Murray drove back down towards Whitton, bone-tired. He had seen enough pigs in the last few days to last him a lifetime, but there was every chance that sheep would rapidly be joining them on his least favourite animals list, for lambing time was beginning to build to its crescendo.

The lanes were clogged with early season visitors, gasping with delight at the banks of primroses and violets and the lambs frisking in the fields, but the sight filled Murray with a nameless dread. Instead of a verdant spring landscape, all he saw was an arid desert of early starts, late finishes and no days off, stretching as far as the eye could see.

He had been hoping for a relaxing cup of coffee and a few minutes' rest before starting work, but when he pulled into the yard of the practice, a glance was enough to tell him that was not remotely likely. He parked in the last remaining space and sidled towards the side door of the practice, hoping at least that he could grab a coffee before being sucked into the maelstrom of work, but Chris had already spotted him and called to him from one of the stables, where a makeshift lambing table had been set up.

Murray groaned inwardly, kissing his coffee goodbye, but hurried over to help Chris, rolling his sleeves up as he went. They lambed one ewe in the shed, and without drawing breath, began working on another one in the back of a farmer's Land Rover in the car-park.

A queue of farmers waited with varying degrees of patience in reception, cheek by jowl with clients holding domestic pets. One farmer kept a wary eye on an alsatian, while clutching a new-born lamb to his chest and feeding it with a baby's bottle. 'What are you going to call him?' asked Clare, laughing, as she handed out mugs of tea.

Amid all the activity, the unassuming figure of a twenty-year-old girl, wearing no make-up and drab functional clothes, had been sitting patiently on the bench for over half an hour, almost hidden from view by a couple of burly farmers.

Jennifer came out of surgery with Laura and glanced around the packed reception, whispering, 'If I'd known that spring brought this mayhem, I'd have stayed in the city.' She was smiling indulgently at the sight of the farmer, unselfconsciously feeding the lamb from a bottle, when she saw the girl on the bench. 'God, I completely forgot about her.'

Laura looked blankly at her.

'It's the student,' explained Jennifer.

Laura groaned. 'They may be students but they know nothing in my experience. The one we had last year was useless.'

Jennifer shrugged. 'Unpaid dogsbodies – I'm not sure I approve anyway.' She moved quickly across to the girl, all smiles. 'Melanie Baxter? I'm terribly sorry to have kept you waiting so long.'

Melanie blushed, almost apologizing for being there. 'That's all right, really, sorry.'

Jennifer looked around. 'We'll go somewhere quieter. Laura, could you do me a favour, and fetch Chris from outside?'

Jennifer led Melanie through the throng to her office, shutting the door gratefully on the bedlam in reception. Melanie looked nervously around.

'Do sit down,' said Jennifer, trying to put her at her ease. 'So you're third year, are you? Bet you can't wait to qualify, I couldn't.'

'I love college though, I do really,' replied Melanie.

'Well, as you saw, we can use all the help we can get at the moment, but the work won't be that interesting, I'm afraid. You never know, though, you might learn something.'

'I don't mind, honestly. I'm dying to start.'

Chris came hurrying in. 'Chris Lennox, we spoke when you phoned. Welcome to bedlam.'

Melanie gave another nervous smile but said nothing.

'Melanie's very keen to begin working her fingers to the bone for us,' said Jennifer, rescuing her from her shyness.

'Work experience, nothing like it,' said Chris briskly. 'Right, now only because we've never met before, we will need some sort of reference from the college, as I said on the phone.'

'They told me it was in the post,' replied Melanie. 'I'll bring it in as soon as it arrives.'

'Terrific,' said Chris. He smiled at her and then hurried out again without waiting for the reply.

'Right,' said Jennifer, 'when can you start? Tomorrow morning?'

'I can start now if you want,' said Melanie eagerly.

Jennifer smiled warmly at her enthusiasm. 'Even better. Why not have a look around for twenty minutes or so, while I sort out a couple of things, and then you can come with me on my rounds.'

Melanie wandered outside and began peering into some of the outbuildings, still grinning with pleasure. Clare gave her a puzzled look. 'Who's that girl?' she asked Murray, earning a look of gratitude, bordering on devotion, for the mug of coffee she planted in his hand.

He glanced around. 'She's the student vet joining the team.'

'Nobody tells me anything. Has she been warned about you?' asked Clare with a sly grin, but before Murray could think of a suitably witty rejoinder, he saw a vintage MG sports car pull up in the car-park and shrank back out of sight. 'Oh, no, look who it is.'

'I quite like Major Brooks,' said Clare, as she watched a middle-aged, military type, wearing a flat cap and driving gloves, prise himself out of the bucket seat and stride towards the practice, his bearing ramrod straight.

Murray groaned. 'Last time he was here I had the full story of how he recaptured Port Stanley single-handed with a Swiss Army penknife. Not again, thank you.'

Brooks marched up to the reception desk, booming, 'Morning, Maddy, how's tricks?'

'Hello, Major Brooks. Is Chris expecting you?'

He shook his head, brandishing a cheque. 'I just popped by to settle up.'

As he handed it to Maddy, Chris came hurrying through but changed direction as he saw Brooks and came over. He glanced at the cheque appreciatively. 'Do you know you're the only client who pays his bills on time?'

Brooks smiled, but got straight down to business. 'The cows have bagged up.'

'Good,' said Chris, calling to Jennifer as she appeared from the back, carrying a guinea-pig. 'Oh, Jen, this is Major Brooks. Jennifer Holt, my new partner.'

'Mr Brooks, please.'

'I induced Mr Brooks's Herefords the day before yesterday, so they'll be ready to be Caesared today,' said Chris. 'Can you get out there?'

Jennifer flashed him a far from grateful look.

'I'll be completely tied up all day, unfortunately,' added Chris hastily.

'Of course,' said Jennifer. 'See you later, Mr Brooks.'

'Looking forward to it. Mind he doesn't bite,' said Brooks, gesturing to the guinea-pig.

Jennifer managed to produce a smile in recognition of his feeble joke, as Brooks turned and strode out again. 'I hate doing that job,' she murmured to Chris as they watched him go, 'and he's a bit of a smoothie, isn't he?'

Chris grinned. 'Maddy, tell Jennifer how much we make out of the Major in an average year.'

Jennifer did not wait to find out, but rolled her eyes at Chris and carried on towards her office.

Melanie was standing waiting, clutching a pair of wellingtons, when Jennifer came out a few minutes later.

'You've brought your own wellies, good,' said Jennifer. 'Our spares have all got holes in them. Right, we'd better get moving.'

As she drove them out of Whitton, Jennifer gradually drew Melanie out of herself, until they were chatting quite animatedly. 'I was going to ask,' said Jennifer, 'are you happy to do night visits sometimes? They can be quite fun.'

'I can't, I'm sorry. It's my mum, you see. She's an invalid. She has someone popping in during the day but at night times there's only me.'

'What happens during termtime, when you're not there?'

Melanie hesitated, then said, 'Erm . . . there's an auntie who looks in.'

'What about your dad?'

'He's dead.'

'Oh, I'm sorry.'

'It's all right, Mrs Holt, you weren't to know,' said Melanie. 'He was a vet actually. He had his own practice.'

'It runs in the family then and please call me Jennifer.'

They exchanged smiles.

Brooks's farm was modest in size but the hi-tech equipment, gleaming new sheds and pure-bred Aberdeen Angus grazing in the pasture alongside the farm showed that it was also a very lucrative one. As Jennifer and Melanie arrived, Brooks was ironing his shirts carefully and precisely, adding them to a rack of beautifully pressed shirts, lined up like soldiers on parade. The room was sparsely, spartanly furnished, without a single feminine touch.

He saw Jennifer pull up and came out of the house as the two women were gathering their equipment.

'Good morning again, Mrs Holt.'

'Morning. This is Melanie, she's at vet college on work experience. You don't mind, do you?'

'Never say no to female company, livens up the old place,' said Brooks with regimental charm. 'Tea, coffee?'

'No thanks,' said Jennifer, 'we'd better get on.'

He led them into the barn, where Jennifer quickly checked the cows then said briskly, 'Right. We'll do these four today and the rest tomorrow.'

She put the first cow into a head collar and started to give it an injection, explaining each step to Melanie as she worked. 'We give the old girls a mil each of sedative and then a local anaesthetic to block out the nerves on the flank while we perform the Caesarean section. It's easier if they're standing, and less stressful for the cow too.'

'How can you tell she needs a Caesarean?' asked Melanie, puzzled by Jennifer's swift and superficial examination.

'They all do, I'm afraid, it's deliberate. These cows are Hereford Crosses which have been implanted with the embryos of Belgian Blues.'

'An arm and a leg those embryos cost,' interjected Brooks. 'Not literally, we hope.'

Jennifer smiled politely at his continued attempts at humour and carried on with the explanation. 'But Belgian Blue calves are too big for these cows to give birth to naturally so we have to . . .

cut them out.' There was a faint but unmistakable hint of disapproval in her choice of phrase.

'Why?' said Melanie, still baffled.

'Because the calf is too big for the pelvis.'

'No, I mean why use surrogate mothers for the calves if they don't fit properly?'

'Because Belgian Blues are very valuable. If you can get more of them by growing them inside cheap cows like these girls here, well . . . it's good business. Isn't that right, Mr Brooks?'

'Absolutely,' said Brooks, 'and call me Gerrard, please.' He watched intently as Jennifer prepared to perform the Caesarean on the first cow, giving it three syringes of local anaesthetic and clipping the hair along the abdomen ready for the cut.

'So, Melanie,' said Brooks, 'looking forward to becoming a glamorous country vet like our Mrs Holt here?'

Melanie was too shy to reply and Jennifer managed to stifle her own 'pass the sick bag' expression before Brooks noticed.

'A bit of a splash she's made in the area, I can tell you,' added Brooks, laying it on with a trowel.

Jennifer took out the scalpel and gave Melanie an encouraging smile. 'Not for the squeamish, this.' She made the incision and worked deftly and confidently under the fascinated gaze of Brooks and the horrified one of Melanie, pulling out the calf and laying it gently on the straw. Jennifer set Melanie to administering drops of a stimulant under the calf's tongue while she completed the stitching on the mother.

Brooks glanced at his watch. 'I've some urgent calls to make. I'll have to leave you alone for ten minutes. Any problems with the next one, do whatever you have to but get the calf out, won't you?' He gave Jennifer an ingratiating smile as he left the barn.

'What did he mean?' whispered Melanie, as soon as he was out of sight.

'He means that the mothers are expendable,' said Jennifer, moving on to another cow.

A couple of hours later Jennifer and Melanie were driving back to the practice. Melanie stared out of the window, pale, quiet, and still a little upset from the visit.

Jennifer glanced sideways at her. 'You did well, Melanie.'

'It was horrible though.'

'I know. Look, you needn't go back out there tomorrow with me, I'll bring Clare.'

Melanie set her jaw. 'No, I'll go back. I have to learn.'

When they got back to the practice, they found Chris and Murray in the middle of an emergency in the lambing shed, dealing with a ewe having a breech birth. Chris was struggling to get his hands inside the ewe to turn the lamb round, and when he saw Jennifer getting out of the car, he called out, 'Just what we need. The feminine touch.'

Jennifer and Melanie walked over to the lambing table.

'He's got his head back,' said Chris, 'I can't bring it round.'

Jennifer stepped up to the table and started to roll up her sleeves.

'Can I help?' asked Melanie.

'Er, I don't think . . .' began Chris, but Jennifer interrupted him.

'Yes, you can. Come round here.'

Chris raised an eyebrow at Jennifer but she smiled his silent protest away and Melanie started helping her deliver the lamb while Chris looked on apprehensively.

'Can you feel the head?' asked Jennifer.

Melanie nodded.

'Good. Try to straighten it and pull it towards the back.'

Melanie's slim wrists and hands were better suited to the task than Chris's and she worked carefully, absorbed in her task.

'How did the visit go?' Chris asked Jennifer quietly.

'No problem, four delivered.' She broke off to encourage Melanie. 'That's it, Melanie, good . . .'

They brought out the lamb safely, bringing an appreciative nod from Chris, a quiet smile of satisfaction from Jennifer and a beam of pure delight to Melanie's face.

Melanie stuck to Jennifer's side like a limpet throughout the afternoon and looked disappointed when Jennifer finally sent her home. She caught the bus back into Plymouth and walked through the streets day-dreaming, apparently lost to the bustle and noise of the evening traffic about her. When she reached a large, old-fashioned office block, however, she turned in through the gates.

The building was deserted apart from a few cleaners hoovering and dusting. They gave Melanie hostile looks as she walked past them. She took a uniform from her locker and put it on, picked up a bucket of cleaning materials and walked down a dark, empty corridor into a large open-plan office. She stopped by a desk and started to polish it half-heartedly, while she looked carefully around her. Satisfied, she sat down at the desk, took a blank piece of headed notepaper out of her bag, and began typing a letter: 'TO WHOM IT MAY CONCERN'.

When she had completed it, she folded it carefully, put it in her pocket, and then began to clean the office. She finished a couple of hours later and made her way to the locker room, where the other cleaners were sitting around, laughing and chatting. The conversation died away as Melanie walked in. No one talked to her and she kept her head down, making eye contact with none of them.

She took off her cleaning uniform and went to hang it up in her locker. There was an expectant silence as she opened the door. She recoiled, screaming. Inside the locker was a dead rat hanging by its tail. The other cleaners sniggered and laughed at the success of their horrible practical joke, while Melanie ran from the room, shaking and crying.

She was still tearful as she arrived home at a terraced house in a nondescript row. She paused for a moment, trying to collect herself, then opened the door. The house was cheaply furnished but tidy and spotlessly clean. The television was on in the front room and she quietly hung up her coat, trying not to be heard, but her mother, Liz, came into the hall before Melanie could sneak upstairs.

Liz was almost fifty and bore the marks of a lifelong struggle against the odds. Her face was as lined and worn as her clothes and her iron grey hair was carelessly gathered into a bun. She pushed a stray strand of hair out of her eyes and looked fondly at her daughter. 'You're late. There's some food in the oven.'

'Not hungry, thanks,' muttered Melanie, backing towards the stairs, but Liz had already seen the tearstains on her face.

'What's the matter, darling?' she asked, putting a hand on Melanie's arm.

'Nothing.'

Liz shook her head wearily. 'What did they do this time?'

Melanie said nothing but began to sob again.

Liz went to her and put her arms around her. 'There, there, it's all right now. You're better than they are, Melanie, remember that. You're worth so much more.'

She stroked her hair tenderly. 'You know what, darling? I think you should give up that cleaning job. It's doing you no good at all and we certainly don't need the money.'

'We do need the money, Mum.'

'But those horrible women.'

'They're not so bad.'

Liz snorted. 'You're a sensitive girl, you oughtn't to spend time with people like that.'

'I can manage,' said Melanie, dabbing at her eyes. 'Please.'

Liz shrugged and smiled. 'All right. Now, what did you get up to today?'

Although her mother's tone was friendly rather than inquisitorial, Melanie immediately stiffened and said guardedly, 'Nothing much.'

'You left at the crack of dawn, where did you go?'

'Nowhere.'

'You must have gone somewhere, darling.'

Liz waited expectantly but Melanie didn't reply, her lips set in a stubborn line.

'Well, if you don't want me to know, I can't force you . . .' said Liz wearily, a little hurt.

'I'm going to try again,' said Melanie reluctantly, 'for veterinary college.'

'They won't have you, Melanie. They rejected you once before.'

'Only because I didn't try hard enough.'

Liz's voice was pleading. 'You did try hard enough. You studied all the hours God sent.'

'You were pleased, weren't you? You never wanted me to be a vet, not deep down, because it's what me and Dad shared and you never could. That's right, isn't it?'

Liz gazed at her daughter uncomprehendingly, determined not to be drawn into a fight. 'This is a ridiculous fantasy, Melanie, you're never going to be a vet.'

'I already am. You should have seen me today,' crowed Melanie, stopping Liz in her tracks.

'What? What are you talking about?' she asked.

'None of your business,' said Melanie, stalking upstairs to her room.

Liz pursued her, still demanding, 'Where were you today?' but Melanie just gave her a sly grin.

'That's our secret. Me and Dad's.'

Liz was close to tears. 'Since he left, I've fed you, I've clothed you, I've protected you. I've done everything I can to make you happy and this is how you reward me.'

'Get out of my room,' said Melanie, hard-faced.

Liz stared balefully at her for a second. 'You really are an ungrateful little bitch,' she said and walked out.

Melanie slammed the door. She walked over to her desk, surrounded by animal posters and pictures. Cages containing hamsters, gerbils and mice stood on the shelves and the bookshelf was filled with books about animals and veterinary textbooks. She sat down at the desk and began intently studying one of them. She heard a faint cheer from outside and, looking up, saw the glow from the lights of the greyhound stadium, lighting up the night sky.

Wilf Morgan and his wife Danielle heard the cheer as well, from rather closer at hand, and redoubled their pace.

'Come on, girl, we're late, the meeting's started,' said Wilf, tugging at the lead of a greyhound which was lying in the back of his estate car.

Wilf, middle-aged, a touch overweight and more than a touch wide, made his money retailing tiles throughout the south-west. Danielle was a few years younger, good looking but vastly over-perfumed, over-made-up and over-dressed. She could and did spend Wilf's money almost as fast as he could earn it, but even she could not compete with the absurd sums of money that Wilf himself lavished on his obsessive and ever-changing hobbies.

This year's model was racing greyhounds and Wilf was struggling with his star performer Nell Gwynn, an 'extremely promising bitch' according to the man who had sold her to him.

'Maybe she doesn't want to race today,' said Danielle sympathetically, staring at the dog. 'Maybe she doesn't feel like it.'

Wilf redoubled his efforts, muttering, 'She's a greyhound, of course she feels like it. Don't you, sweetie pie?'

Danielle looked to the heavens while Nell Gwynn reluctantly allowed herself to be dragged out.

As Wilf stood there panting in triumph, a car-park attendant approached them. 'Nice dog.'

'Nell Gwynn,' said Wilf, his chest swelling with pride. 'Do yourself a favour, pal. The last race, can't lose.'

'Thanks,' said the attendant.

'Don't be going telling the world, will you?' said Wilf, tapping the side of his nose, as he started to move away.

'Not thinking of parking there, are you?' asked the attendant imperturbably.

Danielle returned her gaze to the heavens as Wilf, red-faced and angry, said, 'Oh for God's sake, here's a tenner.'

'That'll do nicely,' said the attendant mockingly as he pocketed the note and sauntered away. 'I'll put it on your dog.'

Having handed Nell Gwynn over to her handler, Wilf and Danielle took their seats in the stand, waiting with very different levels of excitement for the last race. Wilf was proud and full of expectation. 'That's a very competitive field out there, Danielle. This'll be a good test for Nell. She needs to be pushed to bring the best out of her.'

'How do you know?' asked Danielle, bored.

'That's what the man said, didn't he?'

'I mean how do you know that's a competitive field? You haven't seen them race yet.'

'I know about greyhounds and form,' said Wilf loftily, breaking off to doff his hat to another punter, who stared back blankly and then turned away.

After four or five other races, in which Wilf intently studied form while Danielle polished her nails and yawned, Nell Gwynn was finally led to the starting stalls with the other runners and loaded into her trap. The hare began its metallic glide from the far side of the track, the greyhounds barking excitedly as they heard it coming. It rattled past the stalls and there was a clang as the traps sprang open and six dogs came flying out.

Wilf was on his feet, waving his hands excitedly in the air, but as the dogs hurtled around the track he gradually became frozen into immobility, his hands still held above his head as Nell Gwynn lagged further and further behind the field. She eventually trailed in last by twelve lengths. Wilf was absolutely crestfallen, unable to believe his eyes.

Danielle put her arm through his and laid her head affectionately on his shoulder. 'I'm so sorry, cherub. Maybe Nell Gwynn knows the hare isn't real – very intelligent animals, greyhounds.'

Wilf looked slowly round in disbelief that she could say something so stupid. 'There's something wrong with that dog, Danielle, and I'll have the vet out first thing in the morning to find out what it is.'

The short straw was drawn by Murray. As he bustled about on another frenetically busy morning, Chris called him over. Chris broke off from lambing yet another recalcitrant ewe in the back of yet another Land Rover and said, 'House call for you, Murray, as soon as things quieten down here, a greyhound.'

Murray groaned. 'Why can't he bring it into the practice? It's only a greyhound.'

'The man insists on home visits,' said Chris, 'and he's prepared to pay through the nose for it. So take Clare with you and make a fuss of him.'

Murray sighed but went in search of Clare.

Wilf's home was a sprawling modern house on the outskirts of Whitton, with a spectacular view out towards Dartmoor. It was also a racing certainty for an award for the worst-taste house in Devon and possibly the world, a mock-Tudor nightmare with carriage lamps, Doric columns by the front door and a plastic heron by the pond.

Wilf led Nell Gwynn out on to the manicured front lawn and stood anxiously by, fretting like an expectant parent, as Murray examined her. Danielle lay reading a magazine on a sun-lounger near by, fully dressed, since it was only April.

'She's a beautiful greyhound, Mr Morgan,' said Murray, who lacked nothing in diplomatic skills.

'Of course she is,' said Wilf proudly, 'she was sired by Hercules the Second.'

'And who's the dam?'

'Excuse me?' said Wilf, thrown momentarily.

'The dam. The mother.'

'Oh, the dam, right. Who's she out of, you mean?' said Wilf, recovering fast. 'She's out of Crazy Lady. Excellent pedigree. So what's wrong with her?'

'As far as I can see, nothing.'

Wilf acted as if Murray had not even spoken. 'She's obviously got some sort of virus.'

'Well . . .'

'She's not lame, is she?'

Murray shook his head.

'So what did she come in last for?' He supplied his own answer. 'Because she's ill. Maybe she's got hypocalcemia,' he said, cocking an eye at Danielle to see if she was impressed by his medical knowledge.

She was not. She yawned and turned the pages of her magazine listlessly.

'Not if she hasn't had puppies in the last three weeks, Mr Morgan,' said Murray. 'Nell Gwynn appears to be a perfectly healthy bitch.'

Danielle put down the magazine with a sigh and said, 'Listen to the man, he's a vet, he knows what he's talking about.'

'I didn't pay two grand for a dog just to be told there's nothing wrong with it when it runs slower than a catatonic St Bernard,' said Wilf angrily.

Murray and Clare exchanged glances, with Clare mouthing in silent disbelief, 'Two thousand?'

'If you can't find out what's wrong with her, I might have to go elsewhere,' said Wilf abruptly.

'Why don't I take Nell Gwynn back to the vet centre, take a blood sample and run some tests?' said Murray, winking at Clare. 'We'll get to the bottom of this, don't you worry, Mr Morgan.'

Wilf smiled at him. 'That's more like it.'

As Wilf waved off Murray, Clare and Nell Gwynn, Danielle stretched languidly, uncurled herself from the sun-lounger and said huskily, 'Wilf, do you have to go in to work today?'

'I er . . . I don't suppose the business'd collapse without me for an hour or two,' he said, as she gave him a sultry smile. He followed her into the house and up the stairs.

They were locked in a passionate embrace on the bed when Wilf suddenly sat bolt upright and said, 'Hang on, I'll just be a minute.' He wrapped himself in his dressing-gown, a multicoloured monstrosity that would have made even Chris Eubank blush, and disappeared along the landing and down the stairs again. Danielle exhaled heavily and waited for him with mounting impatience. Finally she leaped out of bed, put on her own, rather more flattering silk dressing-gown and followed him downstairs.

She found him rummaging about in the depths of a huge chest freezer, his head and torso completely submerged in frozen food.

'Wilf,' said Danielle, tapping her foot impatiently.

'What?' said Wilf, his voice almost inaudible.

'We were in the middle of making love and you told me you had to go somewhere for a minute. I assumed you meant the bathroom but here you are with your head in the freezer.'

'I had something on my mind,' said Wilf, struggling to extricate himself.

'Evidently not what I had on my mind,' sighed Danielle.

Wilf reappeared triumphantly, holding up some packs of frozen meat. 'I thought I'd defrost some extra fillet steak for Nell Gwynn.'

'Why?' said Danielle.

'Well, when Murray has done his blood tests and found something wrong, he'll probably want to do an operation or something and I don't want to leave Nell Gwynn there without any proper food.'

'Wilfred, my cherub,' said Danielle, draping her arms around his neck, 'last year it was racing pigeons. The year before, a fully trained sheepdog. These hobbies of yours . . . they're getting in the way.' She recoiled sharply as her breast made contact with the frozen steak.

'Of what?'

'Of you and me. Of us.'

'But you'd like to see me happy, wouldn't you?' protested Wilf.

'I'd like to see you, full stop.'

He paused, deep in thought, while Danielle waited hopefully. Then he held up the two packets of meat. 'I thought we had three of these left. We didn't have one ourselves for dinner, did we?'

Danielle shook her head in resignation and went back upstairs to get dressed.

Unlike those of Wilf and Danielle, Jennifer's dressing-gown was built for comfort rather than speed. She sat wearing it at the kitchen table the next morning, absent-mindedly eating a piece of toast as she studied a textbook. Steven appeared in the doorway, stuffing schoolbooks into his bag.

'How much of the trigonometry you learned at school can you remember?' he asked, gesturing at a textbook.

'Absolutely nothing,' said Jennifer, 'but I don't remember a single page of *Anna Karenina* either and I'm still glad I read it.'

She closed her own book as Steven sat down, reading the title to him. '*Nasogastric Tube Fixation and Protection* – Tolstoy it ain't.'

'Mum,' he said warily. 'I spoke to Dad while you were in the shower and he's going to be in Bristol on Thursday.'

Jennifer frowned and began, 'Steven, listen . . .'

'I thought it would be nice for the three of us to go out for the evening,' Steven rattled out hastily.

She gave him a suspicious look. 'I don't know.'

'Nothing heavy, just for dinner,' he said innocently.

'Steven, what are you up to?'

'Nothing.'

'I thought you'd come to terms with our separation.'

'I have really. I want you two to be friends, that's all.'

Jennifer stared at him, trying to probe behind his disarming smile.

'I said I'd phone him soon,' said Steven, 'and let him know. Must dash, I'll be late for school.'

He was out of the door before she could speak again, leaving his smile hanging in the air like the Cheshire Cat's while Jennifer stared after him, troubled. She had no time to dwell on it however, for she was running late for work. She raced upstairs, threw her clothes on and headed for the practice. As she hurried in through the door, Melanie rose from the bench where she had been waiting and Maddy called from behind the desk. 'Major Brooks just phoned, Jennifer. There's a problem with one of the cows that was Caesared yesterday.'

When Maddy had relayed the rest of the message, Jennifer turned to Melanie. 'Post-operative trauma from the sound of it. The shock from us cutting her open yesterday – it happens, I'm afraid. Come on, we'll have to hurry.' They were on the road within five minutes, Jennifer gunning the car as fast the morning traffic would allow.

Brooks was waiting for them and led them through to the barn. He stood by impassively as Jennifer went to work, taking the cow's temperature and doing a routine rectal examination.

'She's got a temperature and a high pulse,' she said. 'It might be peritonitis – fluid from the uterus dripping into the abdomen.'

'She's not going to die, is she?' asked Melanie, quite distressed.

'Not if she's lucky,' said Jennifer, administering an anti-inflammatory for the wound.

Brooks turned to Melanie. 'I wouldn't fret, lass. She's served her purpose.' Jennifer herself winced at Brooks's insensitivity, but Melanie's reaction still stunned her.

'How can you say that?' shouted Melanie angrily. 'She's still got a right to life. How could you be so cruel?'

'Melanie,' barked Jennifer, giving her a fierce warning look. 'I'm sorry, Mr Brooks, it's her first time.'

To her surprise, Brooks seemed completely unperturbed. 'No, no, don't worry, Mrs Holt. That's what I like to see, a bit of spirit. You stick to your guns, girl.'

Melanie scowled at him, trembling with anger, but Brooks merely smiled across at Jennifer.

She did not return the smile as she stepped away from the cow. 'With luck, she'll show some improvement in a day or so.'

'If you pop by tomorrow,' said Brooks, 'you wouldn't fancy a spot of lunch, would you?'

Jennifer summoned up a polite but distinctly cool smile. 'Thanks for the offer, but I don't mix business with pleasure.'

Brooks shrugged. 'Can't win 'em all.'

As he left the cattle shed, Jennifer rounded on Melanie, saying sternly, 'It doesn't matter how much you disapprove, you never ever talk to a client like that.'

'But how could he say those things?'

'What he said was nothing compared to what you're going to have to get used to.'

'Well, I think animals should be reared naturally,' said Melanie, pouting her disapproval.

'For the record, I disapprove of this particular practice too, but as long as transplanting embryos is legal, our job is to see it carried out as humanely as possible. Do you understand?'

Still sullen, Melanie nodded grudgingly.

'Right,' said Jennifer briskly, 'let's get on. When we've finished here, I'm going to drop you off back at the practice and you can shadow Clare for the rest of the day, and get a feeling for her job.' She caught Melanie's hurt look and said, 'It's not a punishment, Melanie, you need to see as much of the work of the whole practice as possible, that's all.'

Melanie softened a little and even managed a weak smile, as Jennifer continued chatting to her while she packed up the equipment.

Wilf was pacing anxiously up and down in reception when they got back, waiting for Murray's verdict on Nell Gwynn. Maddy gave him an encouraging smile, saying, 'He won't be long,' but Wilf was beyond reassurance. He did not even break step in his pacing, mentally running through every terminal canine condition he had ever read about and staring unblinkingly at the closed door leading through to the rest of the practice.

On the other side of the door, Chris was looking carefully at the greyhound while Murray stood next to him, reciting a litany of tests carried out. 'I've done a full blood profile, the haematology is normal and the biochemistry is all in range.'

'You've done a full physical?' queried Chris.

'Of course, but Mr Morgan wants me to test her chromosomes.'

Chris gave him a sideways look and Murray shrugged helplessly. 'He's been reading all these books.'

'Well, we can either do more tests and make more money,' said Chris, adding slightly reluctantly, 'or you can tell the man what's wrong with his dog.'

'What is wrong with the dog?' said Murray.

'It's slow,' said Chris, grinning. 'That's what's wrong with it. It's a slow greyhound.'

Murray took a deep breath, then walked through to reception and led Wilf outside, on to the terrace by the river. Wilf, though, had no eyes for the view. 'Well?' he asked expectantly.

'Well,' said Murray. 'We could take some cell samples and send them to a laboratory . . .'

'Terrific, great,' interrupted Wilf.

'. . . Or we could even look closely at the muscle tissue.'

'Yeah?' said Wilf, like a schoolboy who's just been given free seats at the circus.

'But,' said Murray.

'But what?'

'But it'd be money down the drain. The harsh truth is that Nell Gwynn is slow.'

'Slow?' shouted Wilf, sending a family of moorhens diving for cover on the far bank of the river.

'Relatively, that's all,' said Murray hastily. 'I mean, obviously she can run very quickly but . . .'

'No, no, no, this can't be right,' said Wilf, pressing his hands to his forehead in despair.

'She's still a beautiful greyhound,' said Murray, trying to offer consolation, but Wilf shrugged it off, pleading, 'She's got form, she's won races.'

Murray could think of nothing else to say, but when he looked up there was a triumphant gleam in Wilf's eye. 'X-rays!' he said happily. 'We haven't done any X-rays.'

Murray sighed and gave up. 'All right, I'll do some X-rays. Come back tomorrow morning.'

Wilf went home a happy man while Murray resignedly went back inside to do the X-rays, passing Laura, who was on her way out with an equally hangdog expression.

Alan was waiting for her outside in her car. 'What is it, Alan?' said Laura irritably as she got into the driving seat. 'We're up to our ears in work at the moment, couldn't it have waited till tonight?'

He shook his head.

'All right. I haven't got much time, though, and this had better be important.'

'It is. Drive down to the estuary.'

'Oh, for heaven's sake, Alan,' began Laura, but he gave her such a desperate, pleading look that she relented and drove off, following the winding narrow road that led downstream, alongside the river.

She pulled up overlooking the estuary. The tide was on its way out and the recently exposed mud gleamed black as wading birds trekked across it, leaving neat lines of footprints on its glistening surface. Laura turned expectantly to Alan, saying 'Well?' but he continued to stare through the windscreen, saying dreamily, 'We used to come here during our early snogging days, remember?'

'Alan!' said Laura impatiently.

He turned to face her, took her hand and said flatly, 'I've resigned. I wrote the letter this morning and left it on Harris's desk.'

'Hang on. Are you serious?' demanded Laura, struggling to take this on board.

'I've had enough. Ever since I turned down that Alabama posting, he's had it in for me. Dumping the crap cases in my lap, taking away the juicy ones. It was a question of pride really – dignity, or something.'

'I don't believe I'm hearing this. You resigned? What about us? What are we going to live on till you find a new job? How the hell could you even think about it without talking it over with me?'

He gave her a sad smile. 'What a short memory. You did exactly the same thing, didn't you?'

Laura glared at him, then started the engine and drove back, crunching the gears angrily.

She stomped into reception, startling Melanie, Clare and Maddy, who were sharing a joke over the five-minute sandwich break that passed for lunch hour during lambing time. Clare was recounting the story of Murray and the deer farmer's wife for Melanie's benefit, giving it her full mock Scottish accent. 'So Murray says to her, "Oh, Mrs McMahon, I would sleep with you really, but the thing is . . . I'm gay." Which he isn't, by the way. I know.'

The laughter died at the sight of Laura's thunderous face. She scowled at them, barked, 'I'm on visits all afternoon, Maddy. If you need me, don't bother, get one of the others,' and marched out again. As Laura drove away, tyres squealing, a truck pulled up and a farmer jumped out, grabbing a ewe from the back and running into the practice. As he came in through the door he shouted, 'She's breeching. We ain't got much time.'

Clare and Melanie hurried across to look at the ewe while Maddy picked up the phone. 'I'll call Chris . . . Er . . . no, maybe Jennifer would get here quicker.'

'Call Murray,' said Clare, 'he's only in Ivybridge.'

Melanie was peering at the ewe. 'There's no time,' she said. 'The lamb's turned blue, I can see the cord wrapped round the neck. I'll do it myself.'

'No, Melanie, you can't . . .' began Clare but Melanie cut her off.

'I can. I did it this morning, didn't I?'

'If we wait, it'll be too late,' said the farmer.

Clare and Maddy looked helplessly at each other, then Clare shrugged and followed Melanie to the lambing table outside. With Clare's help, Melanie slowly eased the lamb out as the farmer looked on anxiously. The lamb lay still, apparently lifeless, but Melanie gave it mouth to mouth resuscitation and after a worrying few seconds it started to breathe. The farmer beamed his appreciation as Melanie stood back smiling triumphantly, close to tears.

There were few smiles a couple of hours later, however, as Clare haltingly tried to explain what had happened to a jury of Chris and Jennifer. Chris was furious that an unsupervised student had been let loose on an animal, and Clare was becoming increasingly upset as he interrogated her.

'I'm not blaming you, Clare,' said Chris, not wholly convincingly, 'I only wish you'd phoned through first.'

'Melanie said there wasn't time,' protested Clare. 'I mean, I'm only a nurse, she's training to be a vet, isn't she?'

She looked to Jennifer for support. 'It's OK, Clare, don't worry,' said Jennifer. 'Could you leave us alone for a few minutes?'

As soon as the door had shut behind Clare, Chris rounded on Jennifer. 'If anything had happened to that lamb, or the ewe for that matter . . .'

'But it didn't,' said Jennifer. 'She delivered the lamb safely and none of us would have made it back here in time.'

'That's hardly the point, Jen, she's a student,' said Chris, intransigent.

Jennifer pointed to the reference letter on the desk. 'And a bloody good one if this tutor's reference is anything to go by.' She gave him a reassuring smile. 'I'll have a word with her, don't worry.'

'No,' said Chris firmly. 'We can't risk it. We should let her go.'

'Oh, now come on, Chris. Give the girl a chance. She's going to be a good vet, I'm sure of it. Like her late father apparently.'

'Who was that?' asked Chris, suspiciously.

She shrugged. 'Somebody Baxter, I presume.'

'The only Baxter I know of is a vet in Okehampton who went bankrupt. I didn't know he'd died.'

'Look, I'll give her a formal warning and let's be done with it.'

'OK,' said Chris reluctantly, 'but keep an eye on her, will you?'

As Jennifer started to leave the room, Chris hesitantly called her back. 'Er . . . Jen, there was something else I wanted to talk to you about.'

She waited as he floundered around for a few seconds.

'Erm . . . it's been so busy here this past couple of weeks . . . and I've been wanting to talk about . . .' He ground to a halt.

'About what?' prompted Jennifer, smiling.

'About what happened in the car.'

'The car?' she said blankly, but then realized what he was talking about. 'Oh, right, that.'

Both were embarrassed by the memory and they began to talk at once, a little too quickly, neither allowing the other to complete a sentence.

'It was stupid, you know . . .' began Chris.

'No, no, that's OK . . .' soothed Jennifer.

'No, really stupid, you know . . .'

'It was only . . .'

'A kiss? I know, but . . .'

'It doesn't matter, it wasn't important.'

'No. I'm embarrassed.'

'There's no need, really, there's . . .'

'It's not like I'm harbouring a big crush on you or . . .'

'No, of course you're not. I mean it happens, I've done that, you know . . .'

'There's nothing going on here . . .' He stopped in mid-sentence, intrigued. 'Have you done that? Really?'

'Well, not often but, you know.'

She laughed, embarrassed, and they both fell silent, avoiding each other's eyes.

'Well . . .' said Jennifer, finally.

'Right,' said Chris.

'No problem, then.'

'No problem,' said Chris, doubtfully.

They exchanged a quick, nervous smile. Jennifer turned to go, leaving Chris even more riven by doubts, but after closing the door she also paused, confused and troubled.

As Chris was driving home, he abruptly turned off his normal route and drove across town to the Catholic church. He hurried inside, dropped to his knee to cross himself, then sat in the pew as he waited his turn in the confessional. He could hear the faint, indistinct murmur of voices from the confessional and then the curtain was pulled aside. A woman came out, averting her eyes from Chris's face and hurried away as he took her place and began his confession.

'Forgive me, Father, for I have sinned. It's two months since my last confession.'

He began a litany of minor misdeeds. 'It's been a hectic time at the practice and I've been very hard on my staff, critical of their work and not giving them credit where it's due. I expect too much of them sometimes; I expect too much of myself.'

'Something else is troubling you,' prompted the priest.

'I did something stupid, which I regret . . .'

Chris's voice trailed off for a moment, then picked up again, the words suddenly tumbling out of him. 'I made a pass at my partner, Jennifer. I am attracted to her, I know I am, but maybe that's only because we work so closely together.'

'These things happen,' interjected the priest, 'we're none of us made of stone.'

'But I love my wife and I would never do anything to threaten my marriage.'

'Are you in love with this woman?' asked the priest.

'No,' said Chris loudly, then, embarrassed, he repeated more softly, 'No.'

When Chris got home he was instantly surrounded by Abby and Charlotte, running around in their pyjamas and dressing-gowns. Chris hugged them tightly to him for a moment, closing his eyes, then released them and poured himself a drink. Patricia came through from the kitchen, kissed him and scooped up Charlotte. 'Bed and one story only, it's late.'

'We want Daddy to read.'

Chris nodded. 'Daddy will read. Go and clean your teeth and I'll be up in two minutes. Up!'

As the girls ran up the stairs, Patricia turned to Chris, scanning his face anxiously. 'You look absolutely beat.'

'Completely exhausted.'

'Why don't we go away for a week when the lambing's done?'

He nodded, preoccupied.

Patricia still kept studying his face. 'There's nothing wrong, is there?' she said carefully. 'Apart from work?'

'There's nothing else,' he said flatly, wandering into the front room.

Patricia followed him through. 'Tomorrow night's the dinner. You haven't forgotten, have you?'

Chris looked blank and then grinned sheepishly at her, not having a clue what she was talking about.

Patricia sighed. 'The leader of the group, the prospective parliamentary candidate and the party official . . .'

'The party official from London,' said Chris, dredging it up from the recesses of his mind. 'I remember now. It was in there. It was just hiding.' He tapped his forehead. 'Do you know something? I've been thinking about this. You'd make a very good MP.'

'Do you mean that?' said Patricia, both surprised and pleased.

'Yes, I do. You would.'

Patricia sat down next to him on the sofa. 'Supposing an opportunity arose,' she asked, in a way that convinced him it was far from a rhetorical question. 'What would you say? I mean, would you actually encourage me?'

'Yes,' said Chris, firmly.

'What about the disruption, the changes it would mean to our lives?'

'We'd manage,' smiled Chris. 'Put the kids into care, take on a cook . . .'

'It might happen, don't joke about it. There's a vacancy in a West Country seat – a winnable one.'

'I'm not joking,' said Chris. 'You have much to offer, why should I get it all?'

'You never cease to surprise me,' said Patricia, huskily. 'One of the reasons why I love you.'

Chris silently raised his glass to her, then went upstairs to read the girls their bedtime story.

Chapter 20

Steven and Scott were sitting in Whitton's premier night-spot – the burger bar – drinking Cokes and chatting, slightly bored but not yet bored enough or late enough to go home. 'There's a do out at Barry Neville's tomorrow night,' said Scott. 'Do you fancy it?'

'No, I can't,' said Steven, 'I'm seeing my dad tomorrow in Bristol. I'm taking my mum with me.'

'Really?' said Scott, more than a little surprised.

'She hasn't actually agreed to go yet,' admitted Steven reluctantly.

'Why are you taking her?'

'Well, I think the two of them want to get back together again but are too proud to say so. My dad's chucked his girlfriend and he's on his own now.'

Scott gave him a sceptical look. 'Did he say he wanted your mum back?'

'He didn't exactly say it but I'm sure he still loves her and Mum's lonely. I'm playing it cool though, making out I only want them to be friends.'

Scott shook his head in disbelief. 'Your mother moved two hundred miles to get away from him. She's hardly tripping over herself to get him back. It sounds like a bloody stupid idea if you ask me.'

Steven glared at him. 'Anyway it's late, I'm off home,' he said irritably.

As soon as he got home, he began trying to persuade Jennifer to come with him, but the more he wheedled, the more she dug her heels in. Within five minutes they were shouting at each other. 'Do you expect me not to see him?' demanded Steven.

'No, of course not, don't be stupid.'

'So why won't you come with me?'

'Because you love him and I don't, that's why.'

'It wouldn't worry you if he was dead, would it?'

'Don't be ridiculous,' said Jennifer, trying to get a grip on her rising temper.

'If the two of you are never going to live together again, why should I live with you and not with him?'

'Don't blackmail me, Steven. Your father and I are never going to get back together. I thought you knew that by now.'

Steven stared at her moodily. 'You loved each other once.'

'Life doesn't work like that.'

'It'd be easier for you if I'd never been born, wouldn't it?' said Steven histrionically. 'Maybe you'd be happier if I wasn't around for a while. You're out working all the time anyway.'

He turned and ran up to his room, leaving Jennifer sitting on the stairs, distraught. For once, though, she did not follow him upstairs and try to mend the broken fences.

Steven was up and out of the house while she was still in the shower the next morning, leaving her a note stating ambiguously: 'Gone to Bristol. Don't know when I'll be back.'

She sighed resignedly and left for work, heartsick and worried.

The last thing she needed was to be dragged into a discussion between Murray and Wilf about Nell Gwynn, but she walked right into the middle of it. They were standing looking at the X-rays of the dog when Jennifer came in.

'Well?' said Wilf expectantly.

'A perfect specimen of a greyhound,' said Murray. 'I'm sorry.'

'What's that then?' said Wilf suspiciously, pointing to a dark patch on one of the X-rays.

Murray drew deep upon his reserves of patience. 'That's the left ventricle.'

'That'd slow her down,' said Wilf hopefully. 'Look at the size of it.'

'If it wasn't there, it'd slow her down completely. It's her heart.'

Jennifer tried to slip past them but Wilf was too quick for her. 'Morning, are you a vet?'

She gave him a brief smile. 'Jennifer Holt, how do you do?'

'Would you have a look at these?' he asked, handing her the X-rays.

As Murray opened his mouth to complain, Wilf muttered, 'Only a second opinion, no offence.'

Jennifer studied the X-rays and then looked quizzically at Wilf. 'Can you see anything wrong with her?' he asked.

'No.'

Wilf's face crumpled in disappointment, baffling Jennifer completely.

'I don't understand,' she whispered, turning to Murray. 'Why did he get upset when I told him his dog was all right?'

'She lost a race,' said Murray, out of the side of his mouth.

As Jennifer nodded and made good her escape, Wilf walked to the window, gazing out wistfully across the river. 'I have to face it, don't I?' he said, without turning round.

'I am sorry,' said Murray gently, 'but she's still a very sweet dog.'

Wilf nodded fondly. 'But she's a crap greyhound. How am I going to tell Danielle?'

Murray patted him on the shoulder and started to slip away, but Wilf turned back to him suddenly. 'She wouldn't have an allergy, would she?'

Murray shook his head and Wilf muttered sadly, 'No, no, of course not,' and went back to his gloomy contemplation of the river.

Murray tiptoed through to reception, where Maddy proffered Wilf's enormous bill. Murray shook his head. 'Leave him for a while, he's grieving enough already.'

'Why, is the greyhound sick?'

'Unfortunately not.'

Maddy had no time to dwell on this conundrum, for Melanie and Chris arrived in rapid succession and the phone began ringing. She picked it up. 'Vet centre, hello? Yes, Major Brooks, yes, just a minute.'

She gestured to Jennifer, who had just come through from the back. Jennifer nodded and picked up the phone. 'Hello . . . I'm sorry, Mr Brooks, I won't be able to make it over this afternoon, I'm afraid. I know I meant to finish yesterday but I was called away on an emergency . . . I don't think I'll be able to get to you before about half past six or seven this evening . . . Yes, well, I'll do my best, Mr Brooks. Bye.'

'Problems?' asked Chris.

'I have to go out there again unfortunately. I only managed to do three of them yesterday.'

'What about the cow who went into shock?' asked Melanie.

'She sounds better, I'll be able to see her later.' Jennifer turned to Chris and said, 'He asked me for a date, can you believe it?'

'He's lonely, that's all, he's not a bad sort,' said Chris.

Jennifer rolled her eyes. 'If you're so sorry for him, why don't you go and have lunch with him then?'

Chris grinned and was about to go through to his office when Melanie cleared her throat nervously. 'I'm sorry about yesterday, Mr Lennox.'

'Forget it,' said Chris. 'You've learned your lesson and you did well with the breech birth. By the way, I know your tutor, Graham Delgado. His reference certainly sings your praises.'

Melanie started nervously but forced a weak smile.

'Give him my regards when you go back next term, won't you?' said Chris. She nodded, eyes downcast.

Melanie arrived alone at Brooks's farm in mid-afternoon. She rang the bell and waited nervously for a reply. Suddenly she heard a voice behind her.

'Melanie.'

She jumped in surprise then turned to see Brooks, who had come round from the side of the house. 'Oh, good afternoon, Mr Brooks. I arranged to meet Mrs Holt here.'

'You're very early,' said Brooks, 'she's not due for a couple of hours.'

'No, she told me she was going to be able to get here by teatime after all,' said Melanie.

'Good. So why don't you come and wait in the house and . . .'

'No, no, it's all right,' said Melanie hastily, 'I'll wait with the animals. I'd rather.'

Brooks followed her into the barn and chatted to her for a few minutes. He noted with mild amusement her flushed face and nervous manner, but put it down to the effects of his roguish charm. 'So you're fifth year already?' he asked.

Melanie nodded. 'Mr Lennox and Mrs Holt have invited me to join the practice when I qualify.'

'Really? Well, I'm very pleased for you, Melanie.'

'I am sorry about what I said yesterday,' she said timidly.

'Damned if I can remember what it was,' replied Brooks, offering her a big smile.

She smiled back gratefully and said, 'I really don't mind waiting here on my own, you know, if you've got things to do.'

He looked at his watch. 'Actually, I ought to be getting on. You'll probably hear Mrs Holt arrive yourself.'

Melanie stood watching as Brooks disappeared into the house, then hurried back into the barn. She opened her bag, prepared a syringe and administered an injection to the last pregnant cow.

She waited twenty minutes, glancing repeatedly out at the house and up the drive, then braced herself for what she had come to do. She pulled on an arm-length plastic glove and whispered, 'No one's going to butcher you,' as she moved to the rear of the cow and started carefully sliding her arm inside it.

Brooks had been absorbed at his desk for some time when he glanced at his watch, then yawned, stretched and stood up. He came out of the house and was starting to walk over to the barn when he heard a car and saw Jennifer driving down the lane. He stood to one side as she pulled up and got out clutching her bag.

'Afternoon,' he said, 'I was expecting you earlier.'

Jennifer checked, puzzled, but then saw the other car in the drive. 'That's Melanie's car, isn't it?'

'That's right,' said Brooks. 'I offered her some tea but she chose to wait for you in the barn.'

'She's not supposed to be here,' said Jennifer, suddenly worried and hurrying towards the barn.

Brooks raised an eyebrow at the note of alarm in Jennifer's voice and followed close behind her. As they rushed in, Melanie looked up, sweating and frightened.

'God almighty, what have you done?' said Jennifer, running to the cow.

'What's happening?' asked Brooks.

'The waters have broken, the cow's trying to give birth naturally,' said Jennifer, grabbing her mobile phone.

'I only wanted . . .' began Melanie but Jennifer snarled, 'Shut up, you stupid bloody girl, you've as good as killed this animal.'

Melanie put her head in her hands and began to sob, ignored by both Jennifer and Brooks.

*

Patricia was pouring a drink for her guests when the phone began ringing. Chris slipped out of the room to take the call in the kitchen while Patricia carried on chatting animatedly to the three party officials. As the minutes ticked by and Chris did not return, however, she excused herself and went out into the hall. Chris was standing there putting on his coat.

'Oh no,' said Patricia, 'not this evening of all evenings.'

He shrugged his shoulders sheepishly. 'It's an emergency.'

'I need you here for this,' said Patricia. 'So much for your encouragement. Sort of fell at the first hurdle really, didn't we?'

'I'm sorry . . . Look, I can't explain now, there's no time. Good luck.'

She gave him a bleak, wintry smile as he hurried out of the door, then composed her features before returning to her guests.

Chris drove like a lunatic up to Brooks's farm and raced from his car to the barn. He gave Melanie a single chilling look as she sat hunched on a straw bale and nodded curtly to Brooks.

Jennifer gave him a grateful smile. 'I can feel a big tear in the uterus. We'll have to stitch it up or she'll die.'

Chris nodded, pulling on his surgical gloves. 'Have the waters broken?'

'A while ago. The calf's probably hypoxic.'

Working fast, without a wasted word or an unnecessary move, Jennifer and Chris delivered the calf by Caesarean section. Chris checked it over carefully as it lay on the ground, while Jennifer started to inject some stimulants into it. Chris looked over his shoulder towards Brooks. 'It's showing signs of anoxia – brain damage due to oxygen starvation.'

'But is it going to survive?' asked Brooks testily.

'There's a good chance. We'll know tomorrow.'

Brooks exhaled and then gave vent to the anger that had been building in him. 'I hope for your sake you're right. You let a bloody student loose on my Belgian Blues. That calf's worth a thousand pounds.'

Chris knew he had no option but to take whatever Brooks was dishing out. 'I can only say how sorry I am. We had no idea how irresponsible she'd be. She came with the highest recommendations.'

'Did she really?' said Brooks sarcastically, rounding on Melanie. 'Is this what they teach you in college, you bloody little idiot?'

As Melanie cowered even further into a corner, Jennifer looked up from stitching the cow. 'She's made a bad mistake and will be reprimanded for it, Mr Brooks. There's no need to be abusive.'

'I don't think you're in any position to start lecturing me, Mrs Holt,' said Brooks icily.

'Come on, let's keep the lid on this,' said Chris, giving Jennifer an imploring look.

Brooks swung back to face him and snapped, 'You've not heard the last of this,' before storming out of the barn.

Chris turned furiously to Jennifer hissing, 'Did you have to?'

'Did I have to?' said Jennifer. 'Are you taking his side in this?'

Chris raised his eyes to heaven. 'It's our fault, for God's sake.'

Jennifer turned her back on him and began packing up her things in a silence broken only by Melanie's sniffs and sobs.

After a few moments Chris turned on his heel and went in search of Brooks, leaving Jennifer and Melanie alone. If Melanie thought she might get some sympathy from Jennifer, however, she was to be disappointed.

'What do you think being a vet is all about, Melanie?' asked Jennifer. 'Loving animals? St Francis of Assisi, is that how you see yourself?'

Melanie shook her head mutely.

'Embryonic transplants, veal calf exports, steroids in cattle, these are the realities of veterinary practice. You'd better start getting used to them. Now come on.'

Melanie followed Jennifer out of the barn, keeping as far away as possible from Brooks and Chris, who were talking by the front door. Brooks glared at them, then disappeared inside the house, slamming the door behind him as Chris walked over to them.

'If that calf's not better by tomorrow, we're up shit creek,' he said gloomily.

'Why do I think that sounds like a threat?' asked Jennifer, looking at him sharply.

Chris ignored her and turned to Melanie. 'You'd better get off home . . . and I'll have to let your college know what happened, you realize that?'

He saw the panic in her eyes as she started to protest but then turned, got into her car and drove off without another word.

As Chris turned back he caught Jennifer's fierce look.

'You blame me for this, don't you?' she said accusingly.

'I said we should have let her go, didn't I?'

She looked away for a moment then snapped, 'I'm covered in blood, I'm dirty and I'm exhausted and I'm not discussing this now.'

They both marched indignantly to their cars and got in, slamming the doors and driving off, revving furiously.

Jennifer drove straight to the deserted practice and was scrubbing down, cleaning away the day, when she heard Chris's Range Rover pull into the yard. She frowned and walked through into the reception area, still in a bad mood, as Chris came in from the car-park.

'I thought you had an important dinner this evening,' said Jennifer.

Chris ignored the remark. 'If this business gets out, Brooks will have a field day.'

'Did you come all the way back here just to tell me that?'

'I should have followed my instincts, I knew there was something wrong with that girl.'

Jennifer stared angrily at him, then said coldly, 'There's no problem here, Chris. Blame me for this balls-up. Then your reputation's intact, isn't it? Goodnight.'

She regretted it as soon as the words were out of her mouth, but Chris did not flare up in retaliation. He looked at her for a long moment, then nodded slowly and said quietly, 'I'm angry and I'm upset, I'm sorry . . .' He paused as if about to say more but then fell silent.

'Well, that makes two of us,' said Jennifer. 'So let's call it a day. In the morning things'll seem more manageable.'

Neither of them made any move to leave, however. The silence grew between them as they gazed steadily into each other's eyes.

'But I'm glad you phoned,' said Chris.

Jennifer looked searchingly at him.

'I'd rather have had the terrible two hours we've just had than been at Patricia's dinner,' he went on.

'What are you saying, Chris?'

'I think you know.'

She nodded, a gentle smile playing around the corners of her mouth. 'I'm glad I phoned too.'

For a moment neither of them moved, then Chris took her arm and pulled her gently towards him. They began an unprompted, unplanned, but passionate kiss. Jennifer could feel Chris's heart pounding against hers and for a moment she gave herself up to the feeling of wanting and being wanted, but then she put her fingers to his lips and gently eased herself away from him. She moved away a few paces and sat down, as Chris stared ahead of him, his eyes unfocused.

For a few seconds neither of them spoke, alone with their own thoughts, but then Jennifer stood up and said, 'I'd better go.'

'Don't go, please.'

'Chris, I can't handle this.'

He spoke more to himself than to her. 'I thought everything was as it should be – the practice, my family, all of it.'

She smiled tenderly but shook her head. 'You fancy me, that's all. It happens.'

'No, that's not all. I respect you, I admire you. I love working with you, sharing all this.'

'I'm your partner, that's what it means.'

'No, it's more. You're part of my life now.'

Jennifer suddenly became angry. 'Chris. Stop this. I'm hanging on by my fingertips here. I've got a son who's threatening to leave home, I've got an ex-husband who gives me a migraine every time I hear his name . . .'

'I know, Jen, listen . . .'

'And now you're suggesting I have sex with my boss. Great, that would be a really smart move, wouldn't it?'

'I'm not just talking about sex.'

'What then?' she asked indignantly. 'Love? Come on, you're a married man, for God's sake, what do you think you're doing?'

'I don't know.'

There was another long silence, as she stared into his face. 'I don't know either. But right now, I have to pretend that I've got it all under control.'

She walked out, leaving him standing there motionless as he listened to the door slam and her car drive away.

Jennifer drove for a few minutes, then parked by the river and spent a long time staring into the darkness, listening to the water lapping against the bank. Finally she sighed, started the car and drove home. She was surprised to find the lights on and called, 'Steven? Are you back already? How was your trip?' as she opened the door.

Steven came out of the kitchen. 'I never went.'

She looked at him, trying to fathom his mood, then said, 'I've had a hell of an evening. We've got this student with us at the moment and she . . .' Her voice trailed off as she realized he was not even pretending to listen.

'I'm stupid, aren't I?' said Steven suddenly, 'and selfish.'

'I don't think you're either.'

'No, I am. Why should I expect you and Dad to be unhappy together just for my sake?'

He gazed past her unseeingly, musing, 'It's funny, because when I think back now on when we were in Craven Road, I remember how bad the atmosphere was. I don't want that again.'

'Neither do I,' said Jennifer, putting her arm around him.

He began to cry, sobbing, 'I'm sorry, Mum.'

'You've got me going now as well,' sniffed Jennifer. 'A couple of cry-babies, aren't we?' She hugged him closer. 'We've got each other, and for the moment, that's enough.'

She held him until he pulled away, embarrassed, wiping his eyes. Then she said cheerfully, 'I'm famished. I could murder a curry and a pint of lager.'

'Yeah. Me too.'

Arm in arm, she led him out of the house. 'So how far did you get?'

He smiled. 'Not very. I sat on the platform for two hours, and then came home again.'

Chapter 21

Chris stayed at the practice for a long time after Jennifer had gone, lost in thought. Finally he straightened up, switched off the lights and went home. He opened the front door warily, cocking an ear at the noise and laughter from the front room, and was about to slip upstairs when Patricia came out and stood looking questioningly at him.

He summoned up a smile. 'Sounds a success.'

'It has been. Are you coming in?'

Chris shook his head apologetically. 'Your world, not mine.'

Her mouth tightened a little, then she shrugged and asked, 'So how was the emergency?'

'Grim, but OK. Do you mind if I go straight up?'

'Of course not.' She looked at him quizzically. 'What's the matter?'

'Nothing.'

He turned and went upstairs, leaving Patricia staring thoughtfully after him until a loud laugh from the front room shook her out of her reverie. She went back to her guests, closing the door behind her.

When she got home, Melanie was as uncommunicative as Chris had been. Liz immediately saw the bloodstains and dirt on her working clothes, but fought back her worry and curiosity, waiting expectantly as Melanie made herself a sandwich.

Finally Liz's patience ran out. 'Where have you been, Mel? Why are your clothes so dirty? Enough playing games, I insist you tell me what you've been up to.'

Melanie still said nothing.

'Right,' said her mother. 'You leave me no alternative but to stop you from going out.'

'I'm twenty-one, you can't stop me.'

Liz shook her head. 'You're still a child, you don't know what's best for yourself.'

'My dad wanted me to be a vet . . .' began Melanie.

'No, he didn't,' countered Liz. 'He was a drunk, he didn't give a damn about you.'

'You liar! How dare you?' screamed Melanie, sweeping everything off the kitchen table, sending plates and cutlery clattering on to the floor. 'You killed him, you made him drink.'

She started smashing the ornaments on the sideboard as well, shrugging off her mother as she tried to stop her, screaming, 'Get off me! I hate you!' Liz slapped her face but Melanie just screamed at her incoherently and ran round the room, sending things flying in all directions. 'I hate you! I hate this house! I wish I was dead!'

She ran from the room, leaving Liz shaking as she stood amongst the debris.

Ten minutes later Liz tiptoed upstairs and into Melanie's room, finding her lying on her bed crying.

'I've tidied up the worst of the damage,' said Liz.

She waited, but Melanie said nothing.

'Your father never loved me, Melanie,' Liz said gently. 'I didn't mind, I got used to it, but I expected him to love you.'

Melanie raised a tearstained face. 'He did love me.'

'No. He hated both of us and he hated himself, which is why he started drinking. And when he left for the last time, do you know what his departing words were? "I never want to see either of you again."'

'He'd never say that,' murmured Melanie.

'You were there. You heard him say it,' said Liz, sitting by her on the bed and putting her arms around her.

Just about the only relationship in Whitton that seemed to be on a level course that night was that of Wilf and Danielle. They were floating in their heated swimming-pool, with a bottle of champagne in an ice bucket within easy reach and gazing rapt into each other's eyes.

'After all that,' said Wilf, 'do you know what was wrong with the dog?'

'What?' asked Danielle uneasily.

'Arthritis. That's what Murray said, and this other vet backed him up. Very rapid onset of arthritis.'

'And they're sure it was the arthritis that caused her to lose the race?' said Danielle.

'Without a shadow.'

Danielle thought for a moment. 'You'll have to take her back, Wilf, get your money refunded.'

'No, I can't really do that,' said Wilf nervously. 'I er . . . want to keep her. As a pet, you know?'

'Pricey pet, cherub,' said Danielle, but then went on throatily, 'I'm glad she's not going to be racing again. No more hobbies for a while, eh, Wilf? Just you and me?'

He gazed into her eyes and said, 'Just you and me, Dani,' reaching out to top up their champagne glasses. 'To us.'

Danielle dimpled and toasted him, but then said, 'Wilf . . . cherub. I've been meaning to tell you something. When you told me Nell Gwynn had arthritis I was ever so pleased because I thought it was me who made her lose that race. I didn't want her to be a winner. I didn't want you to spend the next year going to greyhound meetings every night of the week, so . . .' she paused, gulped and carried on '. . . so I fed Nell Gwynn two pounds of fillet steak ten minutes before the race. To slow her down.'

The look on Wilf's face was a picture that would have needed a Leonardo to capture.

'But if she wouldn't have won anyway 'cos of the arthritis, I don't feel so bad about it. Can you forgive me?' asked Danielle.

Wilf knew when he was beaten. 'Dani. I forgive you.'

She took the two glasses and put them on the side, then slid her arms around him and gave him a long, lingering kiss.

Early the next morning, Danielle woke with a blissful smile on her face. Still with her eyes closed, she murmured, 'Oh Wilfy, you do know how to make a girl happy. From now on it's going to be just you and me . . .'

She rolled over and opened her eyes, but Wilf was not there.

As she lay there, she heard the sound of a heavy vehicle arriving outside the house. Curious, Danielle got out of bed and went to the window in time to see Wilf standing with a manic grin on his face as a racehorse was led down the ramp of a large transporter.

A sixth sense made Wilf turn and look up to the window,

where he saw his doom written unmistakably on Danielle's face.

Chris was already out at Brooks's farm taking a close look at the calf, while Brooks stood near by, tapping a sheaf of correspondence against his leg.

Chris looked up and smiled. 'He's going to be all right.'

'That's a relief,' said Brooks. 'Of course you know I don't much take to being spoken to that way.'

'I'm sorry,' murmured Chris, anxious to soothe Brooks's ruffled feathers. 'Melanie's a student, she doesn't really know any better.'

'I'm not talking about her,' said Brooks, drawing himself up to his full military bearing. 'Your partner had the nerve to tell me how to behave.'

Chris stood there, uncertain what he could say, but while his mind was racing, a thaw had set in with Brooks. He relaxed his stance and confided, 'Mind you, I never was very good at talking to women. Public school, army, and all that.'

'I apologize on both their behalves,' said Chris, feeling he ought to pinch himself to make sure he was not dreaming.

'No need. The matter's closed. Now, can I interest you in a spot of breakfast?'

Chris declined politely. 'I really ought to be getting back to the practice.'

'Very wise,' smiled Brooks, 'I'd probably burn it.'

Jennifer had an equally difficult mission to carry out. She stood outside Melanie's house, composing herself before she rang the bell. When Liz answered the door, however, Jennifer was momentarily taken aback to see an able-bodied person standing there. 'Mrs Baxter?' she asked, uncertainly.

'Yes.'

'Jennifer Holt, from the vet centre,' said Jennifer, mentally notching up another of Melanie's strange tales.

'Ah yes, of course,' said Liz. 'You'd better come in.'

Liz led her into the house and called up the stairs, 'Melanie, a visitor for you.'

'You know why I'm here then?' said Jennifer.

She nodded. 'She's not a bad girl . . .'

'I know,' said Jennifer.

Melanie came to the top of the stairs, saw Jennifer and disappeared straight back into her room. Jennifer looked inquiringly at Liz and, receiving a nod of assent, went upstairs and opened the door.

'May I come in?'

Melanie said nothing, so Jennifer walked in and perched on the edge of the bed.

She looked round for a moment, taking in the animals and the piles of books, then asked abruptly, 'How did you forge the reference?'

Melanie darted her an anxious look but said, 'From a rejection letter I got from the college.'

'There's no shame in the rejection,' said Jennifer. 'Not everyone's cut out to be a vet.'

'Are you going to report me to the police?'

She shook her head. 'For impersonating a veterinary student? I'm not even sure it's illegal, but you did betray our trust and you nearly killed two animals.'

'I'm sorry. I didn't mean to be cruel.'

'I know you didn't,' said Jennifer gently. 'I only want you to realize how stupid you've been.'

'Are the calf and mother all right?'

Jennifer nodded.

There was a silence, then Melanie said dreamily, 'It wasn't like I imagined it would be.'

'Didn't you go on visits with your dad?'

'No.'

'But he really was a vet?'

Melanie flashed her an embarrassed look. 'Yeah. He only died last year but I hadn't seen him for years. He wasn't really interested in me. I suppose I thought I had something to prove.' She looked out of the window for a moment, then asked, 'What happens now?'

'I'll have a word with your mother, and tell her we won't take it any further,' said Jennifer. She left Melanie sitting in her room, still staring out of the window.

When Jennifer got back to the practice, she found Chris already finishing off yet another lambing. She waited as the farmer closed up his truck and drove off. Chris looked expectantly at her. 'Well?'

She shook her head disbelievingly. 'Extraordinary girl. Her bedroom's full of animals and veterinary textbooks. To live out a fantasy like that, to want something so much that you just go off and do it . . .'

'It almost sounds like you admire her,' said Chris half indignantly.

'I'm jealous really. I couldn't do it, I always have to be the sensible one . . .'

She left the words hanging in the air and there was a long silence. Chris nodded, smiling wistfully to himself. Jennifer looked at him, aware of what he was thinking, then said gently, 'I'd better get on.' She walked towards the building, leaving Chris standing alone.

He watched her go, then walked round the side of the building and stood on the terrace by the river, staring unseeingly at the water cascading over the weir. Two courting swans sailed serenely by, in perfect harmony, mimicking each other's movements. He watched them moodily, then sighed and turned away, squaring his shoulders as he walked inside the practice.